In the early years of this century, such a linen-weaver, named Silas Marner, worked at his vocation in a stone cottage that stood among the nutty hedgerows near the village of Raveloe, and not far from the edge of a deserted stone-pit. The questionable sound of Silas's loom, so unlike the natural cheerful trotting of the winnowing-machine, or the simpler rhythm of the flail, had a half-fearful fascination for the Raveloe boys, who would often leave off their nutting or birds'-nesting to peep in at the window of the stone cottage, counterbalancing a certain awe at the mysterious action of the loom, by a pleasant sense of scornful superiority, drawn from the mockery of its alternating noises, along with the bent, tread-mill attitude of the weaver.   (from *Silas Marner*, page 4)

He seemed to weave, like the spider, from pure impulse, without reflection. Every man's work, pursued steadily, tends in this way to become an end in itself, and so to bridge over the loveless chasms of his life.

(from *Silas Marner*, page 15)

"Robbed!" said Silas, gaspingly. "I've been robbed!"

(from *Silas Marner*, page 52)

"You're very hard-hearted, Nancy," said Godfrey, pettishly. "You might encourage me to be a better fellow. I'm very miserable—but you've no feeling."   (from *Silas Marner*, page 101)

In utter amazement, Silas fell on his knees and bent his head low to examine the marvel: it was a sleeping child. (from *Silas Marner*, page 105)

Unlike the gold which needed nothing, and must be worshipped in close-locked solitude—which was hidden away from the daylight, was deaf to the song of birds, and started to no human tones—Eppie was a creature of endless claims and ever-growing desires, seeking and loving sunshine, and living sounds, and living movements; making trial of everything, with trust in new joy, and stirring the human kindness in all eyes that looked on her. (from *Silas Marner*, page 120)

"I wasn't worth doing wrong for—nothing is in this world. Nothing is so good as it seems beforehand—not even our marrying wasn't, you see." (from *Silas Marner*, page 155)

"You must make sure as you won't ever be sorry, because you've made your choice to stay among poor folks, and with poor clothes and things, when you might ha' had everything o' the best." (from *Silas Marner*, page 163)

"What a pretty home ours is! I think nobody could be happier than we are." (from *Silas Marner*, page 172)

Just a month from this day, on the twentieth of September, 1850, I shall be sitting in this chair, in this study, at ten o'clock at night, longing to die, weary of incessant insight and foresight, without delusions and without hope. (from "The Lifted Veil," page 175)

I felt a sort of pitying anguish over the pathos of my own lot: the lot of a being finely organized for pain, but with hardly any fibers that responded to pleasure—to whom the idea of future evil robbed the present of its joy, and for whom the idea of future good did not still the uneasiness of a present yearning or a present dread. (from "The Lifted Veil," page 197)

David could invent delightful things in the way of drop-cakes, and he had the widest views of the sugar department; but in other directions he certainly felt hampered by the want of knowledge and practical skill; and the world is so inconveniently constituted that the vague consciousness of being a fine fellow is no guarantee of success in any line of business. (from "Brother Jacob," page 220)

"Come, come, if he's your brother, tell the truth, man," said Mr. Prettyman, with growing suspicion. "Don't be ashamed of your own flesh and blood." (from "Brother Jacob," page 255)

SILAS MARNER
AND TWO SHORT STORIES

George Eliot

WITH AN INTRODUCTION AND NOTES
BY GEORGE LEVINE

GEORGE STADE
CONSULTING EDITORIAL DIRECTOR

BARNES & NOBLE CLASSICS
NEW YORK

ℬ
BARNES & NOBLE CLASSICS
NEW YORK

Published by Barnes & Noble Books
122 Fifth Avenue
New York, NY 10011

www.barnesandnoble.com/classics

Silas Marner: The Weaver of Raveloe was first published in 1861. The present text is that of the Cabinet edition, which includes all of George Eliot's revisions. The Cabinet volume (1878), published as part of Eliot's collected works, also comprised "The Lifted Veil," which had first appeared in 1859, and "Brother Jacob," which had first appeared in 1864.

Published in 2005 by Barnes & Noble Classics with new Introduction, Notes, Biography, Chronology, Inspired By, Comments & Questions, and For Further Reading.

Silas Marner and Two Short Stories
ISBN-10: 1-59308-251-7
ISBN-13: 978-1-59308-251-2
LC Control Number 2005922121

Produced and published in conjunction with:
Fine Creative Media, Inc.
322 Eighth Avenue
New York, NY 10001

Michael J. Fine, President and Publisher

Printed in the United States of America

QM

3   5   7   9   10   8   6   4   2

GEORGE ELIOT

George Eliot was the nom de plume of Mary Anne Evans, born the youngest of five children on a farm in Warwickshire, England, on November 22, 1819. Her father, Robert, a carpenter and land manager, strongly influenced his daughter's early upbringing and education. Mary Anne was educated at religious schools and given access to the large library of her father's employer. From early on, Mary Anne excelled at languages, music, and writing. Her mother's death in 1836, along with her father's declining health, forced her to drop out of school at age sixteen and to become the lady of the house. While nursing her father and learning German and Italian, Mary Anne wrote poetry; her earliest work appeared in the *Christian Observer*. In 1841 she was invited to the home of liberal thinkers Charles and Caroline Bray, who proved to have a deep and lasting influence in her life; the Brays, along with Charles Hennell, Caroline's husband, gave voice and sympathy to Mary Anne's growing disillusionment with Christianity and introduced her to some of the day's advanced ideas and thinkers. After Mary Anne refused to attend church the following year, relations with her father became strained, and they remained that way until his death in 1849.

Having achieved modest success with publication of an anonymous translation of David Friedrich Strauss's *Das Leben Jesu* (*The Life of Jesus*), Mary Anne, now calling herself Marian, moved to London and became assistant editor and later editor of the *Westminster Review*. Her interests broadened along with her intellectual circle, and her work with the *Review* reflected her intelligence and wide range of interests, including literature, religion, music, and art. A fateful meeting in 1851 with critic and author George Henry Lewes turned out to have a deep and abiding effect on her life. Lewes was estranged from his wife but unable to divorce because he had condoned her adultery. Shunning convention and recognizing that the choice would provoke denunciation by Marian's friends and family, the lovers left England to live temporarily in Weimar, Germany.

Upon her return to England with Lewes, Marian was cut off by the majority of her relatives. Yet she was happy with Lewes, who encouraged her to write. Her first novel, *Scenes of Clerical Life* (1858), was published under the pseudonym George Eliot, and she carefully guarded her true identity. The publication of *Adam Bede* (1859) made George Eliot a best-selling author. As her identity became known, Eliot at first received as much scorn for her private life as she did praise for her novels, but tolerance increased with the years. Her masterpiece, *Middlemarch*, appeared in installments in 1871 and 1872 to public acclaim. Called by Virginia Woolf "one of the few English novels written for grown-up people," *Middlemarch* established George Eliot as one of England's great authors, one who combined philosophical ideas and psychological insight with astute observation of society and its effect on the individual. *Daniel Deronda* was published in installments in 1876 and in one volume in 1877.

Sought after by many admirers of her work, Eliot continued to write and enjoy a quiet life with Lewes and a small circle of friends. In 1878 she was devastated by the death of Lewes. She married John Walter Cross in May 1880 and died on December 22 of that year. She was buried alongside George Lewes in Highgate Cemetery, London.

TABLE OF CONTENTS

THE WORLD OF GEORGE ELIOT
AND SILAS MARNER

1819 Mary Anne Evans, who will later be known as George Eliot, is born on November 22, in Warwickshire, the youngest child of Robert and Christiana Evans.

1824 Mary Anne joins her sister, Christiana, at Miss Lathom's boarding school. Recalled later as an unhappy time, her stint there fills her with feelings of abandonment and fearful nightmares.

1828 Mary Anne enters Mrs. Wallington's school, where she meets the inspiring teacher and Evangelical Christian Maria Lewis. A talented but shy student, Mary Anne excels in French, music instruction, and writing. Her education is supplemented by instruction at home and, later, at Miss Franklin's school in Coventry.

1836 After her mother dies, Mary Anne moves home to take care of her ailing father. She receives Holy Communion in the Anglican Church, and her religious views at this time are rigid and righteous; she later describes them as "my stern, ascetic hard views."

1840 She studies German, Latin, and Italian while reading widely, especially in religious works, including the Bible, which she reads daily. Elizabeth Evans, an aunt and Methodist preacher, visits; she later becomes the basis for Dinah Morris in *Adam Bede*. Mary Anne's first published work, a religious poem entitled "As o'er the Fields," appears in the *Christian Observer*.

1841 After moving with her father to the town of Foleshill, Mary Anne meets Charles and Caroline Bray. The couple's intellectual circle and their religious skepticism open Mary Anne's eyes to a world of new ideas. She shortly rejects organized religion.

1842 Mary Anne ceases attending church—a decision that shocks and angers her devout father. A truce is struck in this "holy war" when she agrees to attend church if he will allow her her personal beliefs.

1844 While maintaining the home and nursing her father, Mary Anne agrees to complete the translation of David Friedrich Strauss's *Das Leben Jesu, kritisch bearbeitet* (1835–1836) that was started by Rufa Hennell.

1846 Eliot's translation of Strauss's *The Life of Jesus Critically Examined*, is published anonymously.

1847 Charlotte Brontë's *Jane Eyre*, Anne Brontë's *Agnes Grey*, and Emily Brontë's *Wuthering Heights* are published.

1848 In July, Mary Anne meets Ralph Waldo Emerson at the Brays' home, Rosehill. Emerson praises her "calm, serious soul," and she refers to Emerson as "the first man I have ever seen."

1849 Mary Anne begins translating Baruch Spinoza's *Tractatus Theologico-Politicus* (1670), from the Latin, during her father's final illness; he dies in June. Five days after his funeral, Mary Anne travels with the Brays to Europe and lives in Geneva for eight months after the Brays return to England.

1851 Now calling herself Marian Evans, she moves to London, lodges with *Westminster Review* editor John Chapman, and, in her first major publication, writes on Robert William Mackay's *Progress of the Intellect, as Exemplified in the Religious Development of the Greeks and Hebrews* for the *Westminster Review*. She becomes a regular contributor and editor for that quarterly and meets a variety of well-known thinkers, including Herbert Spencer and her future companion, George Henry Lewes. Herman Melville's *Moby Dick* is published.

1852 Marian begins translating Ludwig Feuerbach's *Das Wesen des Christentums* (1841), which is published as *The Essence of Christianity*, under the name Marian Evans, the only work to carry her given name.

1853 Marian decides to leave her rooms at *Westminster Review* publisher John Chapman's house in order to live alone and pursue her relationship with Lewes. The fact that he is married, although estranged from his wife, makes this move a socially dangerous decision.

1854 Following the publication of the Feuerbach translation, Marian lives with George Lewes for three months in Weimar, Germany.

1855   Upon her return to England, she is ostracized by friends and family for living openly with Lewes.

1857   Happy nonetheless, Marian publishes her first story, "The Sad Fortunes of the Reverend Amos Barton," in *Blackwood's Magazine*. Lewes recommends this story and two others to a publisher, saying they are written by a male friend who wishes to publish anonymously.

1858   *Scenes of Clerical Life*, which collects "The Sad Fortunes of the Reverend Amos Barton," "Mr. Gilfil's Love-Story," and "Janet's Repentance," is published in two volumes under the pseudonym George Eliot. The work receives critical acclaim, and speculation about the true author is a popular topic of conversation in London.

1859   *Adam Bede*, a novel set in rural England, is published in three volumes, to great success. Darwin's *On the Origin of Species* is published. Charles Dickens's *A Tale of Two Cities* is published.

1860   Eliot travels to Italy with Lewes to conduct research for the novel *Romola*. The *Mill on the Floss*, also set in the countryside, is published. By this time, the public knows George Eliot's true identity. Although her novels are celebrated, she endures criticism for her private life.

1861   *Silas Marner*, a third provincial novel, is published.

1863   *Romola*, a novel set in the time of fifteenth-century Italian religious reformer Savonarola, is published in three volumes.

1865   Eliot and Lewis travel to Paris and Brittany.

1866   *Felix Holt, the Radical*, a political novel set in the 1830s, is published. Lewes and Eliot travel in Holland, Belgium, Germany, and Spain. Eliot meets Emanuel Deutsch, later a model for Mordecai Cohen in *Daniel Deronda*.

1867   A Reform Bill doubles the number of people who can vote in Great Britain.

1868   Eliot publishes the long dramatic poem *The Spanish Gypsy*, set during the Spanish Inquisition.

1869   Eliot and Lewes journey to Italy, where Eliot first meets John Walter Cross. She has been considering ideas for *Middlemarch* for some time and now begins to write the novel.

1871   The first book of *Middlemarch* appears, to great acclaim, and the novel is published in installments over the next year. Eliot's status as one of England's great living authors helps ease the scandal surrounding her relationship with Lewes.

1872 The concluding installments of *Middlemarch* are published, and the novel is issued in complete form in four volumes.

1873 Eliot reads books on Jewish history and religion while vacationing in France and Germany. She attends Friday evening synagogue services in Frankfurt, and at Mainz she and Lewes attend Sabbath services. In November she informs Blackwood that she is "slowly simmering towards another big book."

1874 *The Legend of Jubal and Other Poems* is published. The first one-volume edition of *Middlemarch* is published and becomes an immediate best-seller. Eliot begins work on *Daniel Deronda* and tours southern England for settings.

1876 *Daniel Deronda* is published in eight monthly parts beginning in February.

1877 The one-volume edition of *Daniel Deronda* published.

1878 Lewes becomes ill in June and dies in November.

1879 Eliot publishes *Impressions of Theophrastus Such*, a book of essays by the fictional character Theophrastus Such. She devotes a great deal of time to Lewes's unfinished *Problems of Life and Mind*.

1880 Although he is twenty years her junior, Eliot marries her close friend John Walter Cross on May 6. George Eliot dies on December 22.

INTRODUCTION

Of all George Eliot's novels, *Silas Marner* (1861) is the shortest and perhaps the most accessible to modern readers. That is partly because it is the only one of her novels that has the atmosphere of a fable, and indeed seems to have been deliberately written as one. The very qualities of apparent simplicity, clarity, and directness that have always made it among the most popular of her novels have also made it seem as though it is not quite as serious, not quite as "real" as the other much longer and more complex works, most notably *Middlemarch* (1872), universally recognized as her masterpiece and arguably the greatest nineteenth-century English novel.

Unusual as it seems, among Eliot's other more imposing works, *Silas Marner* is not as atypical as it at first appears to be. In fact, no book of Eliot's gives more immediate access to the mysteries of her art, or rather, to the central preoccupations, formal and thematic, that determine the shape and style of her novels, and to the difficulties and potential contradictions they confront. *Silas Marner*, for all its fairy-tale aspects, is also a "realistic" novel, firmly set in time and place, sharply observed, focused not on the extraordinary, but on the everyday. And just as *Silas Marner* has elements of realism, so the larger works reveal elements of the kind of fable we find here. It does not take very close reading (which every book of George Eliot always deserves and requires) to detect the "fabulous" qualities behind the massive and complex structures of her more evidently realistic work: There is more than a touch of the legendary in *Romola* (1863, written just after *Silas Marner*), and even in *Middlemarch*, where fable is more elaborately disguised, and certainly in her last great work, *Daniel Deronda* (1877). *Silas Marner*, then, is interestingly representative of the work of one of the greatest of nineteenth-century novelists, at the same time as it is satisfyingly brief, precisely constructed, and yet full of the intelligence and circumstantial precision that mark all of Eliot's earlier fiction.

The great late books struggle—usually brilliantly, sometimes with "the odor of the lamp" upon them, as Henry James complained—to get the details of context right and full. The very abundance of contextual detail, of plot and of character, complicates and largely disguises the directness of the moral passion that drives them. George Eliot, a novelist with a moral mission, was too wise to think that morality was a simple matter of right and wrong. And yet, while *Silas Marner* is brilliantly crafted, it gives off an air of spontaneity and ease that her contemporaries greatly admired (and they often complained that the later novels had lost just that sense of spontaneity as they grew more apparently solemn and philosophical). While all of Eliot's fiction (except for the remarkable short story "The Lifted Veil," included in this volume) are written from the point of view of a sage narrator who does not often hesitate to intrude and comment on the action, *Silas Marner's* narrator is quite restrained, although also notably learned and sophisticated. Her eye is on the action, and for the most part, she simply tells the story, swiftly and efficiently, commenting on it only occasionally, though pithily.

Throughout her career, Eliot was committed, as she claimed, to keep her stories from lapsing from "the picture to the diagram." She did not want to preach abstractly but, believing that truth is the basis of all moral life, to render faithfully the real world and the real people who lived in it. True morality, she argued, entails recognition of the realities of the world we live in. "Depend upon it," she wrote in her first published story, "The Sad Fortunes of the Reverend Amos Barton": "You would gain unspeakably if you would learn with me to see some of the poetry and pathos, the tragedy and the comedy, lying in the experience of a human soul that looks out through dull grey eyes, and that speaks in a voice of quite ordinary tones." Her "strongest effort," she wrote in *Adam Bede* (1859) "is to give a faithful account of men and things as they have mirrored themselves in my mind."

Why then, one might ask, does *Silas Marner* feel so much like a fable with a moral? Doesn't it, as it deals out its punishment for Godfrey Cass's youthful failure or redeems Silas from the moral isolation caused by his friend's betrayal and his own subsequent miserliness, feel just a bit too much like a "diagram"? It is easy to take this remarkable novel as itself too easy, rendering a bit too much "poetic justice." But the texture of the narrative belies the simplicity of its apparent moralizing. Although this is a fable, it contains all its characters within a clearly defined historical and social context, and it allows nobody the kind of heroism that fables usually require. Only Eppie may seem unnaturally endowed with virtue and education, and happily, unlike Dickens with his Oliver Twist, she speaks with the same dialect as those among whom she has lived all her life. Nevertheless, Nancy Lammeter points out that Eppie "doesn't look like a strapping girl come of working parents" (p. 159).

Even there, however, her voice remains strikingly distant from that of the narrator. Right from the start, that voice moves to an almost anthropological description of the Raveloe culture. In "that far off time," the narrator notes, "superstition clung easily round every person or thing that was at all unwonted" (p. 3). While creating a sense of a romantically remote past, that is, the narrator speaks with the voice of enlightenment, finding among the inhabitants, for example, "strange lingering echoes of the old demon-worship." "The rude mind," she notes with the abstract language of the ethnographer, "with difficulty associates the ideas of power and benignity." The narrator, then, has the double, perhaps triple task of recording the habits and manners of a past epoch, demonstrating their backwardness and intellectual "rudeness," commenting upon that rudeness from an enlightened position, and sustaining our care and concern for the rude characters anyway. Who better than Silas Marner himself can be described as looking out at the world with dull grey eyes (except that Silas's happen to be brown)? What duller eyes are there than Silas's?

Nor does the fabulous quality of Silas Marner preclude it from being an historical novel as well. The narrator, in her great sophistication, is careful to give us a sense (if we are paying attention) of the precise historical moment in which the action is set. But the book is not historical in the sense of putting the great events of the world at center stage; it might be better to say that history flows through the very veins of the story. Eliot wants us to know what is going on in the greater world outside of Raveloe even as the central characters seem to know almost nothing about it, certainly nothing about the great historical forces of transformation of which their own lives are a small part. The narrative is sprinkled with historical allusions that suggest major social transformations going on beyond the view of the dull brown eyes. History, Eliot believed, is always at work, even in the texture of personal life, even when people are not aware of it.

It is for that reason that Silas Marner is as committed to historical context as Middlemarch, and part of the role such context plays is to contrast with the personal story. The Napoleonic Wars go on offstage, and the small dramas of Silas and Godfrey—so carefully and tactfully juxtaposed—are the focus of our attention. The little urban enclave in which Silas lived fifteen years before the story opens has disappeared by the time, thirty years later, he goes back to look for it. The growth and transformation of cities happen while the citizens of Raveloe continue to live in the traditions of feudalism.

By the end of the novel, for example, it is briefly noted that "there was less and less flax spun" (p. 133). This seems like a casual fact, but it marks a quiet recognition of the new commercial and industrial life that was rapidly outdating the feudal conditions in Raveloe and making Silas's kind of weaving unnecessary. The transformation of the Cass estate, under Nancy's direction, into a working farm with a dairy suggests both a social and a moral transformation. While we worry about the sale of Godfrey's horse, or the loss of Silas's hoard, the Napoleonic Wars are going on, and indeed, Silas's slow redemption from isolation and miserliness to full absorption into the community begins just before or about the time of the final defeat of Napoleon. There is an explicit allusion (p. 92) to the illness and (probably) death of King George III (in 1811) during the party that is interrupted by the announcement of the death of Godfrey's secret wife. The narrative doesn't talk about these things except as characters within the story are consciously affected by the events, which they do not interpret except in very personal terms, but readers should be alert to how much history looms over the little lives of the characters. The implicit comparison of great things to small illuminates both.

The "once upon a time" quality of Silas Marner, then, is not any old time. Silas's story up to the time of the loss of the gold and the appearance of Eppie takes fifteen years, from about 1797 to the moments just before Waterloo. It is the period of the Regency in England, the period of mad King George, and the period in which, climaxing in Wellington's victory over Napoleon at Waterloo, England ascends unequivocally to modernity and power. The fifteen years of Eppie's growing up with Silas are a period of change and urbanization in England, the introduction of the railroads, the expansion of industry, and the approach to the First Reform Act, which begins expanding suffrage, and it precedes by only a few years the ascension of Victoria to the throne. While Silas lives and works out his redemption, England transforms from a feudal to a bourgeois society. These changes account for the falloff in flax spinning, and implicitly, as Silas sinks into old age and his son-in-law Aaron takes over, they suggest that Silas's trade will no longer be necessary, that his peculiar fate will no longer be possible.

The shrewdness and sophistication of the narrator of Silas Marner comes as a surprise to readers, like me, who as adolescents were taught it as a moral fable. But if Eliot is telling a fairy story, a fable with a moral, she is doing it in a way consistent with the extraordinary complexity of her thinking and with the great philosophical novels Middlemarch and Daniel Deronda, with which her writing career concluded. Silas Marner does not, like Middlemarch, have four intersecting plots, and it is not played out on as large a scale, but it does have two plots, which, like the plots in both Middlemarch and Daniel Deronda, intersect and comment on each other. And the wise anthropological vision of the narrator makes Silas Marner, like Middlemarch—though on a much smaller scale—"a study of provincial life."

That the story is no minor fable for adolescents was recognized immediately by Eliot's contemporaries. There was no condescension in its reception by her first reviewers and readers. After the remarkable success of her first two full-length novels, Adam Bede and The Mill on the Floss (1860), Eliot had established herself as one of the finest novelists of the time. Here is how R. H. Hutton, a highly intelligent and distinguished Victorian critic, began his review:

> This tale is a permanent and no trifling addition to the wealth of English literature. There is no element of power wanting to make it more impressive, and no element of beauty wanting to make it more attractive. The conception is as fine as the execution is marvelous. . . . No book we have ever read combines so completely the broadest masculine power with the most delicate feminine insight and finish.[1]

(Hutton's insistence on both masculine and feminine qualities in the book would have registered clearly with his readers, for it was only a year before that it had been made public that "George Eliot" was a woman. But by that time, it was much too late to condescend to her as a woman novelist. She had fooled everyone but Charles Dickens and a close friend or two).

Hutton's praise may sound like hyperbole, but he was not in his other criticism lavish with praise. His enthusiasm for *Silas Marner* is partly a consequence of his awareness of the superb intelligence lying behind the simple and ostensibly sentimental aspects of the narrative. To an adolescent, Silas's mistaking of Eppie's golden hair for his lost gold may be just too easy, obvious, and gooey, but the idea of punishing Godfrey by giving him fifteen years of good fortune and then dramatizing his wish that he had acted differently appealed to Hutton as a realistic rather than crudely "poetic" handling of the problem. Along with Silas and Eppie's perhaps too neat happy ending, we experience also something of the barrenness of Godfrey and Nancy's marriage after the discovery. Yet no other work of George Eliot resolves its narrative tensions with so unequivocally happy a resolution. No other story could have concluded with the ripely happy line that Eppie is given to speak: "O father . . . what a pretty home ours is! I think nobody could be happier than we are." But such is the form of fable, and Hutton was right in seeing these apparent simplifications as part of a large conception that made "no trifling addition to the wealth of English literature."

2

It will be useful, before attempting to get closer to the qualities that evoked Hutton's admiration, to take a look briefly at the book's prehistory, at the development of George Eliot from Mary Anne Evans, the daughter of a provincial land agent, into a leading intellectual and famous novelist. As a provincial, and as a woman, Eliot had to contend with the prejudices and assumptions of her own time. Very few women of her time, and indeed very few women in Western history, had achieved the degree of learning and philosophical sophistication that Eliot achieved, largely on her own. Mrs. Wallington's school in Nuneaton, after all, did not produce a great many intellectuals. In her early youth, largely under the influence of a governess and teacher, Maria Lewis, Mary Anne Evans became almost excessively pious even as she excelled in her provincial schools. She began planning a universal religious history when she was in her teens.

Her striking intellectual achievements notwithstanding, she was not at all exempt from women's domestic responsibilities, and after her mother died in 1836, when Mary Anne was seventeen, she bore the primary responsibility for her father's care, a responsibility she fulfilled until his death in 1849. Sharing the culture's assumptions, Mr. Evans was not given to encouraging Mary Anne in her intellectual pursuits, except as they reflected her piety, and when she came into contact with a group of advanced thinkers in the city of Coventry, quite close to where they had moved, serious divisions between father and daughter developed. The brother of one of her new friends, Charles Hennell, had investigated the Bible from an historical perspective, and Mary Anne's view of the world was opened to the possibility of a newly secular understanding. This led to a gradual severing of connections with Maria Lewis.

Her increased skepticism precipitated a crisis that clearly affected her thought and feelings for the rest of her life. When she became aware that she could no longer believe in the literal truth of Christianity, she decided not to attend church. This resulted in what she later called a "holy war" with her family. Both her father and her brother were deeply offended, and her father attempted to persuade her back to faith by bringing learned clergymen to persuade her. Even the most learned of them failed before the power of her astonishing intelligence and learning. But in deep need of the emotional support of her family, she ultimately returned to church-going, although only on the condition that her father would leave her to her own private beliefs. As she explained in a phrase that can account for a great deal of what goes on in *Silas Marner*, what mattered finally was not so much rational truth, as "truth of feeling."

This strange combination of a passionate commitment to intellectual and rational precision with an equally passionate commitment to the value of feeling over that of mere rationality marks all of her work, but it is particularly important to an understanding of *Silas Marner* and of "The Lifted Veil" as well. The young Mary Anne Evans was a child of romanticism. She read Wordsworth and Scott with excitement and deep sympathy, and shared their complicated sense of the way feelings and ideas interweave. The formulation "truth of feeling" is a brilliant attempt to combine her sense of the enormous value of the new knowledge, including especially science, with her more deeply rooted sense of the value of human community and love. Part of her discovery during this period of family crisis was that it is perfectly possible to be an entirely good person while at the same time entertaining absolutely mistaken ideas about such things as religion and politics. Ironically, Eliot claimed that she learned this lesson not from tracts of moral philosophy or religion, but from Scott's novels.

This idea reverberates out into her own fiction. What matters is not whether people are educated and capable of fine rational discriminations, but what kind of people they are. Christianity may be literally wrong, but it is morally right, and its roots go down so deep into the lives of even the least reflective of people in the England of her time that to tear it out just because it is not literally true is to cause irreparable moral damage. "What has grown up historically," she wrote in an important essay, "can only die out historically, by the gradual operation of necessary laws."[2] Family, memory, roots in a community, one's first impressions while growing up—all of these were essential elements in all of Eliot's thought and in all of her fictions. Loss of connection with one's past is for her characters—as it felt to be for her when she once again accompanied her father to church on Sundays—a moral and spiritual disaster.

Important as fiction was to her in her youth, and as central as it became to her identity as "George Eliot," her early writing was of a very different sort. At the age of twenty-five she translated from the German David Strauss's *Leben Jesu*, the major book in the development of early nineteenth-century Higher Criticism, devoted to unearthing the historical Jesus and understanding the Bible historically, rather than as a sacred text. Strauss's work, he claimed, was to determine to what degree the mythical enters into the ostensibly historical account of Jesus in the New Testament. Eliot always remained sensitive to how people's account of actions is infused with the "mythical." Consider, for example, the ways in which the Raveloe people speculate about who stole Silas's money; or consider more generally the way in which Silas's story, from the very start, is wrapped in a mythology that the narrative in part attempts to dispel. The very texture of the narrative derives from Eliot's characteristic double view of the importance of rational truth and empirical fact. Characteristically, as she labored at her translation of the "scientific" Strauss, a large crucifix by the Danish neoclassical sculptor Bertel Thorwaldsen (1770–1844) hung over her desk.

When, after her father's death, she moved to London and began working as an editor of the *Westminster Review*, a journal that published the ideas of the most advanced intellectuals of her time, she did not lose her interest in religion. The only book she published under her own name, which had by then moved from Mary Anne Evans, to Mary Ann Evans, to Marian Evans, was a translation of Ludwig Feuerbach's *Das wesen des Christentums*—that is, *The Essence of Christianity* (1854). Feuerbach argued that Christianity was a projection of human ideals so that when people worshiped God as a spirit external to them they were in fact worshiping humanity, the very highest of human ideals. Eliot's religion, then, was a religion of humanity, a religion that rejected Christian history and theology but took Christian moral teaching as the highest expression of human values. In *Silas Marner* we can see from the touching discussions of religion between Silas and Dolly that what matters humanly is not the wildly confused theologies in which each has been brought up, but the moral conditions facilitated by Christianity, which is very much a human institution—although the narrator carefully says nothing like this but only represents the characters' understanding. "There's dealings," says Dolly, and Silas agrees.

The most famous episode of George Eliot's life is her elopement with the married intellectual George Henry Lewes, an elopement that caused sufficient scandal that it took many years before she would be accepted back into the polite society of women. The normal social life of women was inaccessible to her, but through the years, well after she had become famous, she and Lewes held soirees for artists and intellectuals—all men. Only a very few of her women friends continued to be her confidantes. Lewes had been in an unhappy marriage and was separated from his wife, but at that time it was virtually impossible to get a divorce. The elopement satisfied the needs of two very different but emotionally needy people, and yet in her novels Eliot would never dramatize or sanction such a liaison. Recognizing her own quite unusual talents and history, she determined to focus her attention on those without such talents and such histories.

Lewes was, however, an almost perfect partner for her, and he not only encouraged her desire to switch from translation, editing, and essay composition to writing fiction but also took the responsibility of negotiating its sale as he protected her anonymity.

There were obvious reasons why Mary Anne Evans would adopt a pseudonym. The most obvious, of course, was the scandal of her elopement, but perhaps equally important, Marian Evans's fame as a freethinking intellectual would likely have been very damaging to her early reputation. The translator of Strauss and Feuerbach seemed not exactly someone to turn to for morally satisfying fiction. Moreover— and in this Marian was like many Victorian women novelists—she believed that women writers simply would not be taken seriously. We recall how the Brontë sisters all published under male pseudonyms: Emily Brontë, Anne Brontë, and Charlotte Brontë became Ellis, Acton, and Currer Bell.

George Eliot had written for the *Westminster Review* a sharp, funny, and even bitter essay, "Silly Novels by Lady Novelists," in which she ferociously, with a self-consciously masculine irony, devastates the third-rate fiction produced by many women. But the point of the essay is, in the long run, not to denigrate women but to ensure that they be treated with the same seriousness and hold themselves to the same standards as men. As she puts it in "Silly Novels by Lady Novelists": "Fiction is a department of literature in which women can, after their kind, fully equal men."[3] The essay was written almost contemporaneously with her first foray into fiction, "The Sad Fortunes of the Reverend Amos Barton," and surely for Eliot it served as a kind of statement about how she wanted to be read and understood. She wanted to be criticized if she wrote badly; she wanted desperately not to write the sort of shallow and unrealistic novels that she mocked in the essay. Many early readers did indeed assume that the author was a man, and it wasn't until a clergyman from her own part of the country was being given credit for *Scenes of Clerical Life* and *Adam Bede* that she allowed it to be known that George Eliot was Marian Evans.

So behind the potentially simplistic fable of *Silas Marner* lay a career that would seem the very antithesis of the novel's substance: a fallen-away Christian, an avant-garde intellectual, a translator from German of difficult, controversial, and even atheistic works, a woman who was morally compromised by her elopement with a married man. We find nothing, evidently, of this figure in the materials of *Silas Marner*. The story's piety seems obvious, its disapproval of moral laxity is the center of its whole structure, and its relentless concern with dull, ordinary, unimaginative people is perhaps the most striking thing about it. The book makes drama out of drab unintelligence manifested in a culture that appears to be totally unconnected with the modernity and cosmopolitanism of Eliot's society.

3

Reading *Silas Marner* as if it were a simple fable is appropriate, but by itself this misses some of the book's special strengths. It is always a mistake to ignore the fact that behind every sentence of George Eliot's fiction there is a powerful and deeply learned mind. Although the sophistication of the narrative is handled unobtrusively, one needs to recognize that the intellectual distance between the narrator and her subjects is enormous. The narrator speaks from a scientific modernity about a society into which most of the social and intellectual advances of the nineteenth-century have not entered. The characters live inside their world without any larger perspective on it. The narrator, attempting faithfully to register that world and to portray precisely but sympathetically its characters, always either implies or asserts a far broader vision. She studies the behavior of her characters with scientific precision. Recall that the book's first sentence has a "once upon a time" texture ("In the days when the spinning-wheels hummed busily in the farmhouses . . ."). But while the tone, evoking the buzzing of those pre-industrial looms has a comforting, remote, and generalizing quality about it, the point is historically specific. The story is set at a moment (the very beginning of the nineteenth century) before the development of cotton mills and mass production had proceeded far enough to change the whole society's habits of consumption. The "fable" is firmly set inside history. In those days, we learn, "certain pallid undersized men" walked the lanes with bags thrown over their backs. Dogs barked at them. Shepherds thought of them as somehow in league with the "Evil one." Again, there is something pastoral and pre-modern here, but to understand the fable fully it is important to recognize that these men, entirely misunderstood by the community, which continues to dwell in a feudal culture, are part of an economic system that made their work as weavers indispensable to rural communities.

They seem to be aliens because they are rootless, their pallid faces reflecting their indoor work in a culture of hard-working peasantry whose lives depend on the land and the weather. Consequently they are figures of fear and superstition to the natives, while to the narrator, sympathetically noting the natives' ignorance, they are symptoms of fundamental social changes, and there is no mystery about them, although there is pathos as they mark an early collision between modernity and a dying feudal culture. These urban itinerants, without the roots in place, family, and home that for Eliot were an indispensable source of moral character and social cohesion, were extremely useful in rural areas where the work of farming left little time for activities like weaving. But the cost of this tentative modernity, as Eliot describes it, is moral isolation, a cost that would in later years be experienced intensely by a whole new working class of cotton mill workers. The fable of *Silas Marner* partly explores, with a sense of the value of traditional society, the cost of that isolation and perhaps the possibility of overcoming it.

Silas's sudden miserliness is an indication of that moral isolation. The primary fact of Marner's history is his loss of all connection with his past. Silas's past, as it is narrated in the first two chapters, has failed him. He loses faith in the only god he knew, the god of his independent urban sect, so that he cuts himself off from all familiar things. At his work in Raveloe his life had been reduced "to the unquestioning activity of a spinning insect. He hated the thought of the past; there was nothing that called out his love and fellowship toward the strangers he had come amongst" (p. 15). Marner, in effect, anticipates the anomie of modern urban life that later modernist writers would make their focus. But for Eliot, the aim is both to understand it (which means for her recognizing the importance of tradition and the past in building identity and character), and to overcome it (which means re-assimilation into a human community).

Eliot makes Silas a kind of everyman, full of deep needs, puzzled by the complexities of the world, frustrated by failures, but with the potential for redemption. It is, of course, a human redemption that the narrative offers, but the pattern is distinctly religious. In effect,

Silas sinks into despair about the world and his mind closes to almost everything. Some small stirring of possibility develops as his instinct for loving and connection are converted to miserliness. The only pleasant thing that comes into his insect-like life is the money he earns for his weaving—more particularly, the tactile and visual attractiveness of the gold coins. The moral energies that had gone into his relation with William Dane and his religious community are compressed and diminished but find a first opening in his miserliness.

When he was poor and part of a community, Silas barely cared about money, "but now, when all purpose was gone, that habit of looking toward the money and grasping it with a sense of fulfilled effort made a loam that was deep enough for the seeds of desire" (p. 16). This remarkable metaphor does a lot of work. The seeds of desire are active even in the radically disillusioned weaver; the "loam" of beautiful gold coins is of course shallow, but "deep enough" to allow the rooting of some human desire.

Though money allows no growth of connection and no inter-weaving of deep roots, the passage makes clear that the "seeds of desire" remain germinating in Silas and in the right soil might reconnect him with people and society. The plot is manipulated in such a way as to assure that the soil becomes available. In this respect, the "fable" might be extended out to a consideration of the moral condition of modern factory workers, they too having to work with insect-like narrowness, they too, as urban dwellers, cut off from the kind of traditional society that gave Mary Anne Evans her sense of self and of value. Where, however, is the possibility of human connection, of life-giving soil rather than the merely material soil of coins? Much of Eliot's ultimate political conservatism emerges from her sense that the resolution of the moral emptiness of relations built entirely on money can come only from the reinstatement of the kind of community and tradition that she is fully aware are being displaced and are becoming extinct. She is at the same time fully aware that these valuable community traditions also have their own constricting, unimaginative, and sometimes even destructive powers (her own life, in conflict with her family and with moral conventions, was evidence of that).

In its detailed evocation and description of the ways of a dying culture, *Silas Marner* reflects the influence of the novels of Walter Scott, which, some forty years before Eliot began writing hers, had a revolutionary impact on fiction writing throughout Europe. No novelist before had been more popular than Scott, who, beginning with the first of his series, *Waverley* (1814), described in the most elaborate, sometimes even pedantic detail the way of life of the Scots Highlanders and of the Scots people in general before the unification of Scotland with England. A literal realism, applied to a dying culture and a past irrevocably lost, with its description of costume, customs, manners, and setting, was also inevitably potently romantic. And if, on the one hand, both Scott and Eliot recognize the importance and value of the changes that have effectually extinguished that past, on the other both feel and imply a deep sense of the value of the past culture now lost. It is not a coincidence that *Waverley*'s subtitle, '*Tis Sixty Years Since*, also describes the time difference between the writing of *Silas Marner* and the time in which the narrative takes place.

In considering Eliot's double sense of the past, it is interesting to briefly look at an important essay she wrote in 1856, the year when her writing career was shifting from nonfiction to fiction. Critics have long taken "The Natural History of German Life" as a kind of manifesto for the fiction she was just undertaking; it is also a social and political manifesto, insisting that only "natural," historical change can produce permanent effects, and that sudden, revolutionary rejection of the past would be morally disastrous. It is in this essay also that she complains about "how little the real characteristics of the working classes are known to those who are outside them" and calls for a "natural history" of England's peasants. Writers, she complains, look for their subject "into literature instead of life."[4] In *Silas Marner*, as in her earlier novels of midlands life, Eliot seeks to find her models not in earlier literature (Scott, perhaps, an exception), but in the world of her childhood. And in perhaps the most direct and clearest statement of her view of the function of art, Eliot argues:

> The greatest benefit we owe to the artist, whether painter, poet, or novelist, is the extension of our sympathies. Appeals founded on generalizations and statistics require a sympathy ready-made, a moral sentiment already in activity; but a picture of human life such as a great artist can give, surprises even the trivial and the selfish into that attention to what is apart from themselves, which may be called the raw material of moral sentiment. . . . Art is the nearest thing to life.[5]

"Realism" for George Eliot, then, has a moral and a social function. False representation of the people, she claims, violates the artist's
responsibility to extend our sympathies "beyond the bounds of our
personal lot." "We want to be taught to feel, not for the heroic artisan or the sentimental peasant, but for the peasant in all his coarse
apathy, and the artisan in all his suspicious selfishness." *Silas Marner*,
particularly in the distance between the narrator's voice and the
voices of her "coarse" and apathetic peasant characters, seems to be
attempting to enact this program.

She asks for sympathy in *spite of* the distance, and while from the
perspective of modern social thought Eliot's sense of the absolute difference in sensibility and intelligence between the peasantry (among
whom she herself grew up) and the sophisticated urban intellectual
seems itself prejudiced, *Silas Marner* tries to take an unsentimental look
at a traditional rural community; but at the same time, it attempts to
make her characters colorful in their ignorance and sympathetic in
their narrowness. The book, that is, goes after just the kind of sympathy Eliot argues should be the objective of art.

4

Beyond history, George Eliot always seeks what she believes to be the
timeless principles of human behavior. The particularizing ethnographical eye that portrays the community with the sort of realism
she calls for in "The Natural History of German Life" is also the fab-
ulist finding meaning and moral significance in what might otherwise be seen as random facts. It is a potential contradiction through
all her work that although she believes strongly in the importance of
particular circumstances and thus, as we have seen, becomes an historical novelist, she also believes in the fundamental unity of human
nature and thus seeks qualities that are beyond history. The fable form
produces an interesting kind of tension in Eliot's work, and most obviously in *Silas Marner*.

Every important event in Silas's life is connected to his catalepsy,
momentary lapses in which he is left open to life in ways that his
closed and narrow habits otherwise preclude. As the story unfolds,
the catalepsy that left him vulnerable to William Dane's lies also

makes him susceptible to Dunstan's robbery and then to Eppie's entrance into his cottage. From the perspective of the natives of Raveloe, it would be possible to view these fits as divine visitations, as though every accident were in fact part of the meaningful action of the world. But in giving us the episode of the sect drawing lots to determine the truth of the accusations against Silas, Eliot is clearly rejecting the idea that behind every chance event there is a divine order. What matters, within Eliot's fable, is what the characters do when chance exposes them to new possibilities and dangers, or, put more generally, when history takes its particular and peculiar turns.

To deal with this problem, Eliot juxtaposes two plots in *Silas Marner*: Silas's and Godfrey Cass's. They run parallel in time as well as in events. The plots intersect at two significant points: first when Godfrey's brother, Dunstan, steals Silas's money, and then when Godfrey's child crawls across Silas's threshold, replacing the lost money with a different sort of gold. The conclusion of the novel is the moment in which the question of how each character deals with chance events (with which every human life is filled) determines the turn of the narrative and the moral implications of the fable.

As Silas has a mysterious past that alienates him from the people of Raveloe, so does Godfrey. In George Eliot's fiction (as in Nathaniel Hawthorne's *Scarlet Letter*), it is secrecy, the refusal of openness, that both disguises and encourages morally disruptive action. Godfrey, unlike Silas, has actually been part of "an ugly story of low passion, delusion, and waking from delusion" (p. 28), and as a result he is at the mercy of his crude and conscienceless, blackmailing brother, Dunstan. As Silas is betrayed by William Dane, so Godfrey is betrayed by Dunstan, but obviously Silas is an innocent man and Godfrey a guilty one. Godfrey can be blackmailed because he is afraid to reveal the fact of his misguided marriage. Disguising the past is the worst of sins, and in George Eliot, the past will always return. This return, which seems to work out as "poetic justice" follows theoretically from her belief that all events are tied together in an elaborate web of cause and effect; every act will have consequences well beyond anything that the actor can predict or imagine.

Godfrey relies on chance to keep his secret. And "chance" is a key element both in Eliot's moral theory and in her shaping of the novel. "Favorable Chance," the narrator says, "is the god of all men who follow their own devices instead of obeying a law they believe in . . . the evil principle deprecated in that religion is the orderly sequence by which the seed brings forth a crop after its kind" (p. 69). While this passage applies directly to Godfrey, it also evokes the drawing of lots that concluded Silas's guilt. Morally lazy people, in Eliot's world, assume (or hope) that things will work out to their benefit without taking the trouble to try to produce the conditions that might make that happen; often that means resisting immediate temptation. Chance plays a crucial role in the lives of all the characters, just as it determines the shape of the novel.

In virtually every George Eliot novel, chance enters as a kind of Nemesis, and the effect on the narrative is to make it feel like a fable, or at least to make it feel "contrived." What is more chancy than Silas's door just happening to be open on the one night in which Dunstan might come in to steal, and Eppie might crawl in from the snow? And what more chancy than that the events are balanced within the Cass family, the one taking away, the other giving? The actions of chance in *Silas Marner* seem very much like authorial manipulation, although Eliot would have it that the representation of chance in her narratives simply enacts the way the world really works. In one sense, from her point of view, there is no chance anywhere, for every event is the result of a series of causes. But from the point of view of any individual, incapable of knowing what all the causes are, events will seem merely accidental. In *Silas Marner*, chance, in this sense, works ultimately to determine the way in which events have their inevitably moral effects. Those, like Godfrey and Dunstan, who rely on mere accident to satisfy their desires, are sure to be frustrated, for they assume the world is somehow designed to satisfy their egocentric needs. But chance, the mysterious process of cause and effect, works in utter indifference to ego. But the "seed brings forth a crop after its kind."

As the narrative works out its balances, the parallel stories of Godfrey and Silas reflect each other exactly in this respect. Both are passive in the face of events and unable to speak of their feelings to anyone. But Silas's cataleptic fits are the antitheses to Godfrey's failure to speak, or to act. And where Godfrey says nothing of his child to anyone, particularly to Nancy Lammeter, whom he truly loves, as soon as that child enters Silas's life, Silas claims her for his own, instantaneously and without reflection. This obviously exists, with painful irony, in counterpoint to Godfrey's refusal to claim her and to confess that the dead woman is his wife. "No—no—I can't part with it," says Silas, "It's come to me—I've a right to keep it" (p. 109).

True to Eliot's commitment to be psychologically precise and consistent, she gives Silas the language appropriate to a miser. But the moment makes clear how miserliness was in fact an indication of the possibility of Silas's redemption. The claiming of Eppie as his own, an echo of his claims for the gold he lost, marks the full beginning of Silas's reassimilation into society, and his moral awakening. It should be noted, too, that in choosing to be the only parent of Eppie, Silas instinctively takes up woman's work, the work of nurturing, with which he has no experience. The claim comes from a depth of his character that surprises Silas himself: It "was almost like a revelation." It is such moments of sudden instinctive action that reveal the true nature of character in the work of George Eliot, for, she believes, what one does in such critical instants when there is no time to think reflects the deep moral habits that have been developed over a lifetime.

They are not accidents or chance, but the result of a long-developed moral habit. In *Silas Marner*, this instinctive action is juxtaposed with Godfrey's behavior at the same moment. Godfrey squelches instinct and reflects: He is aware "that he ought not to be waiting . . . that he ought to accept the consequences of his deeds, own the miserable wife, and fulfill the claims of the helpless child" (p. 111). Instead he relies on mere chance to keep his past secret—his great good luck is that his wife is dead. And so, at the end of the chapter, he lapses back into the rationalization that marks the behavior of almost all of Eliot's morally weak characters: "Perhaps," he thinks of Eppie, "it would be just as happy in life without being owned by its father, seeing that nobody could tell how things would turn out, and that—is there any other reason wanted?—well, then, that the father would be much happier without owning the child" (p. 114). The last line rings with a bitterness uncharacteristic of the book, and while for most of the sequence Eliot uses what is called "free indirect discourse" to register Godfrey's thoughts—the narrator representing without comment Godfrey's mind—the last clause, intended to dive below the level of the transparent rationalization, seems more likely to be coming from the narrator than from Godfrey himself.

So ironically, the "favorable chance" that the narrator rejects for her characters actually works to allow Silas to keep Eppie. But the "favorable chance" leads Godfrey to perpetuate his lie, while it evokes from Silas the redeeming qualities that reinvolve him in the life of a community. It is not, then, chance in itself that carries value, but it is how the characters respond to it. By wanting the baby, taking responsibility for it, loving it, determining to bring it up, Silas humanizes himself in the eyes of the Raveloe community.

Ironically, then, Silas's redemption is begun by Dunstan because when the townspeople sitting about in the Rainbow Inn see Silas's distress, they for the first time treat him as a neighbor; and he is further redeemed by Godfrey because Godfrey renounces his own daughter and leaves her to Silas, and it will be Eppie who brings Silas fully back into the community. He even attends church, although he has no idea that the religion of the church in Raveloe has anything to do with the religion of his urban church. The ironies pile upon each other because, while Godfrey does manage to marry Nancy Lammeter, and they have an excellent marriage, the marriage proves to be infertile. Godfrey then wants his child, and the story's crisis comes when Eppie herself has to decide whether to stay with Silas or return to her natural father. Eliot gives us a world in which, even without God, deeds have their consequences and moral errors are punished, moral goodness rewarded.

Most people, Eliot believed (and she shows this in Silas) have the full potential for a good moral life. None of her major characters is willfully immoral, willfully wants to cause other people pain. The function of rationalization among her morally weak characters—like Godfrey—is to allow them to talk themselves into believing that are behaving well, that they are not inflicting pain on others. Godfrey is not a bad man. He is a weak man. And he discovers at the end that his weakness cuts him off from what he really wants. "It's part of my punishment . . . for my daughter to dislike me" (p. 166). And Nancy does not try to soften that pain because she believes it is true. All that is required to ease her pain is that Godfrey should give up his aspiration to have what he has not deserved.

For so small a book, *Silas Marner* is impressively rich in narrative complications, in humor, in historical detail. It is just the book that Hutton claimed it to be. I have focused here on the outlines of the fable, its relation to history, and the moral implications of the story. But the story is far more than I have been able to suggest: Its ethnographical detail is remarkable because Eliot manages to capture the sense of tradition and community, the sense of the combined harshness and narrowness of the local characters gathered in the Rainbow Inn (perhaps the most celebrated part of the story), and the psychological complexities of a cluster of characters, and to bring all these qualities together in a brilliantly structured short novel that continues to give pleasure after close to 150 years, and that can serve as a splendid introduction to the rest of George Eliot's remarkable novels.

5

There will be space here for only a brief discussion of the two short stories included in this volume, both of which were collected with *Silas Marner* in a single volume in the "Cabinet Edition," the last edition of her collected works that George Eliot oversaw. "The Lifted Veil" was written shortly after the great success of *Adam Bede*, in 1859; a year later, breaking off the work that would eventually become *Romola* (1863), Eliot wrote "Brother Jacob," which was not published until 1864. These are the only short stories that Eliot ever wrote, and in her lifetime they received very little attention.

They deserve and in recent years have received more. Although the stories seem to reveal a writer very different from the author of *Silas Marner* and the other novels, they can be taken as fascinating complications of her continuing preoccupations, while at the same time they have their own intrinsic value. Much of current interest in "The Lifted Veil" has derived from the modern fascination with the "Gothic." Nowhere else, even in the smallest episodes, does Eliot turn to the uncanny, the horrific, or the monstrous. "Brother Jacob," in sharp contrast, is almost light-hearted in its moral ironies. The narrative voice has a quality of satiric detachment, a voice that, though comically directed at hypocrisies and absurdities, might at times be heard as almost bitter. Only in that strange final work of her career, *The*

Confessions of Theophrastus Such (1879), does Eliot assume again the voice of the masculine satirist, somewhat embittered, rather funny, and almost too worldly wise, that marks "Brother Jacob."

The striking differences in narrative voice do not, however, take Eliot far from her primary concerns: the importance of roots, of the past, of community, of tradition, of knowledge as a means to sympathy, of getting beyond the self, of checking one's own perspective against that of others, of understanding the social context in which people live and define themselves. We have seen these matters played out in *Silas Marner*, but part of the interest of these stories is that they suggest important problems with Eliot's usual way of dealing with them.

"The Lifted Veil" came as something of a shock to her publisher, John Blackwood, who was expecting a rather different sort of story as a follow-up to the great success of *Adam Bede*. Its lurid quality, the darkness and bleakness of the vision, its almost claustrophobic lingering inside a single morose consciousness, and the very Gothic elements that now seem to make it appealing to new audiences—all of these seemed out of character for the author of a book that looked with such a sharp and sympathetic eye on the life of the midland peasantry. The voice of Latimer, which tells the story, and breaks off almost in midsentence as his foreseen death descends upon him, is that of a highly sophisticated and depressive aesthete, and has none of the healthy breadth of vision that the narrator of *Adam Bede* displayed. In fact, the story is unique in the George Eliot canon in that it is told in the first person, whereas for the most part, Eliot needed an (almost) omniscient narrator who could descend sympathetically into the perspectives of a wide range of characters.

But the story is particularly disturbing because it calls into question a fundamental value of her work: the function of art as a means to extending one's sympathies, exactly by teaching us to understand differences, by learning to see with others' eyes. The poetic epigraph, composed by Eliot (though it was added more than ten years after the story was first published), is startling in its suggestion that increased knowledge might be incompatible with extended sympathy: "Give me no light, great Heaven, but such as turns / To energy of human fellowship." If *Silas Marner* can be seen as in part a sort of

ethnographical study in order to produce aesthetic and thus moral
sympathy, "The Lifted Veil" seems a kind of warning that understanding others might lead not to sympathy but to cynical distrust.
Latimer's gift of second sight turns out to be a curse to him.

In a sort of backward way, the epigraph points toward the tradition of the obsessed scientist in science fiction stories (and to Victor
Frankenstein himself), who becomes dangerous or even villainous
just because he seeks knowledge regardless of its moral consequences. Although Latimer's best friend, Meunier, is not much developed in the story, his character introduces science directly into the
narrative, and it is he who conducts the climactic, horrific, Frankensteinian experiment in reanimation. Science would seem to be precisely the sort of knowledge that does not turn "to energy of human
fellowship," and so it is dramatized in that last scene. In a striking, almost throw-away line at the end of the scene in which her reani-
mated servant accuses Bertha, Latimer's wife, of planning to poison
him, Latimer writes: "Even Meunier looked paralyzed; life for that
moment ceased to be a scientific problem to him" (p. 215).

Science figures more importantly in this story than in any other
George Eliot work except *Middlemarch*, where the scientifically ambitious Lydgate seeks to discover the tissue of all tissues. There are hints
in that book, also, about the Frankensteinian nature of the work, but
here Eliot, herself scientifically very well informed and committed to
the work of science, clearly thematizes the danger of the pursuit of
knowledge without full commitment to increasing the "energy of
human fellowship."

But it would be a mistake to read the story as an argument for
the superiority of art to science, in particular because while Meunier
clearly is not the ideal scientist, Latimer is hardly the ideal artist. And
yet there is no question that he stands in for the artist, as Eliot in her
bleaker moments of depression about her work saw him. Latimer's
role as artist manqué is suggested early, in his reflections on his first
vision:

> No, it was not a dream; was it—the thought was full of tremulous
> exultation—was it the poet's nature in me. . . . Surely it was in this way
> that Homer saw the plain of Troy, that Dante saw the abodes of the de-
> parted, that Milton saw the earthward flight of the Tempter (p. 182).

This neurasthenia is an extreme version of the artist's sensibility, and his fate reveals some of the dangers of the artist's powers. As Helen Small puts it, "Latimer is the only artist protagonist in her fiction, but he fails to produce a single work of art, becoming instead the vehicle for an extraordinary pathologization of the ideals one finds elsewhere in George Eliot's work."[6] On the other hand, while for Eliot modern science is a potential liberator from the narrow and ignorant constraints of traditional culture, it also threatens just that "revolutionary" approach to the culture that (as we have seen in the discussion of *Silas Marner*) she feared would end by being destructive of the best qualities in those traditions.

Recalling Mary Anne Evans's conversion *away* from Christianity, we need to keep in mind as well the strong pull the Christian tradition continued to exercise on her mind and spirit. Latimer's predicament and the peculiar role science plays in this story suggest an alternative, if much more depressing, way in which she imagined handling the disappearance of God from her world. She had committed herself to the validity of scientific evidence, and to the central scientific idea of the laws of "sequence": Every event has its cause, and the laws of cause and effect operate at every level, in human behavior as well as the movement of the stars. Latimer is fascinated by science even as he aspires to art, and although his visionary powers would seem to lie, inexplicably, beyond the realms of science, the knowledge those powers produce exposes an entirely determined world, the very world scientific explanation describes. In such a world, the spiritual emptiness is overwhelming.

It is for this reason that Latimer falls in love with Bertha, a figure who, in her self-centeredness, anticipates later Eliot protagonists like Rosamond Vincy of *Middlemarch*. But whereas in *Middlemarch* Rosamond's effective destruction of Lydgate's scientific ambitions is registered as a loss, in "The Lifted Veil" Bertha's selfishness is part of a narrative that would seem to be seeking ignorance. In no other story is ignorance so positively affirmed. Latimer seeks desperately for something he *doesn't* know. Bertha is particularly attractive to him because "she was my oasis of mystery in the dreary desert of knowledge" (p. 191).

Of course, Bertha's pettiness and even villainy are exposed at the end of the narrative (although there has been little doubt of it for the reader almost from the start); but it takes a Frankensteinian experiment to bring the truth out. Whether, then, it be magic, art, or science, the striking fact about "The Lifted Veil" is that it dramatizes the *failure* of insight into others to produce sympathy. It is as though Eliot were exploring the possibility of a world absolutely opposed to the one she tried for most of her writing career to describe precisely, with the moral energy of realism. Human nature turns out to be fundamentally nasty and self-interested. This bleak possibility gives the story its pervasive darkness. The narrator's limited perspective, beyond which the story does not allow us to see, does not in the end allow the reader to feel much sympathy even for him. That is, just as Latimer sees into others and discovers nothing worth caring for, so the reader, hearing Latimer's voice and looking into him, finds nothing worth caring for.

For modern readers, this strange, bleak story, exploring the most depressive possibilities of the artist's vocation and vision and acquiescing in the view that full knowledge is incompatible with moral being and the meaningfulness of life, has a peculiar fascination. It reveals to us the other side of George Eliot, artist and thinker, the side that distrusts *both* art and science. The artist's visionary possibilities, dramatized through the inadequate artist Latimer, can reveal only the baseness of human nature. In "The Lifted Veil" Eliot expresses directly some of her worst fears as an artist, in particular that the artist's power of vision dries up the artistic creativity that vision has been thought to make possible. It is obviously not the vision that Eliot, in *Silas Marner* and her other great works, attempts to disseminate. But anyone reading Eliot's correspondence will recognize in Latimer's dark depression the Eliot who never fully believed in her own artistic powers, and who, after *Silas Marner*, struggled wretchedly with *Romola*, the book that she said transformed her from a young woman to an old one.

Constrained by a single point of view, "The Lifted Veil" offers no way out but a rejection of the knowledge that would expel spirit and hope from the world. This is not the George Eliot who achieved fame as a novelist; nevertheless, the question of the dangers of full knowledge troubles Eliot's narratives even in the greater novels, although it is never anywhere else handled so painfully and directly. There is, however, one particularly famous passage from *Middlemarch* that captures something of the pain and the fear that produced "The Lifted Veil":

If we had a keen vision and feeling of all ordinary human life, it would be like hearing the grass grow and the squirrel's heart beat, and we should die of that roar which lies on the other side of silence. As it is, the quickest of us walk about well wadded with stupidity.[7]

In the context of George Eliot's complete work, "Brother Jacob" is obviously less bleak and less surprising than the "The Lifted Veil." Although the voice of the narrator, omniscient though he is, has a quality of satirical distance quite far from the norms of Eliot's narrative voice, its themes are familiar. In dramatizing the way the past returns as Nemesis to expose the false David Faux (whose last name, of course, means "false") it anticipates a central element in much of Eliot's work. Jacob, the idiot brother returning to humiliate David, is a comic version of Raffles, who returns in *Middlemarch* to expose Bulstrode's sordid past, or of Baldassare returning to expose Tito's falseness in *Romola*. (It might be pointed out that Eliot gave "Brother Jacob" to the publishers of *Cornhill* to compensate in part for the money they lost in publishing *Romola*.)

Where "The Lifted Veil" allows no humor at all, "Brother Jacob" adopts a comic, satiric mode, and the simple, parable-like structure of the story makes it a much simpler and in some ways less interesting work. Nevertheless, despite its differences, both in simplicity and in symbolic obviousness, it is also full of Eliot's usual preoccupations and techniques. If this is true, what of Eliot's commitment to realism both as an aesthetic and a moral responsibility? "The Lifted Veil" takes us into extrasensory perception and powers of divination and reanimation of the dead, and "Brother Jacob" is both satire and moral allegory. The allegorical quality of it is clear in the relation between the brothers. Jacob is obviously the physical embodiment of David's greed and single-minded pursuit of personal satisfactions, the one gluttonous and enamored of sweets, the other making his living through sweets and gluttonous in a different way. Moreover, the story depends on Jacob's being the instrument of David's exposure. David's fiancée is coyly called "pretty Penny." And Nemesis descends, as in Eliot's world, realist or allegorical, it is bound to do. The poetic justice of the piece may almost be too precise, but it reflects Eliot's sense that the laws of "sequence" include the idea that deeds have their consequence, and that immoral actions will both reveal themselves and be punished. No doubt, "Brother Jacob" is far more a "fable" even than *Silas Marner*.

But as with *Silas Marner*, the fable gains interest as we note that Eliot sets it inside a very carefully conceived social and historical moment. Although the parable focuses on questions of selfishness and personal greed (even gluttony), there is a wonderful and wise sequence in which the narrator traces the way in which "Edward Freely's" new confectionery is established in Grimworth. We watch here, in a few brilliantly concise pages, a particularized explanation of the sort of economic transition that is implicit in *Silas Marner*. Although the story does not give us the precise historical dating we can infer from *Silas Marner*, it traces the transition of the small town as its economy expands beyond the self-sustaining conventions of a feudal, peasant culture.

When David arrives in Grimworth, there is "no competition," for there are no other sweet shops in town (p. 231). We learn that a new charity school is going to be set up (the Yellow School parodies real charity schools in England, which were given the name of other colors). Population is increasing (and the expansion gets mixed reactions from the natives). Again, the power of traditional ways of doing business is set against a new trading economy, which is bringing new fashions and new ways of life to the provincial town. All of this, moreover, confuses the traditional class hierarchies, for not only were tradespeople considered lower than landed gentry, but each trade had a different ranking. Freely, as he attempts to break into an established town family, enacts fraudulently the kinds of breakdowns of social hierarchies that the new economy was forcing upon traditional communities (and that became one of the central subjects of virtually all Victorian fiction). Freely's display windows also mark a social difference, for the traditional trades did not exploit show windows: "What a sight to dawn upon the eyes of Grimworth children! They almost forgot to go to their dinner that day" (pp. 233–234).

Here again, then, the parable is not only about the price to be paid for selfishness but about the relation between the moral issues in David Faux's behavior and the way in which modern advertising and trade and industry were transforming the society. The parable, suggesting a universal moral condition and universal actors, extends to comment upon contemporary social issues. The breakdown of traditional class hierarchies, the substitution of money for traditional hierarchical values, the moral compromises entailed in achieving success in the new economy—all of these questions provide a commentary on the new commercialism.

"Brother Jacob" can also be crudely funny in its excessive ironic sharpness and in the conception of the massive idiot manipulated by sweets but then unmanipulable when he descends on "Davy." But behind its comedy and its experimental form, as behind the form of "The Lifted Veil," there lies the extraordinary subtlety and richness of George Eliot's mind. But these stories show her attempting in a way to get beyond the conventions and theories of her own work, to look into the perhaps unredeemable darkness of human nature. Along with *Silas Marner*, these stories make a remarkable trio of variations in the work of one of England's greatest novelists.

George Levine is Kenneth Burke Professor of English Literature at Rutgers University, and director of the University's Center for the Critical Analysis of Contemporary Culture. He has written extensively about Victorian literature and culture, and has for a long time focused attention on Darwin and the relations between science and literature, particularly in his *Darwin and the Novelists*. He has written and edited many books, on subjects ranging from *Frankenstein* to the works of Thomas Pynchon. Most recently, he has edited *The Cambridge Companion to George Eliot* and written a study of Victorian scientific thought and literature, *Dying to Know*. His earlier volume, *The Realistic Imagination*, which focuses on the development of the English novel in the nineteenth century, also connects that genre with science. His most Darwinian and most personal book, *Lifebirds*, is his volume of birding memoirs, illustrated by his wife, Marge. He is currently at work on a second book on Darwin and the way his thought has been used and misused.

Notes to the Introduction

1. R. H. Hutton, unsigned review in *Economist* (April 27, 1861), reprinted in David Carroll, ed., *George Eliot: The Critical Heritage*, London: Routledge and Kegan Paul, 1971, p. 175.

2. "The Natural History of German Life," *Essays of George Eliot*, edited by Thomas Pinney, New York: Columbia University Press, 1963, p. 287.
3. In *Essays*, p. 324.
4. "The Natural History of German Life," in *Essays*, pp. 268–269.
5. "The Natural History of German Life," in *Essays*, p. 271.
6. Helen Small, "Introduction," in George Eliot, *The Lifted Veil, Brother Jacob*, Oxford: Oxford University Press, 1999, p. xii.
7. George Eliot, *Middlemarch*, New York: Barnes and Noble Classics, 2003, chapter 20, p. 185.

SILAS MARNER:

THE WEAVER OF RAVELOE

"A child, more than all other gifts
That earth can offer to declining man,
Brings hope with it, and forward-looking thoughts."

—*WORDSWORTH.**

---

*Lines 146–148 of William Wordsworth's "Michael, a Pastoral Poem."

PART I

CHAPTER I

IN THE DAYS WHEN the spinning-wheels hummed busily in the farmhouses—and even great ladies, clothed in silk and thread-lace, had their toy spinning-wheels of polished oak—there might be seen in districts far away among the lanes, or deep in the bosom of the hills, certain pallid undersized men, who, by the side of the brawny country-folk, looked like the remnants of a disinherited race.[1] The shepherd's dog barked fiercely when one of these alien-looking men appeared on the upland, dark against the early winter sunset; for what dog likes a figure bent under a heavy bag?— and these pale men rarely stirred abroad without that mysterious burden. The shepherd himself, though he had good reason to believe that the bag held nothing but flaxen thread, or else the long rolls of strong linen spun from that thread, was not quite sure that this trade of weaving, indispensable though it was, could be carried on entirely without the help of the Evil One. In that far-off time superstition clung easily round every person or thing that was at all unwonted, or even intermittent and occasional merely, like the visits of the peddler or the knife-grinder. No one knew where wandering men had their homes or their origin; and how was a man to be explained unless you at least knew somebody who knew his father and mother? To the peasants of old times, the world outside their own direct experience was a region of vagueness and mystery: to their untraveled thought a state of wandering was a conception as dim as the winter life of the swallows that came back with the spring; and even a settler, if he came from distant parts, hardly ever ceased to be viewed with a remnant of distrust, which would have prevented any surprise if a long course of inoffensive conduct on his part had ended in the commission of a crime; especially if he had any reputation for knowledge, or showed any skill in handicraft. All cleverness, whether in the rapid use of that difficult instrument the tongue, or in some other art unfamiliar to villagers, was in itself suspicious: honest folk, born and bred in a visible manner, were mostly not overwise or clever—at least, not beyond such a matter as knowing the signs of the weather; and the process by which rapidity and dexterity of any kind were acquired was so wholly hidden, that they partook of the nature of conjuring. In this way it came to pass that those scattered linen-weavers— emigrants from the town into the country—were to the last regarded as aliens by their rustic neighbors, and usually contracted the eccentric habits which belong to a state of loneliness.

In the early years of this century, such a linen-weaver, named Silas Marner, worked at his vocation in a stone cottage that stood among the nutty hedgerows near the village of Raveloe, and not far from the edge of a deserted stone-pit. The questionable sound of Silas's loom, so unlike the natural cheerful trotting of the winnowing-machine, or the simpler rhythm of the flail, had a half-fearful fascination for the Raveloe boys, who would often leave off their nutting or birds'-nesting to peep in at the window of the stone cottage, counterbalancing a certain awe at the mysterious action of the loom, by a pleasant sense of scornful superiority, drawn from the mockery of its alternating noises, along with the bent, tread-mill attitude of the weaver. But sometimes it happened that Marner, pausing to adjust an irregularity in his thread, became aware of the small scoundrels, and, though chary of his time, he liked their intrusion so ill that he would descend from his loom, and, opening the door, would fix on them a gaze that was always enough to make them take to their legs in terror. For how was it possible to believe that those large brown protuberant eyes in Silas Marner's pale face really saw nothing very distinctly that was not close to them, and not rather that their dreadful stare could dart cramp, or rickets, or a wry mouth at any boy who happened to be in the rear? They had, perhaps, heard their fathers and mothers hint that Silas Marner could cure folk's rheumatism if he had a mind, and add, still more darkly, that if you could only speak the devil fair enough, he might save you the cost of the doctor. Such strange lingering echoes of the old demon worship might perhaps even now be caught by the diligent listener among the gray-haired peasantry; for the rude mind with difficulty associates the ideas of power and benignity. A shadowy conception of power that by much persuasion can be induced to refrain from inflicting harm, is the shape most easily taken by the sense of the Invisible in the minds of men who have always been pressed close by primitive wants, and to whom a life of hard toil has never been illuminated by any enthusiastic religious faith. To them pain and mishap present a far wider range of possibilities than gladness and enjoyment: their imagination is almost barren of the images that feed desire and hope, but is all overgrown by recollections that are a perpetual pasture to fear. "Is there anything you can fancy that you would like to eat?" I once said to an old laboring man, who was in his last illness, and who had refused all the food his wife had offered him. "No," he answered, "I've never been used to nothing but common victual, and I can't eat that." Experience had bred no fancies in him that could raise the phantasm of appetite.

And Raveloe was a village where many of the old echoes lingered, undrowned by new voices. Not that it was one of those barren parishes lying on the outskirts of civilization—inhabited by meagre sheep and thinly-scattered shepherds: on the contrary, it lay in the rich central plain of what we are pleased to call Merry England, and held farms which, speaking from a spiritual point of view, paid highly-desirable tithes. But it was nestled in a snug well-wooded hollow, quite an hour's journey on horseback from any turnpike, where it was never reached by the vibrations of the coach-horn, or of public opinion. It was an important-looking village, with a fine old church and large churchyard in the heart of it, and two or three large brick and stone homesteads, with well-walled orchards and ornamental weathercocks, standing close upon the road, and lifting more imposing fronts than the rectory, which peeped from among the trees on the other side of the churchyard:—a village which showed at once the summits of its social life, and told the practiced eye that there was no great park and manor-house in the vicinity, but that there were several chiefs in Raveloe who could farm badly quite at their ease, drawing enough money from their bad farming, in those war times,[2] to live in a rollicking fashion, and keep a jolly Christmas, Whitsun and Easter tide.

It was fifteen years since Silas Marner had first come to Raveloe; he was then simply a pallid young man, with prominent short-sighted brown eyes, whose appearance would have had nothing strange for people of average culture and experience, but for the villagers near whom he had come to settle it had mysterious peculiarities which corresponded with the exceptional nature of his occupation, and his advent from an unknown region called "North'-ard." So had his way of life:—he invited no comer to step across his door-sill, and he never strolled into the village to drink a pint at the Rainbow, or to gossip at the wheelwright's: he sought no man or woman, save for the purposes of his calling, or in order to supply himself with necessaries; and it was soon clear to the Raveloe lasses that he would never urge one of them to accept him against her will—quite as if he had heard them declare that they would never marry a dead man come to life again. This view of Marner's personality was not without another ground than his pale face and unexampled eyes; for Jem Rodney, the mole-catcher, averred that one evening as he was returning homeward he saw Silas Marner leaning against a stile with a heavy bag on his back, instead of resting the bag on the stile as a man in his senses would have done; and that, on coming up to him, he saw that Marner's eyes were set like a dead man's, and he spoke to him, and shook him, and his limbs were stiff, and his hands clutched the bag as if they'd been made of iron; but just as he had made up his mind that the weaver was dead, he came all right again, like, as you might say, in the winking of an eye, and said "Good night," and walked off. All this Jem swore he had seen, more by token that it was the very day he had been mole-catching on Squire Cass's land, down by the old saw-pit. Some said Marner must have been in a "fit," a word which seemed to explain things otherwise incredible; but the argumentative Mr. Macey, clerk of the parish, shook his head, and asked if anybody was ever known to go off in a fit and not fall down.[3] A fit was a stroke, wasn't it? and it was in the nature of a stroke to partly take away the use of a man's limbs and throw him on the parish, if he'd got no children to look to. No, no; it was no stroke that would let a man stand on his legs, like a horse between the shafts, and then walk off as soon as you can say "Gee!" But there might be such a thing as a man's soul being loose from his body, and going out and in, like a bird out of its nest and back; and that was how folks got over-wise, for they went to school in this shell-less state to those who could teach them more than their neighbors could learn with their five senses and the parson. And where did Master Marner get his knowledge of herbs from—and charms too, if he liked to give them away? Jem Rodney's story was no more than what might have been expected by anybody who had seen how Marner had cured Sally Oates, and made her sleep like a baby, when her heart had been beating enough to burst her body, for two months and more, while she had been under the doctor's care. He might cure more folks if he would; but he was worth speaking fair, if it was only to keep him from doing you a mischief.

It was partly to this vague fear that Marner was indebted for protecting him from the persecution that his singularities might have drawn upon him, but still more to the fact that, the old linen-weaver in the neighboring parish of Tarley being dead, his handicraft made him a highly welcome settler to the richer housewives of the district and even to the more provident cottagers, who had their little stock of yarn at the year's end. Their sense of his usefulness would have counteracted any repugnance or suspicion which was not confirmed by a deficiency in the quality or the tale of the cloth he wove for them. And the years had rolled on without producing any change in the impressions of the neighbors concerning Marner, except the change from novelty to habit. At the end of fifteen years[4] the Raveloe men said just the same things about Silas Marner as at the beginning: they did not say them quite so often, but they believed them much more strongly when they did say them. There was only one important addition which the years had brought: it was, that Master Marner had laid by a fine sight of money somewhere, and that he could buy up "bigger men" than himself.

But while opinion concerning him had remained nearly stationary, and his daily habits had presented scarcely any visible change, Marner's inward life had been a history and a metamorphosis, as that of every fervid nature must be when it has fled, or been condemned to solitude. His life, before he came to Raveloe, had been filled with the movement, the mental activity, and the close fellowship, which in that day as in this, marked the life of an artisan early incorporated in a narrow religious sect, where the poorest layman has the chance of distinguishing himself by gifts of speech, and has, at the very least, the weight of a silent voter in the government of his community. Marner was highly thought of in that little hidden world, known to itself as the church assembling in Lantern Yard,* he was believed, to be a young man of exemplary life and ardent faith; and a peculiar interest

---

*One of many independent sects that sprang up in that era, almost always in towns or cities; these churches typically were not connected with any formal church hierarchies and were committed to the direct experience of God through the Bible.

had been centered in him ever since he had fallen, at a prayer-meeting, into a mysterious rigidity and suspension of consciousness, which, lasting for an hour or more, had been mistaken for death. To have sought a medical explanation for this phenomenon would have been held by Silas himself, as well as by his minister and fellow-members, a willful self-exclusion from the spiritual significance that might lie therein. Silas was evidently a brother selected for a peculiar discipline; and though the effort to interpret this discipline was discouraged by the absence, on his part, of any spiritual vision during his outward trance, yet it was believed by himself and others that its effect was seen in an accession of light and fervor. A less truthful man than he might have been tempted into the subsequent creation of a vision in the form of resurgent memory; a less sane man might have believed in such a creation; but Silas was both sane and honest, though, as with many honest and fervent men, culture had not defined any channels for his sense of mystery, and so it spread itself over the proper pathway of inquiry and knowledge. He had inherited from his mother some acquaintance with medicinal herbs and their preparation—a little store of wisdom which she had imparted to him as a solemn bequest—but of late years he had had doubts about the lawfulness of applying this knowledge, believing that herbs could have no efficacy without prayer, and that prayer might suffice without herbs; so that his inherited delight to wander through the fields in search of foxglove and dandelion and coltsfoot, began to wear to him the character of a temptation.

Among the members of his church there was one young man, a little older than himself, with whom he had long lived in such close friendship that it was the custom of their Lantern Yard brethren to call them David and Jonathan. The real name of the friend was William Dane, and he, too, was regarded as a shining instance of youthful piety, though somewhat given to over-severity toward weaker brethren, and to be so dazzled by his own light as to hold himself wiser than his teachers. But whatever blemishes others might discern in William, to his friend's mind he was faultless; for Marner had one of those impressible self-doubting natures which, at an inexperienced age, admire imperativeness and lean on contradiction. The expression of trusting simplicity in Marner's face, heightened by that absence of special observation, that defenseless, deer-like gaze which belongs to large prominent eyes, was strongly contrasted by the self-complacent suppression of inward triumph that lurked in the narrow slanting eyes and compressed lips of William Dane. One of the most frequent topics of conversation between the two friends was Assurance of salvation: Silas confessed that he could never arrive at anything higher than hope mingled with fear, and listened with longing wonder when William declared that he had possessed un-shaken assurance ever since, in the period of his conversion, he had dreamed that he saw the words "calling and election sure"* standing by themselves on a white page in the open Bible. Such colloquies have occupied many a pair of pale-faced weavers, whose unnurtured souls have been like young winged things, fluttering forsaken in the twilight.

It had seemed to the unsuspecting Silas that the friendship had suffered no chill even from his formation of another attachment of a closer kind. For some months he had been engaged to a young servant-woman, waiting only for a little increase to their mutual sav-ings in order to their marriage; and it was a great delight to him that Sarah did not object to William's occasional presence in their Sunday interviews. It was at this point in their history that Silas's cataleptic fit occurred during the prayer-meeting; and amidst the various queries and expressions of interest addressed to him by his fellow-members, William's suggestion alone jarred with the general sympathy toward a brother thus singled out for special dealings. He observed that, to him, this trance looked more like a visitation of Satan than a proof of divine favor, and exhorted his friend to see that he had no accursed thing within his soul. Silas, feeling bound to accept rebuke and ad-monition as a brotherly office, felt no resentment, but only pain, at his friend's doubts concerning him; and to this was soon added some anxiety at the perception that Sarah's manner toward him began to exhibit a strange fluctuation between an effort at an increased mani-festation of regard and involuntary signs of shrinking and dislike. He asked her if she wished to break off their engagement; but she de-nied this: their engagement was known to the church, and had been

---

*See the Bible, 2 Peter 1:10: "Wherefore the rather, brethren, give diligence to make your calling and election sure: for if ye do these things, ye shall never fall" (King James Version; henceforth, KJV).

recognized in the prayer-meetings; it could not be broken off without strict investigation, and Sarah could render no reason that would be sanctioned by the feeling of the community. At this time the senior deacon was taken dangerously ill, and, being a childless widower, he was tended night and day by some of the younger brethren or sisters. Silas frequently took his turn in the night-watching with William, the one relieving the other at two in the morning. The old man, contrary to expectation, seemed to be on the way to recovery, when one night Silas, sitting up by his bedside, observed that his usual audible breathing had ceased. The candle was burning low, and he had to lift it to see the patient's face distinctly. Examination convinced him that the deacon was dead—had been dead some time, for the limbs were rigid. Silas asked himself if he had been asleep, and looked at the clock: it was already four in the morning. How was it that William had not come? In much anxiety he went to seek for help, and soon there were several friends assembled in the house, the minister among them, while Silas went away to his work, wishing he could have met William to know the reason of his non-appearance. But at six o'clock, as he was thinking of going to seek his friend, William came, and with him the minister. They came to summon him to Lantern Yard, to meet the church members there; and to his inquiry concerning the cause of the summons the only reply was, "You will hear." Nothing further was said until Silas was seated in the vestry, in front of the minister, with the eyes of those who to him represented God's people fixed solemnly upon him. Then the minister, taking out a pocket-knife, showed it to Silas, and asked him if he knew where he had left that knife. Silas said he did not know that he had left it anywhere out of his own pocket—but he was trembling at this strange interrogation. He was then exhorted not to hide his sin, but to confess and repent. The knife had been found in the bureau by the departed deacon's bedside—found in the place where the little bag of church money had lain, which the minister himself had seen the day before. Some hand had removed that bag; and whose hand could it be, if not that of the man to whom the knife belonged? For some time Silas was mute with astonishment. Then he said, "God will clear me. I know nothing about the knife being there, or the money being gone. Search me and my dwelling; you will find nothing but three pound five of my own savings, which William Dane knows I have had these six months." At this William groaned, but the minister said, "The proof is heavy against you, brother Marner. The money was taken in the night last past, and no man was with our departed brother but you, for William Dane declares to us that he was hindered by sudden sickness from going to take his place as usual, and you yourself said that he had not come; and, moreover, you neglected the dead body."

"I must have slept," said Silas. Then, after a pause, he added, "Or I must have had another visitation like that which you have all seen me under, so that the thief must have come and gone while I was not in the body, but out of the body. But I say again, search me and my dwelling, for I have been nowhere else."

The search was made, and it ended—in William Dane's finding the well-known bag, empty, tucked behind the chest of drawers in Silas's chamber! On this William exhorted his friend to confess, and not to hide his sin any longer. Silas turned a look of keen reproach on him, and said, "William, for nine years that we have gone in and out together, have you ever known me tell a lie? But God will clear me."

"Brother," said William, "how do I know what you may have done in the secret chambers of your heart, to give Satan an advantage over you?"

Silas was still looking at his friend. Suddenly a deep flush came over his face, and he was about to speak impetuously, when he seemed checked again by some inward shock that sent the flush back and made him tremble. But at last he spoke feebly, looking at William.

"I remember now—the knife wasn't in my pocket."

William said, "I know nothing of what you mean." The other persons present, however, began to inquire where Silas meant to say that the knife was, but he would give no further explanation: he only said, "I am sore stricken; I can say nothing. God will clear me."

On their return to the vestry there was further deliberation. Any resort to legal measures for ascertaining the culprit was contrary to the principles of the church in Lantern Yard, according to which prosecution was forbidden to Christians, even had the case held less scandal to the community. But the members were bound to take other measures for finding out the truth, and they resolved on praying and drawing lots. This resolution can be a ground of surprise only to those who are unacquainted with that obscure religious life which has gone on in the alleys of our towns. Silas knelt with his brethren, relying on his own innocence being certified by immediate divine interference, but feeling that there was sorrow and mourning behind for him even then—that his trust in man had been cruelly bruised. *The lots declared that Silas Marner was guilty.* He was solemnly suspended from church-membership, and called upon to render up the stolen money: only on confession, as the sign of repentance, could he be received once more within the folds of the church. Marner listened in silence. At last, when everyone rose to depart, he went toward William Dane and said, in a voice shaken by agitation—

"The last time I remember using my knife, was when I took it out to cut a strap for you. I don't remember putting it in my pocket again. You stole the money, and you have woven a plot to lay the sin at my door. But you may prosper, for all that: there is no just God that governs the earth righteously, but a God of lies, that bears witness against the innocent."

There was a general shudder at this blasphemy.

William said meekly, "I leave our brethren to judge whether this is the voice of Satan or not. I can do nothing but pray for you, Silas."

Poor Marner went out with that despair in his soul—that shaken trust in God and man, which is little short of madness to a loving nature. In the bitterness of his wounded spirit, he said to himself, "*She* will cast me off too." And he reflected that, if she did not believe the testimony against him, her whole faith must be upset as his was. To people accustomed to reason about the forms in which their religious feeling has incorporated itself, it is difficult to enter into that simple, untaught state of mind in which the form and the feeling have never been severed by an act of reflection. We are apt to think it inevitable that a man in Marner's position should have begun to question the validity of an appeal to the divine judgment by drawing lots; but to him this would have been an effort of independent thought such as he had never known; and he must have made the effort at a moment when all his energies were turned into the anguish of disappointed faith. If there is an angel who records the sorrows of men as well as their sins, he knows how many and deep are the sorrows that spring from false ideas for which no man is culpable.

Marner went home, and for a whole day sat alone, over-come by despair, without any impulse to go to Sarah and attempt to win her belief in his innocence. The second day he took refuge from be-numbing unbelief, by getting into his loom and working away as usual; and before many hours were past, the minister and one of the deacons came to him with the message from Sarah, that she held her engagement to him at an end. Silas received the message mutely, and then turned away from the messengers to work at his loom again. In little more than a month from that time, Sarah was married to William Dane; and not long afterward it was known to the brethren in Lantern Yard that Silas Marner had departed from the town.

CHAPTER II

EVEN PEOPLE WHOSE LIVES have been made various by learning, sometimes find it hard to keep a fast hold on their habitual views of life, on their faith in the Invisible, nay, on the sense that their past joys and sorrows are a real experience, when they are suddenly transported to a new land, where the beings around them know nothing of their history, and share none of their ideas—where their mother earth shows another lap, and human life has other forms than those on which their souls have been nour-ished. Minds that have been unhinged from their old faith and love, have perhaps sought this Lethean influence of exile, in which the past becomes dreamy because its symbols have all vanished, and the present too is dreamy because it is linked with no memories.[5] But even their experience may hardly enable them thoroughly to imagine what was the effect on a simple weaver like Silas Marner, when he left his own country and people and came to settle in Raveloe. Noth-ing could be more unlike his native town, set within sight of the widespread hillsides, than this low wooded region, where he felt hidden even from the heavens by the screening trees and hedgerows. There was nothing here, when he rose in the deep morning quiet and looked out on the dewy brambles and rank tufted grass, that seemed to have any relation with that life centering in Lantern Yard, which had once been to him the altar-place of high dispensations. The whitewashed walls; the little pews where well-known figures en-tered with a subdued rustling, and where first one well-known voice and then another, pitched in a peculiar key of petition, uttered phrases at once occult and familiar, like the amulet worn on the heart; the pulpit where the minister delivered unquestioned doctrine, and swayed to and fro, and handled the book in a long accustomed manner; the very pauses between the couplets of the hymn, as it was given out, and the recurrent swell of voices in song: these things had been the channel of divine influences to Marner—they were the fostering home of his religious emotions—they were Christianity and God's kingdom upon earth. A weaver who finds hard words in his hymn-book knows nothing of abstractions; as the little child knows nothing of parental love, but only knows one face and one lap toward which it stretches its arms for refuge and nurture.

And what could be more unlike that Lantern Yard world than the world in Raveloe?—orchards looking lazy with neglected plenty; the large church in the wide church-yard, which men gazed at lounging at their own doors in service-time; the purple-faced farmers jogging along the lanes or turning in at the Rainbow; homesteads, where men supped heavily and slept in the light of the evening hearth, and where women seemed to be laying up a stock of linen for the life to come. There were no lips in Raveloe from which a word could fall that would stir Silas Marner's benumbed faith to a sense of pain. In the early ages of the world, we know, it was believed that each territory was inhabited and ruled by its own divinities, so that a man could cross the bordering heights and be out of the reach of his native gods, whose presence was confined to the streams and the groves and the hills among which he had lived from his birth. And poor Silas was vaguely conscious of something not unlike the feeling of primitive men, when they fled thus, in fear or in sullenness, from the face of an unpropitious deity. It seemed to him that the Power he had vainly trusted in among the streets and at the prayer-meetings, was very far away from this land in which he had taken refuge, where men lived in careless abundance, knowing and needing nothing of that trust, which, for him, had been turned to bitterness. The little light he possessed spread its beams so narrowly, that frustrated belief was a curtain broad enough to create for him the blackness of night.

His first movement after the shock had been to work in his loom; and he went on with this unremittingly, never asking himself why, now he was come to Raveloe, he worked far on into the night to finish the tale of Mrs. Osgood's table-linen sooner than she expected— without contemplating beforehand the money, she would put into his hand for the work. He seemed to weave, like the spider, from pure impulse, without reflection. Every man's work, pursued steadily, tends in this way to become an end in itself, and so to bridge over the loveless chasms of his life. Silas's hand satisfied itself with throwing the shuttle, and his eye with seeing the little squares in the cloth complete themselves under his effort. Then there were the calls of hunger; and Silas, in his solitude, had to provide his own breakfast, dinner, and supper, to fetch his own water from the well, and put his own kettle on the fire; and all these immediate promptings helped, along with the weaving, to reduce his life to the unquestioning activity of a spinning insect. He hated the thought of the past; there was nothing that called out his love and fellowship toward the strangers he had come amongst; and the future was all dark, for there was no Unseen Love that cared for him. Thought was arrested by utter bewilderment, now its old narrow pathway was closed, and affection seemed to have died under the bruise that had fallen on its keenest nerves.

But at last Mrs. Osgood's table-linen was finished, and Silas was paid in gold. His earnings in his native town, where he worked for a wholesale dealer, had been after a lower rate; he had been paid weekly, and of his weekly earnings a large proportion had gone to objects of piety and charity. Now, for the first time in his life, he had five bright guineas put into his hand; no man expected a share of them, and he loved no man that he should offer him a share. But what were the guineas to him who saw no vista beyond countless days of weaving? It was needless for him to ask that, for it was pleasant to him to feel them in his palm, and look at their bright faces, which were all his own: it was another element of life, like the weaving and the satisfaction of hunger, subsisting quite aloof from the life of belief and love from which he had been cut off. The weaver's hand had known the touch of hard-won money even before the palm had grown to its full breadth; for twenty years, mysterious money had stood to him as the symbol of earthly good, and the immediate object of toil. He had seemed to love it little in the years when every penny had its purpose for him; for he loved the *purpose* then. But now, when all purpose was gone, that habit of looking toward the money and grasping it with a sense of fulfilled effort made a loam that was deep enough for the seeds of desire; and as Silas walked homeward across the fields in the twilight, he drew out the money and thought it was brighter in the gathering gloom.[6]

About this time an incident happened which seemed to open a possibility of some fellowship with his neighbors. One day, taking a pair of shoes to be mended, he saw the cobbler's wife seated by the fire, suffering from the terrible symptoms of hear-disease and dropsy, which he had witnessed as the precursors of his mother's death. He felt a rush of pity at the mingled sight and remembrance, and, recalling the relief his mother had found from a simple preparation of foxglove, he promised Sally Oates to bring her something that would ease her, since the doctor did her no good. In this office of charity, Silas felt, for the first time since he had come to Raveloe, a sense of unity between his past and present life, which might have been the beginning of his rescue from the insect-like existence into which his nature had shrunk. But Sally Oates's disease had raised her into a personage of much interest and importance among the neighbors, and the fact of her having found relief from drinking Silas Marner's "stuff" became a matter of general discourse. When Doctor Kimble gave physic, it was natural that it should have an effect; but when a weaver, who came from nobody knew where, worked wonders with a bottle of brown waters, the occult character of the process was evident. Such a sort of thing had not been known since the Wise Woman at Tarley died; and she had charms as well as "stuff"; everybody went to her when their children had fits. Silas Marner must be a person of the same sort, for how did he know what would bring back Sally Oates's breath, if he didn't know a fine sight more than that? The Wise Woman had words that she muttered to herself, so that you couldn't hear what they were, and if she tied a bit of red thread round the child's toe the while, it would keep off the water in the head. There were women in Raveloe, at that present time, who had worn one of the Wise Woman's little bags round their necks, and, in consequence, had never had an idiot child, as Ann Coulter had. Silas Marner could very likely do as much, and more; and now it was all clear how he should have come from unknown parts, and be so "comical-looking." But Sally Oates must mind and not tell the doctor, for he would be sure to set his face against Marner; he was always angry about the Wise Woman, and used to threaten those who went to her that they should have none of his help any more.

Silas now found himself and his cottage suddenly beset by mothers who wanted him to charm away the whooping-cough, or bring back the milk; and by men who wanted stuff against the rheumatics or the knots in the hands; and to secure themselves against a refusal, the applicants brought silver in their palms. Silas might have driven a profitable trade in charms as well as in his small list of drugs; but money on this condition was no temptation to him; he had never known an impulse toward falsity, and he drove one after another away with growing irritation, for the news of him as a wise man had spread even to Tarley, and it was long before people ceased to take long walks for the sake of asking his aid. But the hope in his wisdom was at length changed into dread, for no one believed him when he said he knew no charms and could work no cures, and every man and woman who had an accident or a new attack after applying to him, set the misfortune down to Master Marner's ill-will and irritated glances. Thus it came to pass that his movement of pity toward Sally Oates, which had given him a transient sense of brotherhood, heightened the repulsion between him and his neighbors, and made his isolation more complete.

Gradually the guineas, the crowns, and the half-crowns grew to a heap, and Marner drew less and less for his own wants, trying to solve the problem of keeping himself strong enough to work sixteen hours a day on as small an outlay as possible. Have not men, shut up in solitary imprisonment, found an interest in marking the moments by straight strokes of a certain length on the wall, until the growth of the sum of straight strokes, arranged in triangles, has become a mastering purpose? Do we not wile away moments of inanity or fatigued waiting by repeating some trivial movement or sound, until the repetition has bred a want, which is incipient habit? That will help us to understand how the love of accumulating money grows an absorbing passion in men whose imaginations, even in the very beginning of their hoard, showed them no purpose beyond it. Marner wanted the heaps of ten to grow into a square, and then into a larger square; and every added guinea, while it was itself a satisfaction, bred a new desire. In this strange world, made a hopeless riddle to him, he might, if he had had a less intense nature, have sat weaving, weaving—looking toward the end of his pattern, or toward the end of his web, till he forgot the riddle, and everything else but his immediate sensations; but the money had come to mark off his weaving into periods, and the money not only grew, but it remained with him. He began to think it was conscious of him, as his loom was, and he would on no account have exchanged those coins, which had become his familiars, for other coins with unknown faces. He handled them, he counted them, till their form and color were like the satisfaction of a thirst to him; but it was only in the night, when his work was done, that he drew them out to enjoy their companionship. He had taken up some bricks in his floor underneath his loom, and here he had made a hole in which he set the iron pot that contained his guineas and silver coins, covering the bricks with sand whenever he replaced them. Not that the idea of being robbed presented itself often or strongly to his mind: hoarding was common in country districts in those days; there were old laborers in the parish of Raveloe who were known to have their savings by them, probably inside their flock-beds; but their rustic neighbors, though not all of them as honest as their ancestors in the days of King Alfred, had not imaginations bold enough to lay a plan of burglary. How could they have spent the money in their own village without betraying themselves? They would be obliged to "run away"—a course as dark and dubious as a balloon journey.

So, year after year, Silas Marner had lived in this solitude, his guineas rising in the iron pot, and his life narrowing and hardening itself more and more into a mere pulsation of desire and satisfaction that had no relation to any other being. His life had reduced itself to the functions of weaving and hoarding, without any contemplation of an end toward which the functions tended. The same sort of process has perhaps been undergone by wiser men, when they have been cut off from faith and love—only, instead of a loom and a heap of guineas, they have had some erudite research, some ingenious project, or some well-knit theory. Strangely Marner's face and figure shrank and bent themselves into a constant mechanical relation to the objects of his life, so that he produced the same sort of impression as a handle or a crooked tube, which has no meaning standing apart. The prominent eyes that used to look trusting and dreamy, now looked as if they had been made to see only one kind of thing that was very small, like tiny grain, for which they hunted everywhere; and he was so withered and yellow, that, though he was not yet forty, the children always called him "Old Master Marner."

Yet even in this stage of withering a little incident happened, which showed that the sap of affection was not all gone. It was one of his daily tasks to fetch his water from a well a couple of fields off, and for this purpose, ever since he came to Raveloe, he had had a brown earthenware pot, which he held as his most precious utensil among the very few conveniences he had granted himself. It had been his companion for twelve years, always standing on the same spot, always lending its handle to him in the early morning, so that its form had an expression for him of willing helpfulness, and the impress of its handle on his palm gave a satisfaction mingled with that of having the fresh clear water. One day as he was returning from the well, he stumbled against the step of the stile, and his brown pot, falling with force against the stones that overarched the ditch below him, was broken in three pieces. Silas picked up the pieces and carried them home with grief in his heart. The brown pot could never be of use to him any more, but he stuck the bits together and propped the ruin in its old place for a memorial.

This is the history of Silas Marner, until the fifteenth year after he came to Raveloe. The livelong day he sat in his loom, his ear filled with its monotony, his eyes bent close down on the slow growth of sameness in the brownish web, his muscles moving with such even repetition that their pause seemed almost as much a constraint as the holding of his breath. But at night came his revelry: at night he closed his shutters, and made fast his doors, and drew forth his gold. Long ago the heap of coins had become too large for the iron pot to hold them, and he had made for them two thick leather bags, which wasted no room in their resting-place, but lent themselves flexibly to every corner. How the guineas shone as they came pouring out of the dark leather mouths! The silver bore no large proportion in amount to the gold, because the long pieces of linen which formed his chief work were always partly paid for in gold, and out of the silver he supplied his own bodily wants, choosing always the shillings and sixpences to spend in this way. He loved the guineas best, but he would not change the silver—the crowns and half-crowns that were his own earnings, begotten by his labor; he loved them all. He spread them out in heaps and bathed his hands in them; then he counted them and set them up in regular piles, and felt their rounded outlines between his thumb and fingers, and thought fondly of the guineas that were only half earned by the work in his loom, as if they had been unborn children—thought of the guineas that were coming slowly through the coming years, through all his life, which spread far away before him, the end quite hidden by countless days of weaving. No wonder his thoughts were still with his loom and his money when he made his journeys through the fields and the lanes to fetch and carry home his work, so that his steps never wandered to the hedge-banks and the lane-side in search of the once familiar herbs: these too belonged to the past, from which his life had shrunk away, like a rivulet that has sunk far down from the grassy fringe of its old breadth into a little shivering thread, that cuts a groove for itself in the barren sand.

But about the Christmas of that fifteenth year, a second great change came over Marner's life, and his history became blent in a singular manner with the life of his neighbors.[7]

CHAPTER III

THE GREATEST MAN IN Raveloe was Squire Cass, who lived in the large red house with the handsome flight of stone steps in front and the high stables behind it, nearly opposite the church. He was only one among several landed parishioners, but he alone was honored with the title of Squire; for though Mr. Osgood's family was also understood to be of timeless origin—the Raveloe imagination having never ventured back to that fearful blank when there were no Osgoods—still he merely owned the farm he occupied; whereas Squire Cass had a tenant or two, who complained of the game to him quite as if he had been a lord.

It was still that glorious war-time which was felt to be a peculiar favor of Providence toward the landed interest, and the fall of prices had not yet come to carry the race of small squires and yeomen down that road to ruin for which extravagant habits and bad husbandry were plentifully anointing their wheels.[8] I am speaking now in relation to Raveloe and the parishes that resembled it; for our old-fashioned country life had many different aspects, as all life must have when it is spread over a various surface, and breathed on variously by multitudinous currents, from the winds of heaven to the thoughts of men, which are forever moving and crossing each other with incalculable results. Raveloe lay low among the bushy trees and the rutted lanes, aloof from the currents of industrial energy and Puritan earnestness: the rich ate and drank freely, accepting gout and apoplexy as things that ran mysteriously in respectable families, and the poor thought that the rich were entirely in the right of it to lead a jolly life; besides, their feasting caused a multiplication of orts, which were the heirlooms of the poor. Betty Jay scented the boiling of Squire Cass's hams, but her longing was arrested by the unctuous liquor in which they were boiled; and when the seasons brought round the great merry-makings, they were regarded on all hands as a fine thing for the poor. For the Raveloe feasts were like the rounds of beef and the barrels of ale—they were on a large scale, and lasted a good while especially in the winter-time. After ladies had packed up their best gowns and top-knots in bandboxes; and had incurred the risk of fording streams on pillions with the precious burden in rainy or snowy weather, when there was no knowing how high the water would rise, it was not to be supposed that they looked forward to a brief pleasure. On this ground it was always contrived in the dark seasons, when there was little work to be done, and the hours were long, that several neighbors should keep open house in succession. So soon as Squire Cass's standing dishes diminished in plenty and freshness, his guests had nothing to do but to walk a little higher up the village to Mr. Osgood's, at the Orchards, and they found hams and chines uncut, pork-pies with the scent of the fire in them, spun butter in all its freshness—everything, in fact, that appetites at leisure could desire, in perhaps greater perfection, though not in greater abundance, than at Squire Cass's.

For the Squire's wife had died long ago, and the Red House was without that presence of the wife and mother which is the fountain of wholesome love and fear in parlor and kitchen; and this helped to account not only for there being more profusion than finished excellence in the holiday provisions, but also for the frequency with which the proud Squire condescended to preside in the parlor of the Rainbow rather than under the shadow of his own dark wainscot; perhaps, also, for the fact that his sons had turned out rather ill. Raveloe was not a place where moral censure was severe, but it was thought a weakness in the Squire that he had kept all his sons at home in idleness; and though some license was to be allowed to young men whose fathers could afford it, people shook their heads at the courses of the second son, Dunstan, commonly called Dunsey Cass, whose taste for swopping and betting might turn out to be a sowing of something worse than wild oats. To be sure the neighbors said, it was no matter what became of Dunsey—a spiteful, jeering fellow, who seemed to enjoy his drink the more when other people went dry—always provided that his doings did not bring trouble on a family like Squire Cass's with a monument in the church, and tankards older than King George. But it would be a thousand pities if Mr. Godfrey, the eldest, a fine open-faced good-natured young man who was to come into the land some day, should take to going along the same road with his brother, as he had seemed to do of late. If he went on in that way, he would lose Miss Nancy Lammeter; for it was well known that she had looked very shyly on him ever since last Whitsuntide twelvemonth, when there was so much talk about his being away from home days and days together. There was something wrong, more than common—that was quite clear; for Mr. Godfrey didn't look half so fresh-colored and open as he used to do. At one time everybody was saying, What a handsome couple he and Miss Nancy Lammeter would make! and if she could come to be mistress at the Red House, there would be a fine change, for the Lammeters had been brought up in that way, that they never suffered a pinch of salt to be wasted, and yet everybody in their household had of the best, according to his place. Such a daughter-in-law would be a saving to the old Squire, if she never brought a penny to her fortune; for it was to be feared that, notwithstanding his incomings, there were more holes in his pocket than the one where he put his own hand in. But if Mr. Godfrey didn't turn over a new leaf, he might say "Good-bye" to Miss Nancy Lammeter.

It was the once hopeful Godfrey who was standing, with his hands in his side-pockets and his back to the fire, in the dark wainscoted parlor, one late November afternoon in that fifteenth year of

Silas Marner's life at Raveloe. The fading gray light fell dimly on the walls decorated with guns, whips, and foxes' brushes, on coats and hats flung on the chairs, on tankards sending forth a scent of flat ale, and on a half-choked fire, with pipes propped up in the chimney-corners: signs of a domestic life destitute of any hallowing charm, with which the look of gloomy vexation on Godfrey's blonde face was in sad accordance. He seemed to be waiting and listening for some one's approach, and presently the sound of a heavy step, with an accompanying whistle, was heard across the large empty entrance-hall.

The door opened, and a thick-set, heavy-looking young man entered, with the flushed face and the gratuitously elated bearing which mark the first stage of intoxication. It was Dunsey, and at the sight of him Godfrey's face parted with some of its gloom to take on the more active expression of hatred. The handsome brown spaniel that lay on the hearth retreated under the chair in the chimney-corner.

"Well, Master Godfrey, what do you want with me?" said Dunsey, in a mocking tone. "You're my elders and betters, you know; I was obliged to come when you sent for me."

"Why, this is what I want—and just shake yourself sober and listen, will you?" said Godfrey, savagely. He had himself been drinking more than was good for him, trying to turn his gloom into uncalculating anger. "I want to tell you, I must hand over that rent of Fowler's to the Squire, or else tell him that I gave it to you; for he's threatening to distrain for it, and it'll all be out soon, whether I tell him or not. He said, just now, before he went out, he should send word to Cox to distrain, if Fowler didn't come and pay up his arrears this week. The Squire's short o' cash, and in no humor to stand any nonsense; and you know what he threatened, if ever he found you making away with his money again. So, see and get the money, and pretty quickly, will you?"

"Oh?" said Dunsey, sneeringly, coming nearer to his brother and looking in his face. "Suppose, now, you get the money yourself, and save me the trouble, eh? Since you was so kind as to hand it over to me, you'll not refuse me the kindness to pay it back for me: it was your brotherly love made you do it, you know."

Godfrey bit his lips and clenched his fist. "Don't come near me with that look, else I'll knock you down."

"Oh no, you won't," said Dunsey, turning away on his heel, however. "Because I'm such a good-natured brother, you know. I might get you turned out of house and home, and cut off with a shilling any day. I might tell the Squire how his handsome son was married to that nice young woman, Molly Farren, and was very unhappy because he couldn't live with his drunken wife, and I should slip into your place as comfortable as could be. But you see, I don't do it—I'm so easy and good-natured. You'll take any trouble for me. You'll get the hundred pounds for me—I know you will."

"How can I get the money?" said Godfrey, quivering. "I haven't a shilling to bless myself with. And it's a lie that you'd slip into my place: you'd get yourself turned out, too, that's all. For if you begin telling tales, I'll follow. Bob's my father's favorite—you know that very well. He'd only think himself well rid of you."

"Never mind," said Dunsey, nodding his head sideways, as he looked out of the window. "It 'ud be very pleasant to me to go in your company—you're such a handsome brother, and we've always been so fond of quarreling with one another, I shouldn't know what to do without you. But you'd like better for us both to stay at home together; I know you would. So you'll manage to get that little sum o' money, and I'll bid you good-bye, though I'm sorry to part."

Dunstan was moving off, but Godfrey rushed after him, and seized him by the arm, saying with an oath—

"I tell you, I have no money: I can get no money."

"Borrow of old Kimble."

"I tell you, he won't lend me any more, and I shan't ask him."

"Well, then, sell Wildfire."

"Yes, that's easy talking. I must have the money directly."

"Well, you've only got to ride him to the hunt to-morrow. There'll be Bryce and Keating there, for sure. You'll get more bids than one."

"I dare say, and get back home at eight o'clock, splashed up to the chin. I'm going to Mrs. Osgood's birthday dance."

"Oho!" said Dunsey, turning his head on one side, and trying to speak in a small mincing treble. "And there's sweet Miss Nancy coming; and we shall dance with her, and promise never to be naughty again, and be taken into favor, and ———"

"Hold your tongue about Miss Nancy, you fool," said Godfrey, turning red, "else I'll throttle you."

"What for?" said Dunsey, still in an artificial tone, but taking a whip from the table and beating the butt-end of it on his palm. "You've a very good chance. I'd advise you to creep up her sleeve again: it 'ud be saving time, if Molly should happen to take a drop too much laudanum some day, and make a widower of you. Miss Nancy wouldn't mind being a second, if she didn't know it. And you've got a good-natured brother, who'll keep your secret well, because you'll be so very obliging to him."

"I'll tell you what it is," said Godfrey, quivering and pale again, "my patience is pretty near at an end. If you'd a little more sharpness in you, you might know that you may urge a man a bit too far, and make one leap as easy as another. I don't know but what it is so now: I may as well tell the Squire everything myself—I should get you off my back, if I got nothing else. And, after all, he'll know some time. She's been threatening to come herself and tell him. So, don't flatter yourself that your secrecy's worth any price you choose to ask. You drain me of money till I have got nothing to pacify her with, and she'll do as she threatens some day. It's all one. I'll tell my father everything myself, and you may go to the devil."

Dunsey perceived that he had overshot his mark, and that there was a point at which even the hesitating Godfrey might be driven into decision. But he said, with an air of unconcern—

"As you please; but I'll have a draught of ale first." And ringing the bell, he threw himself across two chairs, and began to rap the window-seat with the handle of his whip.

Godfrey stood, still with his back to the fire, uneasily moving his fingers among the contents of his side-pockets, and looking at the floor. That big muscular frame of his held plenty of animal courage, but helped him to no decision when the dangers to be braved were such as could neither be knocked down nor throttled. His natural ir-resolution and moral cowardice were exaggerated by a position in which dreaded consequences seemed to press equally on all sides, and his irritation had no sooner provoked him to defy Dunstan and anticipate all possible betrayals, than the miseries he must bring on himself by such a step seemed more unendurable to him than the present evil. The results of confession were not contingent, they were certain; whereas betrayal was not certain. From the near vision of that certainty he fell back on suspense and vacillation with a sense of repose. The disinherited son of a small squire, equally disinclined to dig and to beg, was almost as helpless as an uprooted tree, which, by the favor of earth and sky, has grown to a handsome bulk on the spot where it first shot upward. Perhaps it would have been possible to think of digging with some cheerfulness if Nancy Lammeter were to be won on those terms; but, since he must irrevocably lose her as well as the inheritance, and must break every tie but the one that degraded him and left him without motive for trying to recover his better self, he could imagine no future for himself on the other side of confession but that of " 'listing for a soldier"—the most desperate step, short of suicide, in the eyes of respectable families. No! he would rather trust to casualties[9] than to his own resolve—rather go on sitting at the feast, and sipping the wine he loved, though with the sword hanging over him and terror in his heart, than rush away into the cold darkness where there was no pleasure left. The utmost concession to Dunstan about the horse began to seem easy, compared with the fulfillment of his own threat. But his pride would not let him recommence the conversation otherwise than by continuing the quarrel. Dunstan was waiting for this, and took his ale in shorter draughts than usual.

"It's just like you," Godfrey burst out, in a bitter tone, "to talk about my selling Wildfire in that cool way—the last thing I've got to call my own, and the best bit of horse-flesh I ever had in my life. And if you'd got a spark of pride in you, you'd be ashamed to see the stables emptied, and everybody sneering about it. But it's my belief you'd sell yourself, if it was only for the pleasure of making somebody feel he'd got a bad bargain."

"Ay, ay," said Dunstan, very placably, "you do me justice, I see. You know I'm a jewel for 'ticing people into bargains. For which reason I advise you to let me sell Wildfire. I'd ride him to the hunt tomorrow for you, with pleasure. I shouldn't look so handsome as you in the saddle, but it's the horse they'll bid for, and not the rider."

"Yes, I dare say—trust my horse to you!"

"As you please," said Dunstan, rapping the window-seat again with an air of great unconcern. "It's you have got to pay Fowler's money; it's none of my business. You received the money from him when you went to Bramcote, and you told the Squire it wasn't paid. I'd nothing to do with that; you chose to be so obliging as to give it me, that was all. If you don't want to pay the money, let it alone; it's all one to me. But I was willing to accommodate you by untertaking to sell the horse, seeing it's not convenient to you to go so far to-morrow."

Godfrey was silent for some moments. He would have liked to spring on Dunstan, wrench the whip from his hand, and flog him to within an inch of his life; and no bodily fear could have deterred him; but he was mastered by another sort of fear, which was fed by feelings stronger even than his resentment. When he spoke again it was in a half-conciliatory tone.

"Well, you mean no nonsense about the horse, eh? You'll sell him all fair, and hand over the money? If you don't, you know, everything 'ull go to smash, for I've got nothing else to trust to. And you'll have less pleasure in pulling the house over my head, when your own skull's to be broken too."

"Ay, ay," said Dunstan, rising; "all right. I thought you'd come round. I'm the fellow to bring old Bryce up to the scratch. I'll get you a hundred and twenty for him, if I get you a penny."

"But it'll perhaps rain cats and dogs to-morrow, as it did yesterday, and then you can't go," said Godfrey, hardly knowing whether he wished for that obstacle or not.

"Not it," said Dunstan. "I'm always lucky in my weather. It might rain if you wanted to go yourself. You never hold trumps, you know—I always do. You've got the beauty, you see, and I've got the luck, so you must keep me by you for your crooked sixpence;* you'll ne-ver get along without me."

"Confound you, hold your tongue!" said Godfrey, impetuously. "And take care to keep sober to-morrow, else you'll get pitched on your head coming home, and Wildfire might be the worse for it."

"Make your tender heart easy," said Dunstan, opening the door. "You never knew me see double when I'd got a bargain to make; it 'ud spoil the fun. Besides, whenever I fall, I'm warranted to fall on my legs."

---

*Taken to be good luck charms.

With that, Dunstan slammed the door behind him, and left Godfrey to that bitter rumination on his personal circumstances which
was now unbroken from day to day save by the excitement of sporting, drinking, card-playing, or the rarer and less oblivious pleasure of
seeing Miss Nancy Lammeter. The subtle and varied pains springing
from the higher sensibility that accompanies higher culture, are perhaps less pitiable than that dreary absence of impersonal enjoyment
and consolation which leaves ruder minds to the perpetual urgent
companionship of their own griefs and discontents. The lives of those
rural forefathers, whom we are apt to think very prosaic figures—men
whose only work was to ride round their land, getting heavier and
heavier in their saddles, and who passed the rest of their days in the
half-listless gratification of senses dulled by monotony—had a certain pathos in them nevertheless. Calamities came to them too, and
their early errors carried hard consequences: perhaps the love of
some sweet maiden, the image of purity, order, and calm, had opened
their eyes to the vision of a life in which the days would not seem
too long, even without rioting; but the maiden was lost, and the vision passed away, and then what was left to them, especially when
they had become too heavy for the hunt, or for carrying a gun over
the furrows, but to drink and get merry, or to drink and get angry, so
that they might be independent of variety, and say over again with
eager emphasis the things they had said already any time that twelvemonth? Assuredly, among these flushed and dull-eyed men there
were some whom—thanks to their native human-kindness—even
riot could never drive into brutality; men who, when their cheeks
were fresh, had felt the keen point of sorrow or remorse, had been
pierced by the reeds they leaned on, or had lightly put their limbs
in fetters from which no struggle could loose them; and under
these sad circumstances, common to us all, their thoughts could find
no resting-place outside the ever-trodden round of their own petty
history.

     That, at least, was the condition of Godfrey Cass in this six-and-
twentieth year of his life. A movement of compunction, helped by
those small indefinable influences which every personal relation
exerts on a pliant nature, had urged him into a secret marriage,
which was a blight on his life. It was an ugly story of low passion,
delusion, and waking from delusion, which needs not to be dragged

from the privacy of Godfrey's bitter memory. He had long known that the delusion was partly due to a trap laid for him by Dunstan, who saw in his brother's degrading marriage the means of gratifying at once his jealous hate and his cupidity. And if Godfrey could have felt himself simply a victim, the iron bit that destiny had put into his mouth would have chaffed him less intolerably. If the curses he muttered half aloud when he was alone had had no other object than Dunstan's diabolical cunning, he might have shrunk less from the consequences of avowal. But he had something else to curse—his own vicious folly, which now seemed as mad and unaccountable to him as almost all our follies and vices do when their promptings have long passed away. For four years he had thought of Nancy Lammeter, and wooed her with tacit patient worship, as the woman who made him think of the future with joy: she would be his wife, and would make home lovely to him, as his father's home had never been; and it would be easy, when she was always near, to shake off those foolish habits that were no pleasures, but only a feverish way of annulling vacancy. Godfrey's was an essentially domestic nature, bred up in a home where the hearth had no smiles, and where the daily habits were not chastised by the presence of household order. His easy disposition made him fall in unresistingly with the family courses, but the need of some tender permanent affection, the longing for some influence that would make the good he preferred easy to pursue, caused the neatness, purity, and liberal orderliness of the Lammeter household, sunned by the smile of Nancy, to seem like those fresh bright hours of the morning when temptations go to sleep and leave the ear open to the voice of the good angel, inviting to industry, sobriety, and peace. And yet the hope of this paradise had not been enough to save him from a course which shut him out of it forever. Instead of keeping fast hold of the strong silken rope by which Nancy would have drawn him safe to the green banks where it was easy to step firmly, he had let himself be dragged back into mud and slime, in which it was useless to struggle. He had made ties for himself which robbed him of all wholesome motive and were a constant exasperation.

Still, there was one position worse than the present: it was the position he would be in when the ugly secret was disclosed; and

the desire that continually triumphed over every other was that of
warding off the evil day, when he would have to bear the consequences of his father's violent resentment for the wound inflicted
on his family pride—would have, perhaps, to turn his back on that
hereditary ease and dignity which, after all, was a sort of reason for
living, and would carry with him the certainty that he was banished
forever from the sight and esteem of Nancy Lammeter. The longer
the interval, the more chance there was of deliverance from some,
at least, of the hateful consequences to which he had sold himself;
the more opportunities remained for him to snatch the strange
gratification of seeing Nancy, and gathering some faint indications
of her lingering regard. Toward this gratification he was impelled,
fitfully, every now and then, after having passed weeks in which
he had avoided her as the far-off bright-winged prize that only
made him spring forward and find his chain all the more galling.
One of those fits of yearning was on him now, and it would have
been strong enough to have persuaded him to trust Wildfire to
Dunstan rather than disappoint the yearning, even if he had not had
another reason for his disinclination toward the morrow's hunt.
That other reason was the fact that the morning's meet was near
Batherley, the market-town where the unhappy woman lived,
whose image became more odious to him every day; and to his
thought the whole vicinage was haunted by her. The yoke a man
creates for himself by wrong-doing will breed hate in the kindliest
nature; and the good-humored, affectionate-hearted Godfrey Cass
was fast becoming a bitter man, visited by cruel wishes, that
seemed to enter and depart, and enter again, like demons who had
found in him a ready-garnished home.

What was he to do this evening to pass the time? He might as
well go to the Rainbow and hear the talk about the cock-fighting;
everybody was there, and what else was there to be done? Though,
for his own part, he did not care a button for cock-fighting. Snuff,
the brown spaniel, who had placed herself in front of him, and
had been watching him for some time, now jumped up in impatience for the expected caress. But Godfrey thrust her away without looking at her, and left the room, followed humbly by the
unresenting Snuff—perhaps because she saw no other career open
to her.

CHAPTER IV

DUNSTAN CASS, SETTING OFF in the raw morning, at the judiciously quiet pace of a man who is obliged to ride to cover on his hunter, had to take his way along the lane which, at its farther extremity, passed by the piece of unenclosed ground called the Stone-pit, where stood the cottage, once a stone-cutter's shed, now for fifteen years inhabited by Silas Marner. The spot looked very dreary at this season, with the moist trodden clay about it, and the red, muddy water high up in the deserted quarry. That was Dunstan's first thought as he approached it; the second was that the old fool of a weaver, whose loom he heard rattling already, had a great deal of money hidden somewhere. How was it that he, Dunstan Cass, who had often heard talk of Marner's miserliness, had never thought of suggesting to Godfrey that he should frighten or persuade the old fellow into lending the money on the excellent security of the young Squire's prospects? The resource occurred to him now as so easy and agreeable, especially as Marner's hoard was likely to be large enough to leave Godfrey a handsome surplus beyond his immediate needs, and enable him to accommodate his faithful brother, that he had almost turned the horse's head toward home again. Godfrey would be ready enough to accept the suggestion: he would snatch eagerly at a plan that might save him from parting with Wildfire. But when Dunstan's meditation reached this point, the inclination to go on grew strong and prevailed. He didn't want to give Godfrey that pleasure: he preferred that Master Godfrey should be vexed. Moreover, Dunstan enjoyed the self-important consciousness of having a horse to sell, and the opportunity of driving a bargain, swaggering, and possibly taking somebody in. He might have all the satisfaction attendant on selling his brother's horse, and not the less have the further satisfaction of setting Godfrey to borrow Marner's money. So he rode on to cover.

Bryce and Keating were there, as Dunstan was quite sure they would be—he was such a lucky fellow.

"Heyday!" said Bryce, who had long had his eye on Wildfire, "you're on your brother's horse to-day: how's that?"

"Oh, I've swopped with him," said Dunstan, whose delight in lying, grandly independent of utility, was not to be diminished by the likelihood that his hearer would not believe him—"Wildfire's mine now."

"What! has he swopped with you for that big-boned hack of yours?" said Bryce, quite aware that he should get another lie in answer.

"Oh, there was a little account between us," said Dunsey, carelessly, "and Wildfire made it even. I accommodated him by taking the horse, though it was against my will, for I'd got an itch for a mare o' Jortin's—as rare a bit o' blood as ever you threw your leg across. But I shall keep Wildfire, now I've got him, though I'd a bid of a hundred and fifty for him the other day, from a man over at Flitton—he's buying for Lord Cromleck—a fellow with a cast in his eye, and a green waistcoat. But I mean to stick to Wildfire: I shan't get a better at a fence in a hurry. The mare's got more blood, but she's a bit too weak in the hind-quarters."

Bryce of course divined that Dunstan wanted to sell the horse, and Dunstan knew that he divined it (horse-dealing is only one of many human transactions carried on in this ingenious manner); and they both considered that the bargain was in its first stage, when Bryce replied ironically—

"I wonder at that now; I wonder you mean to keep him; for I never heard of a man who didn't want to sell his horse getting a bid of half as much again as the horse was worth. You'll be lucky if you get a hundred."

Keating rode up now, and the transaction became more complicated. It ended in the purchase of the horse by Bryce for a hundred and twenty, to be paid on the delivery of Wildfire, safe and sound, at the Batherley stables. It did occur to Dunsey that it might be wise for him to give up the day's hunting, proceed at once to Batherley, and having waited for Bryce's return, hire a horse to carry him home with the money in his pocket. But the inclination for a run, encouraged by confidence in his luck, and by a draught of brandy from his pocket-pistol at the conclusion of the bargain, was not easy to overcome, especially with a horse under him that would take the fences to the admiration of the field. Dunstan, however, took one fence too many, and got his horse pierced with a hedge-stake. His own ill-favored person, which was quite unmarketable, escaped without injury; but poor Wildfire, unconscious of his price, turned on his flank and painfully panted his last. It happened that Dunstan, a short time before, having had to get down to arrange his stirrup, had muttered a good many curses at this interruption, which had thrown him in the rear of the hunt near the moment of glory, and under this exasperation had taken the fences more blindly. He would soon have been up with the hounds again, when the fatal accident happened; and hence he was between eager riders in advance, not troubling themselves about what happened behind them, and far-off stragglers, who were as likely as not to pass quite aloof from the line of road in which Wildfire had fallen. Dunstan, whose nature it was to care more for immediate annoyances than for remote consequences, no sooner recovered his legs and saw that it was all over with Wildfire, than he felt a satisfaction at the absence of witnesses to a position which no swaggering could make enviable. Reinforcing himself, after his shake, with a little brandy and much swearing, he walked as fast as he could to a coppice on his right hand, through which it occurred to him that he could make his way to Batherley without danger of encountering any member of the hunt. His first intention was to hire a horse there and ride home forthwith, for to walk many miles without a gun in his hand and along an ordinary road, was as much out of the question to him as to other spirited young men of his kind. He did not much mind about taking the bad news to Godfrey, for he had to offer him at the same time the resource of Marner's money; and if Godfrey kicked, as he always did, at the notion of making a fresh debt from which he himself got the smallest share of advantage, why, he wouldn't kick long: Dunstan felt sure he could worry Godfrey into anything. The idea of Marner's money kept growing in vividness, now the want of it had become immediate; the prospect of having to make his appearance with the muddy boots of a pedestrian at Batherley, and to encounter the grinning queries of stablemen, stood unpleasantly in the way of his impatience to be back at Raveloe and carry out his felicitous plan; and a casual visitation of his waistcoat-pocket, as he was ruminating, awakened his memory to the fact that the two or three small coins his forefinger encountered there, were of too pale a color to cover that small debt, without payment of which the stable-keeper had declared he would never do any more business with Dunsey Cass. After all, according to the direction in which the run had brought him, he was not so very much farther from home than he was from Batherley; but Dunsey, not being remarkable for clearness of head, was only led to this conclusion by the gradual perception that there were other reasons for choosing the unprecedented course of walking home. It was now nearly four o'-clock, and a mist was gathering: the sooner he got into the road the better. He remembered having crossed the road and seen the finger-post only a little while before Wildfire broke down; so, buttoning his coat, twisting the lash of his hunting-whip compactly round the handle, and rapping the tops of his boots with a self-possessed air, as if to assure himself that he was not at all taken by surprise, he set off with the sense that he was undertaking a remarkable feat of bodily exertion, which somehow and at some time he should be able to dress up and magnify to the admiration of a select circle at the Rainbow. When a young gentleman like Dunsey is reduced to so exceptional a mode of locomotion as walking, a whip in his hand is a desirable corrective to a too bewildering dreamy sense of unwontedness in his position; and Dunstan, as he went along through the gathering mist, was always rapping his whip somewhere. It was Godfrey's whip, which he had chosen to take without leave because it had a gold handle; of course no one could see, when Dunstan held it, that the name *Godfrey Cass* was cut in deep letters on that gold handle—they could only see that it was a very handsome whip. Dunsey was not without fear that he might meet some acquaintance in whose eyes he would cut a pitiable figure, for mist is no screen when people get close to each other; but when he at last found himself in the well-known Raveloe lanes without having met a soul, he silently remarked that that was part of his usual good luck. But now the mist, helped by the evening darkness, was more of a screen than he desired, for it hid the ruts into which his feet were liable to slip—hid everything, so that he had to guide his steps by dragging his whip along the low bushes in advance of the hedgerow. He must soon, he thought, be getting near the opening at the Stone-pits: he should find it out by the break in the hedgerow. He found it out, however, by another circumstance which he had not expected—namely, by certain gleams of light, which he presently guessed to proceed from Silas Marner's cottage. That cottage and the money hidden within it had been in his mind continually during his walk, and he had been imagining ways of cajoling and tempting the weaver to part with the immediate possession of his money for the sake of receiving interest. Dunstan felt as if there must be a little frightening added to the cajolery, for his own arithmetical convictions were not clear enough to afford him any forcible demonstration as to the advantages of interest; and as for security, he regarded it vaguely as a means of cheating a man by making him believe that he would be paid. Altogether, the operation on the miser's mind was a task that Godfrey would be sure to hand over to his more daring and cunning brother: Dunstan had made up his mind to that; and by the time he saw the light gleaming through the chinks of Marner's shutters, the idea of a dialogue with the weaver had become so familiar to him, that it occurred to him as quite a natural thing to make the acquaintance forthwith. There might be several conveniences attending this course: the weaver had possibly got a lantern, and Dunstan was tired of feeling his way. He was still nearly three-quarters of a mile from home, and the lane was becoming unpleasantly slippery, for the mist was passing into rain. He turned up the bank, not without some fear lest he might miss the right way, since he was not certain whether the light were in front or on the side of the cottage. But he felt the ground before him cautiously with his whip-handle, and at last arrived safely at the door. He knocked loudly, rather enjoying the idea that the old fellow would be frightened at the sudden noise. He heard no movement in reply: all was silence in the cottage. Was the weaver gone to bed, then? If so, why had he left a light? That was a strange forgetfulness in a miser. Dunstan knocked still more loudly, and, without pausing for a reply, pushed his fingers through the latch-hole, intending to shake the door and pull the latch-string up and down, not doubting that the door was fastened. But, to his surprise, at this double motion the door opened, and he found himself in front of a bright fire which lit up every corner of the cottage—the bed, the loom, the three chairs, and the table—and showed him that Marner was not there.

Nothing at that moment could be much more inviting to Dunsey than the bright fire on the brick hearth: he walked in and seated himself by it at once. There was something in front of the fire, too,

that would have been inviting to a hungry man, if it had been in a
different stage of cooking. It was a small bit of pork suspended from
the kettle-hanger by a string passed through a large door-key, in a
way known to primitive housekeepers unpossessed of jacks. But the
pork had been hung at the farthest extremity of the hanger, apparently to prevent the roasting from proceeding too rapidly during the
owner's absence. The old staring simpleton had hot meat for his supper, then? thought Dunstan. People had always said he lived on
mouldy bread, on purpose to check his appetite. But where could he
be at this time, and on such an evening, leaving his supper in this
stage of preparation, and his door unfastened? Dunstan's own recent
difficulty in making his way suggested to him that the weaver had
perhaps gone outside his cottage to fetch in fuel, or for some such
brief purpose, and had slipped into the Stone-pit. That was an interesting idea to Dunstan, carrying consequences of entire novelty. If the
weaver was dead, who had a right to his money? Who would know
where his money was hidden? *Who would know that anybody had come to
take it away?* He went no farther into the subtleties of evidence: the
pressing question, "Where is the money?" now took such entire possession of him as to make him quite forget that the weaver's death
was not a certainty. A dull mind, once arriving at an inference that
flatters a desire, is rarely able to retain the impression that the notion
from which the inference started was purely problematic. And Dunstan's mind was as dull as the mind of a possible felon usually is.
There were only three hiding-places where he had ever heard of cottagers' hoards being found: the thatch, the bed, and a hole in the
floor. Marner's cottage had no thatch; and Dunstan's first act, after a
train of thought made rapid by the stimulus of cupidity, was to go up
to the bed; but while he did so, his eyes traveled eagerly over the floor,
where the bricks, distinct in the fire-light, were discernible under the
sprinkling of sand. But not everywhere; for there was one spot, and
one only, which was quite covered with sand, and sand showing the
marks of fingers, which had apparently been careful to spread it over
a given space. It was near the treadles of the loom. In an instant Dunstan darted to that spot, swept away the sand with his whip, and, in-
serting the thin end of the hook between the bricks, found that they
were loose. In haste he lifted up two bricks, and saw what he had no
doubt was the object of his search; for what could there be but

money in those two leathern bags? And, from their weight, they must be filled with guineas. Dunstan felt round the hole, to be certain that it held no more; then hastily replaced the bricks, and spread the sand over them. Hardly more than five minutes had passed since he entered the cottage, but it seemed to Dunstan like a long while; and though he was without any distinct recognition of the possibility that Marner might be alive, and might re-enter the cottage at any moment, he felt an undefinable dread laying hold on him, as he rose to his feet with the bags in his hand. He would hasten out into the darkness, and then consider what he should do with the bags. He closed the door behind him immediately, that he might shut in the stream of light. A few steps would be enough to carry him beyond betrayal by the gleams from the shutter-chinks and the latch-hole. The rain and darkness had got thicker, and he was glad of it; though it was awkward walking with both hands filled, so that it was as much as he could do to grasp his whip along with one of the bags. But when he had gone a yard or two, he might take his time. So he stepped forward into the darkness.

CHAPTER V

WHEN DUNSTAN CASS TURNED his back on the cottage, Silas Marner was not more than a hundred yards away from it, plodding along from the village with a sack thrown round his shoulders as an overcoat, and with a horn lantern in his hand. His legs were weary, but his mind was at ease, free from the presentiment of change. The sense of security more frequently springs from habit than from conviction, and for this reason it often subsists after such a change in the conditions as might have been expected to suggest alarm. The lapse of time during which a given event has not happened, is, in this logic of habit, constantly alleged as a reason why the event should never happen, even when the lapse of time is precisely the added condition which makes the event imminent. A man will tell you that he has worked in a mine for forty years unhurt by an accident as a reason why he should apprehend no danger, though the roof is beginning to sink;

and it is often observable, that the older a man gets, the more difficult it is to him to retain a believing conception of his own death.
This influence of habit was necessarily strong in a man whose life
was so monotonous as Marner's—who saw no new people and
heard of no new events to keep alive in him the idea of the unexpected and the changeful; and it explains simply enough, why his
mind could be at ease, though he had left his house and his treasure
more defenceless than usual. Silas was thinking with double complacency of his supper; first, because it would be hot and savory; and
secondly, because it would cost him nothing. For the little bit of pork
was a present from that excellent housewife, Miss Priscilla Lammeter, to whom he had this day carried home a handsome piece of
linen; and it was only on occasion of a present like this, that Silas in-
dulged himself with roast-meat. Supper was his favorite meal, because it came at his time of revelry, when his heart warmed over his
gold; whenever he had roast-meat, he always chose to have it for
supper. But this evening, he had no sooner ingeniously knotted his
string fast round his bit of pork, twisted the string according to rule
over his door-key, passed it through the handle, and made it fast on
the hanger, than he remembered that a piece of very fine twine was
indispensable to his "setting up" a new piece of work in his loom
early in the morning. It had slipped his memory, because, in coming
from Mr. Lammeter's, he had not had to pass through the village; but
to lose time by going on errands in the morning was out of the
question. It was a nasty fog to turn out into, but there were things
Silas loved better than his own comfort; so, drawing his pork to the
extremity of the hanger, and arming himself with his lantern and his
old sack, he set out on what, in ordinary weather, would have been
a twenty minutes' errand. He could not have locked his door without undoing his well-knotted string and retarding his supper; it was
not worth his while to make that sacrifice. What thief would find his
way to the Stone-pits on such a night as this? and why should he
come on this particular night, when he had never come through all
the fifteen years before? These questions were not distinctly present
in Silas's mind; they merely serve to represent the vaguely-felt foundation of his freedom from anxiety.

He reached his door in much satisfaction that his errand was
done: he opened it, and to his short-sighted eyes everything remained

as he had left it, except that the fire sent out a welcome increase of heat. He trod about the floor while putting by his lantern and throwing aside his hat and sack, so as to merge the marks of Dunstan's feet on the sand in the marks of his own nailed boots. Then he moved his pork nearer to the fire, and sat down to the agreeable business of tending the meat and warming himself at the same time.

Any one who had looked at him as the red light shone upon his pale face, strange straining eyes, and meager form, would perhaps have understood the mixture of contemptuous pity, dread, and suspicion with which he was regarded by his neighbors in Raveloe. Yet few men could be more really harmless than poor Marner. In his truthful and simple soul not even the growing greed and worship of gold could beget any vice directly injurious to others. The light of his faith quite put out, and his affections made desolate, he had clung with all the force of his nature to his work and his money; and like all objects to which a man devotes himself, they had fashioned him into correspondence with themselves. His loom, as he wrought in it without ceasing, had in its turn wrought on him, and confirmed more and more the monotonous craving for its monotonous response. His gold, as he hung over it and saw it grow, gathered his power of loving together into a hard isolation like its own.

As soon as he was warm he began to think it would be a long while to wait till after supper before he drew out his guineas, and it would be pleasant to see them on the table before him as he ate his unwonted feast. For joy is the best of wine, and Silas's guineas were a golden wine of that sort.

He rose and placed his candle unsuspectingly on the floor near his loom, swept away the sand without noticing any change, and removed the bricks. The sight of the empty hole made his heart leap violently, but the belief that his gold was gone could not come at once—only terror, and the eager effort to put an end to the terror. He passed his trembling hand all about the hole, trying to think it possible that his eyes had deceived him; then he held the candle in the hole and examined it curiously, trembling more and more. At last he shook so violently that he let fall the candle, and lifted his hands to his head, trying to steady himself that he might think. Had he put his gold somewhere else, by a sudden resolution last night, and then forgotten it? A man falling into dark waters seeks a momentary footing even on sliding stones; and Silas, by acting as if he believed in false hopes, warded off the moment of despair. He searched in every corner, he turned his bed over, and shook it, and kneaded it; he looked in his brick oven where he laid his sticks. When there was no other place to be searched, he kneeled down again and felt once more all round the hole. There was no untried refuge left for a moment's shelter from the terrible truth.

Yes, there was a sort of refuge which always comes with the prostration of thought under an overpowering passion: it was that expectation of impossibilities, that belief in contradictory images, which is still distinct from madness, because it is capable of being dissipated by the external fact. Silas got up from his knees trembling, and looked round at the table: didn't the gold lie there after all? The table was bare. Then he turned and looked behind him—looked all round his dwelling, seeming to strain his brown eyes after some possible appearance of the bags where he had already sought them in vain. He could see every object in his cottage—and his gold was not there.

Again he put his trembling hands to his head, and gave a wild ringing scream, the cry of desolation. For a few moments after, he stood motionless; but the cry had relieved him from the first maddening pressure of the truth. He turned, and tottered toward his loom, and got into the seat where he worked, instinctively seeking this as the strongest assurance of reality.

And now that all the false hopes had vanished, and the first shock of certainty was past, the idea of a thief began to present itself, and he entertained it eagerly, because a thief might be caught and made to restore the gold. The thought brought some new strength with it, and he started from his loom to the door. As he opened it the rain beat in upon him, for it was falling more and more heavily. There were no footsteps to be tracked on such a night—footsteps? When had the thief come? During Silas's absence in the daytime the door had been locked, and there had been no marks of any inroad on his return by daylight. And in the evening, too, he said to himself, everything was the same as when he had left it. The sand and bricks looked as if they had not been moved. *Was* it a thief who had taken the bags? or was it a cruel power that no hands could reach which had delighted in making him a second time desolate? He shrank from this vaguer dread, and fixed his mind with struggling effort on the robber with hands, who could be reached by hands. His thoughts glanced at all the neighbors who had made any remarks, or asked any questions which he might now regard as a ground of suspicion. There was Jem Rodney, a known poacher, and otherwise disreputable: he had often met Marner in his journeys across the fields, and had said something jestingly about the weaver's money; nay, he had once irritated Marner, by lingering at the fire when he called to light his pipe, instead of going about his business. Jem Rodney was the man—there was ease in the thought. Jem could be found and made to restore the money: Marner did not want to punish him, but only to get back his gold which had gone from him, and left his soul like a forlorn traveler on an unknown desert. The robber must be laid hold of. Marner's ideas of legal authority were confused, but he felt that he must go and proclaim his loss; and the great people in the village—the clergyman, the constable, and Squire Cass—would make Jem Rodney, or somebody else, deliver up the stolen money. He rushed out in the rain, under the stimulus of this hope, forgetting to cover his head, not caring to fasten his door; for he felt as if he had nothing left to lose. He ran swiftly, till want of breath compelled him to slacken his pace as he was entering the village at the turning close to the Rainbow.

The Rainbow, in Marner's view, was a place of luxurious resort for rich and stout husbands, whose wives had superfluous stores of linen; it was the place where he was likely to find the powers and dignities of Raveloe, and where he could most speedily make his loss public. He lifted the latch, and turned into the bright bar or kitchen on the right hand, where the less lofty customers of the house were in the habit of assembling, the parlor on the left being reserved for the more select society in which Squire Cass frequently enjoyed the double pleasure of conviviality and condescension. But the parlor was dark tonight, the personages who ornamented its circle being all at Mrs. Osgood's birthday dance, as Godfrey Cass was. And in consequence of this, the party on the high-screened seats in the kitchen was more numerous than usual; several personages, who would otherwise have been admitted into the parlor and enlarged the opportunity of hectoring and condescension for their betters, being content this evening to vary their enjoyment by taking their spirits-and-water where they could themselves hector and condescend in company that called for beer.

CHAPTER VI

THE CONVERSATION, WHICH WAS at a high pitch of animation when Silas approached the door of the Rainbow, had, as usual, been slow and intermittent when the company first assembled. The pipes began to be puffed in a silence which had an air of severity; the more important customers, who drank spirits and sat nearest the fire, staring at each other as if a bet were depending on the first man who winked; while the beer-drinkers, chiefly men in fustian jackets and smock-frocks, kept their eyelids down and rubbed their hands across their mouths, as if their draughts of beer were a funeral duty attended with embarrassing sadness. At last Mr. Snell, the landlord, a man of a neutral disposition, accustomed to stand aloof from human differences as those of beings who were all alike in need of liquor, broke silence, by saying in a doubtful tone to his cousin the butcher—

"Some folks 'ud say that was a fine beast you druv in yesterday, Bob?"

The butcher, a jolly, smiling, red-haired man, was not disposed to answer rashly. He gave a few puffs before he spat and replied, "And they wouldn't be fur wrong, John."

After this feeble delusive thaw, the silence set in as severely as before.

"Was it a red Durham?" said the farrier, taking up the thread of discourse after the lapse of a few minutes.

The farrier looked at the landlord, and the landlord looked at the butcher as the person who must take the responsibility of answering.

"Red it was," said the butcher, in his good-humored husky treble—"and a Durham it was."

"Then you needn't tell *me* who you bought it of," said the farrier, looking round with some triumph; "I know who it is has got the red Durhams o' this country-side. And she'd a white star on her brow, I'll bet a penny?" The farrier leaned forward with his hands on his knees as he put this question, and his eyes twinkled knowingly.

"Well; yes—she might," said the butcher, slowly, considering that he was giving a decided affirmative. "I don't say contrairy."

"I knew that very well," said the farrier, throwing himself backward again, and speaking defiantly; "if I don't know Mr. Lammeter's cows, I should like to know who does—that's all. And as for the cow you've bought, bargain or no bargain, I've been at the drenching of her—contradick me who will."

The farrier looked fierce, and the mild butcher's conversational spirit was roused a little.

"I'm not for contradicking no man," he said; "I'm for peace and quietness. Some are for cutting long ribs—I'm for cutting 'em short myself; but I don't quarrel with 'em. All I say is, it's a lovely carkiss—and anybody as was reasonable, it 'ud bring tears into their eyes to look at it."

"Well, it's the cow as I drenched, whatever it is," pursued the farrier, angrily; "and it was Mr. Lammeter's cow, else you told a lie when you said it was a red Durham."

"I tell no lies," said the butcher, with the same mild huskiness as before, "and I contradick none—not if a man was to swear himself black: he's no meat o' mine, nor none o' my bargains. All I say is, it's a lovely carkiss. And what I say I'll stick to; but I'll quarrel wi' no man."

"No," said the farrier, with bitter sarcasm, looking at the company generally; "and p'rhaps you arn't pig-headed; and p'rhaps you didn't say the cow was a red Durham; and p'rhaps you didn't say she'd got a star on her brow—stick to that, now you're at it."

"Come, come," said the landlord; "let the cow alone. The truth lies atween you: you're both right and both wrong, as I allays say. And as for the cow's being Mr. Lammeter's, I say nothing to that; but this I say, as the Rainbow's the Rainbow. And for the matter o' that, if the talk is to be o' the Lammeters, you know the most upo' that head, eh, Mr. Macey? You remember when first Mr. Lammeter's father come into these parts, and took the Warrens?"

Mr. Macey, tailor and parish-clerk, the latter of which functions rheumatism had of late obliged him to share with a small-featured young man who sat opposite him, held his white head on one side, and twirled his thumbs with an air of complacency, slightly seasoned with criticism. He smiled pityingly, in answer to the landlord's appeal, and said—

"Ay, ay; I know, I know: but I let other folks talk. I've laid by now, and gev up to the young uns. Ask them as have been to school at Tarley: they've learned pernouncing; that's come up since my day."

"If you're pointing at me, Mr. Macey," said the deputy clerk, with an air of anxious propriety, "I'm nowise a man to speak out of my place. As the psalm says—

> 'I know what's right, nor only so,
> But also practice what I know.' "*

"Well, then, I wish you'd keep hold o' the tune, when it's set for you; if you're for practicing, I wish you'd practice that," said a large jocose-looking man, an excellent wheelwright in his week-day capacity, but on Sundays leader of the choir. He winked, as he spoke, at two of the company, who were known officially as the "bassoon" and the "key-bugle," in the confidence that he was expressing the sense of the musical profession in Raveloe.

Mr. Tookey, the deputy-clerk, who shared the unpopularity common to deputies, turned very red, but replied, with careful moderation—"Mr. Winthrop, if you'll bring me any proof as I'm in the wrong, I'm not the man to say I won't alter. But there's people set up their own ears for a standard, and expect the whole choir to follow 'em. There may be two opinions, I hope."

"Ay, ay," said Mr. Macey, who felt very well satisfied with this attack on youthful presumption; "you're right there, Tookey: there's allays two 'pinions; there's the 'pinion a man has of himsen, and there's the 'pinion other folks have on him. There'd be two 'pinions about a cracked bell, if the bell could hear itself."

"Well, Mr. Macey," said poor Tookey, serious amidst the general laughter, "I undertook to partially fill up the office of parish-clerk by Mr. Crackenthorp's desire, whenever your infirmities should make you unfitting; and it's one of the rights thereof to sing in the choir— else why have you done the same yourself?"

---

*See the Bible, Psalms 106:3; this rhyming version is a popular rewriting of "Blessed are they that keep judgment, and he that doeth righteousness at all times" (KJV).

"Ah! but the old gentleman and you are two folks," said Ben Winthrop. "The old gentleman's got a gift. Why, the Squire used to invite him to take a glass, only to hear him sing the 'Red Rovier'; didn't he, Mr. Macey? It's a nat'ral gift. There's my little lad Aaron, he's got a gift—he can sing a tune off straight, like a throstle. But as for you, Master Tookey, you'd better stick to your 'Amens': your voice is well enough when you keep it up in your nose. It's your inside as isn't right made for music: it's no better nor a hollow stalk."

This kind of unflinching frankness was the most piquant form of joke to the company at the Rainbow, and Ben Winthrop's insult was felt by everybody to have capped Mr. Macey's epigram.

"I see what it is plain enough," said Mr. Tookey, unable to keep cool any longer. "There's a conspiracy to turn me out o' the choir, as I shouldn't share the Christmas money—that's where it is. But I shall speak to Mr. Crackenthorp; I'll not be put upon by no man."

"Nay, nay, Tookey," said Ben Winthrop. "We'll pay you your share to keep out of it—that's what we'll do. There's things folks 'ud pay to be rid on, besides varmin."

"Come, come," said the landlord, who felt that paying people for their absence was a principle dangerous to society; "a joke's a joke. We're all good friends here, I hope. We must give and take. You're both right and you're both wrong, as I say. I agree wi' Mr. Macey here, as there's two opinions; and if mine was asked, I should say they're both right. Tookey's right and Winthrop's right, and they've only got to split the difference and make themselves even."[10]

The farrier was puffing his pipe rather fiercely, in some contempt at this trivial discussion. He had no ear for music himself, and never went to church, as being of the medical profession, and likely to be in requisition for delicate cows. But the butcher, having music in his soul, had listened with a divided desire for Tookey's defeat and for the preservation of the peace.

"To be sure," he said, following up the landlord's conciliatory view, "we're fond of our old clerk; it's nat'ral, and him used to be such a singer, and got a brother as is known for the first fiddler in this country-side. Eh, it's a pity but what Solomon lived in our village, and could give us a tune when we liked; eh, Mr. Macey? I'd keep him in liver and lights for nothing—that I would."

"Ay, ay," said Mr. Macey, in the height of complacency; "our family's been known for musicianers as far back as anybody can tell. But them things are dying out, as I tell Solomon every time he comes round; there's no voices like what there used to be, and there's nobody remembers what we remember, if it isn't the old crows."

"Ay, you remember when first Mr. Lammeter's father come into these parts, don't you, Mr. Macey?" said the landlord.

"I should think I did," said the old man, who had now gone through that complimentary process necessary to bring him up to the point of narration; "and a fine old gentleman he was—as fine, and finer nor the Mr. Lammeter as now is. He came from a bit north'ard, so far as I could ever make out. But there's nobody rightly knows about those parts: only it couldn't be far north'ard, nor much different from this country, for he brought a fine breed o' sheep with him; so there must be pastures there, and everything reasonable. We heared tell as he'd sold his own land to come and take the Warrens, and that seemed odd for a man as had land of his own, to come and rent a farm in a strange place. But they said it was along of his wife's dying; though there's reasons in things as nobody knows on—that's pretty much what I've made out; yet some folks are so wise, they'll find you fifty reasons straight off, and all the while the real reason's winking at 'em in the corner, and they niver see't. Howsomever, it was soon seen as we'd got a new parish'ner as know'd the rights and customs o' things, and kep a good house, and was well looked on by everybody. And the young man—that's the Mr. Lammeter as now is, for he'd niver a sister—soon begun to court Miss Osgood, that's the sister o' the Mr. Osgood as now is, and a fine, handsome lass she was—eh, you can't think—they pretend this young lass is like her, but that's the way wi' people as don't know what come before 'em. I should know, for I helped the old rector, Mr. Drumlow as was, I helped him marry 'em."

Here Mr. Macey paused; he always gave his narrative in instalments, expecting to be questioned according to precedent.

"Ay, and a partic'lar thing happened, didn't it, Mr. Macey, so as you were likely to remember that marriage?" said the landlord, in a congratulatory tone.

"I should think there did—a *very* partic'lar thing," said Mr. Macey, nodding sideways. "For Mr. Drumlow—poor old gentleman, I was fond on him, though he'd got a bit confused in his head, what wi' age and wi' taking a drop o' summat warm when the service come of a cold morning. And young Mr. Lammeter he'd have no way but he must be married in Janiwary, which, to be sure, 's a unreasonable time to be married in, for it isn't like a christening or a burying, as you can't help; and so Mr. Drumlow—poor old gentleman, I was fond on him—but when he come to put the questions, he put 'em by the rule o' contrairy, like, and he says, 'Wilt thou have this man to thy wedded wife?' says he, and then he says, 'Wilt thou have this woman to thy wedded husband?' says he. But the partic'larest thing of all is, as nobody took any notice on it but me, and they answered straight off 'yes,' like as if it had been me saying 'Amen' i' the right place, without listening to what went before."

"But you knew what was going on well enough, didn't you, Mr. Macey? You were live enough, eh?" said the butcher.

"Lor bless you!" said Mr. Macey, pausing, and smiling in pity at the impotence of his hearer's imagination—"why, I was all of a tremble: it was as if I'd been a coat pulled by the two tails, like; for I couldn't stop the parson, I couldn't take upon me to do that; and yet I said to myself, I says, 'Suppose they shouldn't be fast married, cause the words are contrairy?' and my head went working like a mill, for I was allays uncommon for turning things over and seeing all round 'em; and I says to myself, 'Is't the meanin' or the words as makes folks fast i' wedlock?' For the parson meant right, and the bride and bridegroom meant right. But then, when I come to think on it, meanin' goes but a little way i' most things, for you may mean to stick things together and your glue may be bad, and then where are you? And so I says to mysen, 'It isn't the meanin', it's the glue.' And I was worreted as if I'd got three bells to pull at once, when we went into the vestry, and they begun to sign their names. But where's the use o' talking?—you can't think what goes on in a cute man's inside."

"But you held in for all that, didn't you, Mr. Macey?" said the landlord.

"Ay, I held in tight till I was by mysen wi' Mr. Drumlow, and then I out wi' everything, but respectful, as I allays did. And he made light on it, and he says, 'Pooh, pooh, Macey, make yourself easy,' he says; 'it's neither the meaning nor the words—it's the regester does it—that's the glue.' So you see he settled it easy; for parsons and doctors know everything by heart, like, so as they aren't worreted wi' thinking what's the rights and wrongs o' things, as I'n been many and many's the time. And sure enough the wedding turned out all right, on'y poor Mrs. Lammeter—that's Miss Osgood as was—died afore the lasses was growed up; but for prosperity and everything respectable, there's no family more looked on."

Every one of Mr. Macey's audience had heard this story many times, but it was listened to as if it had been a favorite tune, and at certain points the puffing of the pipes was momentarily suspended, that the listeners might give their whole minds to the expected words. But there was more to come; and Mr. Snell, the landlord, duly put the leading question.

"Why, old Mr. Lammeter had a pretty fortin, didn't they say, when he come into these parts?"

"Well, yes," said Mr. Macey; "but I dare say it's as much as this Mr. Lammeter's done to keep it whole. For there was allays a talk as nobody could get rich on the Warrens: though he holds it cheap, for it's what they call Charity Land."

"Ay, and there's few folks know so well as you how it come to be Charity Land, eh, Mr. Macey?" said the butcher.

"How should they?" said the old clerk, with some contempt. "Why, my grandfather made the grooms' livery for that Mr. Cliff as came and built the big stables at the Warrens. Why, they're stables four times as big as Squire Cass's, for he thought o' nothing but hosses and hunting, Cliff didn't—a Lunnon tailor, some folks said, as had gone mad wi' cheating. For he couldn't ride; lor bless you! they said he'd got no more grip o' the hoss than if his legs had been cross-sticks: my grandfather heared old Squire Cass say so many and many a time. But ride he would as if Old Harry had been a-driving him; and he'd a son, a lad o' sixteen; and nothing would his father have him do, but he must ride and ride—though the lad was frighted, they said. And it was a common saying as the father wanted to ride the tailor out o' the lad, and make a gentleman on him—not but what I'm a tailor myself, but in respect as God made me such, I'm proud on it, for 'Macey, tailor,' 's been wrote up over our door since afore the Queen's heads went out on the shillings. But Cliff, he was ashamed o' being called a tailor, and he was sore vexed as his riding was laughed at, and nobody o' the gentlefolks hereabout could abide him. Howsomever, the poor lad got sickly and died, and the father didn't live long after

him, for he got queerer nor ever, and they said he used to go out i'
the dead o' the night, wi' a lantern in his hand, to the stables, and set
a lot o' lights burning, for he got as he couldn't sleep; and there he'd
stand, cracking his whip and looking at his hosses; and they said it
was a mercy as the stables didn't get burned down wi' the poor
dumb creaturs in 'em. But at last he died raving, and they found as
he'd left all his property, Warrens and all, to a Lunnon Charity, and
that's how the Warrens come to be Charity Land; though, as for the
stables, Mr. Lammeter never uses 'em—they're out o' all charicter—
lor bless you! if you was to set the doors a-banging in 'em, it 'ud
sound like thunder half o'er the parish."

"Ay, but there's more going on in the stables than what folks see
by daylight, eh, Mr. Macey?" said the landlord.

"Ay, ay; go that way of a dark night, that's all," said Mr. Macey,
winking mysteriously, "and then make believe, if you like, as you
didn't see lights i' the stables, nor hear the stamping o' the hosses,
nor the cracking o' the whips, and howling, too, if it's tow'rt day-
break. 'Cliff's Holiday' has been the name of it ever sin' I were a
boy; that's to say, some said as it was the holiday Old Harry gev him
from roasting, like. That's what my father told me, and he was
a reasonable man, though there's folks nowadays know what
happened afore they were born better nor they know their own
business."

"What do you say to that, eh, Dowlas?" said the landlord, turning to the farrier, who was swelling with impatience for his cue.
"There's a nut for you to crack."

Mr. Dowlas was the negative spirit in the company, and was
proud of his position.

"Say? I say what a man should say as doesn't shut his eyes to look
at a finger-post. I say, as I'm ready to wager any man ten pound, if
he'll stand out wi' me any dry night in the pasture before the Warren
stables, as we shall neither see lights nor hear noises, if it isn't the
blowing of our own noses. That's what I say, and I've said it many a
time; but there's nobody 'ull ventur a ten-pun' note on their ghos'es
as they make so sure of."

"Why, Dowlas, that's easy betting, that is," said Ben Winthrop.
"You might as well bet a man as he wouldn't catch the rheumatise if
he stood up to's neck in the pool of a frosty night. It 'ud be fine fun

for a man to win his bet as he'd catch the rheumatise. Folks as believe in Cliff's Holiday aren't agoing to ventur near it for a matter o' ten pound."

"If Master Dowlas wants to know the truth on it," said Mr. Macey, with a sarcastic smile, tapping his thumbs together, "he's no call to lay any bet—let him go and stan' by himself—there's nobody 'ull hinder him; and then he can let the parish'ners know if they're wrong."

"Thank you! I'm obliged to you," said the farrier, with a snort of scorn. "If folks are fools, it's no business o' mine. I don't want to make out the truth about ghos'es: I know it a'ready. But I'm not against a bet—everything fair and open. Let any man bet me ten pound as I shall see Cliff's Holiday, and I'll go and stand by myself. I want no company. I'd as lief do it as I'd fill this pipe."

"Ah, but who's to watch you, Dowlas, and see you do it? That's no fair bet," said the butcher.

"No fair bet?" replied Mr. Dowlas, angrily. "I should like to hear any man stand up and say I want to bet unfair. Come now, Master Lundy, I should like to hear you say it."

"Very like you would," said the butcher. "But it's no business o' mine. You're none o' my bargains, and I aren't a-going to try and 'bate your price. If anybody 'll bid for you at your own vallying, let him. I'm for peace and quietness, I am."

"Yes, that's what every yapping cur is, when you hold a stick up at him," said the farrier. "But I'm afraid o' neither man nor ghost, and I'm ready to lay a fair bet. I aren't a turn-tail cur."

"Ay, but there's this in it, Dowlas," said the landlord, speaking in a tone of candor and tolerance. "There's folks, i' my opinion, they can't see ghos'es, not if they stood as plain as a pike-staff before 'em. And there's reason i' that. For there's my wife, now, can't smell, not if she'd the strongest o' cheese under her nose. I never see'd a ghost myself; but then I says to myself, 'Very like I haven't got the smell for 'em.' I mean, putting a ghost for a smell, or else contrairiways. And so, I'm for holding with both sides; for, as I say, the truth lies between 'em. And if Dowlas was to go and stand, and say he'd never seen a wink o' Cliff's Holiday all the night through, I'd back him; and if anybody said as Cliff's Holiday was certain sure for all that, I'd back him too. For the smell's what I go by."

The landlord's analogical argument was not very well received by the farrier—a man intensely opposed to compromise.

"Tut, tut," he said, setting down his glass with refreshed irritation; "what's the smell got to do with it? Did ever a ghost give a man a black eye? That's what I should like to know. If ghos'es want me to believe in 'em, let 'em leave off skulking i' the dark and i' lone places— let 'em come where there's company and candles."

"As if ghos'es 'ud want to be believed in by anybody so ignirant!" said Mr. Macey, in deep disgust at the farrier's crass incompetence to apprehend the conditions of ghostly phenomena.

CHAPTER VII

YET THE NEXT MOMENT there seemed to be some evidence that ghosts had a more condescending disposition than Mr. Macey attributed to them; for the pale thin figure of Silas Marner was suddenly seen standing in the warm light, uttering no word, but looking round at the company with his strange unearthly eyes. The long pipes gave a simultaneous movement, like the antennæ of startled insects, and every man present, not excepting even the skeptical farrier, had an impression that he saw, not Silas Marner in the flesh, but an apparition; for the door by which Silas had entered was hidden by the high-screened seats, and no one had noticed his approach. Mr. Macey, sitting a long way off the ghost, might be supposed to have felt an argumentative triumph, which would tend to neutralize his share of the general alarm. Had he not always said that when Silas Marner was in that strange trance of his, his soul went loose from his body? Here was the demonstration: nevertheless, on the whole, he would have been as well contented without it. For a few moments there was a dead silence, Marner's want of breath and agitation not allowing him to speak. The landlord, under the habitual sense that he was bound to keep his house open to all company, and confident in the protection of his unbroken neutrality, at last took on himself the task of adjuring the ghost.

"Master Marner," he said, in a conciliatory tone, "what's lacking to you? What's your business here?"

"Robbed!" said Silas, gaspingly. "I've been robbed! I want the constable—and the Justice—and Squire Cass—and Mr. Crackenthorp."

"Lay hold on him, Jem Rodney," said the landlord, the idea of a ghost subsiding; "he's off his head, I doubt. He's wet through."

Jem Rodney was the outermost man, and sat conveniently near Marner's standing-place; but he declined to give his services.

"Come and lay hold on him yourself, Mr. Snell, if you've a mind," said Jem, rather sullenly. "He's been robbed, and murdered too, for what I know," he added, in a muttering tone.

"Jem Rodney!" said Silas, turning and fixing his strange eyes on the suspected man.

"Ay, Master Marner, what do you want wi' me?" said Jem, trembling a little, and seizing his drinking-can as a defensive weapon.

"If it was you stole my money," said Silas, clasping his hands entreatingly, and raising his voice to a cry, "give it me back,—and I won't meddle with you. I won't set the constable on you. Give it me back, and I'll let you—I'll let you have a guinea."

"Me stole your money!" said Jem, angrily. "I'll pitch this can at your eye if you talk o' my stealing your money."

"Come, come, Master Marner," said the landlord, now rising resolutely, and seizing Marner by the shoulder, "if you've got any information to lay, speak it out sensible, and show as you're in your right mind, if you expect anybody to listen to you. You're as wet as a drownded rat. Sit down and dry yourself, and speak straight forrard."

"Ah, to be sure, man," said the farrier, who began to feel that he had not been quite on a par with himself and the occasion. "Let's have no more staring and screaming, else we'll have you strapped for a madman. That was why I didn't speak at the first—thinks I, the man's run mad."

"Ay, ay, make him sit down," said several voices at once, well pleased that the reality of ghosts remained still an open question.

The landlord forced Marner to take off his coat, and then to sit down on a chair aloof from every one else, in the centre of the circle and in the direct rays of the fire. The weaver, too feeble to have any distinct purpose beyond that of getting help to recover his money, submitted unresistingly. The transient fears of the company were now forgotten in their strong curiosity, and all faces were turned toward Silas, when the landlord, having seated himself again, said—

"Now then, Master Marner, what's this you've got to say—as you've been robbed? Speak out."

"He'd better not say again as it was me robbed him," cried Jem Rodney, hastily. "What could I ha' done with his money? I could as easy steal the parson's surplice, and wear it."

"Hold your tongue, Jem, and let's hear what he's got to say," said the landlord. "Now then, Master Marner."

Silas now told his story, under frequent questioning as the mysterious character of the robbery became evident.

This strangely novel situation of opening his trouble to his Raveloe neighbors, of sitting in the warmth of a hearth not his own, and feeling the presence of faces and voices which were his nearest promise of help, had doubtless its influence on Marner, in spite of his passionate preoccupation with his loss.[11] Our consciousness rarely registers the beginning of a growth within us any more than without us: there have been many circulations of the sap before we detect the smallest sign of the bud.

The slight suspicion with which his hearers at first listened to him, gradually melted away before the convincing simplicity of his distress: it was impossible for the neighbors to doubt that Marner was telling the truth, not because they were capable of arguing at once from the nature of his statements to the absence of any motive for making them falsely, but because, as Mr. Macey observed, "Folks as had the devil to back 'em were not likely to be so mushed" as poor Silas was. Rather, from the strange fact that the robber had left no traces, and had happened to know the nick of time, utterly incalculable by mortal agent, when Silas would go away from home without locking his door, the more probable conclusion seemed to be, that his disreputable intimacy in that quarter, if it ever existed, had been broken up, and, that, in consequence, this ill turn had been done to Marner by somebody it was quite in vain to set the constable after. Why this preternatural felon should be obliged to wait till the door was left unlocked, was a question which did not present itself.

"It isn't Jem Rodney as has done this work, Master Marner," said the landlord. "You mustn't be a-casting your eye at poor Jem. There may be a bit of a reckoning against Jem for the matter of a hare or so, if anybody was bound to keep their eyes staring open, and niver to wink; but Jem's been a-sitting here drinking his can, like the decentest man i' the parish, since before you left your house, Master Marner, by your own account."

"Ay, ay," said Mr. Macey; "let's have no accusing o' the innicent. That isn't the law. There must be folks to swear again' a man before he can be ta'en up. Let's have no accusing o' the innicent, Master Marner."

Memory was not so utterly torpid in Silas that it could not be awakened by these words. With a movement of compunction as new and strange to him as everything else within the last hour, he started from his chair and went close up to Jem, looking at him as if he wanted to assure himself of the expression in his face.

"I was wrong," he said—"yes, yes—I ought to have thought. There's nothing to witness against you, Jem. Only you'd been into my house oftener than anybody else, and so you came into my head. I don't accuse you—I won't accuse anybody—only," he added, lifting up his hands to his head, and turning away with bewildered misery, "I try—I try to think where my guineas can be."

"Ay, ay, they're gone where it's hot enough to melt 'em, I doubt," said Mr. Macey.

"Tchuh!" said the farrier. And then he asked, with a cross-examining air, "How much money might there be in the bags, Master Marner?"

"Two hundred and seventy-two pounds, twelve and six-pence, last night when I counted it," said Silas, seating himself again, with a groan.

"Pooh! why, they'd be none so heavy to carry. Some tramp's been in, that's all; and as for the no footmarks, and the bricks and the sand being all right—why, your eyes are pretty much like a insect's, Master Marner; they're obliged to look so close, you can't see much at a time. It's my opinion as, if I'd been you, or you'd been me—for it comes to the same thing—you wouldn't have thought you'd found everything as you left it. But what I vote is, as two of the sensiblest o' the company should go with you to Master Kench, the constable's—he's ill i' the bed, I know that much—and get him to appoint one of us his deppity; for that's the law, and I don't think anybody 'ull take upon him to contradick me there. It isn't much of a walk to Kench's; and then, if it's me as is deppity, I'll go back with you, Master Marner, and examine your premises; and if anybody's got any fault to find with that, I'll thank him to stand up and say it out like a man."

By this pregnant speech the farrier had re-established his self-complacency, and waited with confidence to hear himself named as one of the superlatively sensible men.

"Let us see how the night is, though," said the landlord, who also considered himself personally concerned in this proposition. "Why, it rains heavy still," he said, returning from the door.

"Well, I'm not the man to be afraid o' the rain," said the farrier. "For it'll look bad when Justice Malam hears as respectable men like us had a information laid before 'em and took no steps."

The landlord agreed with this view, and after taking the sense of the company, and duly rehearsing a small ceremony known in high ecclesiastical life as the nolo episcopari, he consented to take on himself the chill dignity of going to Kench's. But to the farrier's strong disgust, Mr. Macey now started an objection to his proposing himself as a deputy-constable; for that oracular old gentleman, claiming to know the law, stated, as a fact delivered to him by his father, that no doctor could be a constable.

"And you're a doctor, I reckon, though you're only a cow-doctor—for a fly's a fly, though it may be a hoss-fly," concluded Mr. Macey, wondering a little at his own " 'cuteness."

There was a hot debate upon this, the farrier being of course indisposed to renounce the quality of doctor, but contending that a doctor could be a constable if he liked—the law meant, he needn't be one if he didn't like. Mr. Macey thought this was nonsense, since the law was not likely to be fonder of doctors than of other folks. Moreover, if it was in the nature of doctors more than of other men not to like being constables, how came Mr. Dowlas to be so eager to act in that capacity?

"I don't want to act the constable," said the farrier, driven into a corner by this merciless reasoning; "and there's no man can say it of me, if he'd tell the truth. But if there's to be any jealousy and envying about going to Kench's in the rain, let them go as like it—you won't get me to go, I can tell you."

By the landlord's intervention, however, the dispute was accommodated. Mr. Dowlas consented to go as a second person disinclined to act officially; and so poor Silas, furnished with some old coverings, turned out with his two companions into the rain again, thinking of the long night-hours before him, not as those do who long to rest, but as those who expect to "watch for the morning."*

CHAPTER VIII

WHEN GODFREY CASS RETURNED from Mrs. Osgood's party at midnight, he was not much surprised to learn that Dunsey had not come home. Perhaps he had not sold Wildfire, and was waiting for another chance—perhaps, on that foggy afternoon, he had preferred housing himself at the Red Lion at Batherley for the night, if the run had kept him in that neighborhood; for he was not likely to feel much concern about leaving his brother in suspense. Godfrey's mind was too full of Nancy Lammeter's looks and behavior, too full of the exasperation against himself and his lot, which the sight of her always produced in him, for him to give much thought to Wildfire, or to the probabilities of Dunstan's conduct.

The next morning the whole village was excited by the story of the robbery, and Godfrey, like every one else, was occupied in gathering and discussing news about it, and in visiting the Stone-pits. The rain had washed away all possibility of distinguishing foot-marks, but a close investigation of the spot had disclosed, in the direction opposite to the village, a tinder-box, with a flint and steel, half sunk in the mud. It was not Silas's tinder-box, for the only one he had ever had was still standing on his shelf; and the inference generally accepted was, that the tinder-box in the ditch was somehow connected with the robbery. A small minority shook their heads, and intimated their opinion that it was not a robbery to have much light thrown on it by tinder-boxes, that Master Marner's tale had a queer look with it,

---

*See the Bible, Psalms 130:6: "My soul waiteth for the Lord more than they that watch for the morning" (KJV).

and that such things had been known as a man's doing himself a mischief, and then setting the justice to look for the doer. But when
questioned closely as to their grounds for this opinion, and what
Master Marner had to gain by such false pretenses, they only shook
their heads as before, and observed that there was no knowing what
some folks counted gain; moreover, that everybody had a right to
their own opinions, grounds or no grounds, and that the weaver, as
everybody knew, was partly crazy. Mr. Macey, though he joined in the
defense of Marner against all suspicions of deceit, also pooh-poohed
the tinder-box; indeed, repudiated it as a rather impious suggestion,
tending to imply that everything must be done by human hands,
and that there was no power which could make away with the
guineas without moving the bricks. Nevertheless, he turned round
rather sharply on Mr. Tookey, when the zealous deputy, feeling that
this was a view of the case peculiarly suited to a parish-clerk, carried
it still further, and doubted whether it was right to inquire into a
robbery at all when the circumstances were so mysterious.

"As if," concluded Mr. Tookey—"as if there was nothing but
what could be made out by justices and constables."

"Now, don't you be for overshooting the mark, Tookey," said Mr.
Macey, nodding his head aside admonishingly. "That's what you're allays at; if I throw a stone and hit, you think there's summat better
than hitting, and you try to throw a stone beyond. What I said was
against the tinder-box: I said nothing against justices and constables,
for they're o' King George's making, and it 'ud be ill-becoming a man
in a parish office to fly out again' King George."

While these discussions were going on amongst the group outside the Rainbow, a higher consultation was being carried on within,
under the presidency of Mr. Crackenthorp, the rector, assisted by
Squire Cass and other substantial parishioners. It had just occurred to
Mr. Snell, the landlord—he being, as he observed, a man accustomed
to put two and two together—to connect with the tinder-box, which,
as deputy constable, he himself had had the honorable distinction of
finding, certain recollections of a peddler who had called to drink at
the house about a month before, and had actually stated that he carried a tinder-box about with him to light his pipe. Here, surely, was
a clue to be followed out. And as memory, when duly impregnated
with ascertained facts, is sometimes surprisingly fertile, Mr. Snell

gradually recovered a vivid impression of the effect produced on him
by the peddler's countenance and conversation. He had a "look with
his eye" which fell unpleasantly on Mr. Snell's sensitive organism. To
be sure, he didn't say anything particular—no, except that about the
tinder-box—but it isn't what a man says, it's the way he says it. Moreover, he had a swarthy foreignness of complexion which boded little
honesty.

"Did he wear ear-rings?" Mr. Crackenthorp wished to know, having some acquaintance with foreign customs.

"Well—stay—let me see," said Mr. Snell, like a docile clairvoy-
ante, who would not make a mistake if she could help it. After
stretching the corners of his mouth and contracting his eyes, as if he
were trying to see the ear-rings, he appeared to give up the effort,
and said, "Well, he'd got ear-rings in his box to sell, so it's nat'ral to
suppose he might wear 'em. But he called at every house, a'most, in
the village; there's somebody else, mayhap, saw 'em in his ears,
though I can't take upon me rightly to say."

Mr. Snell was correct in his surmise, that somebody else would
remember the peddler's ear-rings. For on the spread of inquiry
among the villagers it was stated with gathering emphasis, that the
parson had wanted to know whether the peddler wore ear-rings in
his ears, and an impression was created that a great deal depended on
the eliciting of this fact. Of course, every one who heard the question, not having any distinct image of the peddler as without ear-rings,
immediately had an image of him with ear-rings, larger or smaller, as
the case might be; and the image was presently taken for a vivid recollection, so that the glazier's wife, a well-intentioned woman, not
given to lying, and whose house was among the cleanest in the village, was ready to declare, as sure as ever she meant to take the sacrament the very next Christmas that was ever coming, that she had seen
big ear-rings, in the shape of the young moon, in the peddler's two
ears; while Jinny Oates, the cobbler's daughter, being a more imaginative person, stated not only that she had seen them too, but that
they had made her blood creep, as it did at that very moment while
there she stood.

Also, by way of throwing further light on this clue of the tinder-
box, a collection was made of all the articles purchased from the peddler at various houses, and carried to the Rainbow to be exhibited

there. In fact, there was a general feeling in the village, that for the clearing up of this robbery there must be a great deal done at the Rainbow, and that no man need offer his wife an excuse for going there while it was the scene of severe public duties.

Some disappointment was felt, and perhaps a little indignation also, when it became known that Silas Marner, on being questioned by the squire and the parson, had retained no other recollection of the peddler than that he had called at his door, but had not entered his house, having turned away at once when Silas, holding the door ajar, had said that he wanted nothing. This had been Silas's testimony, though he clutched strongly at the idea of the peddler's being the culprit, if only because it gave him a definite image of a whereabout for his gold after it had been taken away from its hiding place; he could see it now in the peddler's box. But it was observed with some irritation in the village, that anybody but a "blind creatur" like Marner would have seen the man prowling about, for how came he to leave his tinder-box in the ditch close by, if he hadn't been lingering there? Doubtless, he had made his observations when he saw Marner at the door. Anybody might know—and only look at him— that the weaver was a half-crazy miser. It was a wonder the peddler hadn't murdered him; men of that sort, with rings in their ears, had been known for murderers often and often; there had been one tried at the 'sizes, not so long ago but what there were people living who remembered it.

Godfrey Cass, indeed, entering the Rainbow during one of Mr. Snell's frequently repeated recitals of his testimony, had treated it lightly, stating that he himself had bought a pen-knife of the peddler, and thought him a merry grinning fellow enough; it was all non-sense, he said, about the man's evil looks. But this was spoken of in the village as the random talk of youth, "as if it was only Mr. Snell who had seen something odd about the peddler!" On the contrary, there were at least half-a-dozen who were ready to go before Justice Malam, and give in much more striking testimony than any the land-lord could furnish. It was to be hoped Mr. Godfrey would not go to Tarley and throw cold water on what Mr. Snell said there, and so pre-vent the justice from drawing up a warrant. He was suspected of in-tending this, when, after midday, he was seen setting off on horseback in the direction of Tarley.

But by this time Godfrey's interest in the robbery had faded before his growing anxiety about Dunstan and Wildfire, and he was going, not to Tarley, but to Batherley, unable to rest in uncertainty about them any longer. The possibility that Dunstan had played him the ugly trick of riding away with Wildfire, to return at the end of a month, when he had gambled away or otherwise squandered the price of the horse, was a fear that urged itself upon him more even than the thought of an accidental injury; and now that the dance at Mrs. Osgood's was past, he was irritated with himself that he had trusted his horse to Dunstan. Instead of trying to still his fears he encouraged them, with that superstitious impression which clings to us all, that if we expect evil very strongly it is the less likely to come; and when he heard a horse approaching at a trot, and saw a hat rising above a hedge beyond an angle of the lane, he felt as if his conjuration had succeeded. But no sooner did the horse come within sight than his heart sank again. It was not Wildfire; and in a few moments more he discerned that the rider was not Dunstan, but Bryce, who pulled up to speak, with a face that implied something disagreeable.

"Well, Mr. Godfrey, that's a lucky brother of yours, that Master Dunsey, isn't he?"

"What do you mean?" said Godfrey, hastily.

"Why, hasn't he been home yet?" said Bryce.

"Home? no. What has happened? Be quick. What has he done with my horse?"

"Ah, I thought it was yours, though he pretended you had parted with it to him."

"Has he thrown him down and broken his knees?" said Godfrey, flushed with exasperation.

"Worse than that," said Bryce. "You see, I'd made a bargain with him to buy the horse for a hundred and twenty—a swinging price, but I always liked the horse. And what does he do but go and stake him—fly at a hedge with stakes in it, atop of a bank with a ditch before it. The horse had been dead a pretty good while when he was found. So he hasn't been home since, has he?"

"Home? no," said Godfrey, "and he'd better keep away. Confound me for a fool! I might have known this would be the end of it."

"Well, to tell you the truth," said Bryce, "after I'd bargained for the horse it did come into my head that he might be riding and selling the horse without your knowledge, for I didn't believe it was his own. I knew Master Dunsey was up to his tricks sometimes. But where can he be gone? He's never been seen at Batherley. He couldn't have been hurt, for he must have walked off."

"Hurt?" said Godfrey, bitterly. "He'll never be hurt—he's made to hurt other people."

"And so you *did* give him leave to sell the horse, eh?" said Bryce.

"Yes; I wanted to part with the horse—he was always a little too hard in the mouth for me," said Godfrey; his pride making him wince under the idea that Bryce guessed the sale to be a matter of necessity. "I was going to see after him—I thought some mischief had happened. I'll go back now," he added, turning the horse's head, and wishing he could get rid of Bryce; for he felt that the long-dreaded crisis in his life was close upon him. "You're coming on to Raveloe, aren't you?"

"Well, no, not now," said Bryce. "I *was* coming round there, for I had to go to Flitton, and I thought I might as well take you in my way, and just let you know all I knew myself about the horse. I suppose Master Dunsey didn't like to show himself till the ill news had blown over a bit. He's perhaps gone to pay a visit at the Three Crowns, by Whitbridge—I know he's fond of the house."

"Perhaps he is," said Godfrey, rather absently. Then rousing himself, he said, with an effort at carelessness, "We shall hear of him soon enough, I'll be bound."

"Well, here's my turning," said Bryce, not surprised to perceive that Godfrey was rather "down"; "so I'll bid you good-day, and wish I may bring you better news another time."

Godfrey rode along slowly, representing to himself the scene of confession to his father from which he felt that there was now no longer any escape. The revelation about the money must be made the very next morning; and if he withheld the rest, Dunstan would be sure to come back shortly, and, finding that he must bear the brunt of his father's anger, would tell the whole story out of spite, even though he had nothing to gain by it. There was one step, perhaps, by which he might still win Dunstan's silence and put off the evil day: he might tell his father that he had himself spent the money paid to him by Fowler; and as he had never been guilty of such an offense before, the affair would blow over after a little storming. But Godfrey could not bend himself to this. He felt that in letting Dunstan have the money, he had already been guilty of a breach of trust hardly less culpable than that of spending the money directly for his own behoof; and yet there was a distinction between the two acts which made him feel that the one was so much more blackening than the other as to be intolerable to him.

"I don't pretend to be a good fellow," he said to himself; "but I'm not a scoundrel—at least, I'll stop short somewhere. I'll bear the consequences of what I *have* done sooner than make believe I've done what I never would have done. I'd never have spent the money for my own pleasure—I was tortured into it."

Through the remainder of this day Godfrey, with only occasional fluctuations, kept his will bent in the direction of a complete avowal to his father, and he withheld the story of Wildfire's loss till the next morning, that it might serve him as an introduction to heavier matter. The old Squire was accustomed to his son's frequent absence from home, and thought neither Dunstan's nor Wildfire's nonappearance a matter calling for remark. Godfrey said to himself again and again, that if he let slip this one opportunity of confession, he might never have another; the revelation might be made even in a more odious way than by Dunstan's malignity: *she* might come as she had threatened to do. And then he tried to make the scene easier to himself by rehearsal: he made up his mind how he would pass from the admission of his weakness in letting Dunstan have the money to the fact that Dunstan had a hold on him which he had been unable to shake off, and how he would work up his father to expect something very bad before he told him the fact. The old Squire was an implacable man: he made resolutions in violent anger, and he was not to be moved from them after his anger had subsided—as fiery volcanic matters cool and harden into rock. Like many violent and implacable men, he allowed evils to grow under favor of his own heedlessness, till they pressed upon him with exasperating force, and then he turned round with fierce severity and became unrelentingly hard. This was his system with his tenants: he allowed them to get into arrears, neglect their fences, reduce their stock, sell their straw, and otherwise go the wrong way,—and then, when he became short of money in consequence of this indulgence, he took the hardest measures and would listen to no appeal. Godfrey knew all this, and felt it with the greater force because he had constantly suffered annoyance from witnessing his father's sudden fits of unrelentingness, for which his own habitual irresolution deprived him of all sympathy. (He was not critical on the faulty indulgence which preceded these fits; *that* seemed to him natural enough.) Still there was just the chance, Godfrey thought, that his father's pride might see this marriage in a light that would induce him to hush it up, rather than turn his son out and make the family the talk of the country for ten miles round.

This was the view of the case that Godfrey managed to keep before him pretty closely till midnight, and he went to sleep thinking that he had done with inward debating. But when he awoke in the still morning darkness he found it impossible to reawaken his evening thoughts; it was as if they had been tired out and were not to be roused to further work. Instead of arguments for confession, he could now feel the presence of nothing but its evil consequences: the old dread of disgrace came back—the old shrinking from the thought of raising a hopeless barrier between himself and Nancy—the old disposition to rely on chances which might be favorable to him, and save him from betrayal. Why, after all, should he cut off the hope of them by his own act? He had seen the matter in a wrong light yesterday. He had been in a rage with Dunstan, and had thought of nothing but a thorough break-up of their mutual understanding; but what it would be really wisest for him to do, was to try and soften his father's anger against Dunsey, and keep things as nearly as possible in their old condition. If Dunsey did not come back for a few days (and Godfrey did not know but that the rascal had enough money in his pocket to enable him to keep away still longer), everything might blow over.

CHAPTER IX

GODFREY ROSE AND TOOK his own breakfast earlier than usual, but lingered in the wainscoted parlor till his younger brothers had finished their meal and gone out; awaiting his father, who always took a walk with his managing man before breakfast. Every one breakfasted at a different hour in the Red House, and the Squire was always the latest, giving a long chance to a rather feeble morning appetite before he tried it. The table had been spread with substantial eatables nearly two hours before he presented himself—a tall, stout man of sixty, with a face in which the knit brow and rather hard glance seemed contradicted by the slack and feeble mouth. His person showed marks of habitual neglect, his dress was slovenly; and yet there was something in the presence of the old Squire distinguishable from that of the ordinary farmers in the parish, who were perhaps every whit as refined as he, but, having slouched their way through life with a consciousness of being in the vicinity of their "betters," wanted that self-possession and authoritativeness of voice and carriage which belonged to a man who thought of superiors as remote existences with whom he had personally little more to do than with America or the stars. The Squire had been used to parish homage all his life, used to the presupposition that his family, his tankards, and everything that was his, were the oldest and best; and as he never associated with any gentry higher than himself, his opinion was not disturbed by comparison.

He glanced at his son as he entered the room, and said, "What, sir! haven't you had your breakfast yet?" but there was no pleasant morning greeting between them; not because of any unfriendliness, but because the sweet flower of courtesy is not a growth of such homes as the Red House.

"Yes, sir," said Godfrey, "I've had my breakfast, but I was waiting to speak to you."

"Ah! well," said the Squire, throwing himself indifferently into his chair, and speaking in a ponderous coughing fashion, which was felt in Raveloe to be a sort of privilege of his rank, while he cut a piece of beef, and held it up before the deer-hound that had come in with him. "Ring the bell for my ale, will you? You youngsters' business is your own pleasure, mostly. There's no hurry about it for anybody but yourselves."

The Squire's life was quite as idle as his sons', but it was a fiction kept up by himself and his contemporaries in Raveloe that youth was exclusively the period of folly, and that their aged wisdom was constantly in a state of endurance mitigated by sarcasm. Godfrey waited, before he spoke again, until the ale had been brought and the door closed—an interval during which Fleet, the deer-hound, had consumed enough bits of beef to make a poor man's holiday dinner.

"There's been a cursed piece of ill-luck with Wildfire," he began; "happened the day before yesterday."

"What! broke his knees?" said the Squire, after taking a draught of ale. "I thought you knew how to ride better than that, sir. I never threw a horse down in my life. If I had, I might ha' whistled for another, for my father wasn't quite so ready to unstring as some other fathers I know of. But they must turn over a new leaf—they must. What with mortgages and arrears, I'm as short o' cash as a roadside pauper. And that fool Kimble says the newspaper's talking about peace. Why, the country wouldn't have a leg to stand on. Prices 'ud run down like a jack, and I should never get my arrears, not if I sold all the fellows up. And there's that damned Fowler, I won't put up with him any longer; I've told Winthrop to go to Cox this very day. The lying scoundrel told me he'd be sure to pay me a hundred last month. He takes advantage because he's on that outlying farm, and thinks I shall forget him."

The Squire had delivered this speech in a coughing and interrupted manner, but with no pause long enough for Godfrey to make it a pretext for taking up the word again. He felt that his father meant to ward off any request for money on the ground of the misfortune with Wildfire, and that the emphasis he had thus been led to lay on his shortness of cash and his arrears was likely to produce an attitude of mind the utmost unfavorable for his own disclosure. But he must go on, now he had begun.

"It's worse than breaking the horse's knees—he's been staked and killed," he said, as soon as his father was silent, and had begun to cut his meat. "But I wasn't thinking of asking you to buy me another horse; I was only thinking I'd lost the means of paying you with the price of Wildfire, as I'd meant to do. Dunsey took him to the hunt to sell him for me the other day, and after he'd made a bargain for a hundred and twenty with Bryce, he went after the hounds, and took some fool's leap or other that did for the horse at once. If it hadn't been for that, I should have paid you a hundred pounds this morning."

The Squire had laid down his knife and fork, and was staring at his son in amazement, not being sufficiently quick of brain to form a probable guess as to what could have caused so strange an inversion of the paternal and filial relations as this proposition of his son to pay him a hundred pounds.

"The truth is, sir—I'm very sorry—I was quite to blame," said Godfrey. "Fowler did pay that hundred pounds. He paid it to me, when I was over there one day last month. And Dunsey bothered me for the money, and I let him have it, because I hoped I should be able to pay it you before this."

The Squire was purple with anger before his son had done speaking, and found utterance difficult. "You let Dunsey have it, sir? And how long have you been so thick with Dunsey that you must *collogue* with him to embezzle my money? Are you turning out a scamp? I tell you I won't have it. I'll turn the whole pack of you out of the house together, and marry again. I'd have you to remember, sir, my property's got no entail on it;—since my grandfather's time the Casses can do as they like with their land.[12] Remember that, sir. Let Dunsey have the money! Why should you let Dunsey have the money? There's some lie at the bottom of it."

"There's no lie, sir," said Godfrey. "I wouldn't have spent the money myself, but Dunsey bothered me, and I was a fool, and let him have it. But I meant to pay it, whether he did or not. That's the whole story. I never meant to embezzle money, and I'm not the man to do it. You never knew me do a dishonest trick, sir."

"Where's Dunsey, then? What do you stand talking there for? Go and fetch Dunsey, as I tell you, and let him give account of what he wanted the money for, and what he's done with it. He shall repent it. I'll turn him out. I said I would, and I'll do it. He shan't brave me. Go and fetch him."

"Dunsey isn't come back, sir."

"What! did he break his own neck, then?" said the Squire, with some disgust at the idea that, in that case, he could not fulfill his threat.

"No, he wasn't hurt, I believe, for the horse was found dead, and Dunsey must have walked off. I dare say we shall see him again by-and-by. I don't know where he is."

"And what must you be letting him have my money for? Answer me that," said the Squire, attacking Godfrey again, since Dunsey was not within reach.

"Well, sir, I don't know," said Godfrey, hesitatingly. That was a

feeble evasion, but Godfrey was not fond of lying, and, not being sufficiently aware that no sort of duplicity can long flourish without the help
of vocal falsehoods, he was quite unprepared with invented motives.

"You don't know? I tell you what it is, sir. You've been up to
some trick, and you've been bribing him not to tell," said the Squire,
with a sudden acuteness which startled Godfrey, who felt his heart
beat violently at the nearness of his father's guess. The sudden alarm
pushed him on to take the next step—a very slight impulse suffices
for that on a downward road.

"Why, sir," he said, trying to speak with careless ease, "it was a
little affair between me and Dunsey; it's no matter to anybody else.
It's hardly worth while to pry into young men's fooleries: it wouldn't
have made any difference to you, sir, if I'd not had the bad luck to
lose Wildfire. I should have paid you the money."

"Fooleries! Pshaw! it's time you'd done with fooleries. And I'd
have you know, sir, you must ha' done with 'em," said the Squire,
frowning and casting an angry glance at his son. "Your goings-on are
not what I shall find money for any longer. There's my grandfather
had his stables full of horses, and kept a good house, too, and in
worse times, by what I can make out; and so might I, if I hadn't four
good-for-nothing fellows to hang on me like horse-leeches. I've been
too good a father to you all—that's what it is. But I shall pull up, sir."

Godfrey was silent. He was not likely to be very penetrating in
his judgments, but he had always had a sense that his father's indulgence had not been kindness, and had had a vague longing for some
discipline that would have checked his own errant weakness and
helped his better will. The Squire ate his bread and meat hastily, took
a deep draught of ale, then turned his chair from the table, and began
to speak again.

"It'll be all the worse for you, you know—you'd need try and
help me keep things together."

"Well, sir, I've often offered to take the management of things,
but you know you've taken it ill always, and seemed to think I wanted
to push you out of your place."

"I know nothing o' your offering or o' my taking it ill," said the
Squire, whose memory consisted in certain strong impressions un-
modified by detail; "but I know, one while you seemed to be thinking
o' marrying, and I didn't offer to put any obstacles in your way, as

some fathers would. I'd as lieve you married Lammeter's daughter as
anybody. I suppose, if I'd said you nay, you'd ha' kept on with it; but,
for want o' contradiction, you've changed your mind. You're a shilly-
shally fellow: you take after your poor mother. She never had a will
of her own; a woman has no call for one, if she's got a proper man
for a husband. But your wife had need have one, for you hardly know
your own mind enough to make both your legs walk one way. The
lass hasn't said downright she won't have you, has she?"

"No," said Godfrey, feeling very hot and uncomfortable; "but I
don't think she will."

"Think! why haven't you the courage to ask her? Do you stick to
it, you want to have *her*—that's the thing?"

"There's no other woman I want to marry," said Godfrey evasively.

"Well, then, let me make the offer for you, that's all, if you
haven't the pluck to do it yourself. Lammeter isn't likely to be loath
for his daughter to marry into my family, I should think. And as for
the pretty lass, she wouldn't have her cousin—and there's nobody
else, as I see, could ha' stood in your way."

"I'd rather let it be, please sir, at present," said Godfrey, in alarm.
"I think she's a little offended with me just now, and I should like to
speak for myself. A man must manage these things for himself."

"Well, speak, then, and manage it, and see if you can't turn over
a new leaf. That's what a man must do when he thinks o' marrying."

"I don't see how I can think of it at present, sir. You wouldn't like
to settle me on one of the farms, I suppose, and I don't think she'd
come to live in this house with all my brothers. It's a different sort of
life to what she's been used to."

"Not come to live in this house? Don't tell me. You ask her, that's
all," said the Squire, with a short, scornful laugh.

"I'd rather let the thing be, at present, sir," said Godfrey. "I hope
you won't try to hurry it on by saying anything."

"I shall do what I choose," said the Squire, "and I shall let you
know I'm master; else you may turn out and find an estate to drop
into somewhere else. Go out and tell Winthrop not to go to Cox's, but
wait for me. And tell 'em to get my horse saddled. And stop: look out
and get that hack o' Dunsey's sold, and hand me the money, will you?
He'll keep no more hacks at my expense. And if you know where he's
sneaking—I dare say you do—you may tell him to spare himself the

journey o' coming back home. Let him turn ostler, and keep himself. He shan't hang on me any more."

"I don't know where he is; and if I did, it isn't my place to tell him to keep away," said Godfrey, moving toward the door.

"Confound it, sir, don't stay arguing, but go and order my horse," said the Squire, taking up a pipe.

Godfrey left the room, hardly knowing whether he were more relieved by the sense that the interview was ended without having made any change in his position, or more uneasy that he had entangled himself still further in prevarication and deceit. What had passed about his proposing to Nancy had raised a new alarm, lest by some after-dinner words of his father's to Mr. Lammeter he should be thrown into the embarrassment of being obliged absolutely to decline her when she seemed to be within his reach. He fled to his usual refuge, that of hoping for some unforeseen turn of fortune, some favorable chance which would save him from unpleasant consequences—perhaps even justify his insincerity by manifesting its prudence.

In this point of trusting to some throw of fortune's dice, Godfrey can hardly be called old-fashioned. Favorable Chance is the god of all men who follow their own devices instead of obeying a law they believe in. Let even a polished man of these days get into a position he is ashamed to avow, and his mind will be bent on all the possible issues that may deliver him from the calculable results of that position. Let him live outside his income, or shirk the resolute honest work that brings wages, and he will presently find himself dreaming of a possible benefactor, a possible simpleton who may be cajoled into using his interest, a possible state of mind in some possible person not yet forthcoming. Let him neglect the responsibilities of his office, and he will inevitably anchor himself on the chance that the thing left undone may turn out not to be of the supposed importance. Let him betray his friend's confidence, and he will adore that same cunning complexity called Chance, which gives him the hope that his friend will never know. Let him forsake a decent craft that he may pursue the gentilities of a profession to which nature never called him, and his religion will infallibly be the worship of blessed Chance, which he will believe in as the mighty creator of success. The evil principle deprecated in that religion is the orderly sequence by which the seed brings forth a crop after its kind.

CHAPTER X

JUSTICE MALAM WAS NATURALLY regarded in Tarley and Raveloe as a man of capacious mind, seeing that he could draw much wider conclusions without evidence than could be expected of his neighbors who were not on the Commission of the Peace. Such a man was not likely to neglect the clue of the tinder-box, and an inquiry was set on foot concerning a peddler, name unknown, with curly black hair and a foreign complexion, carrying a box of cutlery and jewelry, and wearing large rings in his ears. But either because inquiry was too slow-footed to overtake him, or because the description applied to so many peddlers that inquiry did not know how to choose among them, weeks passed away, and there was no other result concerning the robbery than a gradual cessation of the excitement it had caused in Raveloe. Dunstan Cass's absence was hardly a subject of remark: he had once before had a quarrel with his father, and had gone off, nobody knew whither, to return at the end of six weeks, take up his old quarters unforbidden and swagger as usual. His own family, who equally expected this issue, with the sole difference that the Squire was determined this time to forbid him the old quarters, never mentioned his absence; and when his uncle Kimble or Mr. Osgood noticed it, the story of his having killed Wildfire and committed some offense against his father was enough to prevent surprise. To connect the fact of Dunsey's disappearance with that of the robbery occurring on the same day, lay quite away from the track of every one's thought, even Godfrey's, who had better reason than any one else to know what his brother was capable of. He remembered no mention of the weaver between them since the time, twelve years ago, when it was their boyish sport to deride him; and, besides, his imagination constantly created an *alibi* for Dunstan: he saw him continually in some congenial haunt, to which he had walked off on leaving Wildfire—saw him sponging on chance acquaintances, and meditating a return home to the old amusement of tormenting his elder brother. Even if any brain in Raveloe had put the said two facts together, I doubt whether a combination so injurious to the prescriptive respectability of a family with a mural monument and venerable tankards, would not have been suppressed as of unsound tendency. But Christmas puddings, brawn, and abundance of spirituous liquors, throwing the mental originality into the channel of nightmare, are great preservatives against a dangerous spontaneity of waking thought.

When the robbery was talked of at the Rainbow and elsewhere, in good company, the balance continued to waver between the rational explanation founded on the tinder-box, and the theory of an impenetrable mystery that mocked investigation. The advocates of the tinder-box-and-peddler view considered the other side a muddle-headed and credulous set, who, because they themselves were wall-eyed, supposed everybody else to have the same blank outlook; and the adherents of the inexplicable more than hinted that their antagonists were animals inclined to crow before they had found any corn—mere skimming-dishes in point of depth—whose clear-sightedness consisted in supposing there was nothing behind a barn-door because they couldn't see through it; so that, though their controversy did not serve to elicit the fact concerning the robbery, it elicited some true opinions of collateral importance.

But while poor Silas's loss served thus to brush the slow current of Raveloe conversation, Silas himself was feeling the withering desolation of that bereavement about which his neighbors were arguing at their ease. To any one who had observed him before he lost his gold, it might have seemed that so withered and shrunken a life as his could hardly be susceptible of a bruise, could hardly endure any subtraction but such as would put an end to it altogether. But in reality it had been an eager life, filled with immediate purpose which fenced him in from the wide, cheerless unknown. It had been a clinging life; and though the object round which its fibers had clung was a dead disrupted thing, it satisfied the need for clinging. But now the fence was broken down—the support was snatched away. Marner's thoughts could no longer move in their old round, and were baffled by a blank like that which meets a plodding ant when the earth has broken away on its homeward path. The loom was there, and the weaving, and the growing pattern in the cloth; but the bright treasure in the hole under his feet was gone; the prospect of handling and counting it was gone: the evening had no phantasm of delight to still the poor soul's craving. The thought of the money he would get by his actual work could bring no joy, for its meagre image was only a fresh reminder of his loss; and hope was too heavily crushed by the sudden blow, for his imagination to dwell on the growth of a new hoard from that small beginning.

He filled up the blank with grief. As he sat weaving, he every now and then moaned low, like one in pain: it was the sign that his thoughts had come round again to the sudden chasm—to the empty evening time. And all the evening, as he sat in his loneliness by his dull fire, he leaned his elbows on his knees, and clasped his head with his hands, and moaned very low—not as one who seeks to be heard.

And yet he was not utterly forsaken in his trouble. The repulsion Marner had always created in his neighbors was partly dissipated by the new light in which this misfortune had shown him. Instead of a man who had more cunning than honest folks could come by, and, what was worse, had not the inclination to use that cunning in a neighborly way, it was now apparent that Silas had not cunning enough to keep his own. He was generally spoken of as a "poor mushed creatur"; and that avoidance of his neighbors, which had before been referred to his ill-will and to a probable addiction to worse company, was now considered mere craziness.

This change to a kindlier feeling was shown in various ways. The odor of Christmas cooking being on the wind, it was the season when superfluous pork and black puddings are suggestive of charity in well-to-do-families; and Silas's misfortune had brought him uppermost in the memory of house-keepers like Mrs. Osgood. Mr. Crackenthorp, too, while he admonished Silas that his money had probably been taken from him because he thought too much of it and never came to church, enforced the doctrine by a present of pigs' pettitoes, well calculated to dissipate unfounded prejudices against the clerical character. Neighbors who had nothing but verbal consolation to give showed a disposition not only to greet Silas and discuss his misfortune at some length when they encountered him in the village, but also to take the trouble of calling at his cottage and getting him to repeat all the details on the very spot; and then they would try to cheer him by saying, "Well, Master Marner, you're no worse off nor other poor folks, after all; and if you was to be crippled, the parish 'ud give you a 'lowance."

I suppose one reason why we are seldom able to comfort our neighbors with our words is that our goodwill gets adulterated, in spite of ourselves, before it can pass our lips. We can send black puddings and pettitoes without giving them a flavor of our own egoism; but language is a stream that is almost sure to smack of a mingled soil. There was a fair proportion of kindness in Raveloe; but it was often of a beery and bungling sort, and took the shape least allied to the complimentary and hypocritical.

Mr. Macey, for example, coming one evening expressly to let Silas know that the recent events had given him the advantage of standing more favorably in the opinion of a man whose judgment was not formed lightly, opened the conversation by saying, as soon as he had seated himself and adjusted his thumbs—

"Come, Master Marner, why, you've no call to sit a-moaning. You're a deal better off to ha' lost your money, nor to ha' kep it by foul means. I used to think, when you first come into these parts, as you were no better nor you should be; you were younger a deal than what you are now; but you were allays a staring, white-faced creatur, partly like a bald-faced calf, as I may say. But there's no knowing: it isn't every queer-looksed thing as Old Harry's had the making of—I mean, speaking o' toads and such; for they're often harmless, and useful against varmin. And it's pretty much the same wi' you, as fur as I can see. Though as to the yarbs and stuff to cure the breathing, if you brought that sort o' knowledge from distant parts, you might ha' been a bit freer of it. And if the knowledge wasn't well come by, why, you might ha' made up for it by coming to church reg'lar, for as for the children as the Wise Woman charmed, I've been at the christening of 'em again and again, and they took the water just as well. And that's reasonable; for if Old Harry's a mind to do a bit o' kindness for a holiday, like, who's got anything against it? That's my thinking; and I've been clerk o' this parish forty year, and I know, when the parson and me does the cussing of a Ash Wednesday, there's no cussing o' folks as have a mind to be cured without a doctor, let Kimble say what he will. And so, Master Marner, as I was saying—for there's windings i' things as they may carry you to the fur end o' the prayer-book afore you get back to 'em—my advice is, as you keep up your sperrits; for as for thinking you're a deep un, and ha' got more inside you nor 'ull bear daylight, I'm not o' that opinion at all, and so I tell the neighbors.

For, says I, you talk o' Master Marner making out a tale—why, it's nonsense, that is: it 'ud take a 'cute man to make a tale like that; and, says I, he looked as scared as a rabbit."

During this discursive address Silas had continued motionless in his previous attitude, leaning his elbows on his knees, and pressing his hands against his head. Mr. Macey, not doubting that he had been listened to, paused, in the expectation of some appreciatory reply, but Marner remained silent. He had a sense that the old man meant to be good-natured and neighborly; but the kindness fell on him as sunshine falls on the wretched—he had no heart to taste it, and felt that it was very far off him.

"Come, Master Marner, have you got nothing to say to that?" said Mr. Macey at last, with a slight accent of impatience.

"Oh," said Marner, slowly, shaking his head between his hands, "I thank you—thank you—kindly."

"Ay, ay, to be sure: I thought you would," said Mr. Macey; "and my advice is—have you got a Sunday suit?"

"No," said Marner.

"I doubted it was so," said Mr. Macey. "Now let me advise you to get a Sunday suit: there's Tookey, he's a poor creatur, but he's got my tailoring business, and some o' my money in it, and he shall make a suit at a low price, and give you trust, and then you can come to church, and be a bit neighborly. Why, you've never heared me say 'Amen' since you come into these parts, and I recommend you to lose no time, for it'll be poor work when Tookey has it all to himself, for I mayn't be equil to stand i' the desk at all, come another winter." Here Mr. Macey paused, perhaps expecting some sign of emotion in his hearer; but not observing any, he went on. "And as for the money for the suit o' clothes, why, you get a matter of a pound a-week at your weaving, Master Marner, and you're a young man, eh, for all you look so mushed. Why, you couldn't ha' been five-and-twenty when you come into these parts, eh?"

Silas started a little at the change to a questioning tone, and answered mildly, "I don't know; I can't rightly say—it's a long while since."

After receiving such an answer as this, it is not surprising that Mr. Macey observed, later on in the evening at the Rainbow, that Marner's head was "all of a muddle," and that it was to be doubted if he ever knew when Sunday came round, which showed him a worse heathen than many a dog.

Another of Silas's comforters, besides Mr. Macey, came to him with a mind highly charged on the same topic. This was Mrs. Winthrop, the wheelwright's wife. The inhabitants of Raveloe were not severely regular in their church-going, and perhaps there was hardly a person in the parish who would not have held that to go to church every Sunday in the calendar would have shown a greedy desire to stand well with Heaven, and get an undue advantage over their neighbors—a wish to be better than the "common run," that would have implied a reflection on those who had had godfathers and godmothers as well as themselves, and had an equal right to the burying-service. At the same time, it was understood to be requisite for all who were not household servants, or young men, to take the sacrament at one of the great festivals: Squire Cass himself took it on Christmas day; while those who were held to be "good livers" went to church with greater, though still with moderate, frequency.

Mrs. Winthrop was one of these: she was in all respects a woman of scrupulous conscience, so eager for duties that life seemed to offer them too scantily unless she rose at half-past four, though this threw a scarcity of work over the more advanced hours of the morning, which it was a constant problem with her to remove. Yet she had not the vixenish temper which is sometimes supposed to be a necessary condition of such habits: she was a very mild, patient woman, whose nature it was to seek out all the sadder and more serious elements of life, and pasture her mind upon them. She was the person always first thought of in Raveloe when there was illness or death in a family; when leeches were to be applied, or there was a sudden disappointment in a monthly nurse. She was a "comfortable woman"— good-looking, fresh-complexioned, having her lips always slightly screwed, as if she felt herself in a sick-room with the doctor or the clergyman present. But she was never whimpering; no one had seen her shed tears; she was simply grave and inclined to shake her head and sigh, almost imperceptibly, like a funereal mourner who is not a relation. It seemed surprising that Ben Winthrop, who loved his quart-pot and his joke, got along so well with Dolly; but she took her husband's jokes and joviality as patiently as everything else, considering that "men would be so," and viewing the stronger sex in the light of animals whom it had pleased Heaven to make naturally troublesome, like bulls and turkey-cocks.

This good wholesome woman could hardly fail to have her mind drawn strongly toward Silas Marner, now that he appeared in the light of a sufferer; and one Sunday afternoon she took her little boy Aaron with her, and went to call on Silas, carrying in her hand some small lard-cakes, flat paste-like articles much esteemed in Raveloe. Aaron, an apple-cheeked youngster of seven, with a clean starched frill which looked like a plate for the apples, needed all his adventurous curiosity to embolden him against the possibility that the big-eyed weaver might do him some bodily injury; and his dubiety was much increased when, on arriving at the Stone-pits, they heard the mysterious sound of the loom.

"Ah, it is as I thought," said Mrs. Winthrop, sadly.

They had to knock loudly before Silas heard them; but when he did come to the door he showed no impatience, as he would once have done, at a visit that had been unasked for and unexpected. Formerly, his heart had been as a locked casket with its treasure inside; but now the casket was empty, and the lock was broken. Left groping in darkness, with his prop utterly gone, Silas had inevitably a sense, though a dull and half-despairing one, that if any help came to him it must come from without; and there was a slight stirring of expectation at the sight of his fellow-men, a faint consciousness of dependence on their goodwill. He opened the door wide to admit Dolly, but without otherwise returning her greeting than by moving the arm-chair a few inches as a sign that she was to sit down in it. Dolly; as soon as she was seated, removed the white cloth that covered her lard-cakes, and said in her gravest way—

"I'd a baking yesterday, Master Marner, and the lard-cakes turned out better nor common, and I'd ha' asked you to accept some, if you'd thought well. I don't eat such things myself, for a bit o' bread's what I like from one year's end to the other; but men's stomichs are made so comical, they want a change—they do, I know, God help 'em."

Dolly sighed gently as she held out the cakes to Silas, who thanked her kindly and looked very close at them, absently, being accustomed to look so at everything he took into his hand—eyed all the while by the wondering bright orbs of the small Aaron, who had made an outwork of his mother's chair, and was peeping round from behind it.

"There's letters pricked on 'em," said Dolly. "I can't read 'em myself, and there's nobody, not Mr. Macey himself, rightly knows what they mean; but they've a good meaning, for they're the same as is on the pulpit-cloth at church. What are they, Aaron, my dear?"

Aaron retreated completely behind his outwork.

"Oh, go, that's naughty," said his mother, mildly. "Well, whativer the letters are, they've a good meaning; and it's a stamp as has been in our house, Ben says, ever since he was a little un, and his mother used to put it on the cakes, and I've always put it on too; for if there's any good, we've need of it i' this world."

"It's I. H. S.,"* said Silas, at which proof of learning Aaron peeped round the chair again.

"Well, to be sure, you can read 'em off," said Dolly. "Ben's read 'em to me many and many a time, but they slip out o' my mind again; the more's the pity, for they're good letters, else they wouldn't be in the church; and so I prick 'em on all the loaves and all the cakes, though sometimes they won't hold, because o' the rising—for, as I said, if there's any good to be got we've need of it i' this world—that we have; and I hope they'll bring good to you, Master Marner, for it's wi' that will I brought you the cakes; and you see the letters have held better nor common."

Silas was as unable to interpret the letters as Dolly, but there was no possibility of misunderstanding the desire to give comfort that made itself heard in her quiet tones. He said, with more feeling than before: "Thank you—thank you kindly." But he laid down the cakes and seated himself absently—drearily unconscious of any distinct benefit toward which the cakes and the letters, or even Dolly's kindness, could tend for him.

"Ah, if there's good anywhere, we've need of it," repeated Dolly, who did not lightly forsake a serviceable phrase. She looked at Silas pityingly as she went on. "But you didn't hear the church-bells this morning, Master Marner? I doubt you didn't know it was Sunday.

---

*Abbreviation of In *hoc signo vinces*, a Latin phrase meaning "In this sign shall you conquer."

Living so lone here, you lose your count, I dare say; and then, when your loom makes a noise, you can't hear the bells, more partic'lar now the frost kills the sound."

"Yes, I did; I heard 'em," said Silas, to whom Sunday bells were a mere accident of the day, and not part of its sacredness. There had been no bells in Lantern Yard.

"Dear heart!" said Dolly, pausing before she spoke again. "But what a pity it is you should work of a Sunday, and not clean yourself—if you didn't go to church; for if you'd a roasting bit, it might be as you couldn't leave, being a lone man. But there's the bakehus, if you could make up your mind to spend a twopence on the oven now and then—not every week, in course—I shouldn't like to do that my-self—you might carry your bit o' dinner there, for it's nothing but right to have a bit o' summat hot of a Sunday, and not to make it as you can't know your dinner from Saturday. But now, upo' Christmas-day, this blessed Christmas as is ever coming, if you was to take your dinner to the bakehus, and go to church, and see the holly and the yew, and hear the anthim, and then take the sacramen', you'd be a deal the better, and you'd know which end you stood on, and you could put your trust i' Them as knows better nor we do, seein' you'd ha' done what it lies on us all to do."

Dolly's exhortation, which was an unusually long effort of speech for her, was uttered in the soothing persuasive tone with which she would have tried to prevail on a sick man to take his medicine, or a basin of gruel for which he had no appetite. Silas had never before been closely urged on the point of his absence from church, which had only been thought of as a part of his general queerness; and he was too direct and simple to evade Dolly's appeal.

"Nay, nay," he said, "I know nothing o' church. I've never been to church."

"No!" said Dolly, in a low tone of wonderment. Then bethinking herself of Silas's advent from an unknown country, she said, "Could it ha' been as they'd no church where you was born?"

"Oh, yes," said Silas, meditatively, sitting in his usual posture of leaning on his knees, and supporting his head. "There was churches—a many—it was a big town. But I knew nothing of 'em—I went to chapel."

Dolly was much puzzled at this new word, but she was rather afraid of inquiring further, lest "chapel" might mean some haunt of wickedness. After a little thought, she said—

"Well, Master Marner, it's niver too late to turn over a new leaf, and if you've niver had no church, there's no telling the good it'll do you. For I feel so set up and comfortable as niver was, when I've been and heard the prayers, and the singing to the praise and glory o' God, as Mr. Macey gives out—and Mr. Crackenthorp saying good words, and more partic'lar on Sacramen' Day; and if a bit o' trouble comes, I feel as I can put up wi' it, for I've looked for help i' the right quarter, and gev myself up to Them as we must all give ourselves up to at the last; and if we 'n done our part, it isn't to be believed as Them as are above us 'ull be worse nor we are, and come short o' Their'n."

Poor Dolly's exposition of her simple Raveloe theology fell rather unmeaningly on Silas's ears, for there was no word in it that could rouse a memory of what he had known as religion, and his comprehension was quite baffled by the plural pronoun, which was no heresy of Dolly's, but only her way of avoiding a presumptuous familiarity. He remained silent, not feeling inclined to assent to the part of Dolly's speech which he fully understood—her recommendation that he should go to church. Indeed, Silas was so unaccustomed to talk beyond the brief questions and answers necessary for the transaction of his simple business, that words did not easily come to him without the urgency of a distinct purpose.

But now, little Aaron, having become used to the weaver's awful presence, had advanced to his mother's side, and Silas, seeming to notice him for the first time, tried to return Dolly's signs of goodwill by offering the lad a bit of lard-cake. Aaron shrank back a little, and rubbed his head against his mother's shoulder, but still thought the piece of cake worth the risk of putting his hand out for it.

"Oh, for shame, Aaron," said his mother, taking him on her lap, however; "why, you don't want cake again yet awhile. He's wonderful hearty," she went on, with a little sigh—"that he is, God knows. He's my youngest, and we spoil him sadly, for either me or the father must allays hev him in our sight—that we must."

She stroked Aaron's brown head, and thought it must do Master

Marner good to see such a "pictur of a child." But Marner, on the
other side of the hearth, saw the neat-featured rosy face as a mere
dim round, with two dark spots in it.

"And he's got a voice like a bird—you wouldn't think," Dolly
went on; "he can sing a Christmas carril as his father's taught him;
and I take it for a token as he'll come to good, as he can learn the
good tunes so quick. Come, Aaron, stan' up and sing the carril to
Master Marner, come."

Aaron replied by rubbing his forehead against his mother's
shoulder.

"Oh, that's naughty," said Dolly, gently. "Stan' up, when mother
tells you, and let me hold the cake till you've done."

Aaron was not indisposed to display his talents, even to an
ogre, under protecting circumstances; and after a few more signs of
coyness, consisting chiefly in rubbing the backs of his hands over
his eyes, and then peeping between them at Master Marner, to see
if he looked anxious for the "carril," he at length allowed his head
to be duly adjusted, and standing behind the table, which let him
appear above it only as far as his broad frill, so that he looked like
a cherubic head untroubled with a body, he began with a clear
chirp, and in a melody that had the rhythm of an industrious
hammer—

> "God rest you, merry gentlemen,
>   Let nothing you dismay,
> For Jesus Christ our Savior
>   Was born on Christmas-day."

Dolly listened with a devout look, glancing at Marner in some
confidence that this strain would help to allure him to church.

"That's Christmas music," she said, when Aaron had ended, and
had secured his piece of cake again. "There's no other music equil to
the Christmas music—'Hark the erol angils sing.' And you may judge
what it is at church, Master Marner, with the bassoon and the voices,
as you can't help thinking you've got to a better place a'ready—for
I wouldn't speak ill o' this world, seeing as Them put us in it as
knows best—but what wi' the drink, and the quarreling, and the
bad illnesses, and the hard dying, as I've seen times and times, one's

thankful to hear of a better. The boy sings pretty, don't he, Master Marner?"

"Yes," said Silas, absently, "very pretty."

The Christmas carol, with its hammer-like rhythm, had fallen on his ears as strange music, quite unlike a hymn, and could have none of the effect Dolly contemplated. But he wanted to show her that he was grateful, and the only mode that occurred to him was to offer Aaron a bit more cake.

"Oh, no, thank you, Master Marner," said Dolly, holding down Aaron's willing hands. "We must be going home now. And so I wish you good-bye, Master Marner; and if you ever feel anyways bad in your inside, as you can't fend for yourself, I'll come and clean up for you, and get you a bit o' victual, and willing. But I beg and pray of you to leave off weaving of a Sunday, for it's bad for soul and body—and the money as comes i' that way 'ull be a bad bed to lie down on at the last, if it doesn't fly away, nobody knows where, like the white frost. And you'll excuse me being that free with you, Master Marner, for I wish you well—I do. Make your bow, Aaron."

Silas said "Good-bye, and thank you kindly," as he opened the door for Dolly, but he couldn't help feeling relieved when she was gone—relieved that he might weave again and moan at his ease. Her simple view of life and its comforts, by which she had tried to cheer him, was only like a report of unknown objects, which his imagination could not fashion. The fountains of human love and of faith in a divine love had not yet been unlocked, and his soul was still the shrunken rivulet, with only this difference, that its little groove of sand was blocked up, and it wandered confusedly against dark obstruction.

And so, notwithstanding the honest persuasions of Mr. Macey and Dolly Winthrop, Silas spent his Christmas-day in loneliness, eating his meat in sadness of heart, though the meat had come to him as a neighborly present. In the morning he looked out on the black frost that seemed to press cruelly on every blade of grass, while the half-icy red pool shivered under the bitter wind; but toward evening the snow began to fall, and curtained from him even that dreary outlook, shutting him close up with his narrow grief. And he sat in his robbed home through the livelong evening, not caring to close his shutters or lock his door, pressing his head between his hands and moaning, till the cold grasped him and told him that his fire was gray.

Nobody in this world but himself knew that he was the same Silas Marner who had once loved his fellow with tender love, and trusted in an unseen goodness. Even to himself that past experience had become dim.

But in Raveloe village the bells rang merrily, and the church was fuller than all through the rest of the year, with red faces among the abundant dark-green boughs—faces prepared for a longer service than usual by an odorous breakfast of toast and ale. Those green boughs, the hymn and anthem never heard but at Christmas—even the Athanasian Creed, which was discriminated from the others only as being longer and of exceptional virtue, since it was only read on rare occasions—brought a vague exulting sense, for which the grown men could as little have found words as the children, that something great and mysterious had been done for them in heaven above and in earth below, which they were appropriating by their presence. And then the red faces made their way through the black biting frost to their own homes, feeling themselves free for the rest of the day to eat, drink, and be merry, and using that Christian freedom without diffidence.

At Squire Cass's family party that day nobody mentioned Dunstan—nobody was sorry for his absence, or feared it would be too long. The doctor and his wife, uncle and aunt Kimble, were there, and the annual Christmas talk was carried through without any omissions, rising to the climax of Mr. Kimble's experience when he walked the London hospitals thirty years back, together with striking professional anecdotes then gathered. Whereupon cards followed, with aunt Kimble's annual failure to follow suit, and uncle Kimble's irascibility concerning the odd trick which was rarely explicable to him, when it was not on his side, without a general visitation of tricks to see that they were formed on sound principles: the whole being accompanied by a strong steaming odor of spirits-and-water.

But the party on Christmas-day, being a strictly family party, was not the pre-eminently brilliant celebration of the season at the Red House. It was the great dance on New Year's Eve that made the glory of Squire Cass's hospitality, as of his forefathers', time out of mind. This was the occasion when all the society of Raveloe and Tarley, whether old acquaintances separated by long rutty distances, or cooled acquaintances separated by misunderstandings concerning runaway calves, or acquaintances founded on intermittent condescension, counted on meeting and on comporting themselves with mutual appropriateness. This was the occasion on which fair dames who came on pillions sent their bandboxes before them, supplied with more than their evening costume; for the feast was not to end with a single evening, like a paltry town entertainment, where the whole supply of eatables is put on the table at once, and bedding is scanty. The Red House was provisioned as if for a siege; and as for the spare featherbeds ready to be laid on floors, they were as plentiful as might naturally be expected in a family that had killed its own geese for many generations.

Godfrey Cass was looking forward to this New Year's Eve with a foolish reckless longing, that made him half deaf to his importunate companion, Anxiety.

"Dunsey will be coming home soon; there will be a great blow-up, and how will you bribe his spite to silence?" said Anxiety.

"Oh, he won't come home before New Year's Eve, perhaps," said Godfrey; "and I shall sit by Nancy then, and dance with her, and get a kind look from her in spite of herself."

"But money is wanted in another quarter," said Anxiety, in a louder voice, "and how will you get it without selling your mother's diamond pin? And if you don't get it ——?"

"Well, but something may happen to make things easier. At any rate, there's one pleasure for me close at hand: Nancy is coming."

"Yes, and suppose your father should bring matters to a pass that will oblige you to decline marrying her—and to give your reasons?"

"Hold your tongue, and don't worry me. I can see Nancy's eyes, just as they will look at me, and feel her hand in mine already."

But Anxiety went on, though in noisy Christmas company, refusing to be utterly quieted even by much drinking.

CHAPTER XI

SOME WOMEN, I GRANT, would not appear to advantage seated on a pillion, and attired in a drab joseph[13] and a drab beaver-bonnet, with a crown resembling a small stew-pan; for a garment suggesting a coachman's greatcoat, cut out under an exiguity of cloth that would only allow of miniature capes, is not well adapted to conceal deficiencies of contour, nor is drab a color that will throw sallow cheeks into a lively contrast. It was all the greater triumph to Miss Nancy Lammeter's beauty that she looked thoroughly bewitching in that costume, as, seated on the pillion behind her tall, erect father, she held one arm round him, and looked down, with open-eyed anxiety, at the treacherous snow-covered pools and puddles, which sent up formidable splashings of mud under the stamp of Dobbin's foot. A painter would, perhaps, have preferred her in those moments when she was free from self-consciousness; but certainly the bloom on her cheeks was at its highest point of contrast with the surrounding drab when she arrived at the door of the Red House, and saw Mr. Godfrey Cass ready to lift her from the pillion. She wished her sister Priscilla had come up at the same time behind the servant, for then she would have contrived that Mr. Godfrey should have lifted off Priscilla first, and, in the meantime, she would have persuaded her father to go round to the horse-block instead of alighting at the door-steps. It was very painful, when you had made it quite clear to a young man that you were determined not to marry him, however much he might wish it, that he would still continue to pay you marked attentions; besides, why didn't he always show the same attentions, if he meant them sincerely, instead of being so strange as Mr. Godfrey Cass was, sometimes behaving as if he didn't want to speak to her, and taking no notice of her for weeks and weeks, and then, all on a sudden, almost making love again? Moreover, it was quite plain he had no real love for her, else he would not let people have *that* to say of him which they did say. Did he suppose that Miss Nancy Lammeter was to be won by any man, squire or no squire, who led a bad life? That was not what she had been used to see in her own father, who was the soberest and best man in that country-side, only a little hot and hasty now and then, if things were not done to the minute.

All these thoughts rushed through Miss Nancy's mind, in their habitual succession, in the moments between her first sight of Mr. Godfrey Cass standing at the door and her own arrival there. Happily, the Squire came out too and gave a loud greeting to her father, so that, somehow, under cover of this noise she seemed to find concealment for her confusion and neglect of any suitably formal behavior, while she was being lifted from the pillion by strong arms which seemed to find her ridiculously small and light. And there was the best reason for hastening into the house at once, since the snow was beginning to fall again, threatening an unpleasant journey for such guests as were still on the road. These were a small minority; for already the afternoon was beginning to decline, and there would not be too much time for the ladies who came from a distance to attire themselves in readiness for the early tea which was to inspirit them for the dance.

There was a buzz of voices through the house, as Miss Nancy entered, mingled with the scrape of a fiddle preluding in the kitchen; but the Lammeters were guests whose arrival had evidently been thought of so much that it had been watched for from the windows, for Mrs. Kimble, who did the honors at the Red House on these great occasions, came forward to meet Miss Nancy in the hall, and conduct her up-stairs. Mrs. Kimble was the Squire's sister as well as the doctor's wife—a double dignity, with which her diameter was in direct proportion; so that, a journey up-stairs being rather fatiguing to her, she did not oppose Miss Nancy's request to be allowed to find her way alone to the Blue Room, where the Miss Lammeters' bandboxes had been deposited on their arrival in the morning.

There was hardly a bedroom in the house where feminine compliments were not passing and feminine toilets going forward, in various stages, in space made scanty by extra beds spread upon the floor; and Miss Nancy, as she entered the Blue Room, had to make her little formal curtsy to a group of six. On the one hand, there were ladies no less important than the two Miss Gunns, the wine merchant's daughters from Lytherly, dressed in the height of fashion, with the tightest skirts and the shortest waists, and gazed at by Miss

Ladbrook (of the Old Pastures) with a shyness not unsustained by inward criticism. Partly, Miss Ladbrook felt that her own skirt must be regarded as unduly lax by the Miss Gunns, and partly, that it was a pity the Miss Gunns did not show that judgment which she herself would show if she were in their place, by stopping a little on this side of the fashion. On the other hand, Mrs. Ladbrook was standing in skull-cap and front,* with her turban in her hand, curtsying and smiling blandly and saying, "After you, ma'am," to another lady in similar circumstances, who had politely offered the precedence at the looking-glass.

But Miss Nancy had no sooner made her curtsy than an elderly lady came forward, whose full white muslin kerchief, and mob-cap† round her curls of smooth gray hair, were in daring contrast with the puffed yellow satins and top-knotted caps of her neighbors. She approached Miss Nancy with much primness, and said, with a slow, treble suavity—

"Niece, I hope I see you well in health." Miss Nancy kissed her aunt's cheek dutifully, and answered, with the same sort of amiable primness, "Quite well, I thank you, aunt; and I hope I see you the same."

"Thank you, niece; I keep my health for the present. And how is my brother-in-law?"

These dutiful questions and answers were continued until it was ascertained in detail that the Lammeters were all as well as usual, and the Osgoods likewise, also that niece Priscilla must certainly arrive shortly, and that traveling on pillions in snowy weather was unpleasant, though a joseph was a great protection. Then Nancy was formally introduced to her aunt's visitors, the Miss Gunns, as being the daughters of a mother known to their mother, though now for the first time induced to make a journey into these parts; and these ladies were so taken by surprise at finding such a lovely face and figure in an out-of-the-way country place, that they began to feel some curiosity about the dress she would put on when she took off her joseph. Miss Nancy, whose thoughts were always conducted with the propriety and moderation conspicuous in her manners, remarked to

---

*A half wig that covered the front of the head.
†Indoor cap worn by women in the eighteenth and early nineteenth centuries.

herself that the Miss Gunns were rather hard-featured than otherwise, and that such very low dresses as they wore might have been attributed to vanity if their shoulders had been pretty, but that, being as they were, it was not reasonable to suppose that they showed their necks from a love of display, but rather from some obligation not inconsistent with sense and modesty. She felt convinced, as she opened her box, that this must be her aunt Osgood's opinion, for Miss Nancy's mind resembled her aunt's to a degree that everybody said was surprising, considering the kinship was on Mr. Osgood's side; and though you might not have supposed it from the formality of their greeting, there was a devoted attachment and mutual admiration between aunt and niece. Even Miss Nancy's refusal of her cousin Gilbert Osgood (on the ground solely that he was her cousin), though it had grieved her aunt greatly, had not in the least cooled the preference which had determined her to leave Nancy several of her hereditary ornaments, let Gilbert's future wife be whom she might.

Three of the ladies quickly retired, but the Miss Gunns were quite content that Mrs. Osgood's inclination to remain with her niece gave them also a reason for staying to see the rustic beauty's toilette. And it was really a pleasure—from the first opening of the bandbox, where everything smelled of lavender and rose-leaves, to the clasping of the small coral necklace that fitted closely round her little white neck. Everything belonging to Miss Nancy was of delicate purity and nattiness: not a crease was where it had no business to be, not a bit of her linen professed whiteness without fulfilling its profession; the very pins in her pincushion were stuck in after a pattern from which she was careful to allow no aberration; and as for her own person, it gave the same idea of perfect unvarying neatness as the body of a little bird. It is true that her light brown hair was cropped behind like a boy's, and was dressed in front in a number of flat rings, that lay quite away from her face; but there was no sort of coiffure that could make Miss Nancy's cheek and neck look otherwise than pretty; and when at last she stood complete in her silvery twilled silk, her lace tucker, her coral necklace, and coral ear-drops, the Miss Gunns could see nothing to criticise except her hands, which bore the traces of butter-making, cheese-crushing, and even still coarser work. But Miss Nancy was not ashamed of that, for while she was dressing she narrated to her aunt how she and Priscilla had packed their boxes yesterday, because this morning was baking morning, and since they were leaving home, it was desirable to make a good supply of meat-pies for the kitchen; and as she concluded this judicious remark, she turned to the Miss Gunns that she might not commit the rudeness of not including them in the conversation. The Miss Gunns smiled stiffly, and thought what a pity it was that these rich country people, who could afford to buy such good clothes (really Miss Nancy's lace and silk were very costly), should be brought up in utter ignorance and vulgarity. She actually said "mate" for "meat," " 'appen" for "perhaps," and "oss" for "horse," which, to young ladies living in good Lytherly society, who habitually said 'orse, even in domestic privacy, and only said 'appen on the right occasions, was necessarily shocking. Miss Nancy, indeed, had never been to any school higher than Dame Tedman's: her acquaintance with profane literature hardly went beyond the rhymes she had worked in her large sampler under the lamb and the shepherdess; and in order to balance an account, she was obliged to effect her subtraction by removing visible metallic shillings and sixpences from a visible metallic total. There is hardly a servant-maid in these days who is not better informed than Miss Nancy; yet she had the essential attributes of a lady—high veracity, delicate honor in her dealings, deference to others, and refined personal habits,—and lest these should not suffice to convince grammatical fair ones that her feelings can at all resemble theirs, I will add that she was slightly proud and exacting, and as constant in her affection toward a baseless opinion as toward an erring lover.

The anxiety about sister Priscilla, which had grown rather active by the time the coral necklace was clasped, was happily ended by the entrance of that cheerful-looking lady herself, with a face made blowsy by cold and damp. After the first questions and greetings, she turned to Nancy, and surveyed her from head to foot—then wheeled her round, to ascertain that the back view was equally faultless.

"What do you think o' these gowns, aunt Osgood?" said Priscilla, while Nancy helped her to unrobe.

"Very handsome indeed, niece," said Mrs. Osgood, with a slight increase of formality. She always thought niece Priscilla too rough.

"I'm obliged to have the same as Nancy, you know, for all I'm five years older, and it makes me look yellow; for she never will have anything without I have mine just like it, because she wants us to look like sisters. And I tell her, folks 'ull think it's my weakness makes me fancy as I shall look pretty in what she looks pretty in. For I *am* ugly—there's no denying that: I feature my father's family. But, law! I don't mind, do you?" Priscilla here turned to the Miss Gunns, rattling on in too much preoccupation with the delight of talking, to notice that her candor was not appreciated. "The pretty uns do for fly-catchers—they keep the men off us. I've no opinion o' the men, Miss Gunn—I don't know what *you* have. And as for fretting and stewing about what *they'll* think of you from morning till night, and making your life uneasy about what they're doing when they're out o' your sight—as I tell Nancy, it's a folly no woman need be guilty of, if she's got a good father and a good home: let her leave it to them as have got no fortin, and can't help themselves. As I say, Mr. Have-your-own-way is the best husband, and the only one I'd ever promise to obey. I know it isn't pleasant, when you've been used to living in a big way, and managing hogsheads and all that, to go and put your nose in by somebody else's fireside, or to sit down by yourself to a scrag* or a knuckle,† but, thank God! my father's a sober man and likely to live; and if you've got a man by the chimney-corner, it doesn't matter if he's childish—the business needn't be broke up."

The delicate process of getting her narrow gown over her head without injury to her smooth curls, obliged Miss Priscilla to pause in this rapid survey of life, and Mrs. Osgood seized the opportunity of rising and saying—

"Well, niece, you'll follow us. The Miss Gunns will like to go down."

"Sister," said Nancy, when they were alone, "you've offended the Miss Gunns, I'm sure."

"What have I done, child?" said Priscilla, in some alarm.

"Why, you asked them if they minded about being ugly—you're so very blunt."

"Law, did I? Well, it popped out: it's a mercy I said no more, for I'm a bad un to live with folks when they don't like the truth. But as for being ugly, look at me, child, in this silver-colored silk—I told you how it 'ud be—I look as yellow as a daffadil. Anybody 'ud say you wanted to make a mawkin of me."

---

*Lean or inferior end of a neck of mutton or veal.
†End of a bone or a joint.

"No, Priscy, don't say so. I begged and prayed of you not to let us have this silk if you'd like another better. I was willing to have your choice, you know I was," said Nancy, in anxious self-vindication.

"Nonsense, child! you know you'd set your heart on this; and reason good, for you're the color o' cream. It 'ud be fine doings for you to dress yourself to suit my skin. What I find fault with, is that notion o' yours as I must dress myself just like you. But you do as you like with me—you always did, from when first you begun to walk. If you wanted to go the field's length, the field's length you'd go; and there was no whipping you, for you looked as prim and innicent as a daisy all the while."

"Priscy," said Nancy, gently, as she fastened a coral necklace, exactly like her own, round Priscilla's neck, which was very far from being like her own, "I'm sure I'm willing to give way as far as is right, but who shouldn't dress alike if it isn't sisters? Would you have us go about looking as if we were no kin to one another—us that have got no mother and not another sister in the world? I'd do what was right, if I dressed in a gown dyed with cheese-coloring; and I'd rather you'd choose, and let me wear what pleases you."

"There you go again! You'd come round to the same thing if one talked to you from Saturday night till Saturday morning. It'll be fine fun to see how you'll master your husband and never raise your voice above the singing o' the kettle all the while. I like to see the men mastered!"

"Don't talk *so*, Priscy," said Nancy, blushing. "You know I don't mean ever to be married."

"Oh, you never mean a fiddlestick's end!" said Priscilla, as she arranged her discarded dress, and closed her bandbox. "Who shall I have to work for when father's gone, if you are to go and take notions in your head and be an old maid, because some folks are no better than they should be? I haven't a bit o' patience with you—sitting on an addled egg forever, as if there was never a fresh un in the world. One old maid's enough out o' two sisters; and I shall do credit to a single life, for God A'mighty meant me for it. Come, we can go down now. I'm as ready as a mawkin *can* be—there's nothing awanting to frighten the crows, now I've got my ear-droppers in."*

---

*Long, pendant earrings.

As the two Miss Lammeters walked into the large parlor together, any one who did not know the character of both might certainly have supposed that the reason why the square-shouldered, clumsy, high-featured Priscilla wore a dress the facsimile of her pretty sister's, was either the mistaken vanity of the one, or the malicious contrivance of the other in order to set off her own rare beauty. But the good-natured, self-forgetful cheeriness and commonsense of Priscilla would soon have dissipated the one suspicion; and the modest calm of Nancy's speech and manners told clearly of a mind free from all disavowed devices.

Places of honor had been kept for the Miss Lammeters near the head of the principal tea-table in the wainscoted parlor, now looking fresh and pleasant with handsome branches of holly, yew, and laurel, from the abundant growths of the old garden; and Nancy felt an inward flutter, that no firmness of purpose could prevent, when she saw Mr. Godfrey Cass advancing to lead her to a seat between himself and Mr. Crackenthorp, while Priscilla was called to one side between her father and the Squire. It certainly did make some difference to Nancy that the lover she had given up was the young man of quite the highest consequence in the parish—at home in a venerable and unique parlor, which was the extremity of grandeur in her experience, a parlor where she might one day have been mistress, with the consciousness that she was spoken of as "Madam Cass," the Squire's wife. These circumstances exalted her inward drama in her own eyes, and deepened the emphasis with which she declared to herself that not the most dazzling rank should induce her to marry a man whose conduct showed him careless of his character, but that, "love once, love always," was the motto of a true and pure woman, and no man should ever have any right over her which would be a call on her to destroy the dry flowers that she treasured, and always would treasure, for Godfrey Cass's sake. And Nancy was capable of keeping her word to herself under very trying conditions. Nothing but a becoming blush betrayed the moving thoughts that urged themselves upon her as she accepted the seat next to Mr. Crackenthorp; for she was so instinctively neat and adroit in all her actions, and her pretty lips met each other with such quiet firmness that it would have been difficult for her to appear agitated.

It was not the rector's practice to let a charming blush pass without an appropriate compliment. He was not in the least lofty or aristo-cratic, but simply a merry-eyed, small-featured, gray-haired man, with his chin propped by an ample, many-creased white neckcloth which seemed to predominate over every other point in his person, and somehow to impress its peculiar character on his remarks; so that to have considered his amenities apart from his cravat would have been a severe, and perhaps a dangerous, effort of abstraction.

"Ha, Miss Nancy," he said, turning his head within his cravat and smiling down pleasantly upon her, "when anybody pretends this has been a severe winter, I shall tell them I saw the roses blooming on New Year's Eve—eh, Godfrey, what do you say?"

Godfrey made no reply, and avoided looking at Nancy very markedly; for though these complimentary personalities were held to be in excellent taste in old-fashioned Raveloe society, reverent love has a politeness of its own which it teaches to men otherwise of small schooling. But the Squire was rather impatient at Godfrey's showing himself a dull spark in this way. By this advanced hour of the day, the Squire was always in higher spirits than we have seen him in at the breakfast-table, and felt it quite pleasant to fulfill the hereditary duty of being noisily jovial and patronizing: the large silver snuff-box was in active service and was offered without fail to all neighbors from time to time, however often they might have declined the favor. At present, the Squire had only given an express welcome to the heads of families as they appeared; but always as the evening deep-ened, his hospitality rayed out more widely, till he had tapped the youngest guests on the back and shown a peculiar fondness for their presence, in the full belief that they must feel their lives made happy by their belonging to a parish where there was such a hearty man as Squire Cass to invite them and wish them well. Even in this early stage of the jovial mood, it was natural that he should wish to supply his son's deficiencies by looking and speaking for him.

"Ay, ay," he began, offering his snuff-box to Mr. Lammeter, who for the second time bowed his head and waved his hand in stiff re-jection of the offer, "us old fellows may wish ourselves young to-night, when we see the mistletoe-bough in the White Parlor. It's true, most things are gone back'ard in these last thirty years—the coun-try's going down since the old king fell ill.[14] But when I look at Miss Nancy here, I begin to think the lasses keep up their quality—ding me if I remember a sample to match her, not when I was a fine young fellow, and thought a deal about my pigtail. No offense to you, madam," he added, bending to Mrs. Crackenthorp, who sat by him, "I didn't know *you* when you were as young as Miss Nancy here."

Mrs. Crackenthorp—a small blinking woman, who fidgeted incessantly with her lace, ribbons, and gold chain, turning her head about and making subdued noises, very much like a guinea-pig that twitches its nose and soliloquizes in all company indiscriminately—now blinked and fidgeted toward the Squire, and said, "Oh, no—no offense."

This emphatic compliment of the Squire's to Nancy was felt by others besides Godfrey to have a diplomatic significance; and her father gave a slight additional erectness to his back, as he looked across the table at her with complacent gravity. That grave and orderly senior was not going to bate a jot of his dignity by seeming elated at the notion of a match between his family and the Squire's: he was gratified by any honor paid to his daughter; but he must see an alteration in several ways before his consent would be vouchsafed. His spare but healthy person, and high-featured firm face, that looked as if it had never been flushed by excess, was in strong contrast, not only with the Squire's, but with the appearance of the Raveloe farmers generally—in accordance with a favorite saying of his own, that "breed was stronger than pasture."

"Miss Nancy's wonderful like what her mother was, though; isn't she, Kimble?" said the stout lady of that name, looking round for her husband.

But Doctor Kimble (country apothecaries in old days enjoyed that title without authority of diploma), being a thin and agile man, was flitting about the room with his hands in his pockets, making himself agreeable to his feminine patients, with medical impartiality, and being welcomed everywhere as a doctor by hereditary right—not one of those miserable apothecaries who canvass for practice in strange neighborhoods, and spend all their income in starving their one horse, but a man of substance, able to keep an extravagant table like the best of his patients. Time out of mind the Raveloe doctor had been a Kimble; Kimble was inherently a doctor's name; and it was difficult to contemplate firmly the melancholy fact that the actual Kimble had no son, so that his practice might one day be handed over to a successor with the incongruous name of Taylor or Johnson. But in that case the wiser people in Raveloe would employ Dr. Blick of Flitton—as less unnatural.

"Did you speak to me, my dear?" said the authentic doctor, coming quickly to his wife's side; but, as if foreseeing that she would be too much out of breath to repeat her remark, he went on immediately— "Ha, Miss Priscilla, the sight of you revives the taste of that superexcellent pork-pie. I hope the batch isn't near an end."

"Yes, indeed, it is, doctor," said Priscilla; "but I'll answer for it the next shall be as good. My pork-pies don't turn out well by chance."

"Not as your doctoring does, eh, Kimble?—because folks forget to take your physic, eh?" said the Squire, who regarded physic and doctors as many loyal churchmen regard the church and the clergy— tasting a joke against them when he was in health, but impatiently eager for their aid when anything was the matter with him. He tapped his box, and looked round with a triumphant laugh.

"Ah, she has a quick wit, my friend Priscilla has," said the doctor, choosing to attribute the epigram to a lady rather than allow a brother-in-law that advantage over him. "She saves a little pepper to sprinkle over her talk—that's the reason why she never puts too much into her pies. There's my wife, now, she never has an answer at her tongue's end; but if I offend her, she's sure to scarify my throat with black pepper the next day, or else give me the colic with watery greens. That's an awful tit-for-tat." Here the vivacious doctor made a pathetic grimace.

"Did you ever hear the like?" said Mrs. Kimble, laughing above her double chin with much good-humor, aside to Mrs. Crackenthorp, who blinked and nodded, and amiably intended to smile, but the intention lost itself in small twitchings and noises.

"I suppose that's the sort of tit-for-tat adopted in your profession, Kimble, if you've a grudge against a patient," said the rector.

"Never do have a grudge against our patients," said Mr. Kimble, "except when they leave us: and then, you see, we haven't the chance of prescribing for 'em. Ha, Miss Nancy," he continued, suddenly skipping to Nancy's side, "you won't forget your promise? You're to save a dance for me, you know."

"Come, come, Kimble, don't you be too for'ard," said the Squire. "Give the young uns fair play. There's my son Godfrey 'll be wanting to have a round with you if you run off with Miss Nancy. He's be-spoke her for the first dance, I'll be bound. Eh, sir! what do you say?" he continued, throwing himself backward, and looking at Godfrey. "Haven't you asked Miss Nancy to open the dance with you?"

Godfrey, sorely uncomfortable under this significant insistence about Nancy, and afraid to think where it would end by the time his father had set his usual hospitable example of drinking before and after supper, saw no course open but to turn to Nancy and say, with as little awkwardness as possible—

"No; I've not asked her yet, but I hope she'll consent—if some-body else hasn't been before me."

"No, I've not engaged myself," said Nancy, quietly, though blush-ingly. (If Mr. Godfrey founded any hopes on her consenting to dance with him, he would soon be undeceived; but there was no need for her to be uncivil.)

"Then I hope you've no objections to dancing with me," said Godfrey, beginning to lose the sense that there was anything uncom-fortable in this arrangement.

"No, no objections," said Nancy, in a cold tone.

"Ah, well, you're a lucky fellow, Godfrey," said uncle Kimble; "but you're my godson, so I won't stand in your way. Else I'm not so very old, eh, my dear?" he went on, skipping to his wife's side again. "You wouldn't mind my having a second after you were gone—not if I cried a good deal first?"

"Come, come, take a cup o' tea and stop your tongue, do," said good-humored Mrs. Kimble, feeling some pride in a husband who must be regarded as so clever and amusing by the company generally. If he had only not been irritable at cards!

While safe, well-tested personalities were enlivening the tea in this way, the sound of the fiddle approaching within a distance at which it could be heard distinctly, made the young people look at each other with sympathetic impatience for the end of the meal.

"Why, there's Solomon in the hall," said the Squire, "and playing my fav'rite tune, I believe—'The flaxen-headed ploughboy'—he's for giving us a hint as we aren't enough in a hurry to hear him play. Bob," he called out to his third long-legged son, who was at the other end of the room, "open the door, and tell Solomon to come in. He shall give us a tune here."

Bob obeyed, and Solomon walked in, fiddling as he walked, for he would on no account break off in the middle of a tune.

"Here, Solomon," said the Squire, with loud patronage. "Round here, my man. Ah, I knew it was 'The flaxen-headed ploughboy': there's no finer tune."

Solomon Macey, a small, hale old man, with an abundant crop of long white hair reaching nearly to his shoulders, advanced to the indicated spot, bowing reverently while he fiddled, as much as to say that he respected the company though he respected the key-note more. As soon as he had repeated the tune and lowered his fiddle, he bowed again to the Squire and the rector, and said, "I hope I see your honor and your reverence well, and wishing you health and long life and a happy New Year. And wishing the same to you, Mr. Lammeter, sir; and to the other gentlemen, and the madams, and the young lasses."

As Solomon uttered the last words, he bowed in all directions solicitously, lest he should be wanting in due respect. But thereupon he immediately began to prelude, and fell into the tune which he knew would be taken as a special compliment by Mr. Lammeter.

"Thank ye, Solomon, thank ye," said Mr. Lammeter when the fiddle paused again. "That's 'Over the hills and far away,' that is. My father used to say to me, whenever we heard that tune, 'Ah, lad, I come from over the hills and far away.' There's a many tunes I don't make head or tail of; but that speaks to me like the blackbird's whistle. I suppose it's the name: there's a deal in the name of a tune."

But Solomon was already impatient to prelude again, and presently broke with much spirit into "Sir Roger de Coverley,"* at which there was a sound of chairs pushed back, and laughing voices.

"Ay, ay, Solomon, we know what that means," said the Squire, rising. "It's time to begin the dance, eh? Lead the way, then, and we'll all follow you."

So Solomon, holding his white head on one side, and playing vigorously, marched forward at the head of the gay procession into the White Parlor, where the mistletoe bough was hung, and multitudinous

---

*Popular dance of the time.

tallow candles made rather a brilliant effect, gleaming from among the berried holly-boughs, and reflected in the old-fashioned oval mirrors fastened in the panels of the white wainscot. A quaint procession! Old Solomon, in his seedy clothes and long white locks, seemed to be luring that decent company by the magic scream of his fiddle—luring discreet matrons in turban shaped caps, nay, Mrs. Crackenthorp herself, the summit of whose perpendicular feather was on a level with the Squire's shoulder—luring fair lasses complacently conscious of very short waists and skirts blameless of front-folds—luring burly fathers in large variegated waist-coats, and ruddy sons, for the most part shy and sheepish, in short nether garments and very long coat-tails.

Already Mr. Macey and a few other privileged villagers, who were allowed to be spectators on these great occasions, were seated on benches placed for them near the door; and great was the admiration and satisfaction in that quarter when the couples had formed themselves for the dance, and the Squire led off with Mrs. Crackenthorp, joining hands with the rector and Mrs. Osgood. That was as it should be—that was what everybody had been used to—and the charter of Raveloe seemed to be renewed by the ceremony. It was not thought of as an unbecoming levity for the old and middle-aged people to dance a little before sitting down to cards, but rather as part of their social duties. For what were these if not to be merry at appropriate times, interchanging visits and poultry with due frequency, paying each other old-established compliments in sound traditional phrases, passing well-tried personal jokes, urging your guests to eat and drink too much out of hospitality, and eating and drinking too much in your neighbor's house to show that you liked your cheer? And the parson naturally set an example in these social duties. For it would not have been possible for the Raveloe mind, without a peculiar revelation, to know that a clergyman should be a pale-faced memento of solemnities, instead of a reasonably faulty man whose exclusive authority to read prayers and preach, to christen, marry, and bury you, necessarily coexisted with the right to sell you the ground to be buried in and to take tithe in kind; on which last point, of course, there was a little grumbling, but not to the extent of irreligion—not of deeper significance than the grumbling at the rain, which was by no means accompanied with a spirit of impious defiance, but with a desire that the prayer for fine weather might be read forthwith.

There was no reason, then, why the rector's dancing should not be received as part of the fitness of things quite as much as the Squire's, or why, on the other hand, Mr. Macey's official respect should restrain him from subjecting the parson's performance to that criticism with which minds of extraordinary acuteness must necessarily contemplate the doings of their fallible fellow-men.

"The Squire's pretty springe, considering his weight," said Mr. Macey, "and he stamps uncommon well. But Mr. Lammeter beats 'em all for shapes: you see he holds his head like a sodger, and he isn't so cushiony as most o' the oldish gentlefolks—they run fat in general; and he's got a fine leg. The parson's nimble enough, but he hasn't got much of a leg: it's a bit too thick down'ard, and his knees might be a bit nearer wi'out damage; but he might do worse, he might do worse. Though he hasn't that grand way o' waving his hand as the Squire has."

"Talk of nimbleness, look at Mrs. Osgood," said Ben Winthrop, who was holding his son Aaron between his knees. "She trips along with her little steps, so as nobody can see how she goes—it's like as if she had little wheels to her feet. She doesn't look a day older nor last year: she's the finest-made woman as is, let the next be where she will."

"I don't heed how the women are made," said Mr. Macey, with some contempt. "They wear nayther coat nor breeches: you can't make much out o' their shapes."

"Fayder," said Aaron, whose feet were busy beating out the tune, "how does that big cock's-feather stick in Mrs. Crackenthorp's yead? Is there a little hole for it, like in my shuttle-cock?"

"Hush, lad, hush; that's the way the ladies dress theirselves, that is," said the father, adding, however, in an undertone to Mr. Macey, "It does make her look funny, though—partly like a short-necked bottle wi' a long quill in it. Hey, by jingo, there's the young Squire leading off now, wi' Miss Nancy for partners! There's a lass for you!—like a pink-and-white posy—there's nobody 'ud think as anybody could be so pritty. I shouldn't wonder if she's Madam Cass some day, arter all—and nobody more rightfuller, for they'd make a fine match. You can find nothing against Master Godfrey's shapes, Macey, I'll bet a penny."

Mr. Macey screwed up his mouth, leaned his head further on one side, and twirled his thumbs with a presto movement as his eyes followed Godfrey up the dance. At last he summed up his opinion.

"Pretty well down'ard, but a bit too round i' the shoulder-blades. And as for them coats as he gets from the Flitton tailor, they're a poor cut to pay double money for."

"Ah, Mr. Macey, you and me are two folks," said Ben, slightly indignant at this carping. "When I've got a pot o' good ale, I like to swaller it, and do my inside good, i'stead o' smelling and staring at it to see if I can't find faut wi' the brewing. I should like you to pick me out a finer-limbed young fellow nor Master Godfrey—one as 'ud knock you down easier, or 's more pleasanter looksed when he's piert and merry."

"Tchuh!" said Mr. Macey, provoked to increased severity, "he isn't come to his right color yet: he's partly like a slack-baked pie. And I doubt he's got a soft place in his head, else why should he be turned round the finger by that offal Dunsey as nobody's seen o' late, and let him kill that fine hunting hoss as was the talk o' the country? And one while he was allays after Miss Nancy, and then it all went off again, like a smell o' hot porridge, as I may say. That wasn't my way when I went a-coorting."

"Ah, but mayhap Miss Nancy hung off like, and your lass didn't," said Ben.

"I should say she didn't," said Mr. Macey, significantly. "Before I said 'sniff,' I took care to know as she'd say 'snaff,' and pretty quick too. I wasn't a-going to open my mouth, like a dog at a fly, and snap it to again, wi' nothing to swaller."

"Well, I think Miss Nancy's a-coming round again," said Ben, "for Master Godfrey doesn't look so down-hearted to-night. And I see he's for taking her away to sit down, now they're at the end o' the dance: that looks like sweethearting, that does."

The reason why Godfrey and Nancy had left the dance was not so tender as Ben imagined. In the close press of couples a slight accident had happened to Nancy's dress, which, while it was short enough to show her neat ankle in front, was long enough behind to be caught under the stately stamp of the Squire's foot, so as to rend certain stitches at the waist, and cause much sisterly agitation in Priscilla's mind, as well as serious concern in Nancy's. One's thoughts may be much occupied with love-struggles, but hardly so as to be insensible to a disorder in the general framework of things. Nancy had no sooner completed her duty in the figure they were dancing than she said to Godfrey, with a deep blush, that she must go and sit down till Priscilla could come to her; for the sisters had already exchanged a short whisper and an open-eyed glance full of meaning. No reason less urgent than this could have prevailed on Nancy to give Godfrey this opportunity of sitting apart with her. As for Godfrey, he was feeling so happy and oblivious under the long charm of the country-dance with Nancy, that he got rather bold on the strength of her confusion, and was capable of leading her straight away, without leave asked, into the adjoining small parlor, where the card-tables were set.

"O no, thank you," said Nancy, coldly, as soon as she perceived where he was going, "not in there. I'll wait here till Priscilla's ready to come to me. I'm sorry to bring you out of the dance and make myself troublesome."

"Why, you'll be more comfortable here by yourself," said the artful Godfrey: "I'll leave you here till your sister can come." He spoke in an indifferent tone.

That was an agreeable proposition, and just what Nancy desired; why, then, was she a little hurt that Mr. Godfrey should make it? They entered, and she seated herself on a chair against one of the card-tables, as the stiffest and most unapproachable position she could choose.

"Thank you, sir," she said immediately. "I needn't give you any more trouble. I'm sorry you've had such an unlucky partner."

"That's very ill-natured of you," said Godfrey, standing by her without any sign of intended departure, "to be sorry you've danced with me."

"Oh, no, sir, I don't mean to say what's ill-natured at all," said Nancy, looking distractingly prim and pretty. "When gentlemen have so many pleasures; one dance can matter but very little."

"You know that isn't true. You know one dance with you matters more to me than all the other pleasures in the world."

It was a long, long while since Godfrey had said anything so direct as that, and Nancy was startled. But her instinctive dignity and repugnance to any show of emotion made her sit perfectly still, and only throw a little more decision into her voice, as she said—

"No, indeed, Mr. Godfrey, that's not known to me, and I have very good reasons for thinking different. But if it's true, I don't wish to hear it."

"Would you never forgive me, then, Nancy—never think well of me, let what would happen—would you never think the present made amends for the past? Not if I turned a good fellow, and gave up everything you didn't like?"

Godfrey was half conscious that this sudden opportunity of speaking to Nancy alone had driven him beside himself; but blind feeling had got the mastery of his tongue. Nancy really felt much agitated by the possibility Godfrey's words suggested, but this very pressure of emotion that she was in danger of finding too strong for her roused all her power of self-command.

"I should be glad to see a good change in anybody, Mr. Godfrey," she answered, with the slightest discernible difference of tone, "but it 'ud be better if no change was wanted."

"You're very hard-hearted, Nancy," said Godfrey, pettishly. "You might encourage me to be a better fellow. I'm very miserable—but you've no feeling."

"I think those have the least feeling that act wrong to begin with," said Nancy, sending out a flash in spite of herself. Godfrey was delighted with that little flash, and would have liked to go on and make her quarrel with him; Nancy was so exasperatingly quiet and firm. But she was not indifferent to him yet.

The entrance of Priscilla, bustling forward and saying, "Dear heart alive, child, let us look at this gown," cut off Godfrey's hopes of a quarrel.

"I suppose I must go now," he said to Priscilla.

"It's no matter to me whether you go or stay," said that frank lady, searching for something in her pocket, with a preoccupied brow.

"Do you want me to go?" said Godfrey, looking at Nancy, who was now standing up by Priscilla's order.

"As you like," said Nancy, trying to recover all her former coldness, and looking down carefully at the hem of her gown.

"Then I like to stay," said Godfrey, with a reckless determination to get as much of this joy as he could to-night, and think nothing of the morrow.

CHAPTER XII

WHILE GODFREY CASS WAS taking draughts of forget-fulness from the sweet presence of Nancy, willingly losing all sense of that hidden bond which at other moments galled and fretted him so as to mingle irritation with the very sunshine, Godfrey's wife was walking with slow uncertain steps through the snow-covered Raveloe lanes, carrying her child in her arms.

This journey on New Year's Eve was a premeditated act of vengeance which she had kept in her heart ever since Godfrey, in a fit of passion, had told her he would sooner die than acknowledge her as his wife. There would be a great party at the Red House on New Year's Eve, she knew: her husband would be smiling and smiled upon, hiding her existence in the darkest corner of his heart. But she would mar his pleasure: she would go in her dingy rags, with her faded face, once as handsome as the best, with her little child that had its father's hair and eyes, and disclose herself to the Squire as his eldest son's wife. It is seldom that the miserable can help regarding their misery as a wrong inflicted by those who are less miserable. Molly knew that the cause of her dingy rags was not her husband's neglect, but the demon Opium[15] to whom she was enslaved, body and soul, except in the lingering mother's tenderness that refused to give him her hungry child. She knew this well; and yet, in the moments of wretched unbenumbed consciousness, the sense of her want and degradation transformed itself continually into bitterness toward Godfrey. He was well off; and if she had her rights she would be well off too. The belief that he repented his marriage, and suffered from it, only aggravated her vindictiveness. Just and self-reproving thoughts do not come to us too thickly, even in the purest air and with the best lessons of heaven and earth; how should those white-winged delicate messengers make their way to Molly's poisoned chamber, inhabited by no higher memories than those of a barmaid's paradise of pink ribbons and gentlemen's jokes?

She had set out at an early hour, but had lingered on the road, inclined by her indolence to believe that if she waited under a warm shed the snow would cease to fall. She had waited longer than she knew, and now that she found herself belated in the snow-hidden ruggedness of the long lanes, even the animation of a vindictive purpose could not keep her spirit from failing. It was seven o'clock, and by this time she was not very far from Raveloe, but she was not familiar enough with those monotonous lanes to know how near she was to her journey's end. She needed comfort, and she knew but one comforter—the familiar demon in her bosom; but she hesitated a moment, after drawing out the black remnant, before she raised it to her lips. In that moment the mother's love pleaded for painful consciousness rather than oblivion—pleaded to be left in aching weariness, rather than to have the encircling arms benumbed so that they could not feel the dear burden. In another moment Molly had flung something away, but it was not the black remnant—it was an empty phial. And she walked on again under the breaking cloud, from which there came now and then the light of a quickly veiled star, for a freezing wind had sprung up since the snowing had ceased. But she walked always more and more drowsily, and clutched more and more automatically the sleeping child at her bosom.

Slowly the demon was working his will, and cold and weariness were his helpers. Soon she felt nothing but a supreme immediate longing that curtained off all futurity—the longing to lie down and sleep. She had arrived at a spot where her footsteps were no longer checked by a hedgerow, and she had wandered vaguely, unable to distinguish any objects, notwithstanding the wide whiteness around her, and the growing starlight. She sank down against a straggling furze bush, an easy pillow enough; and the bed of snow, too, was soft. She did not feel that the bed was cold, and did not heed whether the child would wake and cry for her. But her arms had not yet relaxed their instinctive clutch; and the little one slumbered on as gently as if it had been rocked in a lace-trimmed cradle.

But the complete torpor came at last: the fingers lost their tension, the arms unbent: then the little head fell away from the bosom, and the blue eyes opened wide on the cold starlight. At first there was a little peevish cry of "mammy," and an effort to regain the pillowing arm and bosom; but mammy's ear was deaf, and the pillow seemed to be slipping away backward. Suddenly, as the child rolled downward on its mother's knees, all wet with snow, its eyes were caught by a bright glancing light on the white ground, and, with the ready transition of infancy, it was immediately absorbed in watching the bright living thing running toward it, yet never arriving. That bright living thing must be caught, and in an instant the child has slipped on all-fours, and held out one little hand to catch the gleam. But the gleam would not be caught in that way, and now the head was held up to see where the cunning gleam came from. It came from a very bright place; and the little one, rising on its legs, toddled through the snow, the old grimy shawl in which it was wrapped trailing behind it, and the queer little bonnet dangling at its back—toddled on to the open door of Silas Marner's cottage, and right up to the warm hearth, where there was a bright fire of logs and sticks, which had thoroughly warmed the old sack (Silas's greatcoat) spread out on the bricks to dry. The little one, accustomed to be left to itself for long hours without notice from its mother, squatted down on the sack, and spread its tiny hands toward the blaze, in perfect contentment, gurgling and making many inarticulate communications to the cheerful fire, like a new-hatched gosling beginning to find itself comfortable. But presently the warmth had a lulling effect, and the little golden head sank down on the old sack, and the blue eyes were vailed by their delicate half-transparent lids.

But where was Silas Marner while this strange visitor had come to his hearth? He was in the cottage, but he did not see the child. During the last few weeks, since he had lost his money, he had contracted the habit of opening his door and looking out from time to time, as if he thought that his money might somehow coming back to him, or that some trace, some news of it, might be mysteriously on the road, and be caught by the listening ear or the straining eye. It was chiefly at night, when he was not occupied in his loom, that he fell into this repetition of an act for which he could have assigned no definite purpose, and which can hardly be understood except by those who have undergone a bewildering separation from a supremely loved object. In the evening twilight, and later, whenever the night was not dark, Silas looked out on that narrow prospect round the Stone-pits, listening and gazing, not with hope, but with mere yearning and unrest.

This morning he had been told by some of his neighbors that it was New Year's Eve, and that he must sit up and hear the old year rung out and the new rung in, because that was good luck, and might bring his money back again. This was only a friendly Raveloe way of jesting with the half-crazy oddities of a miser, but it had perhaps helped to throw Silas into a more than usually excited state. Since the oncoming of twilight he had opened his door again and again, though only to shut it immediately at seeing all distance veiled by the falling snow. But the last time he opened it the snow had ceased, and the clouds were parting here and there. He stood and listened, and gazed for a long while—there was really something on the road coming toward him then, but he caught no sign of it; and the stillness and the wide trackless snow seemed to narrow his solitude, and touched his yearning with the chill of despair. He went in again, and put his right hand on the latch of the door to close it—but he did not close it: he was arrested, as he had been already since his loss, by the invisible wand of catalepsy, and stood like a graven image, with wide but sightless eyes, holding open his door, powerless to resist either the good or the evil that might enter there.

When Marner's sensibility returned, he continued the action which had been arrested, and closed his door, unaware of the chasm in his consciousness, unaware of any intermediate change, except that the light had grown dim, and that he was chilled and faint. He thought he had been too long standing at the door and looking out. Turning toward the hearth, where the two logs had fallen apart, and sent forth only a red uncertain glimmer, he seated himself on his fireside chair, and was stooping to push his logs together, when, to his blurred vision, it seemed as if there were gold on the floor in front of the hearth. Gold!—his own gold—brought back to him as mysteriously as it had been taken away! He felt his heart beat violently, and for a few moments he was unable to stretch out his hand and grasp the restored treasure. The heap of gold seemed to glow and get larger beneath his agitated gaze. He leaned forward at last, and stretched forth his hand; but instead of the hard coin with the familiar resisting outline, his fingers encountered soft warm curls. In utter amazement, Silas fell on his knees and bent his head low to examine the marvel: it was a sleeping child—a round, fair thing, with soft yellow rings all over its head. Could this be his little sister come back to him in a dream—his little sister whom he had carried about in his arms

for a year before she died, when he was a small boy without shoes or
stockings? That was the first thought that darted across Silas's blank
wonderment. *Was* it a dream? He rose to his feet again, pushed his
logs together, and, throwing on some dried leaves and sticks, raised
a flame; but the flame did not disperse the vision—it only lit up more
distinctly the little round form of the child, and its shabby clothing.
It was very much like his little sister. Silas sank into his chair powerless, under the double presence of an inexplicable surprise and a hurrying influx of memories. How and when had the child come in
without his knowledge? He had never been beyond the door. But
along with that question, and almost thrusting it away, there was a vision of the old home and the old streets leading to Lantern Yard—
and within that vision another, of the thoughts which had been
present with him in those far-off scenes. The thoughts were strange
to him now, like old friendships impossible to revive; and yet he had
a dreamy feeling that this child was somehow a message come to him
from that far-off life: it stirred fibres that had never been moved in
Raveloe—old quiverings of tenderness—old impressions of awe at
the presentiment of some Power presiding over his life; for his imagination had not yet extricated itself from the sense of mystery in the
child's sudden presence, and had formed no conjectures of ordinary
natural means by which the event could have been brought about.

But there was a cry on the hearth: the child had awaked, and
Marner stooped to lift it on his knee. It clung round his neck, and
burst louder and louder into that mingling of inarticulate cries with
"mammy" by which little children express the bewilderment of waking. Silas pressed it to him, and almost unconsciously uttered sounds
of hushing tenderness, while he bethought himself that some of his
porridge, which had got cool by the dying fire, would do to feed the
child with if it were only warmed up a little.

He had plenty to do through the next hour. The porridge, sweet-
ened with some dry brown sugar from an old store which he had refrained from using for himself, stopped the cries of the little one, and
made her lift her blue eyes with a wide quiet gaze at Silas, as he put
the spoon into her mouth. Presently she slipped from his knee and
began to toddle about, but with a pretty stagger that made Silas jump
up and follow her lest she should fall against anything that would
hurt her. But she only fell in a sitting posture on the ground, and

began to pull at her boots, looking up at him with a crying face as if the boots hurt her. He took her on his knee again, but it was some time before it occurred to Silas's dull bachelor mind that the wet boots were the grievance, pressing on her warm ankles. He got them off with difficulty, and baby was at once happily occupied with the primary mystery of her own toes, inviting Silas with much chuckling, to consider the mystery too. But the wet boots had at last suggested to Silas that the child had been walking on the snow, and this roused him from his entire oblivion of any ordinary means by which it could have entered or been brought into his house. Under the prompting of this new idea, and without waiting to form conjectures, he raised the child in his arms, and went to the door. As soon as he had opened it, there was the cry of "mammy" again, which Silas had not heard since the child's first hungry waking. Bending forward, he could just discern the marks made by the little feet on the virgin snow, and he followed their track to the furze bushes. "Mammy!" the little one cried again and again, stretching itself forward so as almost to escape from Silas's arms, before he himself was aware that there was something more than the bush before him— that there was a human body, with the head sunk low in the furze, and half-covered with the shaken snow.

CHAPTER XIII

IT WAS AFTER THE early supper-time at the Red House, and the entertainment was in that stage when bashfulness itself had passed into easy jollity, when gentlemen, conscious of unusual accomplishments, could at length be prevailed on to dance a hornpipe, and when the Squire preferred talking loudly, scattering snuff, and patting his visitors' backs, to sitting longer at the whist-table— a choice exasperating to uncle Kimble, who, being always volatile in sober business hours, became intense and bitter over cards and brandy, shuffled before his adversary's deal with a glare of suspicion, and turned up a mean trump-card with an air of inexpressible disgust, as if in a world where such things could happen one might as well enter on a course of reckless profligacy. When the evening had advanced to this pitch of freedom and enjoyment, it was usual for the servants, the heavy duties of supper being well over, to get their share of amusement by coming to look on at the dancing; so that the back regions of the house were left in solitude.

There were two doors by which the White Parlor was entered from the hall, and they were both standing open for the sake of air; but the lower one was crowded with the servants and villagers, and only the upper doorway was left free. Bob Cass was figuring in a hornpipe, and his father, very proud of his lithe son, whom he repeatedly declared to be just like himself in his young days in a tone that implied this to be the very highest stamp of juvenile merit, was the centre of a group who had placed themselves opposite the performer, not far from the upper door. Godfrey was standing a little way off, not to admire his brother's dancing, but to keep sight of Nancy, who was seated in the group, near her father. He stood aloof, because he wished to avoid suggesting himself as a subject for the Squire's fatherly jokes in connection with matrimony and Miss Nancy Lammeter's beauty, which were likely to become more and more explicit. But he had the prospect of dancing with her again when the hornpipe was concluded, and in the meanwhile it was very pleasant to get long glances at her quite unobserved.

But when Godfrey was lifting his eyes from one of those long glances, they encountered an object as startling to him at that moment as if it had been an apparition from the dead. It *was* an apparition from that hidden life which lies, like a dark by-street, behind the goodly ornamented façade that meets the sunlight and the gaze of respectable admirers. It was his own child carried in Silas Marner's arms. That was his instantaneous impression, unaccompanied by doubt, though he had not seen the child for months past; and when the hope was rising that he might possibly be mistaken, Mr. Crackenthorp and Mr. Lammeter had already advanced to Silas, in astonishment at this strange advent. Godfrey joined them immediately, unable to rest without hearing every word—trying to control himself, but conscious that if any one noticed him, they must see that he was white-lipped and trembling.

But now all eyes at that end of the room were bent on Silas Marner; the Squire himself had risen, and asked angrily, "How's this?—what's this?—what do you do coming in here in this way?"

"I'm come for the doctor—I want the doctor," Silas had said, in the first moment, to Mr. Crackenthorp.

"Why, what's the matter, Marner?" said the rector. "The doctor's here; but say quietly what you want him for."

"It's a woman," said Silas, speaking low and half breathlessly, just as Godfrey came up. "She's dead, I think—dead in the snow at the Stone-pits—not far from my door."

Godfrey felt a great throb; there was one terror in his mind at that moment; it was that the woman might *not* be dead. That was an evil terror—an ugly inmate to have found a nestling-place in Godfrey's kindly disposition; but no disposition is a security from evil wishes to a man whose happiness hangs on duplicity.

"Hush, hush!" said Mr. Crackenthorp. "Go out into the hall there. I'll fetch the doctor to you. Found a woman in the snow—and thinks she's dead," he added, speaking low to the Squire. "Better say as little about it as possible; it will shock the ladies. Just tell them a poor woman is ill from cold and hunger. I'll go and fetch Kimble."

By this time, however, the ladies had pressed forward, curious to know what could have brought the solitary linen-weaver there under such strange circumstances, and interested in the pretty child, who, half alarmed and half attracted by the brightness and the numerous company, now frowned and hid her face, now lifted up her head again and looked round placably, until a touch or a coaxing word brought back the frown and made her bury her face with new determination.

"What child is it?" said several ladies at once, and, among the rest, Nancy Lammeter, addressing Godfrey.

"I don't know—some poor woman's who has been found in the snow, I believe," was the answer Godfrey wrung from himself with a terrible effort. ("After all, *am* I certain?" he hastened to add, in anticipation of his own conscience.)

"Why, you'd better leave the child here, then, Master Marner," said good-natured Mrs. Kimble, hesitating, however, to take those dingy clothes into contact with her own ornamented satin bodice. "I'll tell one o' the girls to fetch it."

"No—no—I can't part with it; I can't let it go," said Silas abruptly. "It's come to me—I've a right to keep it."

The proposition to take the child from him had come to Silas quite unexpectedly, and his speech, uttered under a strong sudden impulse, was almost like a revelation to himself: a minute before, he had no distinct intention about the child.

"Did you ever hear the like?" said Mrs. Kimble, in mild surprise, to her neighbor.

"Now, ladies, I must trouble you to stand aside," said Mr. Kimble, coming from the card-room, in some bitterness at the interruption, but drilled by the long habit of his profession into obedience to unpleasant calls, even when he was hardly sober.

"It's a nasty business turning out now, eh, Kimble?" said the Squire. "He might ha' gone for your young fellow—the 'prentice, there—what's his name?"

"Might? ay—what's the use of talking about might?" growled uncle Kimble, hastening out with Marner, and followed by Mr. Crackenthorp and Godfrey. "Get me a pair of thick boots, Godfrey, will you? And stay, let somebody run to Winthrop's and fetch Dolly—she's the best woman to get. Ben was here himself before supper; is he gone?"

"Yes, sir, I met him," said Marner; "but I couldn't stop to tell him anything, only I said I was going for the doctor, and he said the doctor was at the Squire's. And I made haste and ran, and there was nobody to be seen at the back o' the house, and so I went in to where the company was."

The child, no longer distracted by the bright light and the smiling women's faces, began to cry and call for "mammy," though always clinging to Marner, who had apparently won her thorough confidence. Godfrey had come back with the boots, and felt the cry as if some fibre were drawn tight within him.

"I'll go," he said, hastily, eager for some movement; "I'll go and fetch the woman—Mrs. Winthrop."

"Oh, pooh—send somebody else," said uncle Kimble, hurrying away with Marner.

"You'll let me know if I can be of any use, Kimble," said Mr. Crackenthorp. But the doctor was out of hearing.

Godfrey, too, had disappeared. He was gone to snatch his hat and coat, having just reflection enough to remember that he must not look like a madman; but he rushed out of the house into the snow without heeding his thin shoes.

In a few minutes he was on his rapid way to the Stone-pits by the side of Dolly, who, though feeling that she was entirely in her place in encountering cold and snow on an errand of mercy, was much concerned at a young gentleman's getting his feet wet under a like impulse.

"You'd a deal better go back, sir," said Dolly, with respectful compassion. "You've no call to catch cold; and I'd ask you if you'd be so good as to tell my husband to come, on your way back—he's at the Rainbow, I doubt—if you found him anyway sober enough to be o' use. Or else, there's Mrs. Snell 'ud happen send the boy up to fetch and carry, for there may be things wanted from the doctor's."

"No, I'll stay, now I'm once out—I'll stay outside here," said Godfrey, when they came opposite Marner's cottage. "You can come and tell me if I can do anything."

"Well, sir, you're very good: you've a tender heart," said Dolly, going to the door.

Godfrey was too painfully preoccupied to feel a twinge of self-reproach at this undeserved praise. He walked up and down, unconscious that he was plunging ankle-deep in snow, unconscious of everything but trembling suspense about what was going on in the cottage, and the effect of each alternative on his future lot. No, not quite unconscious of everything else. Deeper down, and half-smothered by passionate desire and dread, there was the sense that he ought not to be waiting on these alternatives; that he ought to accept the consequences of his deeds, own the miserable wife, and fulfill the claims of the helpless child. But he had not moral courage enough to contemplate that active renunciation of Nancy as possible for him: he had only conscience and heart enough to make him forever uneasy under the weakness that forbade the renunciation. And at this moment his mind leaped away from all restraint toward the sudden prospect of deliverance from his long bondage.

"Is she dead?" said the voice that predominated over every other within him. "If she is, I may marry Nancy; and then I shall be a good fellow in future, and have no secrets, and the child—shall be taken care of somehow." But across that vision came the other possibility—"She may live, and then it's all up with me."

Godfrey never knew how long it was before the door of the cottage opened and Mr. Kimble came out. He went forward to meet his uncle, prepared to suppress the agitation he must feel, whatever news he was to hear.

"I waited for you, as I'd come so far," he said, speaking first.

"Pooh, it was nonsense for you to come out: why didn't you send one of the men? There's nothing to be done. She's dead—has been dead for hours, I should say."

"What sort of woman is she?" said Godfrey, feeling the blood rush to his face.

"A young woman, but emaciated, with long black hair. Some vagrant—quite in rags. She's got a wedding-ring on, however. They must fetch her away to the workhouse to-morrow. Come, come along."

"I want to look at her," said Godfrey. "I think I saw such a woman yesterday. I'll overtake you in a minute or two."

Mr. Kimble went on, and Godfrey turned back to the cottage. He cast only one glance at the dead face on the pillow, which Dolly had smoothed with decent care; but he remembered that last look at his unhappy hated wife so well, that at the end of sixteen years every line in the worn face was present to him when he told the full story of this night.

He turned immediately toward the hearth, where Silas Marner sat lulling the child. She was perfectly quiet now, but not asleep—only soothed by sweet porridge and warmth into that wide-gazing calm which makes us older human beings, with our inward turmoil, feel a certain awe in the presence of a little child, such as we feel before some quiet majesty or beauty in the earth or sky—before a steady glowing planet, or a full-flowered eglantine, or the bending trees over a silent pathway. The wide-open blue eyes looked up at Godfrey's without any uneasiness or sign of recognition; the child could make no visible audible claim on its father; and the father felt a strange mixture of feelings, a conflict of regret and joy, that the pulse of that little heart had no response for the half-jealous yearning in his own, when the blue eyes turned away from him slowly, and fixed themselves on the weaver's queer face, which was bent low down to look at them, while the small hand began to pull Marner's withered cheek with loving disfiguration.

"You'll take the child to the parish to-morrow?" asked Godfrey, speaking as indifferently as he could.

"Who says so?" said Marner, sharply.—"Will they make me take her?"

"Why, you wouldn't like to keep her, should you—an old bachelor like you?"

"Till anybody shows they've a right to take her away from me," said Marner. "The mother's dead, and I reckon it's got no father; it's a lone thing—and I'm a lone thing. My money's gone, I don't know where—and this is come from I don't know where. I know nothing—I'm partly mazed."

"Poor little thing!" said Godfrey. "Let me give something toward finding it clothes."

He had put his hand in his pocket and found half-a-guinea, and, thrusting it into Silas's hand, he hurried out of the cottage to overtake Mr. Kimble.

"Ah, I see it's not the same woman I saw," he said as he came up. "It's a pretty little child; the old fellow seems to want to keep it; that's strange for a miser like him. But I gave him a trifle to help him out; the parish isn't likely to quarrel with him for the right to keep the child."

"No; but I've seen the time when I might have quarreled with him for it myself. It's too late now, though. If the child ran into the fire, your aunt's too fat to overtake it; she could only sit and grunt like an alarmed sow. But what a fool you are, Godfrey, to come out in your dancing shoes and stockings in this way—and you one of the beaux of the evening, and at your own house! What do you mean by such freaks, young fellow? Has Miss Nancy been cruel, and do you want to spite her by spoiling your pumps?"

"O, everything has been disagreeable to-night. I was tired to death of jigging and gallanting, and that bother about the hornpipes. And I'd got to dance with the other Miss Gunn," said Godfrey, glad of the subterfuge his uncle had suggested to him.

The prevarication and white lies which a mind that keeps itself ambitiously pure is as uneasy under as a great artist under the false touches that no eye detects but his own, are worn as lightly as mere trimmings when once the actions have become a lie.

Godfrey reappeared in the White Parlor with dry feet, and, since the truth must be told, with a sense of relief and gladness that was too strong for painful thoughts to struggle with. For could he not venture now, whenever opportunity offered, to say the tenderest things to

Nancy Lammeter—to promise her and himself that he would always be just what she would desire to see him? There was no danger that his dead wife would be recognized: those were not days of active inquiry and wide report; and as for the registry of their marriage, that was a long way off, buried in unturned pages, away from every one's interest but his own. Dunsey might betray him if he came back; but Dunsey might be won to silence.

And when events turn out so much better for a man than he has had reason to dread, is it not a proof that his conduct has been less foolish and blameworthy than it might otherwise have appeared? When we are treated well, we naturally begin to think that we are not altogether unmeritorious, and that it is only just we should treat ourselves well, and not mar our own good fortune. Where, after all, would be the use of his confessing the past to Nancy Lammeter, and throwing away his happiness?—nay, hers? for he felt some confidence that she loved him. As for the child, he would see that it was cared for: he would never forsake it; he would do everything but own it. Perhaps it would be just as happy in life without being owned by its father, seeing that nobody could tell how things would turn out, and that—is there any other reason wanted?—well, then, that the father would be much happier without owning the child.

CHAPTER XIV

THERE WAS A PAUPER'S burial that week in Raveloe, and up Kench Yard at Batherley it was known that the dark-haired woman with the fair child, who had lately come to lodge there, was gone away again. That was all the express note taken that Molly had disappeared from the eyes of men. But the unwept death which, to the general lot, seemed as trivial as the summer-shed leaf, was charged with the force of destiny to certain human lives that we know of, shaping their joys and sorrows even to the end.

Silas Marner's determination to keep the "tramp's child" was matter of hardly less surprise and iterated talk in the village than the robbery of his money. That softening of feeling toward him which dated from his misfortune, that merging of suspicion and dislike in a rather contemptuous pity for him as lone and crazy, was now accompanied with a more active sympathy, especially amongst the women. Notable mothers, who knew what it was to keep children "whole and sweet"; lazy mothers, who knew what it was to be interrupted in folding their arms and scratching their elbows by the mischievous propensities of children just firm on their legs, were equally interested in conjecturing how a lone man would manage with a two-year-old child on his hands, and were equally ready with their suggestions: the notable chiefly telling him what he had better do, and the lazy ones being emphatic in telling him what he would never be able to do.

Among the notable mothers, Dolly Winthrop was the one whose neighborly offices were the most acceptable to Marner, for they were rendered without any show of bustling instruction. Silas had shown her the half-guinea given to him by Godfrey, and had asked her what he should do about getting some clothes for the child.

"Eh, Master Marner," said Dolly, "there's no call to buy no more nor a pair o' shoes; for I've got the little petticoats as Aaron wore five years ago, and it's ill spending the money on them baby-clothes, for the child 'ul grow like grass i' May, bless it—that it will."

And the same day Dolly brought her bundle, and displayed to Marner, one by one, the tiny garments in their due order of succession, most of them patched and darned, but clean and neat as fresh-sprung herbs. This was the introduction to a great ceremony with soap and water, from which Baby came out in new beauty, and sat on Dolly's knee, handling her toes and chuckling and patting her palms together with an air of having made several discoveries about herself, which she communicated by alternate sounds of "gug-gug-gug," and "mammy." The "mammy" was not a cry of need or uneasiness: Baby had been used to utter it without expecting either tender sound or touch to follow.

"Anybody 'ud think the angils in heaven couldn't be prettier," said Dolly, rubbing the golden curls and kissing them. "And to think of its being covered wi' them dirty rags—and the poor mother—froze to death; but there's Them as took care of it, and brought it to your door, Master Marner. The door was open, and it walked in over the snow, like as if it had been a little starved robin. Didn't you say the door was open?"

"Yes," said Silas, meditatively. "Yes—the door was open. The money's gone, I don't know where, and this is come from I don't know where."

He had not mentioned to any one his unconsciousness of the child's entrance, shrinking from questions which might lead to the fact he himself suspected—namely, that he had been in one of his trances.

"Ah," said Dolly, with soothing gravity, "it's like the night and the morning, and the sleeping and the waking, and the rain and the harvest—one goes and the other comes, and we know nothing how nor where. We may strive and scrat and fend, but it's little we can do arter all—the big things come and go wi' no striving o' our'n—they do, that they do; and I think you're in the right on it to keep the little un, Master Marner, seeing as it's been sent to you, though there's folks as thinks different. You'll happen be a bit moithered with it while it's so little; but I'll come, and welcome, and see to it for you: I've a bit o' time to spare most days, for when one gets up betimes i' the morning, the clock seems to stan' still tow'rt ten, afore it's time to go about the victual. So, as I say, I'll come and see to the child for you, and welcome."

"Thank you———kindly," said Silas, hesitating a little. "I'll be glad if you'll tell me things. But," he added, uneasily, leaning forward to look at Baby with some jealousy, as she was resting her head backward against Dolly's arm, and eyeing him contentedly from a distance—"But I want to do things for it myself, else it may get fond o' somebody else, and not fond o' me. I've been used to fending for myself in the house—I can learn, I can learn."

"Eh, to be sure," said Dolly, gently. "I've see men as are wonderful handy wi' children. The men are awk'ard and contrairy mostly, God help 'em—but when the drink's out of 'em, they aren't unsensible, though they're bad for leeching and bandaging—so fiery and unpatient. You see this goes first, next the skin," proceeded Dolly, taking up the little shirt, and putting it on.

"Yes," said Marner, docilely, bringing his eyes very close, that they might be initiated in the mysteries; whereupon Baby seized his head with both her small arms, and put her lips against his face with purring noises.

"See there," said Dolly, with a woman's tender tact, "she's fondest o' you. She wants to go o' your lap, I'll be bound. Go, then: take her, Master Marner; you can put the things on, and then you can say as you've done for her from the first of her coming to you."

Marner took her on his lap, trembling with an emotion mysterious to himself, at something unknown dawning on his life. Thought and feeling were so confused within him, that if he had tried to give them utterance, he could only have said that the child was come instead of the gold—that the gold had turned into the child. He took the garments from Dolly, and put them on under her teaching; interrupted, of course, by Baby's gymnastics.

"There, then! why, you take to it quite easy, Master Marner," said Dolly; "but what shall you do when you're forced to sit in your loom? For she'll get busier and mischievouser every day—she will, bless her. It's lucky as you've got that high hearth i'stead of a grate, for that keeps the fire more out of her reach: but if you've got anything as can be spilt or broke, or as is fit to cut her fingers off, she'll be at it—and it is but right you should know."

Silas meditated a little while in some perplexity. "I'll tie her to the leg o' the loom," he said at last—"tie her with a good long strip o' something."

"Well, mayhap that'll do, as it's a little gell, for they're easier persuaded to sit i' one place nor the lads. I know what the lads are; for I've had four—four I've had, God knows—and if you was to take and tie 'em up, they'd make a fighting and a crying as if you was ringing the pigs. But I'll bring you my little chair, and some bits o' red rag and things for her to play wi'; an' she'll sit and chatter to 'em as if they was alive. Eh, if it wasn't a sin to the lads to wish 'em made different, bless 'em, I should ha' been glad for one of 'em to be a little gell; and to think as I could ha' taught her to scour, and mend, and the knitting, and everything. But I can teach 'em this little un, Master Marner, when she gets old enough."

"But she'll be *my* little un," said Marner, rather hastily. "She'll be nobody else's."

"No, to be sure; you'll have a right to her, if you're a father to her, and bring her up according. But," added Dolly, coming to a point which she had determined beforehand to touch upon, "you must bring her up like christened folks's children, and take her to church, and let her learn her catechise, as my little Aaron can say off—the 'I believe,' and everything, and 'hurt nobody by word or deed,'—as well as if he was the clerk. That's what you must do, Master Marner, if you'd do the right thing by the orphin child."

Marner's pale face flushed suddenly under a new anxiety. His mind was too busy trying to give some definite bearing to Dolly's words for him to think of answering her.

"And it's my belief," she went on, "as the poor little creature has never been christened, and it's nothing but right as the parson should be spoke to; and if you was noways unwilling, I'd talk to Mr. Macey about it this very day. For if the child ever went anyways wrong, and you hadn't done your part by it, Master Marner—'noculation, and everything to save it from harm—it 'ud be a thorn i' your bed for-ever o' this side the grave; and I can't think as it 'ud be easy lying down for anybody when they'd got to another world, if they hadn't done their part by the helpless children as come wi'out their own asking."

Dolly herself was disposed to be silent for some time now, sor she had spoken from the depths of her own simple belief, and was much concerned to know whether her words would produce the de-sired effect on Silas. He was puzzled and anxious, for Dolly's word "christened" conveyed no distinct meaning to him. He had only heard of baptism, and had only seen the baptism of grown-up men and women.

"What is it as you mean by 'christened'?" he said at last, timidly. "Won't folks be good to her without it?"

"Dear, dear! Master Marner," said Dolly, with gentle distress and compassion. "Had you never no father nor mother as taught you to say your prayers, and as there's good words and good things to keep us from harm?"

"Yes," said Silas, in a low voice; "I know a deal about that—used to, used to. But your ways are different: my country was a good way off." He paused a few moments, and then added, more decidedly, "But I want to do everything as can be done for the child. And what-ever's right for it i' this country, and you think 'ull do it good, I'll act according, if you'll tell me."

"Well, then, Master Marner," said Dolly, inwardly rejoiced, "I'll ask Mr. Macey to speak to the parson about it; and you must fix on a name for it, because it must have a name giv' it when it's christened."

"My mother's name was Hephzibah," said Silas, "and my little sister was named after her."

"Eh, that's a hard name," said Dolly. "I partly think it isn't a christened name."

"It's a Bible name," said Silas, old ideas recurring.*

"Then I've no call to speak again' it," said Dolly, rather startled by Silas's knowledge on this head; "but you see I'm no scholard, and I'm slow at catching the words. My husband says I'm allays like as if I was putting the haft for the handle—that's what he says—for he's very sharp, God help him. But it was awk'ard calling your little sister by such a hard name, when you'd got nothing big to say, like—wasn't it, Master Marner?"

"We called her Eppie," said Silas.

"Well, if it was noways wrong to shorten the name, it 'ud be a deal handier. And so I'll go now, Master Marner, and I'll speak about the christening, afore dark; and I wish you the best o' luck, and it's my belief as it'll come to you if you do what's right by the orphin child;—and there's the 'noculation to be seen to; and as to washing it's bits o' things, you need look to nobody but me, for I can do 'em wi' one hand when I've got my suds about. Eh, the blessed angil! You'll let me bring my Aaron one o' these days, and he'll show her his little cart as his father's made for him, and the black-and-white pup as he's got a-rearing."

Baby *was* christened, the rector deciding that a double baptism was the lesser risk to incur; and on this occasion Silas, making himself as clean and tidy as he could, appeared for the first time within the church, and shared in the observances held sacred by his neighbors. He was quite unable, by means of anything he heard or saw, to identify the Raveloe religion with his old faith; if he could at any time in his previous life have done so, it must have been by the aid of a strong feeling ready to vibrate with sympathy, rather than by a comparison of phrases and ideas: and now for long years that feeling had been dormant. He had no distinct idea about the baptism and the church-going, except that Dolly had said it was for the good of the

---

*See the Bible, Isaiah 62:4: "Thou shalt no more be termed Forsaken; neither shall thy land any more be termed Desolate; but thou shalt be called Hepzibah and thy land Beulah: for the lord delighteth in thee, and thy land shall be married" (KJV).

child; and in this way, as the weeks grew to months, the child created fresh and fresh links between his life and the lives from which he had hitherto shrunk continually into narrower isolation. Unlike the gold which needed nothing, and must be worshiped in close-locked solitude—which was hidden away from the daylight, was deaf to the song of birds, and started to no human tones—Eppie was a creature of endless claims and ever-growing desires, seeking and loving sunshine, and living sounds, and living movements; making trial of everything, with trust in new joy, and stirring the human kindness in all eyes that looked on her. The gold had kept his thoughts in an ever-repeated circle, leading to nothing beyond itself; but Eppie was an object compacted of changes and hopes that forced his thoughts onward, and carried them far away from their old eager pacing toward the same blank limit—carried them away to the new things that would come with the coming years, when Eppie would have learned to understand how her father Silas cared for her; and made him look for images of that time in the ties and charities that bound together the families of his neighbors. The gold had asked that he should sit weaving longer and longer, deafened and blinded more and more to all things except the monotony of his loom and the repetition of his web; but Eppie called him away from his weaving, and made him think all its pauses a holiday, reawakening his senses with her fresh life, even to the old winter-flies that came crawling forth in the early spring sunshine, and warming him into joy because she had joy.

And when the sunshine grew strong and lasting, so that the buttercups were thick in the meadows, Silas might be seen in the sunny midday, or in the late afternoon when the shadows were lengthening under the hedgerows, strolling out with uncovered head to carry Eppie beyond the Stone-pits to where the flowers grew, till they reached some favorite bank where he could sit down, while Eppie toddled to pluck the flowers, and make remarks to the winged things that murmured happily above the bright petals, calling "Dad-dad's" attention continually by bringing him the flowers. Then she would turn her ear to some sudden bird-note, and Silas learned to please her by making signs of hushed stillness, that they might listen for the note to come again: so that when it came, she set up her small back and laughed with gurgling triumph. Sitting on the banks in this way, Silas began to look for the once familiar herbs again; and as the leaves, with their unchanged outline and markings, lay on his palm, there was a sense of crowding remembrances from which he turned away timidly, taking refuge in Eppie's little world, that lay lightly on his enfeebled spirit.

As the child's mind was growing into knowledge, his mind was growing into memory: as her life unfolded, his soul, long stupefied in a cold, narrow prison, was unfolding too, and trembling gradually into full consciousness.

It was an influence which must gather force with every new year: the tones that stirred Silas's heart grew articulate, and called for more distinct answers; shapes and sounds grew clearer for Eppie's eyes and ears, and there was more that "Dad-dad" was imperatively required to notice and account for. Also, by the time Eppie was three years old, she developed a fine capacity for mischief, and for devising ingenious ways of being troublesome, which found much exercise, not only for Silas's patience, but for his watchfulness and penetration. Sorely was poor Silas puzzled on such occasions by the incompatible demands of love. Dolly Winthrop told him that punishment was good for Eppie, and that, as for rearing a child without making it tingle a little in soft and safe places now and then, it was not to be done.

"To be sure, there's another thing you might do, Master Marner," added Dolly, meditatively: "you might shut her up once i' the coal-hole. That was what I did wi' Aaron; for I was that silly wi' the youngest lad, as I could never bear to smack him. Not as I could find i' my heart to let him stay i' the coal-hole more nor a minute, but it was enough to colly him all over, so as he must be new washed and dressed, and it was as good as a rod to him—that was. But I put it upo' your conscience, Master Marner, as there's one of 'em you must choose—ayther smacking or the coal-hole—else she'll get so masterful, there'll be no holding her."

Silas was impressed with the melancholy truth of this last remark; but his force of mind failed before the only two penal methods open to him, not only because it was painful to him to hurt Eppie, but because he trembled at a moment's contention with her, lest she should love him the less for it. Let even an affectionate Goliath get himself tied to a small tender thing, dreading to hurt it by pulling, and dreading still more to snap the cord, and which of the two, pray, will be master? It was clear that Eppie, with her short toddling steps, must lead father Silas a pretty dance on any fine morning when circumstances favored mischief.

For example. He had wisely chosen a broad strip of linen as a means of fastening her to his loom when he was busy: it made a broad belt round her waist, and was long enough to allow of her reaching the truckle bed and sitting down on it, but not long enough for her to attempt any dangerous climbing. One bright summer's morning Silas had been more engrossed than usual in "setting up" a new piece of work, an occasion on which his scissors were in requisition. These scissors, owing to an especial warning of Dolly's, had been kept carefully out of Eppie's reach; but the click of them had had a peculiar attraction for her ear, and watching the results of that click, she had derived the philosophic lesson that the same cause would produce the same effect. Silas had seated himself in his loom, and the noise of weaving had begun; but he had left his scissors on a ledge which Eppie's arm was long enough to reach; and now, like a small mouse, watching her opportunity, she stole quietly from her corner, secured the scissors, and toddled to the bed again, setting up her back as a mode of concealing the fact. She had a distinct intention as to the use of the scissors; and having cut the linen strip in a jagged but effectual manner, in two moments she had run out at the open door where the sunshine was inviting her, while poor Silas believed her to be a better child than usual. It was not until he happened to need his scissors that the terrible fact burst upon him: Eppie had run out by herself—had perhaps fallen into the Stone-pit. Silas, shaken by the worst fear that could have befallen him, rushed out, calling "Eppie!" and ran eagerly about the unenclosed space, exploring the dry cavities into which she might have fallen, and then gazing with questioning dread at the smooth red surface of the water. The cold drops stood on his brow. How long had she been out? There was one hope—that she had crept through the stile and got into the fields, where he habitually took her to stroll. But the grass was high in the meadow, and there was no descrying her, if she were there, except by a close search that would be a trespass on Mr. Osgood's crop. Still, that misdemeanor must be committed; and poor Silas, after peering all round the hedgerows, traversed the grass, beginning with perturbed vision to see Eppie behind every group of red sorrel, and to see her moving always farther off as he approached. The meadow was searched in vain; and he got over the stile into the next field, looking with dying hope toward a small pond which was now reduced to its summer shallowness, so as to leave a wide margin of good adhesive mud. Here, however, sat Eppie, discoursing cheerfully to her own small boot, which she was using as a bucket to convey the water into a deep hoof-mark, while her little naked foot was planted comfortably on a cushion of olive-green mud. A red-headed calf was observing her with alarmed doubt through the opposite hedge.

Here was clearly a case of aberration in a christened child which demanded severe treatment; but Silas, overcome with convulsive joy at finding his treasure again, could do nothing but snatch her up, and cover her with half-sobbing kisses. It was not until he had carried her home, and had begun to think of the necessary washing, that he recollected the need that he should punish Eppie, and "make her remember." The idea that she might run away again and come to harm, gave him unusual resolution, and for the first time he determined to try the coal-hole—a small closet near the hearth.

"Naughty, naughty Eppie," he suddenly began, holding her on his knee, and pointing to her muddy feet and clothes—"naughty to cut with the scissors and run away. Eppie must go into the coal-hole for being naughty. Daddy must put her in the coal-hole."

He half-expected that this would be shock enough, and that Eppie would begin to cry. But instead of that, she began to shake herself on his knee, as if the proposition opened a pleasing novelty. Seeing that he must proceed to extremities, he put her into the coal-hole, and held the door closed, with a trembling sense that he was using a strong measure. For a moment there was silence, but then came a little cry, "Opy, opy!" and Silas let her out again, saying, "Now Eppie 'ull never be naughty again, else she must go in the coal-hole—a black naughty place."

The weaving must stand still a long while this morning, for now Eppie must be washed, and have clean clothes on; but it was to be hoped that this punishment would have a lasting effect, and save time in future—though, perhaps, it would have been better if Eppie had cried more.

In half an hour she was clean again, and Silas having turned his back to see what he could do with the linen band threw it down again, with the reflection that Eppie would be good without fastening for the rest of the morning. He turned round again, and was going to place her in her little chair near the loom, when she peeped out at him with black face and hands again, and said, "Eppie in de toal-hole!"

This total failure of the coal-hole discipline shook Silas's belief in the efficacy of punishment. "She'd take it all for fun," he observed to Dolly, "if I didn't hurt her, and that I can't do, Mrs. Winthrop. If she makes me a bit o' trouble. I can bear it. And she's got no tricks but what she'll grow out of."

"Well, that's partly true, Master Marner," said Dolly, sympathetically; "and if you can't bring your mind to frighten her off touching things, you must do what you can to keep 'em out of her way. That's what I do wi' the pups as the lads are allays a-rearing. They will worry and gnaw—worry and gnaw they will, if it was one's Sunday cap as hung anywhere so as they could drag it. They know no difference, God help 'em: it's the pushing o' the teeth as sets 'em on, that's what it is."

So Eppie was reared without punishment, the burden of her misdeeds being borne vicariously by father Silas. The stone hut was made a soft nest for her, lined with downy patience: and also in the world that lay beyond the stone hut she knew nothing of frowns and denials.

Notwithstanding the difficulty of carrying her and his yarn or linen at the same time, Silas took her with him in most of his journeys to the farmhouses, unwilling to leave her behind at Dolly Winthrop's, who was always ready to take care of her; and little curly-headed Eppie, the weaver's child, became an object of interest at several outlying homesteads, as well as in the village. Hitherto he had been treated very much as if he had been a useful gnome or brownie—a queer and unaccountable creature who must necessarily be looked at with wondering curiosity and repulsion, and with whom one would be glad to make all greetings and bargains as brief as possible, but who must be dealt with in a propitiatory way, and occasionally have a present of pork or garden stuff to carry home with him, seeing that without him there was no getting the yarn woven. But now Silas met with open smiling faces and cheerful questioning, as a person whose satisfactions and difficulties could be understood. Everywhere he must sit a little and talk about the child, and words of interest were always ready for him: "Ah, Master Marner, you'll be lucky if she takes the measles soon and easy!"—or, "Why, there isn't many lone men 'ud ha' been wishing to take up with a little un like

that: but I reckon the weaving makes you handier than men as do
out-door work—you're partly as handy as a woman, for weaving
comes next to spinning." Elderly masters and mistresses, seated ob-
servantly in large kitchen arm-chairs, shook their heads over the difficulties attendant on rearing children, felt Eppie's round arms and
legs, and pronounced them remarkably firm, and told Silas that, if she
turned out well (which, however, there was no telling) it would be a
fine thing for him to have a steady lass to do for him when he got
helpless. Servant maidens were fond of carrying her out to look at the
hens and chickens, or to see if any cherries could be shaken down in
the orchard; and the small boys and girls approached her slowly, with
cautious movement and steady gaze, like little dogs face to face
with one of their own kind, till attraction had reached the point at
which the soft lips were put out for a kiss. No child was afraid of approaching Silas when Eppie was near him: there was no repulsion
around him now, either for young or old; for the little child had
come to link him once more with the whole world. There was love
between him and the child that blent them into one, and there was
love between the child and the world—from men and women with
parental looks and tones, to the red lady-birds and the round pebbles.

Silas began now to think of Raveloe life entirely in relation to
Eppie: she must have everything that was a good in Raveloe; and he
listened docilely that he might come to understand better what this
life was, from which, for fifteen years he had stood aloof as from a
strange thing, wherewith he could have no communion: as some
man who has a precious plant to which he would give a nurturing
home in a new soil, thinks of the rain, and the sunshine, and all influences, in relation to his nursling, and asks industriously for all
knowledge that will help him to satisfy the wants of the searching
roots, or to guard leaf and bud from invading harm. The disposition
to hoard had been utterly crushed at the very first by the loss of his
long-stored gold: the coins he earned afterward seemed as irrelevant
as stones brought to complete a house suddenly buried by an earth-
quake; the sense of bereavement was too heavy upon him for the old
thrill of satisfaction to arise again at the touch of the newly-earned
coin. And now something had come to replace his hoard which gave
a growing purpose to the earnings, drawing his hope and joy continually onward beyond the money.

In old days there were angels who came and took men by the hand and led them away from the city of destruction. We see no white-winged angels now. But yet men are led away from threatening destruction: a hand is put into theirs, which leads them forth gently toward a calm and bright land, so that they look no more backward; and the hand may be a little child's*

CHAPTER XV

T HERE WAS ONE PERSON, as you will believe, who watched with keener though more hidden interest than any other, the prosperous growth of Eppie under the weaver's care. He dared not do anything that would imply a stronger interest in a poor man's adopted child than could be expected from the kindliness of the young Squire, when a chance meeting suggested a little present to a simple old fellow whom others noticed with good-will; but he told himself that the time would come when he might do something toward furthering the welfare of his daughter without incurring suspicion. Was he very uneasy in the meantime at his inability to give his daughter her birthright? I cannot say that he was. The child was being taken care of, and would very likely be happy, as people in humble stations often were—happier, perhaps than those brought up in luxury.

That famous ring† that pricked its owner when he forgot duty and followed desire—I wonder if it pricked very hard when he set out on the chase, or whether it pricked but lightly then, and only pierced to the quick when the chase had long been ended, and hope, folding her wings, looked backward and became regret?

Godfrey Cass's cheek and eye were brighter than ever now. He was so undivided in his aims that he seemed like a man of firmness.

---

*The biblical Sodom. The last line of the chapter is an allusion to Isaiah 11:6: "The wolf also shall dwell with the lamb, and the leopard shall lie down with the kid; and the calf and young lion and the fatling together; and a little child shall lead them" (KJV).

†Allusion to a fairy tale in which Prince Darling is given a ring that pricks him whenever he does something wrong.

No Dunsey had come back: people had made up their minds that he was gone for a soldier, or gone "out of the country," and no one cared to be specific in their inquiries on a subject delicate to a respectable family. Godfrey had ceased to see the shadow of Dunsey across his path; and the path now lay straight forward to the accomplishment of his best, longest-cherished wishes. Everybody said Mr. Godfrey had taken the right turn; and it was pretty clear what would be the end of things, for there were not many days in the week that he was not seen riding to the Warrens. Godfrey himself, when he was asked jocosely if the day had been fixed, smiled with the pleasant consciousness of a lover who could say "yes," if he liked. He felt a reformed man, delivered from temptation; and the vision of his future life seemed to him as a promised land for which he had no cause to fight. He saw himself with all his happiness centered on his own hearth, while Nancy would smile on him as he played with the children.

And that other child, not on the hearth—he would not forget it; he would see that it was well provided for. That was a father's duty.

CHAPTER XVI

IT WAS A BRIGHT autumn Sunday, sixteen years after Silas Marner had found his new treasure on the hearth. The bells of the old Raveloe church were ringing the cheerful peal which told that the morning service was ended; and out of the arched doorway in the tower came slowly, retarded by friendly greetings and questions, the richer parishioners who had chosen this bright Sunday morning as eligible for church-going. It was the rural fashion of that time for the more important members of the congregation to depart first, while their humbler neighbors waited and looked on, stroking their bent heads or dropping their curtsies to any large ratepayer who turned to notice them.

Foremost among these advancing groups of well-clad people, there are some whom we shall recognize, in spite of Time, who has laid his hand on them all. The tall blonde man of forty is not much changed in feature from the Godfrey Cass of six-and-twenty; he is only fuller in flesh, and has only lost the indefinable look of youth— a loss which is marked even when the eye is undulled and the wrinkles are not yet come. Perhaps the pretty woman, not much younger than he, who is leaning on his arm, is more changed than her husband; the lovely bloom that used to be always on her cheek now comes but fitfully, with the fresh morning air or with some strong surprise; yet to all who love human faces best for what they tell of human experience, Nancy's beauty has a heightened interest. Often the soul is ripened into fuller goodness while age has spread an ugly film, so that mere glances can never divine the preciousness of the fruit. But the years have not been so cruel to Nancy. The firm yet placid mouth, the clear, veracious glance of the brown eyes, speak now of a nature that has been tested and has kept its highest quali-

---

*Part II takes up the story fifteen years later, in the early 1830s.

ties; and even the costume, with its dainty neatness and purity, has more significance now the coquetries of youth can have nothing to do with it.

Mr. and Mrs. Godfrey Cass (any higher title has died away from Raveloe lips since the old Squire was gathered to his fathers and his inheritance was divided) have turned round to look for the tall aged man and the plainly dressed woman who are a little behind—Nancy having observed that they must wait for "father and Priscilla"—and now they all turn into a narrower path leading across the churchyard to a small gate opposite the Red House. We will not follow them now; for may there not be some others in this departing congregation whom we should like to see again—some of those who are not likely to be handsomely clad, and whom we may not recognize so easily as the master and mistress of the Red House?

But it is impossible to mistake Silas Marner. His large brown eyes seem to have gathered a longer vision, as is the way with eyes that have been short-sighted in early life, and they have a less vague, a more answering gaze; but in everything else one sees signs of a frame much enfeebled by the lapse of the sixteen years. The weaver's bent shoulders and white hair give him almost the look of advanced age, though he is not more than five-and-fifty; but there is the freshest blossom of youth close by his side—a blonde dimpled girl of eighteen, who has vainly tried to chastise her curly auburn hair into smoothness under her brown bonnet; the hair ripples as obstinately as a brooklet under the March breeze, and the little ringlets burst away from the restraining comb behind and show themselves below the bonnet-crown. Eppie cannot help being rather vexed about her hair, for there is no other girl in Raveloe who has hair at all like it, and she thinks hair ought to be smooth. She does not like to be blameworthy even in small things; you see how neatly her prayer book is folded in her spotted handkerchief.

That good-looking young fellow, in a new fustian suit, who walks behind her, is not quite sure upon the question of hair in the abstract, when Eppie puts it to him, and thinks that perhaps straight hair is the best in general, but he doesn't want Eppie's hair to be different. She surely divines that there is some one behind her who is thinking about her very particularly, and mustering courage to come to her side as soon as they are out in the lane, else why should she look rather shy, and take care not to turn away her head from her father Silas, to whom she keeps murmuring little sentences as to who was at church, and who was not at church, and how pretty the red mountain-ash is over the rectory wall!

"I wish we had a little garden, father, with double daisies in, like Mrs. Winthrop's," said Eppie, when they were out in the lane; "only they say it 'ud take a deal of digging and bringing fresh soil—and you couldn't do that, could you, father? Anyhow, I shouldn't like you to do it, for it 'ud be too hard work for you."

"Yes, I could do it, child, if you want a bit o' garden; these long evenings I could work at taking in a little bit o' the waste, just enough for a root or two o' flowers for you; and again, i' the morning, I could have a turn wi' the spade before I sat down to the loom. Why didn't you tell me before as you wanted a bit o' garden?"

"I can dig it for you, Master Marner," said the young man in fustian, who was now by Eppie's side, entering into the conversation without the trouble of formalities. "It'll be play to me after I've done my day's work, or any odd bits o' time when the work's slack. And I'll bring you some soil from Mr. Cass's garden—he'll let me, and willing."

"Eh, Aaron, my lad, are you there?" said Silas; "I wasn't aware of you; for when Eppie's talking o' things, I see nothing but what she's a-saying. Well, if you could help me with the digging, we might get her a bit o' garden all the sooner."

"Then, if you think well and good," said Aaron, "I'll come to the Stone-pits this afternoon, and we'll settle what land's to be taken in, and I'll get up an hour earlier i' the morning and begin on it."

"But not if you don't promise me not to work at the hard digging, father," said Eppie. "For I shouldn't ha' said anything about it," she added, half-bashfully, half-roguishly, "only Mrs. Winthrop said as Aaron 'ud be so good, and ——"

"And you might ha' known it without mother telling you," said Aaron. "And Master Marner knows, too, I hope, as I'm able and willing to do a turn o' work for him, and he won't do me the unkindness to anyways take it out o' my hands."

"There, now, father, you won't work in it till it's all easy," said Eppie, "and you and me can mark out the beds and make holes and plant the roots. It'll be a deal livelier at the Stone-pits when we've got some flowers, for I always think the flowers can see us and know what we're talking about. And I'll have a bit o' rosemary, and berg-amot, and thyme, because they are so sweet-smelling; but there's no lavender only in the gentlefolks' gardens, I think."

"That's no reason why you shouldn't have some," said Aaron, "for I can bring you slips of anything; I'm forced to cut no end of 'em when I'm gardening, and throw 'em away mostly. There's a big bed o' lavender at the Red House; the missis is very fond of it."

"Well," said Silas, gravely, "so as you don't make free for us, or ask for anything as is worth much at the Red House: for Mr. Cass's been so good to us, and built us up the new end o' the cottage, and given us beds and things, as I couldn't abide to be imposin' for garden-stuff or anything else."

"No, no, there's no imposin'," said Aaron; "there's never a gar-den in all the parish but what there's endless waste in it for want o' somebody as could use everything up. It's what I think to myself sometimes, as there need nobody run short o' victuals if the land was made the most on, and there was never a morsel but what could find its way to a mouth. It sets one thinking o' that—gardening does. But I must go back now, else mother 'ull be in trouble as I aren't there."

"Bring her with you this afternoon, Aaron," said Eppie; "I shouldn't like to fix about the garden, and her not know everything from the first—should you, father?"

"Ay, bring her if you can, Aaron," said Silas; "she's sure to have a word to say as 'll help set things on their right end."

Aaron turned back up the village, while Silas and Eppie went on up the lonely sheltered lane.

"O, daddy!" she began, when they were in privacy, clasping and squeezing Silas's arm, and skipping round to give him an energetic kiss. "My little old daddy! I'm so glad. I don't think I shall want any-thing else when we've got a little garden; and I knew Aaron would dig it for us," she went on with roguish triumph—"I knew that very well."

"You're a deep little puss, you are," said Silas, with the mild pas-sive happiness of love-crowned age in his face; "but you'll make yourself fine and beholden to Aaron."

"O, no, I shan't," said Eppie, laughing and frisking; "he likes it."

"Come, come, let me carry your prayer-book, else you'll be dropping it, jumping i' that way."

Eppie was now aware that her behavior was under observation, but it was only the observation of a friendly donkey, browsing with a log fastened to his foot—a meek donkey, not scornfully critical of human trivialities, but thankful to share in them, if possible, by getting his nose scratched; and Eppie did not fail to gratify him with her usual notice, though it was attended with the inconvenience of his following them, painfully, up to the very door of their home.

But the sound of a sharp bark inside, as Eppie put the key in the door, modified the donkey's views, and he limped away again without bidding. The sharp bark was the sign of an excited welcome that was awaiting them from a knowing brown terrier, who, after dancing at their legs in a hysterical manner, rushed with a worrying noise at a tortoise-shell kitten under the loom, and then rushed back with a sharp bark again, as much as to say, "I have done my duty by this feeble creature, you perceive"; while the lady-mother of the kitten sat sunning her white bosom in the window, and looked round with a sleepy air of expecting caresses, though she was not going to take any trouble for them.

The presence of this happy animal life was not the only change which had come over the interior of the stone cottage. There was no bed now in the living-room, and the small space was well filled with decent furniture, all bright and clean enough to satisfy Dolly Winthrop's eye. The oaken table and three-cornered oaken chair were hardly what was likely to be seen in so poor a cottage: they had come, with the beds and other things, from the Red House; for Mr. Godfrey Cass, as every one said in the village, did very kindly by the weaver; and it was nothing but right a man should be looked on and helped by those who could afford it, when he had brought up an orphan child, and been father and mother to her—and had lost his money, too, so as he had nothing but what he worked for week by week, and when the weaving was going down, too—for there was less and less flax spun—and Master Marner was none so young. Nobody was jealous of the weaver, for he was regarded as an exceptional person, whose claims on neighborly help were not to be matched in Raveloe. Any superstition that remained concerning him had taken an entirely new color; and Mr. Macey, now a very feeble old man of fourscore and six, never seen except in his chimney-corner or sitting in the sunshine at his door-sill, was of opinion that when a man had done what Silas had done by an orphan child, it was a sign that his money would come to light again, or leastwise that the robber would be made to answer for it—for, as Mr. Macey observed of himself, his faculties were as strong as ever.

Silas sat down now and watched Eppie with a satisfied gaze as she spread the clean cloth, and set on it the potatopie, warmed up slowly in a safe Sunday fashion, by being put into a dry pot over a slowly-dying fire, as the best substitute for an oven. For Silas would not consent to have a grate and oven added to his conveniences. He loved the old brick hearth as he had loved his brown pot—and was it not there when he had found Eppie? The gods of the hearth exist for us still; and let all new faith be tolerant of that fetishism, lest it bruise its own roots![16]

Silas ate his dinner more silently than usual, soon laying down his knife and fork, and watching abstractedly Eppie's play with Snap and the cat, by which her own dining was made rather a lengthy business. Yet it was a sight that might well arrest wandering thoughts: Eppie, with the rippling radiance of her hair and the whiteness of her rounded chin and throat set off by the dark-blue cotton gown, laughing merrily as the kitten held on with her four claws to one shoulder, like a design for a jug-handle, while Snap on the right hand and Puss on the other put up their paws toward a morsel which she held out of the reach of both—Snap occasionally desisting in order to remonstrate with the cat by a cogent worrying growl on the greediness and futility of her conduct; till Eppie relented, caressed them both, and divided the morsel between them.

But at last Eppie, glancing at the clock, checked the play, and said, "Oh, daddy, you're wanting to go into the sunshine to smoke your pipe. But I must clear away first, so as the house may be tidy when godmother comes. I'll make haste—I won't be long."

Silas had taken to smoking a pipe daily during the last two years, having been strongly urged to it by the sages of Raveloe, as a practice "good for the fits"; and this advice was sanctioned by Dr. Kimble, on the ground that it was as well to try what could do no harm—a principle which was made to answer for a great deal of work in that gentleman's medical practice. Silas did not highly enjoy smoking, and often wondered how his neighbors could be so fond of it; but a humble sort of acquiescence in what was held to be good, had become a strong habit of that new self which had been developed in him since he had found Eppie on his hearth: it had been the only clew his bewildered mind could hold by in cherishing this young life that had been sent to him out of the darkness into which his gold had departed. By seeking what was needful for Eppie, by sharing the effect that everything produced on her, he had himself come to appropriate the forms of custom and belief which were the mould of Raveloe life, and as, with reawakening sensibilities, memory also reawakened, he had begun to ponder over the elements of his old faith, and blend them with his new impressions, till he recovered a consciousness of unity between his past and present. The sense of presiding goodness and the human trust which come with all pure peace and joy, had given him a dim impression that there had been some error, some mistake, which had thrown that dark shadow over the days of his best years; and as it grew more and more easy to him to open his mind to Dolly Winthrop, he gradually communicated to her all he could describe of his early life. The communication was necessarily a slow and difficult process, for Silas's meagre power of explanation was not aided by any readiness of interpretation in Dolly, whose narrow outward experience gave her no key to strange customs, and made every novelty a source of wonder that arrested them at every step of the narrative. It was only by fragments and at intervals which left Dolly time to revolve what she had heard till it acquired some familiarity for her, that Silas at last arrived at the climax of the sad story—the drawing of lots, and its false testimony concerning him; and this had to be repeated in several interviews, under new questions on her part as to the nature of this plan for detecting the guilty and clearing the innocent.

"And yourn's the same Bible, you're sure o' that, Master Marner—the Bible as you brought wi' you from that country—it's the same as what they've got at church, and what Eppie's a-learning to read in."

"Yes," said Silas, "every bit the same; and there's drawing o' lots in the Bible, mind you," he added in a lower tone.

"O dear, dear," said Dolly in a grieved voice, as if she were hearing an unfavorable report of a sick man's case. She was silent for some minutes; at last she said—

"There's wise folks, happen, as know how it all is; the parson knows, I'll be bound; but it takes big words to tell them things, and such as poor folks can't make much out on. I can never rightly know the meaning o' what I hear at church, only a bit here and there, but I know it's good words—I do. But what lies upo' your mind—it's this, Master Marner: as, if Them above had done the right thing by you, They'd never ha' let you be turned out for a wicked thief when you was innocent."

"Ah!" said Silas, who had now come to understand Dolly's phraseology, "that was what fell on me like as if it had been red-hot iron; because, you see, there was nobody as cared for me or clave to me above nor below. And him as I'd gone out and in wi' for ten year and more, since when we was lads and went halves—mine own familiar friend in whom I trusted, had lifted up his heel again' me, and worked to ruin me."*

"Eh, but he was a bad 'un—I can't think as there's another such," said Dolly. "But I'm o'ercome, Master Marner; I'm like as if I'd waked and didn't know whether it was night or morning. I feel somehow as sure as I do when I've laid something up though I can't justly put my hand on it, as there was a rights in what happened to you, if one could but make it out; and you'd no call to lose heart as you did. But we'll talk on it again; for sometimes things come into my head when I'm leeching or poulticing, or such, as I could never think on when I was sitting still."

Dolly was too useful a woman not to have many opportunities of illumination of the kind she alluded to, and she was not long before she recurred to the subject.

"Master Marner," she said, one day that she came to bring home Eppie's washing, "I've been sore puzzled for a good bit wi' that trouble o' yourn and the drawing o' lots; and it got twisted back'ards and for'ards, as I didn't know which end to lay hold on. But it come to me all clear like, that night when I was sitting up wi' poor Bessy Fawkes, as is dead and left her children behind, God help 'em—it come to me as clear as daylight; but whether I've got hold on it now,

---

*See the Bible, Psalms 41:9: "Yea, mine own familiar friend, in whom I trusted, which did eat of my bread, hath lifted up his heel against me" (KJV).

or can anyways bring it to my tongue's end, that I don't know. For I've often a deal inside me as 'll never come out; and for what you talk o' your folks in your old country niver saying prayers by heart nor saying 'em out of a book, they must be wonderful cliver; for if I didn't know 'Our Father,' and little bits o' good words as I can carry out o' church wi' me, I might down o' my knees every night, but nothing could I say."

"But you can mostly say something as I can make sense on, Mrs. Winthrop," said Silas.

"Well, then, Master Marner, it come to me summat like this: I can make nothing o' the drawing o' lots and the answer coming wrong; it 'ud mayhap take the parson to tell that, and he could only tell us i' big words. But what come to me as clear as the daylight, it was when I was troubling over poor Bessy Fawkes, and it allays comes into my head when I'm sorry for folks, and feel as I can't do a power to help 'em, not if I was to get up i' the middle o' the night—it comes into my head as Them above has got a deal tenderer heart nor what I've got—for I can't be anyways better nor Them as made me; and if anything looks hard to me, it's because there's things I don't know on; and for the matter o' that, there may be plenty o' things I don't know on, for it's little as I know—that it is. And so, while I was thinking o' that, you come into my mind, Master Marner, and it all come pouring in: ——if I felt i' my inside what was the right and just thing by you, and them as prayed and drawed the lots, all but that wicked un, if they'd ha' done the right thing by you if they could, isn't there Them as was at the making on us, and knows better and has a better will? And that's all as ever I can be sure on, and everything else is a big puzzle to me when I think on it. For there was the fever come and took off them as were full-growed, and left the helpless children; and there's the breaking o' limbs; and them as 'ud do right and be sober have to suffer by them as are contrairy—eh, there's trouble i' this world, and there's things as we can niver make out the rights on. And all as we've got to do is to trusten, Master Marner—to do the right thing as fur as we know, and to trusten. For if us as knows so little can see a bit o' good and rights, we may be sure as there's a good and a rights bigger nor what we can know—I feel it i' my own insides as it must be so. And if you could but ha' gone on trustening, Master Marner, you wouldn't ha' run away from your fellow-creaturs and been so lone."

"Ah, but that 'ud ha' been hard," said Silas, in an under-tone; "it 'ud ha' been hard to trusten then."

"And so it would," said Dolly, almost with compunction; "them things are easier said nor done; and I'm partly ashamed o' talking."

"Nay, nay," said Silas, "you're i' the right, Mrs. Winthrop—you're i' the right. There's good i' this world—I've a feeling o' that now; and it makes a man feel as there's a good more nor he can see, i' spite o' the trouble and the wickedness. That drawing o' the lots is dark; but the child was sent to me: there's dealings with us—there's dealings."

This dialogue took place in Eppie's earlier years, when Silas had to part with her for two hours every day, that she might learn to read at the dame school, after he had vainly tried himself to guide her in that first step to learning. Now that she was grown up, Silas had often been led, in those moments of quiet outpouring which come to people who live together in perfect love, to talk with her too of the past, and how and why he had lived a lonely man until she had been sent to him. For it would have been impossible for him to hide from Eppie that she was not his own child: even if the most delicate reticence on the point could have been expected from Raveloe gossips in her presence, her own questions about her mother could not have been parried, as she grew up, without that complete shrouding of the past which would have made a painful barrier between their minds. So Eppie had long known how her mother had died on the snowy ground, and how she herself had been found on the hearth by father Silas, who had taken her golden curls for his lost guineas brought back to him. The tender and peculiar love with which Silas had reared her in almost inseparable companionship with himself, aided by the seclusion of their dwelling, had preserved her from the lowering influences of the village talk and habits, and had kept her mind in that freshness which is sometimes falsely supposed to be an invariable attribute of rusticity. Perfect love has a breath of poetry which can exalt the relations of the least-instructed human beings; and this breath of poetry had surrounded Eppie from the time when she had followed the bright gleam that beckoned her to Silas's hearth; so that it is not surprising if, in other things besides her delicate prettiness,

she was not quite a common village maiden, but had a touch of re-
finement and fervor which came from no other teaching than that of
tenderly-nurtured unvitiated feeling. She was too childish and simple
for her imagination to rove into questions about her unknown father;
for a long while it did not even occur to her that she must have had
a father; and the first time that the idea of her mother having had a
husband presented itself to her, was when Silas showed her the
wedding-ring which had been taken from the wasted finger, and had
been carefully preserved by him in a little lackered box shaped like a
shoe. He delivered this box into Eppie's charge when she had grown
up, and she often opened it to look at the ring: but still she thought
hardly at all about the father of whom it was the symbol. Had she not
a father very close to her, who loved her better than any real fathers
in the village seemed to love their daughters? On the contrary, who
her mother was, and how she came to die in that forlornness, were
questions that often pressed on Eppie's mind. Her knowledge of Mrs.
Winthrop, who was her nearest friend next to Silas, made her
feel that a mother must be very precious; and she had again and
again asked Silas to tell her how her mother looked, whom she was
like, and how he had found her against the furze bush, led toward
it by the little footsteps and the outstretched arms. The furze bush
was there still; and this afternoon, when Eppie came out with Silas
into the sunshine, it was the first object that arrested her eyes and
thoughts.

"Father," she said, in a tone of gentle gravity, which sometimes
came like a sadder, slower cadence across her playfulness, "we shall
take the furze bush into the garden; it'll come into the corner, and
just against it I'll put snowdrops and crocuses, 'cause Aaron says they
won't die out, but 'll always get more and more."

"Ah, child," said Silas, always ready to talk when he had his pipe
in his hand, apparently enjoying the pauses more than the puffs, "it
wouldn't do to leave out the furze bush; and there's nothing prettier
to my thinking, when it's yallow with flowers. But it's just come into
my head what we're to do for a fence—mayhap Aaron can help us to
a thought; but a fence we must have, else the donkeys and things 'ull
come and trample everything down. And fencing's hard to be got at,
by what I can make out."

"Oh, I'll tell you, daddy," said Eppie, clasping her hands suddenly, after a minute's thought. "There's lots o' loose stones about, some of 'em not big, and we might lay 'em atop of one another, and make a wall. You and me could carry the smallest, and Aaron 'ud carry the rest—I know he would."

"Eh, my precious 'un," said Silas, "there isn't enough stones to go all round; and as for you carrying, why, wi' your little arms you couldn't carry a stone no bigger than a turnip. You're dillicate made, my dear," he added, with a tender intonation—"that's what Mrs. Winthrop says."

"Oh, I'm stronger than you think, daddy," said Eppie; "and if there wasn't stones enough to go all round, why they'll go part o' the way, and then it 'll be easier to get sticks and things for the rest. See here, round the big pit, what a many stones!"

She skipped forward to the pit, meaning to lift one of the stones and exhibit her strength, but she started back in surprise.

"Oh, father, just come and look here," she exclaimed—"come and see how the water's gone down since yesterday. Why, yesterday the pit was ever so full!"

"Well, to be sure," said Silas, coming to her side. "Why, that's the draining they've begun on, since harvest, i' Mr. Osgood's fields, I reckon. The foreman said to me the other day, when I passed by 'em, 'Master Marner,' he said, 'I shouldn't wonder if we lay your bit o' waste as dry as a bone.' It was Mr. Godfrey Cass, he said, had gone into the draining: he'd been taking these fields o' Mr. Osgood."

"How odd it 'll seem to have the old pit dried up!" said Eppie, turning away, and stooping to lift rather a large stone. "See, daddy, I can carry this quite well," she said, going along with much energy for a few steps, but presently letting it fall.

"Ah, you're fine and strong, arn't you?" said Silas, while Eppie shook her aching arms and laughed. "Come, come, let us go and sit down on the bank against the stile there, and have no more lifting. You might hurt yourself, child. You'd need have somebody to work for you—and my arm isn't overstrong."

Silas uttered the last sentence slowly, as if it implied more than met the ear; and Eppie, when they sat down on the bank, nestled close to his side, and, taking hold caressingly of the arm that was not over strong, held it on her lap while Silas puffed again dutifully at the pipe, which occupied his other arm. An ash in the hedgerow behind made a fretted screen from the sun, and threw happy playful shadows all about them.

"Father," said Eppie, very gently, after they had been sitting in silence a little while, "if I was to be married, ought I to be married with my mother's ring?"

Silas gave an almost imperceptible start, though the question fell in with the under-current of thought in his own mind, and then said, in a subdued tone, "Why, Eppie, have you been a-thinking on it?"

"Only this last week, father," said Eppie, ingenuously, "since Aaron talked to me about it."

"And what did he say?" said Silas, still in the same subdued way, as if he were anxious lest he should fall into the slightest tone that was not for Eppie's good.

"He said he should like to be married, because he was a-going in four-and-twenty, and had got a deal of gardening work, now Mr. Mott's given up; and he goes twice a-week regular to Mr. Cass's, and once to Mr. Osgood's, and they're going to take him on at the rectory."

"And who is it as he's wanting to marry?" said Silas, with rather a sad smile.

"Why, me, to be sure, daddy," said Eppie, with dimpling laughter, kissing her father's cheek; "as if he'd want to marry anybody else!"

"And you mean to have him, do you?" said Silas.

"Yes, sometime," said Eppie; "I don't know when. Everybody's married some time, Aaron says. But I told him that wasn't true: for, I said, look at father—he's never been married."

"No, child," said Silas, "your father was a lone man till you was sent to him."

"But you'll never be lone again, father," said Eppie, tenderly. "That was what Aaron said—'I could never think o' taking you away from Master Marner, Eppie.' And I said, 'It 'ud be no use if you did, Aaron.' And he wants us all to live together, so as you needn't work a bit, father, only what's for your own pleasure; and he'd be as good as a son to you—that was what he said."

"And should you like that, Eppie?" said Silas, looking at her.

"I shouldn't mind it, father," said Eppie, quite simply. "And I should like things to be so as you needn't work much. But if it wasn't for that, I'd sooner things didn't change. I'm very happy: I like Aaron to be fond of me, and come and see us often, and behave pretty to you—he always *does* behave pretty to you, doesn't he, father?"

"Yes, child, nobody could behave better," said Silas, emphatically. "He's his mother's lad."

"But I don't want any change," said Eppie. "I should like to go on a long, long while, just as we are. Only Aaron does want a change; and he made me cry a bit—only a bit—because he said I didn't care for him, for if I cared for him I should want us to be married, as he did."

"Eh, my blessed child," said Silas, laying down his pipe as if it were useless to pretend to smoke any longer, "you're o'er young to be married. We'll ask Mrs. Winthrop—we'll ask Aaron's mother what *she* thinks: if there's a right thing to do, she'll come at it. But there's this to be thought on, Eppie: things will change, whether we like it or no; things won't go on for a long while just as they are and no difference. I shall get older and helplesser, and be a burden on you, belike, if I don't go away from you altogether. Not as I mean you'd think me a burden—I know you wouldn't—but it 'ud be hard upon you; and when I look for'ard to that, I like to think as you'd have somebody else besides me—somebody young and strong, as'll outlast your own life, and take care on you to the end." Silas paused, and resting his wrists on his knees, lifted his hands up and down meditatively as he looked on the ground.

"Then, would you like me to be married, father?" said Eppie, with a little trembling in her voice.

"I'll not be the man to say no, Eppie," said Silas, emphatically; but we'll ask your godmother. She'll wish the right thing by you and her son, too."

"There they come, then," said Eppie. "Let us go and meet 'em. O, the pipe! won't you have it lit again, father?" said Eppie, lifting that medicinal appliance from the ground.

"Nay, child," said Silas, "I've done enough for to-day. I think, mayhap, a little of it does me more good than so much at once."

CHAPTER XVII

WHILE SILAS AND EPPIE were seated on the bank discoursing in the fleckered shade of the ash tree, Miss Priscilla Lammeter was resisting her sister's arguments, that it would be better to take tea at the Red House, and let her father have a long nap, than drive home to the Warrens so soon after dinner. The family party (of four only) were seated round the table in the dark wainscoted parlor, with the Sunday dessert before them, of fresh filberts, apples and pears, duly ornamented with leaves by Nancy's own hand before the bells had rung for church.

A great change has come over the dark wainscoted parlor since we saw it in Godfrey's bachelor days, and under the wifeless reign of the old Squire. Now all is polish, on which no yesterday's dust is ever allowed to rest, from the yard's width of oaken boards round the carpet, to the old Squire's gun and whips and walking-sticks, ranged on the stag's antlers above the mantel-piece. All other signs of sporting and outdoor occupation Nancy has removed to another room; but she has brought into the Red House the habit of filial reverence, and preserves sacredly in a place of honor these relics of her husband's departed father. The tankards are on the sidetable still, but the bossed silver is undimmed by handling, and there are no dregs to send forth unpleasant suggestions; the only prevailing scent is of the lavender and roseleaves that fill the vases of Derbyshire spar. All is purity and order in this once dreary room, for, fifteen years ago, it was entered by a new presiding spirit.

"Now, father," said Nancy, "is there any call for you to go home to tea? Mayn't you just as well stay with us? Such a beautiful evening as it's likely to be."

The old gentleman had been talking with Godfrey about the increasing poor-rate and the ruinous times, and had not heard the dialogue between his daughters.[17]

"My dear, you must ask Priscilla," he said, in the once firm voice, now become rather broken. "She manages me and the farm too."

"And reason good as I should manage you, father," said Priscilla, "else you'd be giving yourself your death with rheumatism. And as for the farm, if anything turns out wrong, as it can't but do in these times, there's nothing kills a man so soon as having nobody to find fault with but himself. It's a deal the best way o' being master, to let somebody else do the ordering, and keep the blaming in your own hands. It 'ud save many a man a stroke, I believe."

"Well, well, my dear," said her father, with a quiet laugh, "I didn't say you don't manage for everybody's good."

"Then manage so as you may stay to tea, Priscilla," said Nancy, putting her hand on her sister's arm affectionately. "Come now; and we'll go round the garden while father has his nap."

"My dear child, he'll have a beautiful nap in the gig, for I shall drive. And as for staying to tea, I can't hear of it; for there's this dairy-maid, now she knows she's to be married, turned Michaelmas, she'd as lief pour the new milk into the pig-trough as into the pans. That's the way with 'em all; it's as if they thought the world 'ud be new-made because they're to be married. So come and let me put my bonnet on, and there'll be time for us to walk round the garden while the horse is being put in."

When the sisters were treading the neatly-swept garden-walks, between the bright turf that contrasted pleasantly with the dark cones and arches and wall-like hedges of yew, Priscilla said—

"I'm as glad as anything at your husband's making that exchange o' land with cousin Osgood and beginning the dairying. It's a thousand pities you didn't do it before; for it'll give you something to fill your mind. There's nothing like a dairy if folks want a bit o' worrit to make the days pass. For as for rubbing furniture, when you can once see your face in a table there's nothing else to look for; but there's always something fresh with the dairy; for even in the depths o' winter there's some pleasure in conquering the butter, and making it come whether or no. My dear," added Priscilla, pressing her sister's hand affectionately as they walked side by side, "you'll never be low when you've got a dairy."

"Ah, Priscilla," said Nancy, returning the pressure with a grateful glance of her clear eyes, "but it won't make up to Godfrey: a dairy's not so much to a man. And it's only what he cares for that ever makes me low. I'm contented with the blessings we have, if he could be contented."

"It drives me past patience," said Priscilla, impetuously, "that way o' the men—always wanting and wanting, and never easy with what they've got: they can't sit comfortable in their chairs when they've neither ache nor pain, but either they must stick a pipe in their mouths, to make 'em better than well, or else they must be swallowing something strong, though they're forced to make haste before the next meal comes in. But joyful be it spoken, our father was never that sort o' man. And if it had pleased God to make you ugly, like me, so as the men wouldn't ha' run after you, we might have kept to our own family, and had nothing to do with folks as have got uneasy blood in their veins."

"O don't say so, Priscilla," said Nancy, repenting that she had called forth this outburst; "nobody has any occasion to find fault with Godfrey. It's natural he should be disappointed at not having any children: every man likes to have somebody to work for and lay by for, and he always counted so on making a fuss with 'em when they were little. There's many another man would hanker more than he does. He's the best of husbands."

"Oh, I know," said Priscilla, smiling sarcastically, "I know the way o' wives; they set one on to abuse their husbands, and then they turn round on one and praise 'em as if they wanted to sell 'em. But father'll be waiting for me; we must turn now."

The large gig with the steady old gray was at the front door, and Mr. Lammeter was already on the stone steps, passing the time in recalling to Godfrey what very fine points Speckle had when his master used to ride him.

"I always *would* have a good horse, you know," said the old gentleman, not liking that spirited time to be quite effaced from the memory of his juniors.

"Mind you bring Nancy to the Warrens before the week's out, Mr. Cass," was Priscilla's parting injunction, as she took the reins, and shook them gently, by way of friendly incitement to Speckle.

"I shall just take a turn to the fields against the Stone-pits, Nancy, and look at the draining," said Godfrey.

"You'll be in again by tea-time, dear?"

"O yes, I shall be back in an hour."

It was Godfrey's custom on Sunday afternoon to do a little contemplated farming in a leisurely walk. Nancy seldom accompanied him; for the women of her generation—unless, like Priscilla, they took to outdoor management—were not given to much walking beyond their own house and garden, finding sufficient exercise in domestic duties. So, when Priscilla was not with her, she usually sat with Mant's Bible* before her, and after following the text with her eyes for a little while, she would gradually permit them to wander as her thoughts had already insisted on wandering.

But Nancy's Sunday thoughts were rarely quite out of keeping with the devout and reverential intention implied by the book spread open before her. She was not theologically instructed enough to discern very clearly the relation between the sacred documents of the past which she opened without method, and her own obscure, simple life; but the spirit of rectitude, and the sense of responsibility for the effect of her conduct on others, which were strong elements in Nancy's character, had made it a habit with her to scrutinize her past feelings and actions with self-questioning solicitude. Her mind not being courted by a great variety of subjects, she filled the vacant moments by living inwardly, again and again, through all her remembered experience, especially through the fifteen years of her married time, in which her life and its significance had been doubled. She recalled the small details, the words, tones, and looks, in the critical scenes which had opened a new epoch for her by giving her a deeper insight into the relations and trials of life; or which had called on her for some little effort of forbearance, or of painful adherence to an imagined or real duty—asking herself continually whether she had been in any respect blamable. This excessive rumination and self-questioning is perhaps a morbid habit inevitable to a mind of much moral sensibility when shut out from its due share of outward activity and of practical claims on its affections—inevitable to a noble-hearted, childless woman, when her lot is narrow. "I can do so little—have I done it all well?" is the perpetually recurring thought; and there are no voices calling her away from that soliloquy, no peremptory demands to divert energy from vain regret or superfluous scruple.

---

*Published in 1817 with annotations and illustrations, Mant's Bible became very popular.

There was one main thread of painful experience in Nancy's married life, and on it hung certain deeply-felt scenes, which were the oftenest revived in retrospect. The short dialogue with Priscilla in the garden had determined the current of retrospect in that frequent direction this particular Sunday afternoon. The first wandering of her thought from the text, which she still attempted dutifully to follow with her eyes and silent lips, was into an imaginary enlargement of the defense she had set up for her husband against Priscilla's implied blame. The vindication of the loved object is the best balm affection can find for its wounds:—"A man must have so much on his mind," is the belief by which a wife often supports a cheerful face under rough answers and unfeeling words. And Nancy's deepest wounds had all come from the perception that the absence of children from their hearth was dwelt on in her husband's mind as a privation to which he could not reconcile himself.

Yet sweet Nancy might have been expected to feel still more keenly the denial of a blessing to which she had looked forward with all the varied expectations and preparations, solemn and prettily trivial, which fill the mind of a loving woman when she expects to become a mother. Was there not a drawer filled with the neat work of her hands, all unworn and untouched, just as she had arranged it there fourteen years ago—just, but for one little dress, which had been made the burial-dress? But under this immediate personal trial Nancy was so firmly unmurmuring, that years ago she had suddenly renounced the habit of visiting the drawer, lest she should in this way be creating a longing for what was not given.

Perhaps it was this very severity toward any indulgence of what she held to be sinful regret in herself that made her shrink from applying her own standard to her husband. "It is very different—it is much worse for a man to be disappointed in that way: a woman can always be satisfied with devoting herself to her husband, but a man wants something that will make him look forward more—and sitting by the fire is so much duller to him than to a woman." And always, when Nancy reached this point in her meditations—trying, with predetermined sympathy, to see everything as Godfrey saw it—there came a renewal of self-questioning. *Had* she done everything in her power to lighten Godfrey's privation? Had she really been right in the resistance which had cost her so much pain six years ago, and again four years ago—the resistance to her husband's wish that they should adopt a child? Adoption was more remote from the ideas and habits of that time than of our own; still Nancy had her opinion on it. It was as necessary to her mind to have an opinion on all topics, not exclusively masculine, that had come under her notice, as for her to have a precisely marked place for every article of her personal property: and her opinions were always principles to be unwaveringly acted on. They were firm, not because of their basis, but because she held them with a tenacity inseparable from her mental action. On all the duties and proprieties of life, from filial behavior to the arrangements of the evening toilet, pretty Nancy Lammeter, by the time she was three-and-twenty, had her unalterable little code, and had formed every one of her habits in strict accordance with that code. She carried these decided judgments within her in the most unobtrusive way: they rooted themselves in her mind, and grew there as quietly as grass. Years ago, we know, she insisted on dressing like Priscilla, because "it was right for sisters to dress alike," and because "she would do what was right if she wore a gown dyed with cheese-coloring." That was a trivial but typical instance of the mode in which Nancy's life was regulated.

It was one of those rigid principles, and no petty egoistic feeling, which had been the ground of Nancy's difficult resistance to her husband's wish. To adopt a child, because children of your own had been denied you, was to try and choose your lot in spite of Providence: the adopted child, she was convinced, would never turn out well, and would be a curse to those who had willfully and rebelliously sought what it was clear that, for some high reason, they were better without. When you saw a thing was not meant to be, said Nancy, it was a bounden duty to leave off so much as wishing for it. And so far, perhaps, the wisest of men could scarcely make more than a verbal improvement in her principle. But the conditions under which she held it apparent that a thing was not meant to be, depended on a more peculiar mode of thinking. She would have given up making a purchase at a particular place if, on three successive times, rain, or some other cause of Heaven's sending, had formed an obstacle; and she would have anticipated a broken limb or other heavy misfortune to any one who persisted in spite of such indications.

"But why should you think the child would turn out ill?" said Godfrey, in his remonstrances. "She has thriven as well as child can do with the weaver; and *he* adopted her. There isn't such a pretty little girl anywhere else in the parish, or one fitter for the station we could give her. Where can be the likelihood of her being a curse to anybody?"

"Yes, my dear Godfrey," said Nancy, who was sitting with her hands tightly clasped together, and with yearning, regretful affection in her eyes. "The child may not turn out ill with the weaver. But, then, he didn't go to seek her, as we should be doing. It will be wrong: I feel sure it will. Don't you remember what that lady we met at the Royston Baths told us about the child her sister adopted? That was the only adopting I ever heard of: and the child was transported when it was twenty-three. Dear Godfrey, don't ask me to do what I know is wrong: I should never be happy again. I know it's very hard for *you*—it's easier for me—but it's the will of Providence."

It might seem singular that Nancy—with her religious theory pieced together out of narrow social traditions, fragments of church doctrine imperfectly understood, and girlish reasonings on her small experience—should have arrived by herself at a way of thinking so nearly akin to that of many devout people whose beliefs are held in the shape of a system quite remote from her knowledge: singular, if we did not know that human beliefs, like all other natural growths, elude the barriers of system.[18]

Godfrey had from the first specified Eppie, then about twelve years old, as a child suitable for them to adopt. It had never occurred to him that Silas would rather part with his life than with Eppie. Surely the weaver would wish the best to the child he had taken so much trouble with, and would be glad that such good fortune should happen to her: she would always be very grateful to him, and he would be well provided for to the end of his life—provided for as the excellent part he had done by the child deserved. Was it not an appropriate thing for people in a higher station to take a charge off the hands of a man in a lower? It seemed an eminently appropriate thing to Godfrey, for reasons that were known only to himself; and by a common fallacy, he imagined the measure would be easy because he had private motives for desiring it. This was rather a coarse mode of estimating Silas's relation to Eppie; but we must remember that many of the impressions which Godfrey was likely to gather concerning the laboring people around him would favor the idea that deep affections can hardly go along with callous palms and scant means; and he had not had the opportunity, even if he had had the power, of entering intimately into all that was exceptional in the weaver's experience. It was only the want of adequate knowledge that could have made it possible for Godfrey deliberately to entertain an unfeeling project: his natural kindness had outlived that blighting time of cruel wishes, and Nancy's praise of him as a husband was not founded entirely on a willful illusion.

"I was right," she said to herself, when she had recalled all their scenes of discussion—"I feel I was right to say him nay, though it hurt me more than anything; but how good Godfrey has been about it! Many men would have been very angry with me for standing out against their wishes; and they might have thrown out that they'd had ill-luck in marrying me; but Godfrey has never been the man to say me an unkind word. It's only what he can't hide: everything seems so blank to him, I know; and the land—what a difference it 'ud make to him, when he goes to see after things, if he'd children growing up that he was doing it all for! But I won't murmur; and perhaps if he'd married a woman who'd have had children, she'd have vexed him in other ways."

This possibility was Nancy's chief comfort; and to give it greater strength, she labored to make it impossible that any other wife should have had more perfect tenderness. She had been forced to vex him by that one denial. Godfrey was not insensible to her loving effort, and did Nancy no injustice as to the motives of her obstinacy. It was impossible to have lived with her fifteen years and not be aware that an unselfish clinging to the right, and a sincerity clear as the flower-born dew, were her main characteristics; indeed, Godfrey felt this so strongly, that his own more wavering nature, too averse to facing difficulty to be unvaryingly simple and truthful, was kept in a certain awe of this gentle wife who watched his looks with a yearning to obey them. It seemed to him impossible that he should ever confess to her the truth about Eppie: she would never recover from the repulsion the story of his earlier marriage would create, told to her now, after that long concealment. And the child, too, he thought, must become an object of repulsion: the very sight of her would be painful. The shock to Nancy's mingled pride and ignorance of the world's evil might even be too much for her delicate frame. Since he had married her with that secret on his heart, he must keep it there to the last. Whatever else he did, he could not make an irreparable breach between himself and this long-loved wife.

Meanwhile, why could he not make up his mind to the absence of children from a hearth brightened by such a wife? Why did his mind fly uneasily to that void, as if it were the sole reason why life was not thoroughly joyous to him? I suppose it is the way with all men and women who reach middle age without the clear perception that life never *can* be thoroughly joyous: under the vague dullness of the gray hours, dissatisfaction seeks a definite object, and finds it in the privation of an untried good. Dissatisfaction seated musingly on a childless hearth, thinks with envy of the father whose return is greeted by young voices, seated at the meal where the little heads rise one above another like nursery plants, it sees a black care hovering behind every one of them, and thinks the impulses by which men abandon freedom, and seek for ties, are surely nothing but a brief madness. In Godfrey's case there were further reasons why his thoughts should be continually solicited by this one point in his lot: his conscience, never thoroughly easy about Eppie, now gave his childless home the aspect of a retribution; and as the time passed on, under Nancy's refusal to adopt her, any retrieval of his error became more and more difficult.

On this Sunday afternoon it was already four years since there had been any allusion to the subject between them, and Nancy supposed that it was forever buried.

"I wonder if he'll mind it less or more as he gets older," she thought; "I'm afraid more. Aged people feel the miss of children: what would father do without Priscilla? And if I die, Godfrey will be very lonely—not holding together with his brothers much. But I won't be over-anxious, and trying to make things out beforehand: I must do my best for the present."

With that last thought Nancy roused herself from her reverie, and turned her eyes again toward the forsaken page. It had been forsaken longer than she imagined, for she was presently surprised by the appearance of the servant with the tea-things. It was, in fact, a little before the usual time for tea; but Jane had her reasons.

"Is your master come into the yard, Jane?"

"No 'm, he isn't," said Jane, with a slight emphasis, of which, however, her mistress took no notice.

"I don't know whether you've seen 'em, 'm," continued Jane, after a pause, "but there's folks making haste all one way, afore the front window. I doubt something's happened. There's niver a man to be seen i' the yard, else I'd send and see. I've been up into the top attic, but there's no seeing anything for trees. I hope nobody's hurt, that's all."

"Oh, no, I dare say there's nothing much the matter," said Nancy. "It's perhaps Mr. Snell's bull got out again, as he did before."

"I wish he mayn't gore anybody then, that's all," said Jane, not altogether despising a hypothesis which covered a few imaginary calamities.

"That girl is always terrifying me," thought Nancy; "I wish Godfrey would come in."

She went to the front window and looked as far as she could see along the road, with an uneasiness which she felt to be childish, for there were now no such signs of excitement as Jane had spoken of, and Godfrey would not be likely to return by the village road, but by the fields. She continued to stand, however, looking at the placid churchyard with the long shadows of the gravestones across the bright green hillocks, and at the glowing autumn colors of the rectory trees beyond. Before such calm external beauty the presence of a vague fear is more distinctly felt—like a raven flapping its slow wing across the sunny air. Nancy wished more and more that Godfrey would come in.

CHAPTER XVIII

SOME ONE OPENED THE door at the other end of the room, and Nancy felt that it was her husband. She turned from the window with gladness in her eyes, for the wife's chief dread was stilled.

"Dear, I'm so thankful you're come," she said, going toward him. "I began to get ———"

She paused abruptly, for Godfrey was laying down his hat with trembling hands, and turned toward her with a pale face and a strange unanswering glance, as if he saw her indeed, but saw her as part of a scene invisible to herself. She laid her hand on his arm, not daring to speak again; but he left the touch unnoticed, and threw himself into his chair.

Jane was already at the door with the hissing urn. "Tell her to keep away, will you?" said Godfrey; and when the door was closed again he exerted himself to speak more distinctly.

"Sit down, Nancy—there," he said, pointing to a chair opposite him. "I came back as soon as I could, to hinder anybody's telling you but me. I've had a great shock—but I care most about the shock it'll be to you."

"It isn't father and Priscilla?" said Nancy, with quivering lips, clasping her hands together tightly on her lap.

"No, it's nobody living," said Godfrey, unequal to the considerate skill with which he would have wished to make his revelation. "It's Dunstan—my brother Dunstan, that we lost sight of sixteen years ago. We've found him—found his body—his skeleton."

The deep dread Godfrey's look had created in Nancy made her feel these words a relief. She sat in comparative calmness to hear what else he had to tell. He went on:

"The Stone-pit has gone dry suddenly—from the draining, I suppose; and there he lies—has lain for sixteen years, wedged between two great stones. There's his watch and seals, and there's my gold handled hunting-whip, with my name on; he took it away, without my knowing, the day he went hunting on Wildfire, the last time he was seen."

Godfrey paused: it was not so easy to say what came next. "Do you think he drowned himself?" said Nancy, almost wondering that her husband should be so deeply shaken by what had happened all those years ago to an unloved brother, of whom worse things had been augured.

"No, he fell in," said Godfrey, in a low but distinct voice, as if he felt some deep meaning in the fact. Presently he added: "Dunstan was the man that robbed Silas Marner."

The blood rushed to Nancy's face and neck at this surprise and shame, for she had been bred up to regard even a distant kinship with crime as a dishonor.

"O, Godfrey!" she said, with compassion in her tone, for she had immediately reflected that the dishonor must be felt still more keenly by her husband.

"There was the money in the pit," he continued—"all the weaver's money. Everything's been gathered up, and they're taking the skeleton to the Rainbow. But I came back to tell you: there was no hindering it; you must know."

He was silent, looking on the ground for two long minutes. Nancy would have said some words of comfort under this disgrace, but she refrained, from an instinctive sense that there was something behind—that Godfrey had something else to tell her. Presently he lifted his eyes to her face, and kept them fixed on her, as he said—

"Everything comes to light, Nancy, sooner or later. When God Almighty wills it, our secrets are found out. I've lived with a secret on my mind, but I'll keep it from you no longer. I wouldn't have you know it by somebody else, and not by me—I wouldn't have you find it out after I'm dead. I'll tell you now. It's been 'I will' and 'I won't' with me all my life—I'll make sure of myself now."

Nancy's utmost dread had returned. The eyes of the husband and wife met with awe in them, as at a crisis which suspended affection.

"Nancy," said Godfrey, slowly, "when I married you, I hid something from you—something I ought to have told you. That woman Marner found dead in the snow—Eppie's mother—that wretched woman—was my wife: Eppie is my child."

He paused, dreading the effect of his confession. But Nancy sat quite still, only that her eyes dropped and ceased to meet his. She was pale and quiet as a meditative statue, clasping her hands on her lap.

"You'll never think the same of me again," said Godfrey, after a little while, with some tremor in his voice.

She was silent.

"I oughtn't to have left the child unowned: I oughtn't to have kept it from you. But I couldn't bear to give you up, Nancy. I was led away into marrying her—I suffered for it."

Still Nancy was silent, looking down; and he almost expected that she would presently get up and say she would go to her father's.

How could she have any mercy for faults that must seem so black to her, with her simple, severe notions?

But at last she lifted up her eyes to his again and spoke. There was no indignation in her voice—only deep regret.

"Godfrey, if you had but told me this six years ago, we could have done some of our duty by the child. Do you think I'd have refused to take her in, if I'd known she was yours?"

At that moment Godfrey felt all the bitterness of an error that was not simply futile, but had defeated its own end. He had not measured this wife with whom he had lived so long. But she spoke again, with more agitation.

"And—O, Godfrey—if we'd had her from the first, if you'd taken to her as you ought, she'd have loved me for her mother—and you'd have been happier with me: I could better have bore my little baby dying, and our life might have been more like what we used to think it 'ud be."

The tears fell, and Nancy ceased to speak.

"But you wouldn't have married me then, Nancy, if I'd told you," said Godfrey, urged, in the bitterness of his self-reproach, to prove to himself that his conduct had not been utter folly. "You may think you would now, but you wouldn't then. With your pride and your father's, you'd have hated having anything to do with me after the talk there'd have been."

"I can't say what I should have done about that, Godfrey. I should never have married anybody else. But I wasn't worth doing wrong for—nothing is in this world. Nothing is so good as it seems beforehand—not even our marrying wasn't, you see." There was a faint sad smile on Nancy's face as she said the last words.

"I'm a worse man than you thought I was, Nancy," said Godfrey, rather tremulously. "Can you forgive me ever?"

"The wrong to me is but little, Godfrey: you've made it up to me—you've been good to me for fifteen years. It's another you did the wrong to; and I doubt it can never be all made up for."

"But we can take Eppie now," said Godfrey. "I won't mind the world knowing at last. I'll be plain and open for the rest o' my life."

"It'll be different coming to us, now she's grown up," said Nancy, shaking her head sadly. "But it's your duty to acknowledge her and provide for her; and I'll do my part by her, and pray to God Almighty to make her love me."

"Then we'll go together to Silas Marner's this very night, as soon as everything's quiet at the Stone-pits."

CHAPTER XIX

B ETWEEN EIGHT AND NINE o'clock that evening, Eppie and Silas were seated alone in the cottage. After the great excitement the weaver had undergone from the events of the afternoon, he had felt a longing for this quietude, and had even begged Mrs. Winthrop and Aaron, who had naturally lingered behind every one else, to leave him alone with his child. The excitement had not passed away: it had only reached that stage when the keenness of the susceptibility makes external stimulus intolerable—when there is no sense of weariness, but rather an intensity of inward life, under which sleep is an impossibility. Any one who has watched such moments in other men remembers the brightness of the eyes and the strange definiteness that comes over coarse features from that transient influence. It is as if a new fineness of ear for all spiritual voices had sent wonder-working vibrations through the heavy mortal frame—as if "beauty born of murmuring sound"* had passed into the face of the listener.

Silas's face showed that sort of transfiguration, as he sat in his arm-chair and looked at Eppie. She had drawn her own chair toward his knees, and leaned forward, holding both his hands, while she looked up at him. On the table near them, lit by a candle, lay the recovered gold—the old long-loved gold, ranged in orderly heaps, as Silas used to range it in the days when it was his only joy. He had been telling her how he used to count it every night, and how his soul was utterly desolate till she was sent to him.

"At first, I'd a sort o' feeling come across me now and then," he was saying, in a subdued tone, "as if you might be changed into the

---

*From Wordsworth's poem that begins "Three years she grew . . ."

gold again; for sometimes, turn my head which way I would, I seemed to see the gold; and I thought I should be glad if I could feel it, and find it was come back. But that didn't last long. After a bit, I should have thought it was a curse come again, if it had drove you from me, for I'd got to feel the need o' your looks and your voice and the touch o' your little fingers. You didn't know then, Eppie, when you were such a little un—you didn't know what your old father Silas felt for you."

"But I know now, father," said Eppie. "If it hadn't been for you, they'd have taken me to the workhouse, and there'd have been nobody to love me."

"Eh, my precious child, the blessing was mine. If you hadn't been sent to save me, I should ha' gone to the grave in my misery. The money was taken away from me in time; and you see it's been kept—kept till it was wanted for you. It's wonderful—our life is wonderful."

Silas sat in silence a few minutes, looking at the money. "It takes no hold of me now," he said, ponderingly—"the money doesn't. I wonder if it ever could again—I doubt it might, if I lost you, Eppie. I might come to think I was forsaken again, and lose the feeling that God was good to me."

At that moment there was a knocking at the door; and Eppie was obliged to rise without answering Silas. Beautiful she looked, with the tenderness of gathering tears in her eyes, and a slight flush on her cheeks, as she stepped to open the door. The flush deepened when she saw Mr. and Mrs. Godfrey Cass. She made her little rustic curtsy, and held the door wide for them to enter.

"We're disturbing you very late, my dear," said Mrs. Cass, taking Eppie's hand and looking in her face with an expression of anxious interest and admiration. Nancy herself was pale and tremulous.

Eppie, after placing chairs for Mr. and Mrs. Cass, went to stand against Silas, opposite to them.

"Well, Marner," said Godfrey, trying to speak with perfect firmness, "it's a great comfort to me to see you with your money again, that you've been deprived of so many years. It was one of my family did you the wrong—the more grief to me—and I feel bound to make up to you for it in every way. Whatever I can do for you will be nothing but paying a debt, even if I looked no further than the robbery.

But there are other things I'm beholden—shall be beholden to you for, Marner."

Godfrey checked himself. It had been agreed between him and his wife that the subject of his fatherhood should be approached very carefully, and that, if possible, the disclosure should be reserved for the future, so that it might be made to Eppie gradually. Nancy had urged this, because she felt strongly the painful light in which Eppie must inevitably see the relation between her father and mother.

Silas, always ill at ease when he was being spoken to by "betters," such as Mr. Cass—tall, powerful, florid men, seen chiefly on horseback—answered with some constraint—

"Sir, I've a deal to thank you for a'ready. As for the robbery, I count it no loss to me. And if I did, you couldn't help it: you aren't answerable for it."

"You may look at it in that way, Marner, but I never can; and I hope you'll let me act according to my own feeling of what's just. I know you're easily contented: you've been a hard-working man all your life."

"Yes, sir, yes," said Marner, meditatively. "I should ha' been bad off without my work: it was what I held by when everything else was gone from me."

"Ah," said Godfrey, applying Marner's words simply to his bodily wants, "it was a good trade for you in this country, because there's been a great deal of linen-weaving to be done. But you're getting rather past such close work, Marner: it's time you laid by and had some rest. You look a good deal pulled down, though you're not an old man, *are* you?"

"Fifty-five, as near as I can say, sir," said Silas.

"Oh, why, you may live thirty years longer—look at old Macey! And that money on the table, after all, is but little. It won't go far either way—whether it's put out to interest, or you were to live on it as long as it would last: it wouldn't go far if you'd nobody to keep but yourself, and you've had two to keep for a good many years now."

"Eh, sir," said Silas, unaffected by anything Godfrey was saying, "I'm in no fear o' want. We shall do very well—Eppie and me 'ull do well enough. There's few working-folks have got so much laid by as that. I don't know what it is to gentlefolks, but I look upon it as a deal—almost too much. And as for us, it's little we want."

"Only the garden, father," said Eppie, blushing up to the ears the moment after.

"You love a garden, do you, my dear?" said Nancy, thinking that this turn in the point of view might help her husband. "We should agree in that: I give a deal of time to the garden."

"Ah, there's plenty of gardening at the Red House," said Godfrey, surprised at the difficulty he found in approaching a proposition which had seemed so easy to him in the distance. "You've done a good part by Eppie, Marner, for sixteen years. It 'ud be a great comfort to you to see her well provided for, wouldn't it? She looks blooming and healthy, but not fit for any hardships: she doesn't look like a strapping girl come of working parents. You'd like to see her taken care of by those who can leave her well off, and make a lady of her; she's more fit for it than for a rough life, such as she might come to have in a few years' time."

A slight flush came over Marner's face, and disappeared, like a passing gleam. Eppie was simply wondering Mr. Cass should talk so about things that seemed to have nothing to do with reality, but Silas was hurt and uneasy.

"I don't take your meaning, sir," he answered, not having words at command to express the mingled feelings with which he had heard Mr. Cass's words.

"Well, my meaning is this, Marner," said Godfrey, determined to come to the point. "Mrs. Cass and I, you know, have no children—nobody to be the better for our good home and everything else we have—more than enough for ourselves. And we should like to have somebody in the place of a daughter to us—we should like to have Eppie, and treat her in every way as our own child. It 'ud be a great comfort to you in your old age, I hope, to see her fortune made in that way, after you've been at the trouble of bringing her up so well. And it's right you should have every reward for that. And Eppie, I'm sure, will always love you and be grateful to you: she'd come and see you very often, and we should all be on the lookout out to do everything we could toward making you comfortable."

A plain man like Godfrey Cass, speaking under some embarrassment, necessarily blunders on words that are coarser than his intentions, and that are likely to fall gratingly on susceptible feelings. While he had been speaking, Eppie had quietly passed her arm behind Silas's head, and let her hand rest against it caressingly: she felt him trembling violently. He was silent for some moments when Mr. Cass had ended—powerless under the conflict of emotions, all alike painful. Eppie's heart was swelling at the sense that her father was in distress; and she was just going to lean down and speak to him, when one struggling dread at last gained the mastery over every other in Silas, and he said, faintly—

"Eppie, my child, speak. I won't stand in your way. Thank Mr. and Mrs. Cass."

Eppie took her hand from her father's head, and came forward a step. Her cheeks were flushed, but not with shyness this time, the sense that her father was in doubt and suffering banished that sort of self-consciousness. She dropped a low curtsy, first to Mrs. Cass and then to Mr. Cass, and said—

"Thank you, ma'am—thank you, sir. But I can't leave my father, nor own anybody nearer than him. And I don't want to be a lady— thank you all the same" (here Eppie dropped another curtsy.) "I couldn't give up the folks I've been used to."

Eppie's lip began to tremble a little at the last words. She retreated to her father's chair again, and held him round the neck: while Silas, with a subdued sob, put up his hand to grasp hers.

The tears were in Nancy's eyes, but her sympathy with Eppie was, naturally, divided with distress on her husband's account. She dared not speak, wondering what was going on in her husband's mind.

Godfrey felt an irritation inevitable to almost all of us when we encounter an unexpected obstacle. He had been full of his own penitence and resolution to retrieve his error as far as the time was left to him; he was possessed with all-important feelings, that were to lead to a predetermined course of action which he had fixed on as the right, and he was not prepared to enter with lively appreciation into other people's feelings counteracting his virtuous resolves. The agitation with which he spoke again was not quite unmixed with anger.

"But I've a claim on you, Eppie—the strongest of all claims. It's my duty, Marner, to own Eppie as my child, and provide for her. She's my own child: her mother was my wife. I've a natural claim on her that must stand before every other."

Eppie had given a violent start, and turned quite pale. Silas, on the contrary, who had been relieved, by Eppie's answer, from the dread lest his mind should be in opposition to hers, felt the spirit of resistance in him set free, not without a touch of parental fierceness. "Then, sir," he answered, with an accent of bitterness that had been silent in him since the memorable day when his youthful hope had perished—"then, sir, why didn't you say so sixteen year ago, and claim her before I'd come to love her, i'stead o' coming to take her from me now, when you might as well take the heart out o' my body? God gave her to me because you turned your back upon her, and He looks upon her as mine: you've no right to her! When a man turns a blessing from his door, it falls to them as take it in."

"I know that, Marner. I was wrong. I've repented of my conduct in that matter," said Godfrey, who could not help feeling the edge of Silas's words.

"I'm glad to hear it, sir," said Marner, with gathering excitement; "but repentance doesn't alter what's been going on for sixteen year. Your coming now and saying 'I'm her father' doesn't alter the feelings inside us. It's me she's been calling her father ever since she could say the word."

"But I think you might look at the thing more reasonably, Marner," said Godfrey, unexpectedly awed by the weaver's direct truth-speaking. "It isn't as if she was to be taken quite away from you, so that you'd never see her again. She'll be very near you, and come to see you very often. She'll feel just the same toward you."

"Just the same?" said Marner, more bitterly than ever. "How'll she feel just the same for me as she does now, when we eat o' the same bit, and drink o' the same cup, and think o' the same things from one day's end to another? Just the same? that's idle talk. You'd cut us i' two."

Godfrey, unqualified by experience to discern the pregnancy of Marner's simple words, felt rather angry again. It seemed to him that the weaver was very selfish (a judgment readily passed by those who have never tested their own power of sacrifice) to oppose what was undoubtedly for Eppie's welfare; and he felt himself called upon, for her sake, to assert his authority.

"I should have thought, Marner," he said, severely—"I should have thought your affection for Eppie would make you rejoice in what was for her good, even if it did call upon you to give up something. You ought to remember your own life's uncertain, and she's at an age now when her lot may soon be fixed in a way very different from what it would be in her father's home: she may marry some low working-man, and then, whatever I might do for her, I couldn't make her well-off. You're putting yourself in the way of her welfare; and though I'm sorry to hurt you after what you've done, and what I've left undone, I feel now it's my duty to insist on taking care of my own daughter. I want to do my duty."

It would be difficult to say whether it were Silas or Eppie that was more deeply stirred by this last speech of Godfrey's. Thought had been very busy in Eppie as she listened to the contest between her old long-loved father and this new unfamiliar father who had suddenly come to fill the place of that black featureless shadow which had held the ring and placed it on her mother's finger. Her imagination had darted backward in conjectures, and forward in previsions, of what this revealed fatherhood implied; and there were words in Godfrey's last speech which helped to make the previsions especially definite. Not that these thoughts, either of past or future, determined her resolution—*that* was determined by the feelings which vibrated to every word Silas had uttered; but they raised, even apart from these feelings, a repulsion toward the offered lot and the newly-revealed father.

Silas, on the other hand, was again stricken in conscience, and alarmed lest Godfrey's accusation should be true—lest he should be raising his own will as an obstacle to Eppie's good. For many moments he was mute, struggling for the self-conquest necessary to the uttering of the difficult words. They came out tremulously.

"I'll say no more. Let it be as you will. Speak to the child. I'll hinder nothing."

Even Nancy, with all the acute sensibility of her own affections, shared her husband's view, that Marner was not justifiable in his wish to retain Eppie, after her real father had avowed himself. She felt that it was a very hard trial for the poor weaver, but her code allowed no question that a father by blood must have a claim above that of any foster-father. Besides, Nancy used all her life to plenteous circumstances and the privileges of "respectability," could not enter into the pleasures which early nurture and habit connect with all the little aims and efforts of the poor who are born poor: to her mind, Eppie, in being restored to her birthright, was entering on a too long withheld but unquestionable good. Hence she heard Silas's last words with relief, and thought, as Godfrey did, that their wish was achieved.

"Eppie, my dear," said Godfrey, looking at his daughter, not without some embarrassment, under the sense that she was old enough to judge him, "it'll always be our wish that you should show your love and gratitude to one who's been a father to you so many years, and we shall want to help you to make him comfortable in every way. But we hope you'll come to love us as well; and though I haven't been what a father should ha' been to you all these years, I wish to do the utmost in my power for you for the rest of my life, and provide for you as my only child. And you'll have the best of mothers in my wife—that'll be a blessing you haven't known since you were old enough to know it."

"My dear, you'll be a treasure to me," said Nancy, in her gentle voice. "We shall want for nothing when we have our daughter."

Eppie did not come forward and curtsy, as she had done before. She held Silas's hand in hers, and grasped it firmly—it was a weaver's hand, with a palm and fingertips that were sensitive to such pressure—while she spoke with colder decision than before.

"Thank you, ma'am—thank you, sir, for your offers—they're very great, and far above my wish. For I should have no delight i' life any more if I was forced to go away from my father, and knew he was sitting at home, a-thinking of me and feeling lone. We've been used to be happy together every day, and I can't think o' no happiness without him. And he says he'd nobody i' the world till I was sent to him, and he'd have nothing when I was gone. And he's took care of me and loved me from the first, and I'll cleave to him as long as he lives, and nobody shall ever come between him and me."

"But you must make sure, Eppie," said Silas, in a low voice—"you must make sure as you won't ever be sorry, because you've made your choice to stay among poor folks, and with poor clothes and things, when you might ha' had everything o' the best."

His sensitiveness on this point had increased as he listened to Eppie's words of faithful affection.

"I can never be sorry, father," said Eppie. "I shouldn't know what to think on or to wish for with fine things about me, as I haven't been used to. And it 'ud be poor work for me to put on things, and ride in a gig, and sit in a place at church, as 'ud make them as I'm fond of think me unfitting company for 'em. What could I care for then?"

Nancy looked at Godfrey with a pained questioning glance. But his eyes were fixed on the floor, where he was moving the end of his stick, as if he were pondering on something absently. She thought there was a word which might perhaps come better from her lips than from his.

"What you say is natural, my dear child—it's natural you should cling to those who've brought you up," she said mildly; "but there's a duty you owe to your lawful father. There's perhaps something to be given up on more sides than one. When your father opens his home to you, I think it's right you shouldn't turn your back on it."

"I can't feel as I've got any father but one," said Eppie, impetuously, while the tears gathered. "I've always thought of a little home where he'd sit i' the corner, and I should fend and do everything for him: I can't think o' no other home. I wasn't brought up to be a lady, and I can't turn my mind to it. I like the working-folks, and their victuals, and their ways. And," she ended passionately, while the tears fell, "I'm promised to marry a working-man, as'll live with father, and help me to take care of him."

Godfrey looked up at Nancy with a flushed face and smarting dilated eyes. This frustration of a purpose toward which he had set out under the exalted consciousness that he was about to compensate in some degree for the greatest demerit of his life, made him feel the air of the room stifling.

"Let us go," he said in an under-tone.

"We won't talk of this any longer now," said Nancy, rising. "We're your well-wishers, my dear—and yours too, Marner. We shall come and see you again. It's getting late now."

In this way she covered her husband's abrupt departure, for Godfrey had gone straight to the door, unable to say more.

CHAPTER XX

NANCY AND GODFREY WALKED home under the starlight in silence. When they entered the oaken parlor, Godfrey threw himself into his chair, while Nancy laid down her bonnet and shawl, and stood on the hearth near her husband, unwilling to leave him even for a few minutes, and yet fearing to utter any word lest it might jar on his feeling. At last Godfrey turned his head toward her, and their eyes met, dwelling in that meeting without any movement on either side. That quiet mutual gaze of a trusting husband and wife is like the first moment of rest or refuge from a great weariness or a great danger—not to be interfered with by speech or action which would distract the sensations from the fresh enjoyment of repose.

But presently he put out his hand, and as Nancy placed hers within it, he drew her toward him, and said—

"That's ended!"

She bent to kiss him, and then said, as she stood by his side, "Yes, I'm afraid we must give up the hope of having her for a daughter. It wouldn't be right to want to force her to come to us against her will. We can't alter her bringing up and what's come of it."

"No," said Godfrey, with a keen decisiveness of tone, in contrast with his usually careless and unemphatic speech—"there's debts we can't pay like money debts, by paying extra for the years that have slipped by. While I've been putting off and putting off, the trees have been growing—it's too late now. Marner was in the right in what he said about a man's turning away a blessing from his door: it falls to somebody else. I wanted to pass for childless once, Nancy—I shall pass for childless now against my wish."

Nancy did not speak immediately, but after a little while she asked—"You won't make it known, then, about Eppie's being your daughter?"

"No: where would be the good to anybody?—only harm. I must do what I can for her in the state of life she chooses. I must see who it is she is thinking of marrying."

"If it won't do any good to make the thing known," said Nancy, who thought she might now allow herself the relief of entertaining a feeling which she had tried to silence before, "I should be very thankful for father and Priscilla never to be troubled with knowing what was done in the past, more than about Dunsey, it can't be helped, their knowing that."

"I shall put it in my will—I think I shall put it in my will. I shouldn't like to leave anything to be found out like this about Dunsey," said Godfrey, meditatively. "But I can't see anything but difficulties that 'ud come from telling it now. I must do what I can to make her happy in her own way. I've a notion," he added, after a moment's pause, "it's Aaron Winthrop she meant she was engaged to. I remember seeing him with her and Marner going away from church."

"Well, he's very sober and industrious," said Nancy, trying to view the matter as cheerfully as possible.

Godfrey fell into thoughtfulness again. Presently he looked up at Nancy sorrowfully, and said—

"She's a very pretty nice girl, isn't she, Nancy?"

"Yes, dear; and with just your hair and eyes: I wondered it had never struck me before."

"I think she took a dislike to me at the thought of my being her father: I could see a change in her manner after that."

"She couldn't bear to think of not looking on Marner as her father," said Nancy, not wishing to confirm her husband's painful impression.

"She thinks I did wrong by her mother as well as by her. She thinks me worse than I am. But she *must* think it: she can never know all. It's part of my punishment, Nancy, for my daughter to dislike me. I should never have got into that trouble if I'd been true to you—if I hadn't been a fool. I'd no right to expect anything but evil could come of that marriage—and when I shirked doing a father's part too."

Nancy was silent: her spirit of rectitude would not let her try to soften the edge of what she felt to be a just compunction. He spoke again after a little while, but the tone was rather changed: there was tenderness mingled with the previous self-reproach.

"And I got *you*, Nancy, in spite of all; and yet I've been grumbling and uneasy because I hadn't something else—as if I deserved it."

"You've never been wanting to me, Godfrey," said Nancy, with quiet sincerity. "My only trouble would be gone if you resigned yourself to the lot that's been given us."

"Well, perhaps it isn't too late to mend a bit there. Though it is too late to mend some things, say what they will."

CHAPTER XXI

THE NEXT MORNING, WHEN Silas and Eppie were seated at their breakfast, he said to her—

"Eppie, there's a thing I've had on my mind to do this two year, and now the money's been brought back to us, we can do it. I've been turning it over and over in the night, and I think we'll set out to-morrow, while the fine days last. We'll leave the house and everything for your godmother to take care on, and we'll make a little bundle o' things and set out."

"Where to go, daddy?" said Eppie, in much surprise.

"To my old country—to the town where I was born—up Lantern Yard. I want to see Mr. Paston, the minister: something may ha' come out to make 'em know I was innicent o' the robbery. And Mr. Paston was a man with a deal o' light—I want to speak to him about the drawing o' the lots. And I should like to talk to him about the religion o' this country-side, for I partly think he doesn't know on it."

Eppie was very joyful, for there was the prospect not only of wonder and delight at seeing a strange country, but also of coming back to tell Aaron all about it. Aaron was so much wiser than she was about most things—it would be rather pleasant to have this little advantage over him. Mrs. Winthrop, though possessed with a dim fear of dangers attendant on so long a journey, and requiring many assurances that it would not take them out of the region of carriers' carts and slow wagons, was nevertheless well pleased that Silas should revisit his own country, and find out if he had been cleared from that false accusation.

"You'd be easier in your mind for the rest o' your life, Master Marner," said Dolly—"that you would. And if there's any light to be

got up the Yard as you talk on, we've need of it i' this world, and I'd
be glad on it myself, if you could bring it back."

So on the fourth day from that time, Silas and Eppie, in their
Sunday clothes, with a small bundle tied in a blue linen handkerchief,
were making their way through the streets of a great manufacturing
town. Silas, bewildered by the changes thirty years had brought over
his native place had stopped several persons in succession to ask them
the name of this town, that he might be sure he was not under a mistake about it.

"Ask for Lantern Yard, father—ask this gentleman with the tas-
sels on his shoulders a-standing at the shop door; he isn't in a hurry
like the rest," said Eppie, in some distress at her father's bewilderment, and ill at ease, besides, amidst the noise, the movement, and
the multitude of strange indifferent faces.

"Eh, my child, he won't know anything about it," said Silas;
"gentlefolks didn't ever go up the Yard. But happen somebody can tell
me which is the way to Prison Street, where the jail is. I know the
way out o' that as if I'd seen it yesterday."

With some difficulty, after many turnings and new inquiries,
they reached Prison Street; and the grim walls of the jail, the first object that answered to any image in Silas's memory, cheered him with
the certitude, which no assurance of the town's name had hitherto
given him, that he was in his native place.

"Ah," he said, drawing a long breath, "there's the jail, Eppie;
that's just the same: I aren't afraid now. It's the third turning on the
left hand from the jail doors—that's the way we must go."

"O, what a dark ugly place!" said Eppie. "How it hides the sky!
It's worse than the Workhouse. I'm glad you don't live in this town
now, father. Is Lantern Yard like this street?"

"My precious child," said Silas, smiling, "it isn't a big street like
this. I never was easy i' this street myself, but I was fond o' Lantern
Yard. The shops here are all altered, I think—I can't make 'em out;
but I shall know the turning, because it's the third."

"Here it is," he said, in a tone of satisfaction, as they came to a
narrow alley. "And then we must go to the left again, and then
straight for'ard a bit, up Shoe Lane: and then we shall be at the entry
next to the o'erhanging window, where there's the nick in the road
for the water to run. Eh, I can see it all."

"O father, I'm like as if I was stifled," said Eppie. "I couldn't ha' thought as any folks lived i' this way, so close together. How pretty the Stone-pits 'ull look when we get back!"

"It looks comical to me, child, now—and smells bad. I can't think as it usened to smell so."

Here and there a sallow, begrimed face looked out from a gloomy doorway at the strangers, and increased Eppie's uneasiness, so that it was a longed-for relief when they issued from the alleys into Shoe Lane, where there was a broader strip of sky.

"Dear heart!" said Silas, "why, there's people coming out o' the Yard as if they'd been to chapel at this time o' day—a weekday noon!"

Suddenly he started and stood still with a look of distressed amazement, that alarmed Eppie. They were before an opening in front of a large factory, from which men and women were streaming for their midday meal.

"Father," said Eppie, clasping his arm, "what's the matter?"

But she had to speak again and again before Silas could answer her.

"It's gone, child," he said, at last, in strong agitation—"Lantern Yard's gone. It must ha' been here, because here's the house with the o'erhanging window—I know that—it's just the same; but they've made this new opening; and see that big factory! It's all gone—chapel and all."

"Come into that little brush-shop and sit down, father—they'll let you sit down," said Eppie, always on the watch lest one of her father's strange attacks should come on. "Perhaps the people can tell you all about it."

But neither from the brush-maker, who had come to Shoe Lane only ten years ago, when the factory was already built, nor from any other source within his reach, could Silas learn anything of the old Lantern Yard friends, or of Mr. Paston the minister.

"The old place is all swep' away," Silas said to Dolly Winthrop on the night of his return—"the little graveyard and everything. The old home's gone; I've no home but this now. I shall never know whether they got at the truth o' the robbery, nor whether Mr. Paston could ha' given me any light about the drawing o' the lots. It's dark to me, Mrs. Winthrop, that is; I doubt it'll be dark to the last."

"Well, yes, Master Marner," said Dolly, who sat with a placid listening face, now bordered by gray hairs; "I doubt it may. It's the will o' Them above as a many things should be dark to us; but there's some things as I've never felt i' the dark about, and they're mostly what comes i' the day's work. You were hard done by that once, Master Marner, and it seems as you'll never know the rights of it; but that doesn't hinder there *being* a rights, Master Marner, for all it's dark to you and me."

"No," said Silas, "no; that doesn't hinder. Since the time the child was sent to me and I've come to love her as myself, I've had light enough to trusten by; and-now she says she'll never leave me, I think I shall trusten till I die."

CONCLUSION

THERE WAS ONE TIME of the year which was held in Raveloe to be especially suitable for a wedding. It was when the great lilacs and laburnums in the old-fashioned gardens showed their golden and purple wealth above the lichen-tinted walls, and when there were calves still young enough to want bucketfuls of fragrant milk. People were not so busy then as they must become when the full cheese-making and the mowing had set in; and besides, it was a time when a light bridal dress could be worn with comfort and seen to advantage.

Happily the sunshine fell more warmly than usual on the lilac tufts the morning that Eppie was married, for her dress was a very light one. She had often thought, though with a feeling of renunciation, that the perfection of a wedding-dress would be a white cotton, with the tiniest pink sprig at wide intervals; so that when Mrs. Godfrey Cass begged to provide one, and asked Eppie to choose what it should be, previous meditation had enabled her to give a decided answer at once.

Seen at a little distance as she walked across the churchyard and down the village, she seemed to be attired in pure white, and her hair looked like the dash of gold on a lily. One hand was on her husband's arm, and with the other she clasped the hand of her father Silas.

"You won't be giving me away, father," she had said before they went to church; "you'll only be taking Aaron to be a son to you."

Dolly Winthrop walked behind with her husband; and there ended the little bridal procession.

There were many eyes to look at it, and Miss Priscilla Lammeter was glad that she and her father had happened to drive up to the door of the Red House just in time to see this pretty sight. They had come to keep Nancy company to-day, because Mr. Cass had had to go away to Lytherley, for special reasons. That seemed to be a pity, for otherwise he might have gone, as Mr. Crackenthorp and Mr. Osgood certainly would, to look on at the wedding feast which he had ordered at the Rainbow, naturally feeling a great interest in the weaver who had been wronged by one of his own family.

"I could ha' wished Nancy had had the luck to find a child like that and bring her up," said Priscilla to her father, as they sat in the gig; "I should ha' had something young to think of then, besides the lambs and the calves."

"Yes, my dear, yes," said Mr. Lammeter; "one feels that as one gets older. Things look dim to old folks: they'd need have some young eyes about 'em, to let 'em know the world's the same as it used to be."

Nancy came out now to welcome her father and sister; and the wedding group had passed on beyond the Red House to the humbler part of the village.

Dolly Winthrop was the first to divine that old Mr. Macey, who had been set in his arm-chair outside his own door, would expect some special notice as they passed, since he was too old to be at the wedding feast.

"Mr. Macey's looking for a word from us," said Dolly; "he'll be hurt if we pass him and say nothing—and him so racked with rheumatiz."

So they turned aside to shake hands with the old man. He had looked forward to the occasion, and had his premeditated speech.

"Well, Master Marner," he said, in a voice that quavered a good deal, "I've lived to see my words come true. I was the first to say there was no harm in you, though your looks might be again' you; and I was the first to say you'd get your money back. And it's nothing but rightful as you should. And I'd ha' said the 'Amens,' and willing, at the holy matrimony; but Tookey's done it a good while now, and I hope you'll have none the worse luck."

In the open yard before the Rainbow the party of guests were already assembled, though it was still nearly an hour before the appointed feast time. But by this means they could not only enjoy the slow advent of their pleasure; they had also ample leisure to talk of Silas Marner's strange history, and arrive by due degrees at the conclusion that he had brought a blessing on himself by acting like a father to a lone motherless child. Even the farrier did not negative this sentiment; on the contrary, he took it up as peculiarly his own, and invited any hardy person present to contradict him. But he met with no contradiction; and all differences among the company were merged in a general agreement with Mr. Snell's sentiment, that when a man had deserved his good luck, it was the part of his neighbors to wish him joy.

As the bridal group approached, a hearty cheer was raised in the Rainbow yard; and Ben Winthrop, whose jokes had retained their acceptable flavor, found it agreeable to turn in there and receive congratulations; not requiring the proposed interval of quiet at the Stone-pits before joining the company.

Eppie had a larger garden than she had ever expected there now; and in other ways there had been alterations at the expense of Mr. Cass, the landlord, to suit Silas's larger family. For he and Eppie had declared that they would rather stay at the Stone-pits than go to any new home. The garden was fenced with stones on two sides, but in front there was an open fence, through which the flowers shone with answering gladness, as the four united people came within sight of them.

"O father," said Eppie, "what a pretty home ours is! I think nobody could be happier than we are."

THE LIFTED VEIL

Give me no light, great Heaven, but such as turns
To energy of human fellowship;
No powers beyond the growing heritage
That makes completer manhood.[1]

CHAPTER I

THE TIME OF MY end approaches. I have lately been subject to attacks of *angina pectoris;** and in the ordinary course of things, my physician tells me, I may fairly hope that my life will not be protracted many months. Unless, then, I am cursed with an exceptional physical constitution, as I am cursed with an exceptional mental character, I shall not much longer groan under the wearisome burden of this earthly existence. If it were to be otherwise—if I were to live on to the age most men desire and provide for—I should, for once, have known whether the miseries of delusive expectation can outweigh the miseries of true prevision. For I foresee when I shall die, and everything that will happen in my last moments.

Just a month from this day, on the twentieth of September, 1850, I shall be sitting in this chair, in this study, at ten o'clock at night, longing to die, weary of incessant insight and foresight, without delusions and without hope. Just as I am watching a tongue of blue flame rising in the fire, and my lamp is burning low, the horrible contraction will begin at my chest. I shall only have time to reach the bell and pull it violently, before the sense of suffocation will come. No one will answer my bell. I know why. My two servants are lovers, and will have quarreled. My housekeeper will have rushed out of the house, in a fury, two hours before, hoping that Perry will believe she has gone to drown herself. Perry is alarmed at last, and is gone out after her. The little scullery-maid is asleep on a bench: she never answers the bell; it does not wake her. The sense of suffocation increases: my lamp goes out with a horrible stench: I make a great effort and snatch at the bell again. I long for life, and there is no help. I thirsted for the unknown: the thirst is gone. O God, let me stay with the known, and be weary of it: I am content. Agony of pain and suffocation—and all the while the earth, the fields, the pebbly brook at the bottom of the rookery, the fresh scent after the rain, the

---

*Latin name for a disease of the heart; here it is probably used both literally and symbolically.

light of the morning through my chamber window, the warmth of the hearth after the frosty air—will darkness close over them forever?

Darkness—darkness—no pain—nothing but darkness: but I am passing on and on through the darkness: my thought stays in the darkness, but always with a sense of moving onward ——

Before that time comes, I wish to use my last hours of ease and strength in telling the strange story of my experience. I have never fully unbosomed myself to any human being; I have never been encouraged to trust much in the sympathy of my fellow-men. But we have all a chance of meeting with some pity, some tenderness, some charity when we are dead; it is the living only who cannot be forgiven—the living only from whom men's indulgence and reverence are held off, like the rain by the hard east wind. While the heart beats, bruise it— it is your only opportunity; while the eye can still turn toward you with moist, timid entreaty, freeze it with an icy, unanswering gaze; while the ear, that delicate messenger to the inmost sanctuary of the soul, can still take in the tones of kindness, put it off with hard civility, or sneering compliment, or envious affectation of indifference; while the creative brain can still throb with the sense of injustice, with the yearning for brotherly recognition—make haste—oppress it with your ill-considered judgments, your trivial comparisons, your careless misrepresentations. The heart will by-and-by be still—*ubi sæva indignatio ulterius cor lacerare nequit;** the eye will cease to entreat; the ear will be deaf; the brain will have ceased from all wants as well as from all work. Then your charitable speeches may find vent; then you may remember and pity the toil and the struggle and the failure; then you may give due honor to the work achieved; then you may find extenuation for errors, and may consent to bury them.

That is a trivial schoolboy text; why do I dwell on it? It has little reference to me, for I shall leave no works behind me for men to honor. I have no near relatives who will make up, by weeping over my grave, for the wounds they inflicted on me when I was among them. It is only the story of my life that will perhaps win a little more sympathy from strangers when I am dead, than I ever believed it would obtain from my friends while I was living.

---

*"Where savage indignation can no longer lacerate the heart" (Latin). Inscribed on Swift's tombstone [author's note].

My childhood perhaps seems happier to me than it really was, by contrast with all the after-years. For then the curtain of the future was as impenetrable to me as to other children: I had all their delight in the present hour, their sweet indefinite hopes for the morrow; and I had a tender mother: even now, after the dreary lapse of long years, a slight trace of sensation accompanies the remembrance of her caress as she held me on her knee—her arms round my little body, her cheek pressed against mine. I had a complaint of the eyes that made me blind for a little while, and she kept me on her knee from morning till night. That unequaled love soon vanished out of my life, and even to my childish consciousness it was as if that life had become more chill. I rode my little white pony with the groom by my side as before, but there were no loving eyes looking at me as I mounted, no glad arms open to me when I came back. Perhaps I missed my mother's love more than most children of seven or eight would have done, to whom the other pleasures of life remained as before; for I was certainly a very sensitive child. I remember still the mingled trepidation and delicious excitement with which I was affected by the tramping of the horses on the pavement in the echoing stables, by the loud resonance of the grooms' voices, by the booming bark of the dogs as my father's carriage thundered under the archway of the courtyard, by the din of the gong as it gave notice of luncheon and dinner. The measured tramp of soldiery which I sometimes heard— for my father's house lay near a county town where there were large barracks—made me sob and tremble; and yet when they were gone past, I longed for them to come back again.

I fancy my father thought me an odd child, and had little fondness for me; though he was very careful in fulfilling what he regarded as a parent's duties. But he was already past the middle of life, and I was not his only son. My mother had been his second wife, and he was five-and-forty when he married her. He was a firm, unbending, intensely orderly man, in root and stem a banker, but with a flourishing graft of the active landholder, aspiring to county influence: one of those people who are always like themselves from day to day, who are uninfluenced by the weather, and neither know melancholy nor high spirits. I held him in great awe, and appeared more timid and sensitive in his presence than at other times; a circumstance which, perhaps, helped to confirm him in the intention to educate

me on a different plan from the prescriptive one with which he had
complied in the case of my elder brother, already a tall youth at Eton.
My brother was to be his representative and successor; he must go to
Eton and Oxford, for the sake of making connections, of course: my
father was not a man to underrate the bearing of Latin satirists or
Greek dramatists on the attainment of an aristocratic position. But,
intrinsically, he had slight esteem for "those dead but sceptred spirits"; having qualified himself for forming an independent opinion by
reading Potter's "Æschylus," and dipping into Francis's "Horace." To
this negative view he added a positive one, derived from a recent
connection with mining speculations; namely, that a scientific education was the really useful training for a younger son. Moreover, it was
clear that a shy, sensitive boy like me was not fit to encounter the
rough experience of a public school. Mr. Letherall had said so very
decidedly. Mr. Letherall was a large man in spectacles, who one day
took my small head between his large hands, and pressed it here and
there in an exploratory, suspicious manner—then placed each of his
great thumbs on my temples, and pushed me a little way from him,
and stared at me with glittering spectacles. The contemplation appeared to displease him, for he frowned sternly, and said to my father, drawing his thumbs across my eyebrows—

"The deficiency is there, sir—there; and here," he added, touching the upper sides of my head, "here is the excess. That must be
brought out, sir, and this must be laid to sleep."[2]

I was in a state of tremor, partly at the vague idea that I was the
object of reprobation, partly in the agitation of my first hatred—
hatred of this big, spectacled man, who pulled my head about as if
he wanted to buy and cheapen it.

I am not aware how much Mr. Letherall had to do with the system afterward adopted toward me, but it was presently clear that private tutors, natural history, science, and the modern languages, were
the appliances by which the defects of my organization were to be
remedied. I was very stupid about machines, so I was to be greatly
occupied with them; I had no memory for classification, so it was
particularly necessary that I should study systematic zoology and
botany; I was hungry for human deeds and human emotions, so I
was to be plentifully crammed with the mechanical powers, the ele-
mentary bodies, and the phenomena of electricity and magnetism. A

better-constituted boy would certainly have profited under my intelligent tutors, with their scientific apparatus; and would, doubtless, have found the phenomena of electricity and magnetism as fascinating as I was, every Thursday, assured they were. As it was, I could have paired off, for ignorance of whatever was taught me, with the worst Latin scholar that was ever turned out of a classical academy. I read Plutarch, and Shakespeare, and Don Quixote by the sly, and supplied myself in that way with wandering thoughts, while my tutor was assuring me that "an improved man, as distinguished from an ignorant one, was a man who knew the reason why water ran down-hill." I had no desire to be this improved man; I was glad of the running water; I could watch it and listen to it gurgling among the pebbles, and bathing the bright green water-plants, by the hour together. I did not want to know *why* it ran; I had perfect confidence that there were good reasons for what was so very beautiful.

There is no need to dwell on this part of my life. I have said enough to indicate that my nature was of the sensitive, unpractical order, and that it grew up in an uncongenial medium, which could never foster it into happy, healthy development. When I was sixteen I was sent to Geneva to complete my course of education; and the change was a very happy one to me, for the first sight of the Alps, with the setting sun on them, as we descended the Jura, seemed to me like an entrance into heaven; and the three years of my life there were spent in a perpetual sense of exaltation, as if from a draught of delicious wine, at the presence of Nature in all her awful loveliness. You will think, perhaps, that I must have been a poet, from this early sensibility to Nature. But my lot was not so happy as that. A poet pours forth his song and *believes* in the listening ear and answering soul, to which his song will be floated sooner or later. But the poet's sensibility without his voice—the poet's sensibility that finds no vent but in silent tears on the sunny bank, when the noonday light sparkles on the water, or in an inward shudder at the sound of harsh human tones, the sight of a cold human eye—this dumb passion brings with it a fatal solitude of soul in the society of one's fellow-men. My least solitary moments were those in which I pushed off in my boat, at evening, toward the center of the lake; it seemed to me that the sky, and the glowing mountain-tops, and the wide blue water, surrounded me with a cherishing love such as no human face had shed on me since my mother's love had vanished out of my life. I used to do as Jean Jacques did—lie down in my boat and let it glide where it would,* while I looked up at the departing glow leaving one mountain-top after the other, as if the prophet's chariot of fire were passing over them on its way to the home of light. Then when the white summits were all sad and corpse-like, I had to push home-ward, for I was under careful surveillance, and was allowed no late wanderings. This disposition of mine was not favorable to the forma-tion of intimate friendships among the numerous youths of my own age who are always to be found studying at Geneva. Yet I made one such friendship; and, singularly enough, it was with a youth whose intel-lectual tendencies were the very reverse of my own. I shall call him Charles Meunier; his real surname—an English one, for he was of En-glish extraction—having since become celebrated. He was an orphan, who lived on a miserable pittance while he pursued the medical stud-ies for which he had a special genius. Strange! that with my vague mind, susceptible and unobservant, hating inquiry and given up to contemplation, I should have been drawn toward a youth whose strongest passion was science. But the bond was not an intellectual one; it came from a source that can happily blend the stupid with the bril-liant, the dreamy with the practical: it came from community of feel-ing. Charles was poor and ugly, derided by Genevese *gamins*, and not acceptable in drawing-rooms. I saw that he was isolated, as I was, though from a different cause, and, stimulated by a sympathetic re-sentment, I made timid advances toward him. It is enough to say that there sprang up as much comradeship between us as our different habits would allow; and in Charles's rare holidays we went up the Salève together, or took the boat to Vevay, while I listened dreamily to the monologues in which he unfolded his bold conceptions of future experiment and discovery. I mingled them confusedly in my thought with glimpses of blue water and delicate floating cloud, with the notes of birds and the distant glitter of the glacier. He knew quite well that my mind was half absent, yet he liked to talk to me in this way; for don't we talk of our hopes and our projects even to dogs and birds, when they love us? I have mentioned this one friendship because of its

---

*The *Confessions* of French philosopher Jean-Jacques Rousseau (1712–1778) had an enormous influence on the development of Romantic thought and attitudes.

connection with a strange and terrible scene which I shall have to narrate in my subsequent life.

This happier life at Geneva was put an end to by a severe illness, which is partly a blank to me, partly a time of dimly-remembered suffering, with the presence of my father by my bed from time to time. Then came the languid monotony of convalescence, the days gradually breaking into variety and distinctness as my strength enabled me to take longer and longer drives. On one of these more vividly remembered days, my father said to me, as he sat beside my sofa—

"When you are quite well enough to travel, Latimer, I shall take you home with me. The journey will amuse you and do you good, for I shall go through the Tyrol and Austria, and you will see many new places. Our neighbors, the Filmores, are come; Alfred will join us at Basle, and we shall all go together to Vienna, and back by Prague ———"

My father was called away before he had finished his sentence, and he left my mind resting on the word *Prague*, with a strange sense that a new and wondrous scene was breaking upon me: a city under the broad sunshine, that seemed to me as if it were the summer sunshine of a long-past century arrested in its course—unrefreshed for ages by the dews of night, or the rushing rain-cloud; scorching the dusty, weary, time-eaten grandeur of a people doomed to live on in the stale repetition of memories, like deposed and superannuated kings in their regal gold-inwoven tatters. The city looked so thirsty that the broad river seemed to me a sheet of metal; and the blackened statues, as I passed under their blank gaze, along the unending bridge, with their ancient garments and their saintly crowns, seemed to me the real inhabitants and owners of this place, while the busy, trivial men and women, hurrying to and fro, were a swarm of ephemeral visitants infesting it for a day. It is such grim, stony beings as these, I thought, who are the fathers of ancient faded children, in those tanned time-fretted dwellings that crowd the steep before me; who pay their court in the worn and crumbling pomp of the palace which stretches its monotonous length on the height; who worship wearily in the stifling air of the churches, urged by no fear or hope, but compelled by their doom to be ever old and undying, to live on in the rigidity of habit, as they live on in perpetual midday, without the repose of night or the new birth of morning.

A stunning clang of metal suddenly thrilled through me, and I became conscious of the objects in my room again: one of the fire-irons had fallen as Pierre opened the door to bring me my draught. My heart was palpitating violently, and I begged Pierre to leave my draught beside me: I would take it presently.

As soon as I was alone again, I began to ask myself whether I had been sleeping. Was this a dream—this wonderfully distinct vision—minute in its distinctness down to a patch of rainbow light on the pavement, transmitted through a colored lamp in the shape of a star—of a strange city, quite unfamiliar to my imagination? I had seen no picture of Prague: it lay in my mind as a mere name, with vaguely-remembered historical associations—ill-defined memories of imperial grandeur and religious wars.

Nothing of this sort had ever occurred in my dreaming experience before, for I had often been humiliated because my dreams were only saved from being utterly disjointed and commonplace by the frequent terrors of nightmare. But I could not believe that I had been asleep, for I remembered distinctly the gradual breaking-in of the vision upon me, like the new images in a dissolving view, or the growing distinctness of the landscape as the sun lifts up the veil of the morning mist. And while I was conscious of this incipient vision, I was also conscious that Pierre came to tell my father Mr. Filmore was waiting for him, and that my father hurried out of the room. No, it was not a dream; was it—the thought was full of tremulous exultation—was it the poet's nature in me, hitherto only a troubled, yearning sensibility, now manifesting itself suddenly as spontaneous creation? Surely it was in this way that Homer saw the plain of Troy, that Dante saw the abodes of the departed, that Milton saw the earthward flight of the Tempter. Was it that my illness had wrought some happy change in my organization—given a firmer tension to my nerves—carried off some dull obstruction? I had often read of such effects—in works of fiction at least. Nay; in genuine biographies I had read of the subtilizing or exalting influence of some diseases on the mental powers. Did not Novalis* feel his inspiration intensified under the progress of consumption?

---

*Novalis, whose real name was Friedrich Leopold von Hardenberg, was a central figure in German romantic poetry; born in 1772, he died in 1801 of pulmonary disease.

When my mind had dwelt for some time on this blissful idea, it seemed to me that I might perhaps test it by an exertion of my will. The vision had begun when my father was speaking of our going to Prague. I did not for a moment believe it was really a representation of that city; I believed—I hoped it was a picture that my newly-liberated genius had painted in fiery haste, with the colors snatched from lazy memory. Suppose I were to fix my mind on some other place—Venice, for example, which was far more familiar to my imagination than Prague; perhaps the same sort of result would follow. I concentrated my thoughts on Venice; I stimulated my imagination with poetic memories, and strove to feel myself present in Venice, as I had felt myself present in Prague. But in vain. I was only coloring the Canaletto* engravings that hung in my old bedroom at home; the picture was a shifting one, my mind wandering uncertainly in search of more vivid images; I could see no accident of form or shadow without conscious labor after the necessary conditions. It was all prosaic effort, not rapt passivity, such as I had experienced half an hour before. I was discouraged; but I remembered that inspiration was fitful.

For several days I was in a state of excited expectation, watching for a recurrence of my new gift. I sent my thoughts ranging over my world of knowledge, in the hope that they would find some object which would send a reawakening vibration through my slumbering genius. But no; my world remained as dim as ever, and that flash of strange light refused to come again, though I watched for it with palpitating eagerness.

My father accompanied me every day in a drive, and a gradually lengthening walk as my powers of walking increased; and one evening he had agreed to come and fetch me at twelve the next day, that we might go together to select a musical box, and other purchases rigorously demanded of a rich Englishman visiting Geneva. He was one of the most punctual of men and bankers, and I was always nervously anxious to be quite ready for him at the appointed time. But, to my surprise, at a quarter past twelve he had not appeared. I felt all

---

*Giovanni Antonio Canale or Canal (1697–1768) was an influential Italian painter; his topographical view, particularly of Venice, were internationally known.

the impatience of a convalescent who has nothing particular to do, and who has just taken a tonic in the prospect of immediate exercise that would carry off the stimulus.

Unable to sit still and reserve my strength, I walked up and down the room, looking out on the current of the Rhone, just where it leaves the dark-blue lake; but thinking all the while of the possible causes that could detain my father.

Suddenly I was conscious that my father was in the room, but not alone: there were two persons with him. Strange! I had heard no footstep, I had not seen the door open; but I saw my father, and at his right hand our neighbor Mrs. Filmore, whom I remembered very well, though I had not seen her for five years. She was a common-place middle-aged woman, in silk and cashmere; but the lady on the left of my father was not more than twenty, a tall, slim, willowy fig-ure, with luxuriant blonde hair, arranged in cunning braids and folds that looked almost too massive for the slight figure and the small-featured, thin-lipped face they crowned. But the face had not a girl-ish expression: the features were sharp, the pale gray eyes at once acute, restless, and sarcastic. They were fixed on me in half-smiling curiosity, and I felt a painful sensation as if a sharp wind were cutting me. The pale-green dress, and the green leaves that seemed to form a border about her pale blonde hair, made me think of a Water-Nixie—for my mind was full of German lyrics,* and this pale, fatal-eyed woman, with the green weeds, looked like a birth from some cold sedgy stream, the daughter of an aged river.

"Well, Latimer, you thought me long," my father said ——.

But while the last word was in my ears, the whole group van-ished, and there was nothing between me and the Chinese painted folding-screen that stood before the door I was cold and trembling; I could only totter forward and throw myself on the sofa. This strange new power had manifested itself again ——. But *was* it a power? Might it not rather be a disease—a sort of intermittent delirium, con-centrating my energy of brain into moments of unhealthy activity, and leaving my saner hours all the more barren? I felt a dizzy sense

---

*The Water-Nixie, a familiar figure in German romantic poetry, was particularly frightening because of her dislike of humans.

of unreality in what my eye rested on; I grasped the bell convulsively, like one trying to free himself from nightmare, and rang it twice. Pierre came with a look of alarm in his face.

"Monsieur ne se trouve pas bien?" he said, anxiously.

"I'm tired of waiting, Pierre," I said, as distinctly and emphatically as I could, like a man determined to be sober in spite of wine; "I'm afraid something has happened to my father—he's usually so punctual. Run to the Hôtel des Bergues and see if he is there."

Pierre left the room at once, with a soothing "Bien, Monsieur"; and I felt the better for this scene of simple waking prose. Seeking to calm myself still further, I went into my bedroom, adjoining the *salon*, and opened a case of eau-de-Cologne; took out a bottle; went through the process of taking out the cork very neatly and then rubbed the reviving spirit over my hands and forehead, and under my nostrils, drawing a new delight from the scent because I had procured it by slow details of labor, and by no strange sudden madness. Already I had begun to taste something of the horror that belongs to the lot of a human being whose nature is not adjusted to simple human conditions.

Still enjoying the scent, I returned to the *salon*, but it was not unoccupied, as it had been before I left it. In front of the Chinese folding-screen there was my father, with Mrs. Filmore on his right hand, and on his left —— the slim blonde-haired girl, with the keen face and the keen eyes fixed on me in half-smiling curiosity.

"Well, Latimer, you thought me long," my father said ——

I heard no more, felt no more, till I became conscious that I was lying with my head low on the sofa, Pierre and my father by my side. As soon as I was thoroughly revived, my father left the room, and presently returned, saying—

"I've been to tell the ladies how you are, Latimer. They were waiting in the next room. We shall put off our shopping expedition to-day."

Presently he said, "That young lady is Bertha Grant, Mrs. Filmore's orphan niece. Filmore has adopted her, and she lives with them, so you will have her for a neighbor when we go home—perhaps for a near relation; for there is a tenderness between her and Alfred, I suspect, and I should be gratified by the match, since Filmore means to provide for her in every way as if she were his daughter. It had not occurred to me that you knew nothing about her living with the Filmores."

He made no further allusion to the fact of my having fainted at the moment of seeing her, and I would not for the world have told him the reason: I shrank from the idea of disclosing to anyone what might be regarded as a pitiable peculiarity, most of all from betraying it to my father, who would have suspected my sanity ever after.

I do not mean to dwell with particularity on the details of my experience. I have described these two cases at length; because they had definite, clearly traceable results in my after-lot.

Shortly after this last occurrence—I think the very next day—I began to be aware of a phase in my abnormal sensibility, to which, from the languid and slight nature of my intercourse with others since my illness, I had not been alive before. This was the obtrusion on my mind of the mental process going forward in first one person, and then another, with whom I happened to be in contact: the vagrant, frivolous ideas and emotions of some uninteresting acquaintance— Mrs. Filmore, for example—would force themselves on my consciousness like an importunate, ill-played musical instrument, or the loud activity of an imprisoned insect. But this unpleasant sensibility was fitful, and left me moments of rest, when the souls of my companions were once more shut out from me, and I felt a relief such as silence brings to wearied nerves. I might have believed this importunate insight to be merely a diseased activity of the imagination, but that my prevision of incalculable words and actions proved it to have a fixed relation to the mental process in other minds. But this superadded consciousness, wearying and annoying enough when it urged on me the trivial experience of indifferent people became an intense pain and grief when it seemed to be opening to me the souls of those who were in a close relation to me—when the rational talk, the graceful attentions, the wittily-turned phrases, and the kindly deeds, which used to make the web of their characters, were seen as if thrust asunder by a microscopic vision, that showed all the intermediate frivolities, all the suppressed egoism, all the struggling chaos of puerilities, meanness, vague capricious memories, and indolent make-shift thoughts, from which human words and deeds emerge like leaflets covering a fermenting heap.

At Basle we were joined by my brother Alfred, now a handsome self-confident man of six-and-twenty—a thorough contrast to my fragile, nervous, ineffectual self. I believe I was held to have a sort of half-womanish, half-ghostly beauty; for the portrait-painters, who are thick as weeds at Geneva, had often asked me to sit to them, and I had been the model of a dying minstrel in a fancy picture. But I thoroughly disliked my own *physique*, and nothing but the belief that it was a condition of poetic genius would have reconciled me to it. That brief hope was quite fled, and I saw in my face now nothing but the stamp of a morbid organization, framed for passive suffering— too feeble for the sublime resistance of poetic production. Alfred, from whom I had been almost constantly separated, and who, in his present stage of character and appearance, came before me as a perfect stranger, was bent on being extremely friendly and brother-like to me. He had the superficial kindness of a good-humored, self-satisfied nature, that fears no rivalry, and has encountered no contrarieties. I am not sure that my disposition was good enough for me to have been quite free from envy toward him, even if our desires had not clashed, and if I had been in the healthy human condition which admits of generous confidence and charitable construction. There must always have been an antipathy between our natures. As it was, he became in a few weeks an object of intense hatred to me; and when he entered the room, still more when he spoke, it was as if a sensation of grating metal had set my teeth on edge. My diseased consciousness was more intensely and continually occupied with his thoughts and emotions than with those of any other person who came in my way. I was perpetually exasperated with the petty promptings of his conceit and his love of patronage, with his self-complacent belief in Bertha Grant's passion for him, with his half-pitying contempt for me—seen not in the ordinary indications of intonation and phrase and slight action, which an acute and suspicious mind is on the watch for, but in all their naked skinless complication.

For we were rivals, and our desires clashed, though he was not aware of it. I have said nothing yet of the effect Bertha Grant produced in me on a nearer acquaintance. That effect was chiefly determined by the fact that she made the only exception, among all the human beings about me, to my unhappy gift of insight. About

Bertha I was always in a state of uncertainty: I could watch the expression of her face, and speculate on its meaning; I could ask for
her opinion with the real interest of ignorance; I could listen for her
words and watch for her smile with hope and fear: she had for me
the fascination of an unraveled destiny. I say it was this fact that
chiefly determined the strong effect she produced on me: for, in the
abstract, no womanly character could seem to have less affinity for
that of a shrinking, romantic, passionate youth than Bertha's. She
was keen, sarcastic, unimaginative, prematurely cynical, remaining
critical and unmoved in the most impressive scenes, inclined to dis-
sect all my favorite poems, and especially contemptuous toward the
German lyrics which were my pet literature at that time. To this moment I am unable to define my feeling toward her: it was not ordinary boyish admiration, for she was the very opposite, even to the
color of her hair, of the ideal woman who still remained to me the
type of loveliness; and she was without that enthusiasm for the great
and good, which, even at the moment of her strongest dominion
over me, I should have declared to be the highest element of character. But there is no tyranny more complete than that which a self-
centred negative nature exercises over a morbidly sensitive nature
perpetually craving sympathy and support. The most independent
people feel the effect of a man's silence in heightening their value
for his opinion—feel an additional triumph in conquering the reverence of a critic habitually captious and satirical: no wonder, then,
that an enthusiastic, self-distrusting youth should watch and wait
before the closed secret of a sarcastic woman's face, as if it were the
shrine of the doubtfully benignant deity who ruled his destiny. For
a young enthusiast is unable to imagine the total negation in another
mind of the emotions which are stirring his own: they may be feeble, latent, inactive, he thinks, but they are there—they may be called
forth; sometimes, in moments of happy hallucination, he believes
they may be there in all the greater strength because he sees no outward sign of them. And this effect, as I have intimated, was heightened to its utmost intensity in me, because Bertha was the only
being who remained for me in the mysterious seclusion of soul that
renders such youthful delusion possible. Doubtless there was another sort of fascination at work—that subtle physical attraction
which delights in cheating our psychological predictions, and in

compelling the men who paint sylphs to fall in love with some *bonne et brave femme*,* heavy-heeled and freckled.

Bertha's behavior toward me was such as to encourage all my illusions, to heighten my boyish passion, and make me more and more dependent on her smiles. Looking back with my present wretched knowledge, I conclude that her vanity and love of power were intensely gratified by the belief that I had fainted on first seeing her purely from the strong impression her person had produced on me. The most prosaic woman likes to believe herself the object of a violent, a poetic passion; and without a grain of romance in her, Bertha had that spirit of intrigue which gave piquancy to the idea that the brother of the man she meant to marry was dying with love and jealousy for her sake. That she meant to marry my brother, was what at that time I did not believe; for though he was assiduous in his attentions to her, and I knew well enough that both he and my father had made up their minds to this result, there was not yet an understood engagement—there had been no explicit declaration; and Bertha habitually, while she flirted with my brother, and accepted his homage in a way that implied to him a thorough recognition of its intention, made me believe, by the subtlest looks and phrases—feminine nothings which could never be quoted against her—that he was really the object of her secret ridicule; that she thought him, as I did, a coxcomb, whom she would have pleasure in disappointing. Me she openly petted in my brother's presence, as if I were too young and sickly ever to be thought of as a lover; and that was the view he took of me. But I believe she must inwardly have delighted in the tremors into which she threw me by the coaxing way in which she patted my curls, while she laughed at my quotations. Such caresses were always given in the presence of our friends; for when we were alone together she affected a much greater distance toward me, and now and then took the opportunity, by words or slight actions, to stimulate my foolish timid hope that she really preferred me. And why should she not follow her inclination? I was not in so advantageous a position as my brother, but I had fortune, I was not a year younger than she was, and she was an heiress, who would soon be of age to decide for herself.

---

*Good and worthy woman (French).

The fluctuations of hope and fear, confined to this one channel, made each day in her presence a delicious torment. There was one deliberate act of hers which especially helped to intoxicate me. When we were at Vienna her twentieth birthday occurred, and as she was very fond of ornaments, we all took the opportunity of the splendid jewelers' shops in that Teutonic Paris to purchase her a birthday present of jewelry. Mine, naturally, was the least expensive; it was an opal ring—the opal was my favorite stone, because it seemed to blush and turn pale as if it had a soul. I told Bertha so when I gave it her, and said that it was an emblem of the poetic nature, changing with the changing light of heaven and of woman's eyes. In the evening she appeared elegantly dressed, and wearing conspicuously all the birthday presents except mine. I looked eagerly at her fingers, but saw no opal. I had no opportunity of noticing this to her during the evening; but the next day, when I found her seated near the window alone, after breakfast, I said, "You scorn to wear my poor opal. I should have remembered that you despised poetic natures, and should have given you coral or turquoise, or some other opaque unresponsive stone." "Do I despise it?" she answered, taking hold of a delicate gold chain which she always wore round her neck and drawing out the end from her bosom with my ring hanging to it; "it hurts me a little, I can tell you," she said, with her usual dubious smile, "to wear it in that secret place; and since your poetical nature is so stupid as to prefer a more public position, I shall not endure the pain any longer."

She took off the ring from the chain and put it on her finger, smiling still, while the blood rushed to my cheeks, and I could not trust myself to say a word of entreaty that she would keep the ring where it was before.

I was completely fooled by this, and for two days shut myself up in my room whenever Bertha was absent, that I might intoxicate myself afresh with the thought of this scene and all it implied.

I should mention that during these two months—which seemed a long life to me from the novelty and intensity of the pleasures and pains I underwent—my diseased participation in other people's consciousness continued to torment me; now it was my father, and now my brother, now Mrs. Filmore or her husband, and now our German courier, whose stream of thought rushed upon me like a ringing in the ears not to be got rid of, though it allowed my own impulses and ideas to continue their uninterrupted course. It was like a preternaturally heightened sense of hearing, making audible to one a roar of sound where others find perfect stillness. The weariness and disgust of this involuntary intrusion into other souls was counteracted only by my ignorance of Bertha, and my growing passion for her; a passion enormously stimulated, if not produced, by that ignorance. She was my oasis of mystery in the dreary desert of knowledge. I had never allowed my diseased condition to betray itself, or to drive me into any unusual speech or action, except once, when, in a moment of peculiar bitterness against my brother, I had forestalled some words which I knew he was going to utter—a clever observation, which he had prepared beforehand. He had occasionally a slightly-affected hesitation in his speech, and when he paused an instant after the second word, my impatience and jealousy impelled me to continue the speech for him, as if it were something we had both learned by rote. He colored and looked astonished, as well as annoyed; and the words had no sooner escaped my lips than I felt a shock of alarm lest such an anticipation of words—very far from being words of course, easy to divine—should have betrayed me as an exceptional being, a sort of quiet energumen,* whom every one, Bertha, above all, would shudder at and avoid. But I magnified, as usual, the impression any word or deed of mine could produce on others; for no one gave any sign of having noticed my interruption as more than a rudeness, to be forgiven me on the score of my feeble nervous condition.

While this superadded consciousness of the actual was almost constant with me, I had never had a recurrence of that distinct prevision which I have described in relation to my first interview with Bertha; and I was waiting with eager curiosity to know whether or not my vision of Prague would prove to have been an instance of the same kind. A few days after the incident of the opal ring, we were paying one of our frequent visits to the Lichtenberg Palace. I could never look at many pictures in succession; for pictures, when they are at all powerful, affect me so strongly that one or two exhaust all my

---

*One who is wrought upon or possessed by the devil.

capability of contemplation. This morning I had been looking at
Giorgione's picture of the cruel-eyed woman, said to be a likeness of
Lucrezia Borgia.[3] I had stood long alone before it, fascinated by the
terrible reality of that cunning, relentless face, till I felt a strange poisoned sensation, as if I had long been inhaling a fatal odor, and was
just beginning to be conscious of its effects. Perhaps even then I
should not have moved away, if the rest of the party had not returned
to this room, and announced that they were going to the Belvedere
Gallery to settle a bet which had arisen between my brother and Mr.
Filmore about a portrait. I followed them dreamily, and was hardly
alive to what occurred till they had all gone up to the gallery, leaving
me below; for I refused to come within sight of another picture that
day. I made my way to the Grand Terrace, since it was agreed that we
should saunter in the gardens when the dispute had been decided. I
had been sitting here a short space, vaguely conscious of trim gardens, with a city and green hills in the distance, when, wishing to
avoid the proximity of the sentinel, I rose and walked down the
broad stone steps, intending to seat myself farther on in the gardens.
Just as I reached the gravel walk, I felt an arm slipped within mine,
and a light hand gently pressing my wrist. In the same instant a
strange intoxicating numbness passed over me, like the continuance
or climax of the sensation I was still feeling from the gaze of Lucrezia
Borgia. The gardens, the summer sky, the consciousness of Bertha's
arm being within mine, all vanished, and I seemed to be suddenly in
darkness, out of which there gradually broke a dim firelight, and I felt
myself sitting in my father's leather chair in the library at home. I knew
the fireplace—the dogs for the wood-fire—the black marble chimney-
piece with the white marble medallion of the dying Cleopatra in the
centre. Intense and hopeless misery was pressing on my soul; the light
became stronger, for Bertha was entering with a candle in her hand—
Bertha, my wife—with cruel eyes, with green jewels and green leaves
on her white ball-dress; every hateful thought within her present to
me ——"Madman, idiot! why don't you kill yourself, then?" It was a
moment of hell. I saw into her pitiless soul—saw its barren worldliness, its scorching hate—and felt it clothe me round like an air I was
obliged to breathe. She came with her candle and stood over me with
a bitter smile of contempt; I saw the great emerald brooch on her
bosom, a studded serpent with diamond eyes. I shuddered—I de-

spised this woman with the barren soul and mean thoughts; but I felt helpless before her, as if she clutched my bleeding heart, and would clutch it till the last drop of life-blood ebbed away. She was my wife, and we hated each other. Gradually the hearth, the dim library, the candle-light disappeared—seemed to melt away into a background of light, the green serpent with the diamond eyes remaining a dark image on the retina. Then I had a sense of my eyelids quivering, and the living daylight broke in upon me; I saw gardens, and heard voices; I was seated on the steps of the Belvedere Terrace, and my friends were round me.

The tumult of mind into which I was thrown by this hideous vision made me ill for several days, and prolonged our stay at Vienna. I shuddered with horror as the scene recurred to me; and it recurred constantly, with all its minutiæ, as if they had been burned into my memory; and yet, such is the madness of the human heart under the influence of its immediate desires, I felt a wild hell-braving joy that Bertha was to be mine; for the fulfillment of my former prevision concerning her first appearance before me, left me little hope that this last hideous glimpse of the future was the mere diseased play of my own mind, and had no relation to external realities. One thing alone I looked toward as a possible means of casting doubt on my terrible conviction—the discovery that my vision of Prague had been false—and Prague was the next city on our route.

Meanwhile, I was no sooner in Bertha's society again, than I was as completely under her sway as before. What if I saw into the heart of Bertha, the matured woman—Bertha, my wife? Bertha, the girl, was a fascinating secret to me still: I trembled under her touch; I felt the witchery of her presence; I yearned to be assured of her love. The fear of poison is feeble against the sense of thirst. Nay, I was just as jealous of my brother as before—just as much irritated by his small patronizing ways; for my pride, my diseased sensibility, were there as they had always been, and winced as inevitably under every offense as my eye winced from an intruding mote. The future, even when brought within the compass of feeling by a vision that made me shudder, had still no more than the force of an idea, compared with the force of present emotion—of my love for Bertha, of my dislike and jealousy toward my brother.

It is an old story, that men sell themselves to the tempter, and sign a bond with their blood, because it is only to take effect at a distant day; then rush on to snatch the cup their souls thirst after with an impulse not the less savage because there is a dark shadow beside them forevermore. There is no short cut, no patent tram-road, to wisdom: after all the centuries of invention, the soul's path lies through the thorny wilderness which must be still trodden in solitude, with bleeding feet, with sobs for help, as it was trodden by them of old time.

My mind speculated eagerly on the means by which I should become my brother's successful rival, for I was still too timid, in my ignorance of Bertha's actual feeling, to venture on any step that would urge from her an avowal of it. I thought I should gain confidence even for this, if my vision of Prague proved to have been veracious; and yet, the horror of that certitude! Behind the slim girl Bertha, whose words and looks I watched for, whose touch was bliss, there stood continually that Bertha with the fuller form, the harder eyes, the more rigid mouth,—with the barren selfish soul laid bare; no longer a fascinating secret, but a measured fact, urging itself perpetually on my unwilling sight. Are you unable to give me your sympathy—you who read this? Are you unable to imagine this double consciousness at work within me, flowing on like two parallel streams which never mingle their waters and blend into a common hue? Yet you must have known something of the presentiments that spring from an insight at war with passion; and my visions were only like presentiments intensified to horror. You have known the powerlessness of ideas before the might of impulse; and my visions, when once they had passed into memory, were mere ideas—pale shadows that beckoned in vain, while my hand was grasped by the living and the loved.

In after-days I thought with bitter regret that if I had foreseen something more or something different—if instead of that hideous vision which poisoned the passion it could not destroy, or if even along with it I could have had a foreshadowing of that moment when I looked on my brother's face for the last time, some softening influence would have been shed over my feeling toward him: pride and hatred would surely have been subdued into pity, and the record of those hidden sins would have been shortened. But this is one of the vain thoughts with which we men flatter ourselves. We try to believe that the egoism within us would have easily been melted, and that it was only the narrowness of our knowledge which hemmed in our generosity, our awe, our human piety, and hindered them from submerging our hard indifference to the sensations and emotions of our fellow. Our tenderness and self-renunciation seem strong when our egoism has had its day—when, after our mean striving for a triumph that is to be another's loss, the triumph comes suddenly, and we shudder at it, because it is held out by the chill hand of death.

Our arrival in Prague happened at night, and I was glad of this, for it seemed like a deferring of a terribly decisive moment, to be in the city for hours without seeing it. As we were not to remain long in Prague, but to go on speedily to Dresden, it was proposed that we should drive out the next morning and take a general view of the place, as well as visit some of its specially interesting spots, before the heat became oppressive—for we were in August, and the season was hot and dry. But it happened that the ladies were rather late at their morning toilet, and to my father's politely-repressed but perceptible annoyance, we were not in the carriage till the morning was far advanced. I thought with a sense of relief, as we entered the Jews' quarter, where we were to visit the old synagogue, that we should be kept in this flat, shut-up part of the city, until we should all be too tired and too warm to go farther, and so we should return without seeing more than the streets through which we had already passed. That would give me another day's suspense—suspense, the only form in which a fearful spirit knows the solace of hope. But, as I stood under the blackened, groined arches of that old synagogue, made dimly visible by the seven thin candles in the sacred lamp, while our Jewish cicerone reached down the Book of the Law, and read to us in its ancient tongue,—I felt a shuddering impression that this strange building, with its shrunken lights, this surviving withered remnant of mediæval Judaism, was of a piece with my vision. Those darkened dusty Christian saints, with their loftier arches and their larger candles, needed the consolatory scorn with which they might point to a more shriveled death-in-life than their own.

As I expected, when we left the Jews' quarter the elders of our party wished to return to the hotel. But now, instead of rejoicing in this, as I had done beforehand, I felt a sudden overpowering impulse to go on at once to the bridge, and put an end to the suspense I had been wishing to protract. I declared, with unusual decision, that I would get out of the carriage and walk on alone; they might return without me. My father, thinking this merely a sample of my usual "poetic nonsense," objected that I should only do myself harm by walking in the heat; but when I persisted, he said angrily that I might follow my own absurd devices, but that Schmidt (our courier) must go with me. I assented to this, and set off with Schmidt toward the bridge. I had no sooner passed from under the archway of the grand old gate leading on to the bridge than a trembling seized me, and I turned cold under the midday sun; yet I went on; I was in search of something—a small detail which I remembered with special intensity as part of my vision. There it was—the patch of rainbow light on the pavement transmitted through a lamp in the shape of a star.

CHAPTER II

BEFORE THE AUTUMN WAS at an end, and while the brown leaves still stood thick on the beeches in our park, my brother and Bertha were engaged to each other, and it was understood that their marriage was to take place early in the next spring. In spite of the certainly I had felt from that moment on the bridge at Prague, that Bertha would one day be my wife, my constitutional timidity and distrust had continued to benumb me, and the words in which I had sometimes premeditated a confession of my love had died away unuttered. The same conflict had gone on within me as before—the longing for an assurance of love from Bertha's lips, the dread lest a word of contempt and denial should fall upon me like a corrosive acid. What was the conviction of a distant necessity to me? I trembled under a present glance, I hungered after a present joy, I was clogged and chilled by a present fear. And so the days passed on: I witnessed Bertha's engagement and heard her marriage discussed as if I were under a conscious nightmare—knowing it was a dream that would vanish, but feeling stifled under the grasp of hard-clutching fingers.

When I was not in Bertha's presence—and I was with her very

often, for she continued to treat me with a playful patronage that wakened no jealousy in my brother—I spent my time chiefly in wandering, in strolling, or taking long rides while the daylight lasted, and then shutting myself up with my unread books; for books had lost the power of chaining my attention. My self-consciousness was heightened to that pitch of intensity in which our own emotions take the form of a drama which urges itself imperatively on our contemplation, and we begin to weep, less under the sense of our suffering than at the thought of it. I felt a sort of pitying anguish over the pathos of my own lot: the lot of a being finely organized for pain, but with hardly any fibers that responded to pleasure—to whom the idea of future evil robbed the present of its joy, and for whom the idea of future good did not still the uneasiness of a present yearning or a present dread. I went dumbly through that stage of the poet's suffering, in which he feels the delicious pang of utterance, and makes an image of his sorrows.

I was left entirely without remonstrance concerning this dreamy wayward life: I knew my father's thought about me: "That lad will never be good for anything in life: he may waste his years in an insignificant way on the income that falls to him: I shall not trouble myself about a career for him."

One mild morning in the beginning of November, it happened that I was standing outside the portico patting lazy old Cæsar, a Newfoundland almost blind with age, the only dog that ever took any notice of me—for the very dogs shunned me, and fawned on the happier people about me—when the groom brought up my brother's horse which was to carry him to the hunt, and my brother himself appeared at the door, florid, broad-chested, and self-complacent, feeling what a good-natured fellow he was not to behave insolently to us all on the strength of his great advantages.

"Latimer, old boy," he said to me in a tone of compassionate cordiality, "what a pity it is you don't have a run with the hounds now and then! The finest thing in the world for low spirits!"

"Low spirits!" I thought bitterly, as he rode away; "that is the sort of phrase with which coarse, narrow natures like yours think to describe experience of which you can know no more than your horse knows. It is to such as you that the good of this world falls: ready dullness, healthy selfishness, good-tempered conceit—these are the keys to happiness."

The quick thought came that my selfishness was even stronger than his—it was only a suffering selfishness instead of an enjoying one. But then, again, my exasperating insight into Alfred's self-complacent soul, his freedom from all the doubts and fears, the unsatisfied yearnings, the exquisite tortures of sensitiveness, that had made the web of my life, seemed to absolve me from all bonds toward him. This man needed no pity, no love; those fine influences would have been as little felt by him as the delicate white mist is felt by the rock it caresses. There was no evil in store for him: if he was not to marry Bertha, it would be because he had found a lot pleasanter to himself.

Mr. Filmore's house lay not more than half a mile beyond our own gates, and whenever I knew my brother was gone in another direction, I went there for the chance of finding Bertha at home. Later on in the day I walked thither. By a rare accident she was alone, and we walked out in the grounds together, for she seldom went on foot beyond the trimly-swept gravel-walks. I remember what a beautiful sylph she looked to me as the low November sun shone on her blonde hair, and she tripped along teasing me with her usual light banter, to which I listened half fondly, half moodily; it was all the sign Bertha's mysterious inner self ever made to me. To-day perhaps the moodiness predominated, for I had not yet shaken off the access of jealous hate which my brother had raised in me by his parting patronage. Suddenly I interrupted and startled her by saying, almost fiercely, "Bertha, how can you love Alfred?"

She looked at me with surprise for a moment, but soon her light smile came again, and she answered sarcastically, "Why do you suppose I love him?"

"How can you ask that, Bertha?"

"What! your wisdom thinks I must love the man I'm going to marry? The most unpleasant thing in the world. I should quarrel with him; I should be jealous of him; our ménage would be conducted in a very ill-bred manner. A little quiet contempt contributes greatly to the elegance of life."

"Bertha, that is not your real feeling. Why do you delight in try-ing to deceive me by inventing such cynical speeches?"

"I need never take the trouble of invention in order to deceive you, my small Tasso"* (that was the mocking name she usually gave me). "The easiest way to deceive a poet is to tell him the truth."

She was testing the validity of her epigram in a daring way, and for a moment the shadow of my vision—the Bertha whose soul was no secret to me—passed between me and the radiant girl, the playful sylph whose feelings were a fascinating mystery. I suppose I must have shuddered, or betrayed in some other way my momentary chill of horror.

"Tasso!" she said, seizing my wrist, and peeping round into my face, "are you really beginning to discern what a heartless girl I am? Why, you are not half the poet I thought you were; you are actually capable of believing the truth about me."

The shadow passed from between us, and was no longer the ob-ject nearest to me. The girl whose light fingers grasped me, whose elfish, charming face looked into mine—who, I thought, was betray-ing an interest in my feelings that she would not have directly avowed,—this warm-breathing presence again possessed my senses and imagination like a returning syren melody which had been over-powered for an instant by the roar of threatening waves. It was a mo-ment as delicious to me as the waking up to a consciousness of youth after a dream of middle age. I forgot everything but my passion, and said with swimming eyes—

"Bertha, shall you love me when we are first married? I wouldn't mind if you really loved me only for a little while."

Her look of astonishment, as she loosed my hand and started away from me recalled me to a sense of my strange, my criminal in-discretion.

"Forgive me," I said, hurriedly, as soon as I could speak again; "I did not know what I was saying."

---

*Torquato Tasso (1544–1595), author of *Gerusalemme liberata*, was the greatest Italian poet of the late Renaissance; his career was marked by madness and imprisonment, but he died just before the Pope was to crown him as the king of poets. Tasso became almost a cult figure to the English Romantic poets.

"Ah, Tasso's mad fit has come on, I see," she answered, quietly, for she had recovered herself sooner than I had. "Let him go home and keep his head cool. I must go in, for the sun is setting."

I left her—full of indignation against myself. I had let slip words, which, if she reflected on them, might rouse in her a suspicion of my abnormal mental condition—a suspicion which of all things I dreaded. And besides that, I was ashamed of the apparent baseness I had committed in uttering them to my brother's betrothed wife. I wandered home slowly, entering our park through a private gate instead of by the lodges. As I approached the house, I saw a man dashing off at full speed from the stable-yard across the park. Had any accident happened at home? No; perhaps it was only one of my father's peremptory business errands that required this headlong haste. Nevertheless I quickened my pace without any distinct motive, and was soon at the house. I will not dwell on the scene I found there. My brother was dead—had been pitched from his horse, and killed on the spot by a concussion of the brain.

I went up to the room where he lay, and where my father was seated beside him with a look of rigid despair. I had shunned my father more than any one since our return home, for the radical antipathy between our natures made my insight into his inner self a constant affliction to me. But now, as I went up to him, and stood beside him in sad silence, I felt the presence of a new element that blended us as we had never been blent before. My father had been one of the most successful men in the money-getting world, he had had no sentimental sufferings, no illness. The heaviest trouble that had befallen him was the death of his first wife. But he married my mother soon after and I remember he seemed exactly the same, to my keen childish observation, the week after her death as before. But now, at last, a sorrow had come—the sorrow of old age, which suffers the more from the crushing of its pride and its hopes, in proportion as the pride and hope are narrow and prosaic. His son was to have been married soon—would probably have stood for the borough at the next election. That son's existence was the best motive that could be alleged for making new purchases of land every year to round off the estate. It is a dreary thing to live on doing the same things year after year, without knowing why we do them. Perhaps the tragedy of disappointed youth and passion is less piteous than the tragedy of disappointed age and worldliness.

As I saw into the desolation of my father's heart, I felt a movement of deep pity toward him, which was the beginning of a new affection—an affection that grew and strengthened in spite of the strange bitterness with which he regarded me in the first month or two after my brother's death. If it had not been for the softening influence of my compassion for him—the first deep compassion I had ever felt—I should have been stung by the perception that my father transferred the inheritance of an eldest son to me with a mortified sense that fate had compelled him to the unwelcome course of caring for me as an important being. It was only in spite of himself that he began to think of me with anxious regard. There is hardly any neglected child for whom death has made vacant a more favored place, who will not understand what I mean.

Gradually, however, my new deference to his wishes, the effect of that patience which was born of my pity for him, won upon his affection, and he began to please himself with the endeavor to make me fill my brother's place as fully as my feebler personality would admit. I saw that the prospect which by-and-by presented itself of my becoming Bertha's husband was welcome to him, and he even contemplated in my case what he had not intended in my brother's—that his son and daughter-in-law should make one household with him. My softened feeling toward my father made this the happiest time I had known since childhood;—these last months in which I retained the delicious illusion of loving Bertha, of longing and doubting and hoping that she might love me. She behaved with a certain new consciousness and distance toward me after my brother's death; and I too was under a double constraint—that of delicacy toward my brother's memory, and of anxiety as to the impression my abrupt words had left on her mind. But the additional screen this mutual reserve erected between us only brought me more completely under her power: no matter how empty the adytum,* so that the veil be thick enough. So absolute is our soul's need of something hidden and uncertain for the maintenance of that doubt and hope and effort which

---

*Innermost part of a temple; secret shrine whence oracles were delivered.

are the breath of its life, that if the whole future were laid bare to us beyond to-day, the interest of all mankind would be bent on the hours that lie between; we should pant after the uncertainties of our one morning and our one afternoon; we should rush fiercely to the Exchange for our last possibility of speculation, of success, of disappointment; we should have a glut of political prophets foretelling a crisis or a no-crisis within the only twenty-four hours left open to prophecy. Conceive the condition of the human mind if all propositions whatsoever were self-evident except one, which was to become self-evident at the close of a summer's day, but in the meantime might be the subject of question, of hypothesis, of debate. Art and philosophy, literature and science, would fasten like bees on that one proposition which had the honey of probability in it, and be the more eager because their enjoyment would end with sunset. Our impulses, our spiritual activities, no more adjust themselves to the idea of their future nullity, than the beating of our heart, or the irritability of our muscles.

Bertha, the slim, fair-haired girl, whose present thoughts and emotions were an enigma to me amidst the fatiguing obviousness of the other minds around me, was as absorbing to me as a single unknown to-day—as a single hypothetic proposition to remain problematic till sunset; and all the cramped, hemmed-in belief and disbelief, trust and distrust, of my nature, welled out in this one narrow channel.

And she made me believe that she loved me. Without ever quitting her tone of *badinage* and playful superiority, she intoxicated me with the sense that I was necessary to her, that she was never at ease unless I was near her, submitting to her playful tyranny. It costs a woman so little effort to besot us in this way! A half-repressed word, a moment's unexpected silence, even an easy fit of petulance on our account, will serve us as *hashish* for a long while. Out of the subtlest web of scarcely perceptible signs, she set me weaving the fancy that she had always unconsciously loved me better than Alfred, but that, with the ignorant fluttered sensibility of a young girl, she had been imposed on by the charm that lay for her in the distinction of being admired and chosen by a man who made so brilliant a figure in the world as my brother. She satirized herself in a very graceful way for her vanity and ambition. What was it to me that I had the light of my wretched prevision on the fact that now it was I who possessed at least all but the personal part of my brother's advantages? Our sweet illusions are half of them conscious illusions, like effects of color that we know to be made up of tinsel, broken glass, and rags.

We were married eighteen months after Alfred's death, one cold, clear morning in April, when there came hail and sunshine both together; and Bertha, in her white silk and pale-green leaves, and the pale hues of her hair and face, looked like the spirit of the morning. My father was happier than he had thought of being again: my marriage, he felt sure, would complete the desirable modification of my character, and make me practical and worldly enough to take my place in society among sane men. For he delighted in Bertha's tact and acuteness, and felt sure she would be mistress of me, and make me what she chose: I was only twenty-one, and madly in love with her. Poor father! He kept that hope a little while after our first year of marriage, and it was not quite extinct when paralysis came and saved him from utter disappointment.

I shall hurry through the rest of my story, not dwelling so much as I have hitherto done on my inward experience. When people are well known to each other, they talk rather of what befalls them externally, leaving their feelings and sentiments to be inferred.

We lived in a round of visits for some time after our return home, giving splendid dinner-parties, and making a sensation in our neighborhood by the new luster of our equipage, for my father had reserved this display of his increased wealth for the period of his son's marriage; and we gave our acquaintances liberal opportunity for remarking that it was a pity I made so poor a figure as an heir and a bridegroom. The nervous fatigue of this existence, the insincerities and platitudes which I had to live through twice over—through my inner and outward sense—would have been maddening to me, if I had not had that sort of intoxicated callousness which came from the delights of a first passion. A bride and bridegroom, surrounded by all the appliances of wealth, hurried through the day by the whirl of society, filling their solitary moments with hastily-snatched caresses, are prepared for their future life together as the novice is prepared for the cloister—by experiencing its utmost contrast.

Through all these crowded excited months, Bertha's inward self remained shrouded from me, and I still read her thoughts only through the language of her lips and demeanor: I had still the human interest of wondering whether what I did and said pleased her, of longing to hear a word of affection, of giving a delicious exaggeration of meaning to her smile. But I was conscious of a growing difference in her manner toward me; sometimes strong enough to be called haughty coldness, cutting and chilling me as the hail had done that came across the sunshine on our marriage morning; sometimes only perceptible in the dexterous avoidance of a tête-à-tête walk or dinner to which I had been looking forward. I had been deeply pained by this—had even felt a sort of crushing of the heart, from the sense that my brief day of happiness was near its setting; but still I remained dependent on Bertha, eager for the last rays of a bliss that would soon be gone forever, hoping and watching for some afterglow more beautiful from the impending night.

I remember—how should I not remember?—the time when that dependence and hope utterly left me, when the sadness I had felt in Bertha's growing estrangement became a joy that I looked back upon with longing, as a man might look back on the last pains in a paralyzed limb. It was just after the close of my father's last illness, which had necessarily withdrawn us from society and thrown us more upon each other. It was the evening of my father's death. On that evening the veil which had shrouded Bertha's soul from me—had made me find in her alone among my fellow-beings the blessed possibility of mystery, and doubt, and expectation—was first withdrawn. Perhaps it was the first day since the beginning of my passion for her, in which that passion was completely neutralized by the presence of an absorbing feeling of another kind. I had been watching by my father's deathbed: I had been witnessing the last fitful yearning glance his soul had cast back on the spent inheritance of life—the last faint consciousness of love he had gathered from the pressure of my hand. What are all our personal loves when we have been sharing in that supreme agony? In the first moments when we come away from the presence of death, every other relation to the living is merged, to our feeling, in the great relation of a common nature and a common destiny.

In that state of mind I joined Bertha in her private sitting-room. She was seated in a leaning posture on a settee, with her back toward the door; the great rich coils of her pale blonde hair surmounting her small neck, visible above the back of the settee. I remember, as I closed the door behind me, a cold tremulousness seizing me, and a vague sense of being and lonely—vague and strong, like a presentiment. I know how I looked at that moment, for I saw myself in Bertha's thought as she lifted her cutting gray eyes and looked at me: a miserable ghost-seer, surrounded by phantoms in the noonday, trembling under a breeze when the leaves were still, without appetite for the common objects of human desire, but pining after the moonbeams. We were front to front with each other, and judged each other. The terrible moment of complete illumination had come to me, and I saw that the darkness had hidden no landscape from me, but only a blank prosaic wall: from that evening forth, through the sickening years which followed, I saw all round the narrow room of this woman's soul—saw petty artifice and mere negation where I had delighted to believe in coy sensibilities and in wit at war with latent feeling—saw the light floating vanities of the girl defining themselves into the systematic coquetry, the scheming selfishness, of the woman—saw repulsion and antipathy harden into cruel hatred, giving pain only for the sake of wreaking itself.

For Bertha, too, after her kind, felt the bitterness of disillusion. She had believed that my wild poet's passion for her would make me her slave; and that, being her slave, I should execute her will in all things. With the essential shallowness of a negative, unimaginative nature, she was unable to conceive the fact that sensibilities were anything else than weaknesses. She had thought my weaknesses would put me in her power, and she found them unmanageable forces. Our positions were reversed. Before marriage she had completely mastered my imagination, for she was a secret to me; and I created the unknown thought before which I trembled as if it were hers. But now that her soul was laid open to me, now that I was compelled to share the privacy of her motives, to follow all the petty devices that preceded her words and acts, she found herself powerless with me, except to produce in me the chill shudder of repulsion—powerless, because I could be acted on by no lever within her reach. I was dead to worldly ambitions, to social vanities, to all the incentives within the compass of her narrow imagination, and I lived under influences utterly invisible to her.

She was really pitiable to have such a husband, and so all the world thought. A graceful, brilliant woman, like Bertha, who smiled on morning callers, made a figure in ball-rooms, and was capable of that light repartee which, from such a woman, is accepted as wit, was secure of carrying off all sympathy from a husband who was sickly, abstracted, and, as some suspected, crack-brained. Even the servants in our house gave her the balance of their regard and pity. For there were no audible quarrels between us; our alienation, our repulsion from each other, lay within the silence of our own hearts; and if the mistress went out a great deal, and seemed to dislike the master's society, was it not natural, poor thing? The master was odd. I was kind and just to my dependents, but I excited in them a shrinking, half-contemptuous pity; for this class of men and women are but slightly determined in their estimate of others by general considerations, or even experience, of character. They judge of persons as they judge of coins, and value those who pass current at a high rate.

After a time I interfered so little with Bertha's habits, that it might seem wonderful how her hatred toward me could grow so intense and active as it did. But she had begun to suspect, by some involuntary betrayals of mine, that there was an abnormal power of penetration in me—that fitfully, at least, I was strangely cognizant of her thoughts and intentions, and she began to be haunted by a terror of me, which alternated every now and then with defiance. She meditated continually how the incubus could be shaken off her life—how she could be freed from this hateful bond to a being whom she at once despised as an imbecile, and dreaded as an inquisitor. For a long while she lived in the hope that my evident wretchedness would drive me to the commission of suicide; but suicide was not in my nature. I was too completely swayed by the sense that I was in the grasp of unknown forces, to believe in my power of self-release. Toward my own destiny I had become entirely passive; for my one ardent desire had spent itself, and impulse no longer predominated over knowledge. For this reason I never thought of taking any steps toward a complete separation, which would have made our alienation evident to the world. Why should I rush for help to a new course, when I was only suffering from the consequences of a deed which had been the act of my intensest will? That would have been the logic of one who had desires to gratify, and I had no desires. But Bertha and I lived more and more aloof from each other. The rich find it easy to live married and apart.

That course of our life which I have indicated in a few sentences filled the space of years. So much misery—so slow and hiedous a growth of hatred and sin, may be compressed into a sentence! And men judge of each other's lives through this summary medium. They epitomize the experience of their fellow-mortal, and pronounce judgment on him in neat syntax, and feel themselves wise and virtuous—conquerors over the temptations they define in well-selected predicates. Seven years of wretchedness glide glibly over the lips of the man who has never counted them out in moment of chill disappointment, of head and heart throbbings, of dread and vain wrestling, of remorse and despair. We learn *words* by rote, but not their meaning; *that* must be paid for with our life-blood, and printed in the subtle fibres of our nerves.

But I will hasten to finish my story. Brevity is justified at once to those who readily understand, and to those who will never understand.

Some years after my father's death, I was sitting by the dim firelight in my library one January evening—sitting in the leather chair that used to be my father's—when Bertha appeared at the door, with a candle in her hand, and advanced toward me. I knew the ball-dress she had on—the white ball-dress, with the green jewels, shone upon by the light of the wax candle which lit up the medallion of the dying Cleopatra on the mantelpiece. Why did she come to me before going out? I had not seen her in the library, which was my habitual place, for months. Why did she stand before me with the candle in her hand, with her cruel contemptuous eyes fixed on me, and the glittering serpent, like a familiar demon, on her breast. For a moment I thought this fulfillment of my vision at Vienna marked some dreadful crisis in my fate, but I saw nothing in Bertha's mind, as she stood before me, except scorn for the look of overwhelming misery with which I sat before her. —— "Fool, idiot, why don't you kill yourself, then?"—that was her thought. But at length her thoughts reverted to her errand, and she spoke aloud. The apparently indifferent nature of the errand seemed to make a ridiculous anticlimax to my prevision and my agitation.

"I have had to hire a new maid. Fletcher is going to be married, and she wants me to ask you to let her husband have the public-house and farm at Molton. I wish him to have it. You must give the promise now, because Fletcher is going to-morrow morning—and quickly, because I'm in a hurry."

"Very well; you may promise her," I said, indifferently, and Bertha swept out of the library again.

I always shrank from the sight of a new person, and all the more when it was a person whose mental life was likely to weary my reluctant insight with worldly ignorant trivialities. But I shrank especially from the sight of this new maid, because her advent had been announced to me at a moment to which I could not cease to attach some fatality: I had a vague dread that I should find her mixed up with the dreary drama of my life—that some new sickening vision would reveal her to me as an evil genius. When at last I did unavoidably meet her, the vague dread was changed into definite disgust. She was a tall, wiry, dark-eyed woman, this Mrs. Archer, with a face handsome enough to give her coarse hard nature the odious finish of bold, self-confident coquetry. That was enough to make me avoid her, quite apart from the contemptuous feeling with which she contemplated me. I seldom saw her; but I perceived that she rapidly became a favorite with her mistress, and, after the lapse of eight or nine months, I began to be aware that there had arisen in Bertha's mind toward this woman a mingled feeling of fear and dependence, and that this feeling was associated with ill-defined images of candle-light scenes in her dressing-room, and the locking-up of something in Bertha's cabinet. My interviews with my wife had become so brief and so rarely solitary, that I had no opportunity of perceiving these images in her mind with more definiteness. The recollections of the past become contracted in the rapidity of thought till they sometimes bear hardly a more distinct resemblance to the external reality than the forms of an oriental alphabet to the objects that suggested them.

Besides, for the last year or more a modification had been going forward in my mental condition, and was growing more and more marked. My insight into the minds of those around me was becoming dimmer and more fitful, and the ideas that crowded my double consciousness became less and less dependent on any personal contact. All that was personal in me seemed to be suffering a gradual death, so that I was losing the organ through which the personal agitations and projects of others could affect me. But along with this relief from wearisome insight, there was a new development of what I concluded—as I have since found rightly—to be a prevision of external scenes. It was as if the relation between me and my fellow-men was more and more deadened, and my relation to what we call the inanimate was quickened into new life. The more I lived apart from society, and in proportion as my wretchedness subsided from the violent throb of agonized passion into the dullness of habitual pain, the more frequent and vivid became such visions as that I had had of Prague—of strange cities, of sandy plains, of gigantic ruins, of midnight skies with strange bright constellations, of mountain passes, of grassy nooks flecked with the afternoon sunshine through the boughs: I was in the midst of such scenes, and in all of them one presence seemed to weigh on me in all these mighty shapes—the presence of something unknown and pitiless. For continual suffering had annihilated religious faith within me: to the utterly miserable—the unloving and the unloved—there is no religion possible, no worship but a worship of devils. And beyond all these, and continually recurring, was the vision of my death—the pangs, the suffocation, the last struggle, when life would be grasped at in vain.

Things were in this state near the end of the seventh year. I had become entirely free from insight, from my abnormal cognizance of any other consciousness than my own, and instead of intruding involuntarily into the world of other minds, was living continually in my own solitary future. Bertha was aware that I was greatly changed. To my surprise she had of late seemed to seek opportunities of remaining in my society, and had cultivated that kind of distant yet familiar talk which is customary between a husband and wife who live in polite and irrevocable alienation. I bore this with languid submission, and without feeling enough interest in her motives to be roused into keen observation; yet I could not help perceiving something triumphant and excited in her carriage and the expression of her face—something too subtle to express itself in words or tones, but giving one the idea that she lived in a state of expectation or hopeful suspense. My chief feeling was satisfaction that her inner self was once more shut out from me; and I almost revelled for the moment in the absent melancholy that made me answer her at cross purposes, and betray utter ignorance of what she had been saying. I remember well the look and the smile with which she one day said, after a mistake of this kind on my part: "I used to think you were a clairvoyant, and that was the reason why you were so bitter against other clairvoyants, wanting to keep your monopoly; but I see now you have become rather duller than the rest of the world."

I said nothing in reply. It occurred to me that her recent obtrusion of herself upon me might have been prompted by the wish to test my power of detecting some of her secrets; but I let the thought drop again at once; her motives and her deeds had no interest for me, and whatever pleasures she might be seeking, I had no wish to balk her. There was still pity in my soul for every living thing, and Bertha was living—was surrounded with possibilities of misery.

Just at this time there occurred an event which roused me somewhat from my inertia, and gave me an interest in the passing moment that I had thought impossible for me. It was a visit from Charles Meunier, who had written me word that he was coming to England for relaxation from too strenuous labor, and would like to see me. Meunier had now a European reputation; but his letter to me expressed that keen remembrance of an early regard, an early debt of sympathy, which is inseparable from nobility of character; and I, too, felt as if his presence would be to me like a transient resurrection into a happier pre-existence.

He came, and as far as possible, I renewed our old pleasure of making tête-à-tête excursions, though, instead of mountains and glaciers and the wide blue lake, we had to content ourselves with mere slopes and ponds and artificial plantations. The years had changed us both, but with what different result! Meunier was now a brilliant figure in society, to whom elegant women pretended to listen, and whose acquaintance was boasted of by noblemen ambitious of brains. He repressed with the utmost delicacy all betrayal of the shock which I am sure he must have received from our meeting, or of a desire to penetrate into my condition and circumstances, and sought by the utmost exertion of his charming social powers to make our reunion agreeable. Bertha was much struck by the unexpected facinations of a visitor who she had expected to find presentable only on the score of his celebrity, and put forth all her coquetries and accomplishments. Apparently she succeeded in attracting his admiration, for his manner toward her was attentive and flattering. The effect of his presence on me was so benignant, especially in those renewals of our old tête-à-tête wanderings, when he poured forth to me wonderful narratives of his professional experience, that more than once, when his talk turned on the psychological relations of disease, the thought crossed my mind that, if his stay with me were long enough, I might possibly bring myself to tell this man the secrets of my lot. Might there not lie some remedy for *me*, too, in his science? Might there not at least lie some comprehension and sympathy ready for me in his large and susceptible mind? But the thought only flickered feebly now and then, and died out before it could become a wish. The horror I had of again breaking in on the privacy of another soul, made me, by an irrational instinct, draw the shroud of concealment more closely around my own, as we automatically perform the gesture we feel to be wanting in another.

When Meunier's visit was approaching its conclusion, there happened an event which caused some excitement in our household, owing to the surprisingly strong effect it appeared to produce on Bertha—on Bertha, the self-possessed, who usually seemed inaccessible to feminine agitations, and did even her hate in a self-restrained hygienic manner. This event was the sudden severe illness of her maid, Mrs. Archer. I have reserved to this moment the mention of a circumstance which had forced itself on my notice shortly before Meunier's arrival, namely, that there had been some quarrel between Bertha and this maid, apparently during a visit to a distant family, in which she had accompanied her mistress. I had overheard Archer speaking in a tone of bitter insolence, which I should have thought an adequate reason for immediate dismissal. No dismissal followed; on the contrary, Bertha seemed to be silently putting up with personal inconveniences from the exhibitions of this woman's temper. I was the more astonished to observe that her illness seemed a cause of strong solicitude to Bertha; that she was at the bedside night and day, and would allow no one else to officiate as head nurse. It happened that our family doctor was out on a holiday, an accident which made Meunier's presence in the house doubly welcome, and he apparently entered into the case with an interest which seemed so much stronger than the ordinary professional feeling, that one day when he had fallen into a long fit of silence after visiting her, I said to him—

"Is this a very peculiar case of disease, Meunier?"

"No," he answered, "it is an attack of peritonitis, which will be fatal, but which does not differ physically from many other cases that have come under my observation. But I'll tell you what I have on my mind. I want to make an experiment on this woman, if you will give me permission. It can do her no harm—will give her no pain—for I shall not make it until life is extinct to all purposes of sensation. I want to try the effect of transfusing blood into her arteries after the heart has ceased to beat for some minutes. I have tried the experiment again and again with animals that have died of this disease, with astounding results, and I want to try it on a human subject. I have the small tubes necessary, in a case I have with me, and the rest of the apparatus could be prepared readily. I should use my own blood—take it from my own arm. This woman won't live through the night, I'm convinced, and I want you to promise me your assistance in making the experiment. I can't do without another hand, but it would perhaps not be well to call in a medical assistant from among your provincial doctors. A disagreeable foolish version of the thing might get abroad."

"Have you spoken to my wife on the subject?" I said, "because she appears to be peculiarly sensitive about this woman: she has been a favorite maid."

"To tell you the truth," said Meunier, "I don't want her to know about it. There are always insuperable difficulties with women in these matters, and the effect on the supposed dead body may be startling. You and I will sit up together, and be in readiness. When certain symptoms appear I shall take you in, and at the right moment we must manage to get every one else out of the room."

I need not give our farther conversation on the subject. He entered very fully into the details, and overcame my repulsion from them, by exciting in me a mingled awe and curiosity concerning the possible results of his experiment.

We prepared everything, and he instructed me in my part as assistant. He had not told Bertha of his absolute conviction that Archer would not survive through the night, and endeavored to persuade her to leave the patient and take a night's rest. But she was obstinate, suspecting the fact that death was at hand, and supposing that he wished merely to save her nerves. She refused to leave the sick-room. Meunier and I sat up together in the library, he making frequent visits to the sick-room, and returning with the information that the case was taking precisely the course he expected. Once he said to me, "Can you imagine any cause of ill feeling this woman has against her mistress, who is so devoted to her?"

"I think there was some misunderstanding between them before her illness. Why do you ask?"

"Because I have observed for the last five or six hours—since, I fancy, she has lost all hope of recovery—there seems a strange prompting in her to say something which pain and failing strength forbid her to utter; and there is a look of hideous meaning in her eyes, which she turns continually toward her mistress. In this disease the mind often remains singularly clear to the last."

"I am not surprised at an indication of malevolent feeling in her," I said. "She is a woman who has always inspired me with distrust and dislike, but she managed to insinuate herself into her mistress's favor." He was silent after this, looking at the fire with an air of absorption, till he went up-stairs again. He stayed away longer than usual, and on returning, said to me quietly, "Come now."

I followed him to the chamber where death was hovering. The dark hangings of the large bed made a background that gave a strong relief to Bertha's pale face as I entered. She started forward as she saw me enter, and then looked at Meunier with an expression of angry inquiry; but he lifted up his hand as if to impose silence, while he fixed his glance on the dying woman and felt her pulse. The face was pinched and ghastly, a cold perspiration was on the forehead, and the eyelids were lowered so as almost to conceal the large dark eyes. After a minute or two, Meunier walked round to the other side of the bed where Bertha stood, and with his usual air of gentle politeness toward her begged her to leave the patient under our care—everything should be done for her—she was no longer in a state to be conscious of an affectionate presence. Bertha was hesitating, apparently almost willing to believe his assurance and to comply. She looked round at the ghastly dying face, as if to read the confirmation of that assurance, when for a moment the lowered eyelids were raised again, and it seemed as if the eyes were looking toward Bertha, but blankly. A shudder passed through Bertha's frame, and she returned to her station near the pillow, tacitly implying that she would not leave the room.

The eyelids were lifted no more. Once I looked at Bertha as she watched the face of the dying one. She wore a rich *peignoir*,* and her

---

*Loose woman's dressing gown worn when the hair is being combed (French).

blonde hair was half covered by a lace cap: in her attire she was, as always, an elegant woman, fit to figure in a picture of modern aristocratic life: but I asked myself how that face of hers could ever have seemed to me the face of a woman born of woman, with memories of childhood, capable of pain, needing to be fondled? The features at that moment seemed so preternaturally sharp, the eyes were so hard and eager—she looked like a cruel immortal, finding her spiritual feast in the agonies of a dying race. For across those hard features there came something like a flash when the last hour had been breathed out, and we all felt that the dark veil had completely fallen. What secret was there between Bertha and this woman? I turned my eyes from her with a horrible dread lest my insight should return, and I should be obliged to see what had been breeding about two unloving women's hearts. I felt that Bertha had been watching for the moment of death as the sealing of her secret: I thanked Heaven it could remain sealed for me.

Meunier said quietly: "She is gone." He then gave his arm to Bertha, and she submitted to be led out of the room.

I suppose it was at her order that two female attendants came into the room, and dismissed the younger one who had been present before. When they entered, Meunier had already opened the artery in the long, thin neck that lay rigid on the pillow, and I dismissed them, ordering them to remain at a distance till we rang: the doctor, I said, had an operation to perform—he was not sure about the death. For the next twenty minutes I forgot everything but Meunier and the experiment in which he was so absorbed, that I think his senses would have been closed against all sounds or sights which had no relation to it. It was my task at first to keep up the artificial respiration in the body after the transfusion had been effected, but presently Meunier relieved me, and I could see the wondrous slow return of life; the breast began to heave, the inspirations became stronger, the eyelids quivered, and the soul seemed to have returned beneath them. The artificial respiration was withdrawn: still the breathing continued, and there was a movement of the lips.

Just then I heard the handle of the door moving: I suppose Bertha had heard from the women that they had been dismissed: probably a vague fear had arisen in her mind, for she entered with a look of alarm. She came to the foot of the bed and gave a stifled cry.

The dead woman's eyes were wide open, and met hers in full recognition—the recognition of hate. With a sudden strong effort, the hand that Bertha had thought for ever still was pointed toward her, and the haggard face moved. The gasping eager voice said—

"You mean to poison your husband —— the poison is in the black cabinet —— I got it for you —— you laughed at me, and told lies about me behind my back, to make me disgusting —— because you were jealous —— are you sorry —— now?"

The lips continued to murmur, but the sounds were no longer distinct. Soon there was no sound—only a slight movement: the flame had leaped out, and was being extinguished the faster. The wretched woman's heartstrings had been set to hatred and vengeance; the spirit of life had swept the chords for an instant, and was gone again for ever. Great God! Is this what it is to live again —— to wake up with our unstilled thirst upon us, with our unuttered curses rising to our lips, with our muscles ready to act out their half-committed sins?

Bertha stood pale at the foot of the bed, quivering and helpless, despairing of devices, like a cunning animal whose hiding-places are surrounded by swift-advancing flame. Even Meunier looked paralyzed; life for that moment ceased to be a scientific problem to him. As for me, this scene seemed of one texture with the rest of my existence: horror was my familiar, and this new revelation was only like an old pain recurring with new circumstances.

Since then Bertha and I have lived apart—she in her own neighborhood, the mistress of half our wealth, I as a wanderer in foreign countries, until I came to this Devonshire nest to die. Bertha lives pitied and admired; for what had I against that charming woman, whom every one but myself could have been happy with? There had been no witness of the scene in the dying room except Meunier, and while Meunier lived his lips were sealed by a promise to me.

Once or twice, weary of wandering, I rested in a favorite spot, and my heart went out toward the men and women and children whose faces were becoming familiar to me: but I was driven away again in terror at the approach of my old insight—driven away to live continually with the one Unknown Presence revealed and yet hidden by the moving curtain of the earth and sky. Till at last disease took hold of me and forced me to rest here—forced me to live in dependence on my servants. And then the curse of insight—of my double consciousness, came again, and has never left me. I know all their narrow thoughts, their feeble regard, their half-wearied pity.

It is the twentieth of September, 1850. I know these figures I have just written, as if they were a long familiar inscription. I have seen them on this page in my desk unnumbered times, when the scene of my dying struggle has opened upon me.

BROTHER JACOB

"Trompeurs, c'est pour vous que j'écris,
Attendez vous à la pareille."*

—LA FONTAINE.

---

*From the late-seventeenth-century *Fables* of Jean de La Fontaine: "Deceivers, I write for you / Wait for the same fate"(French).

CHAPTER I

AMONG THE MANY FATALITIES attending the bloom of young desire, that of blindly taking to the confectionery line has not, perhaps, been sufficiently considered. How is the son of a British yeoman, who has been fed principally on salt pork and yeast dumplings, to know that there is satiety for the human stomach even in a paradise of glass jars full of sugared almonds and pink lozenges, and that the tedium of life can reach a pitch where plum-buns at discretion cease to offer the slightest enticement? Or how, at the tender age when a confectioner seems to him a very prince whom all the world must envy—who breakfasts on macaroons, dines on marengs, sups on twelfth-cake,* and fills up the intermediate hours with sugar-candy or peppermint—how is he to foresee the day of sad wisdom, when he will discern that the confectioner's calling is not so-cially influential, or favorable to a soaring ambition? I have known a man who turned out to have a metaphysical genius, incautiously, in the period of youthful buoyancy, commence his career as a dancing-master; and you may imagine the use that was made of this initial mis-take by opponents who felt themselves bound to warn the public against his doctrine of the Inconceivable. He could not give up his dancing-lessons, because he made his bread by them, and metaphysics would not have found him in so much as salt to his bread. It was re-ally the same with Mr. David Faux and the confectionery business. His uncle, the butler at the great house close by Brigford, had made a pet of him in his early boyhood, and it was on a visit to this uncle that the confectioners' shops in that brilliant town had, on a single day, fired his tender imagination. He carried home the pleasing illusion that a confectioner must be at once the happiest and the foremost of men, since the things he made were not only the most beautiful to behold, but the very best eating, and such as the Lord Mayor must always order largely for his private recreation; so that when his father

---

*A cake traditionally eaten on the twelfth night of the Epiphany.

declared he must be put to a trade, David chose his line without a moment's hesitation; and, with a rashness inspired by a sweet tooth, wedded himself irrevocably to confectionery. Soon, however, the tooth lost its relish and fell into blank indifference; and all the while his mind expanded, his ambition took new shapes, which would hardly be satisfied within the sphere his youthful ardor had chosen. But what was he to do? He was a young man of much mental activity, and above all, gifted with a spirit of contrivance; but then, his faculties would not tell with great effect in any other medium than that of candied sugars, conserves and pastry. Say what you will about the identity of the reasoning process in all branches of thought, or about the advantage of coming to subjects with a fresh mind, the adjustment of butter to flour, and of heat to pastry, is not the best preparation for the office of prime minister; besides, in the present imperfectly-organized state of society, there are social barriers. David could invent delightful things in the way of drop-cakes, and he had the widest views of the sugar department; but in other directions he certainly felt hampered by the want of knowledge and practical skill; and the world is so inconveniently constituted that the vague consciousness of being a fine fellow is no guarantee of success in any line of business.

This difficulty pressed with some severity on Mr. David Faux, even before his apprenticeship was ended. His soul swelled with an impatient sense that he ought to become something very remarkable—that it was quite out of the question for him to put up with a narrow lot as other men did: he scorned the idea that he could accept an average. He was sure there was nothing average about him: even such a person as Mrs. Tibbits, the washerwoman, perceived it, and probably had a preference for his linen. At that particular period he was weighing out gingerbread nuts; but such an anomaly could not continue. No position could be suited to Mr. David Faux that was not in the highest degree easy to the flesh and flattering to the spirit. If he had fallen on the present times, and enjoyed the advantages of a Mechanics' Institute,* he would certainly have taken to literature and have written reviews; but his education had not been liberal. He had read some novels from the adjoining circulating library, and had even

---

*Institutes of adult education for working people; the first in was founded in 1821 in Glasgow, the second in London in 1823.

bought the story of "Inkle and Yarico,"[1] which had made him feel very sorry for poor Mr. Inkle; so that his ideas might not have been below a certain mark of the literary calling; but his spelling and diction were too unconventional.

When a man is not adequately appreciated or comfortably placed in his own country, his thoughts naturally turn toward foreign climes; and David's imagination circled round and round the utmost limits of his geographical knowledge, in search of a country where a young gentleman of pasty visage, lipless mouth, and stumpy hair, would be likely to be received with the hospitable enthusiasm which he had a right to expect. Having a general idea of America as a country where the population was chiefly black, it appeared to him the most propitious destination for an emigrant who, to begin with, had the broad and easily recognizable merit of whiteness; and this idea gradually took such strong possession of him that Satan seized the opportunity of suggesting to him that he might emigrate under easier circumstances, if he supplied himself with a little money from his master's till. But that evil spirit, whose understanding, I am convinced, has been much overrated, quite wasted his time on this occasion. David would certainly have liked well to have some of his master's money in his pocket, if he had been sure his master would have been the only man to suffer for it; but he was a cautious youth, and quite determined to run no risks on his own account. So he stayed out his apprenticeship, and committed no act of dishonesty that was at all likely to be discovered, reserving his plan of emigration for a future opportunity. And the circumstances under which he carried it out were in this wise. Having been at home a week or two partaking of the family beans, he had used his leisure in ascertaining a fact which was of considerable importance to him, namely, that his mother had a small sum in guineas painfully saved from her maiden perquisites, and kept in the corner of a drawer where her baby-linen had reposed for the last twenty years—ever since her son David had taken to his feet, with a slight promise of bow-legs, which had not been altogether unfulfilled. Mr. Faux, senior, had told his son very frankly, that he must not look to being set-up in business by him: with seven sons, and one of them a very healthy and well-developed idiot, who consumed a dumpling about eight inches in diameter every day, it was pretty well if they got a hundred apiece at his death. Under these circumstances, what was David to do? It was certainly hard that he should take his mother's money; but he saw no other ready means of getting any, and it was not to be expected that a young man of his merit should put up with inconveniences that could be avoided. Besides, it is not robbery to take property belonging to your mother: she doesn't prosecute you. And David was very well behaved to his mother; he comforted her by speaking highly of himself to her, and assuring her that he never fell into the vices he saw practiced by other youths of his own age, and that he was particularly fond of honesty. If his mother would have given him her twenty guineas as a reward of this noble disposition, he really would not have stolen them from her, and it would have been more agreeable to his feelings. Nevertheless, to an active mind like David's, ingenuity is not without its pleasures: it was rather an interesting occupation to become stealthily acquainted with the wards of his mother's simple key (not in the least like Chubb's patent*), and to get one that would do its work equally well; and also to arrange a little drama by which he would escape suspicion, and run no risk of forfeiting the prospective hundred at his father's death, which would be convenient in the improbable case of his not making a large fortune in the "Indies."

First, he spoke freely of his intention to start shortly for Liverpool and take ship for America; a resolution which cost his good mother some pain, for, after Jacob the idiot, there was not one of her sons to whom her heart clung more than to her youngest-born, David. Next, it appeared to him that Sunday afternoon, when everybody was gone to church except Jacob and the cow-boy, was so singularly favorable an opportunity for sons who wanted to appropriate their mothers' guineas, that he half thought it must have been kindly intended by Providence for such purposes. Especially the third Sunday in Lent; because Jacob had been out on one of his occasional wanderings for the last two days; and David, being a timid young man, had a considerable dread and hatred of Jacob, as of a large personage who went about habitually with a pitchfork in his hand.

---

*The patent (1818) for a newly designed lock that was very successful and underwent successive improvements through the lifetime of its inventor, Charles Chubb (1773–1845).

Nothing could be easier, then, than for David on this Sunday afternoon to decline going to church, on the ground that he was going to tea at Mr. Lunn's, whose pretty daughter Sally had been an early flame of his, and, when the church-goers were at a safe distance, to abstract the guineas from their wooden box and slip them into a small canvas bag—nothing easier than to call to the cow-boy that he was going, and tell him to keep an eye on the house for fear of Sunday tramps. David thought it would be easy, too, to get to a small thicket and bury his bag in a hole he had already made and covered up under the roots of an old hollow ash, and he had, in fact, found the hole without a moment's difficulty, had uncovered it, and was about gently to drop the bag into it, when the sound of a large body rustling toward him with something like a bellow was such a surprise to David, who, as a gentleman gifted with much contrivance, was naturally only prepared for what he expected, that instead of dropping the bag gently he let it fall so as to make it untwist and vomit forth the shining guineas. In the same moment he looked up and saw his dear brother Jacob close upon him, holding the pitchfork so that the bright smooth prongs were a yard in advance of his own body, and about a foot off David's. (A learned friend, to whom I once narrated this history, observed that it was David's guilt which made these prongs formidable, and that the mens nil conscia sibi* strips a pitchfork of all terrors. I thought this idea so valuable, that I obtained his leave to use it on condition of suppressing his name.) Nevertheless, David did not entirely lose his presence of mind; for in that case he would have sunk on the earth or started backward; whereas he kept his ground and smiled at Jacob, who nodded his head up and down, and said, "Hoich, Zavy!" in a painfully equivocal manner. David's heart was beating audibly, and if he had had any lips they would have been pale; but his mental activity, instead of being paralyzed, was stimulated. While he was inwardly praying (he always prayed when he was much frightened)—"Oh, save me this once, and I'll never get into danger again!"—he was thrusting his hand into his pocket in search of a box of yellow lozenges, which he had brought with him from Brigford among other delicacies of the same portable

---

*A mind not conscious of itself (Latin).

kind, as a means of conciliating proud beauty, and more particularly
the beauty of Miss Sarah Lunn. Not one of these delicacies had he
ever offered to poor Jacob, for David was not a young man to waste
his jujubes and barley-sugar in giving pleasure to people from whom
he expected nothing. But an idiot with equivocal intentions and a
pitchfork is as well worth flattering and cajoling as if he were Louis
Napoleon.* So David, with a promptitude equal to the occasion,
drew out his box of yellow lozenges, lifted the lid, and performed a
pantomime with his mouth and fingers, which was meant to imply
that he was delighted to see his dear brother Jacob, and seized the opportunity of making him a small present, which he would find particularly agreeable to the taste. Jacob, you understand, was not an
intense idiot, but within a certain limited range knew how to choose
the good and reject the evil: he took one lozenge by way of test, and
sucked it as if he had been a philosopher; then, in as great an ecstacy
at its new and complex savour as Caliban at the taste of Trinculo's
wine,† chuckled and stroked this suddenly beneficent brother, and held
out his hand for more; for, except in fits of anger, Jacob was not fe-
rocious or needlessly predatory. David's courage half returned, and he
left off praying; pouring a dozen lozenges into Jacob's palm, and trying to look very fond of him. He congratulated himself that he had
formed the plan of going to see Miss Sally Lunn this afternoon, and
that, as a consequence, he had brought with him these propitiatory
delicacies: he was certainly a lucky fellow; indeed, it was always likely
that Providence should be fonder of him than of other apprentices,[2]
and since he *was* to be interrupted, why, an idiot was preferable to any
other sort of witness. For the first time in his life, David thought he
saw the advantage of idiots.

   As for Jacob, he had thrust his pitchfork into the ground, and
had thrown himself down beside it, in thorough abandonment to
the unprecedented pleasure of having five lozenges in his mouth
at once, blinking mean while, and making inarticulate sounds of
gustative content. He had not yet given any sign of noticing the

---

*The nephew of Napoleon Bonaparte was Napoleon III, emperor of France, from
1852 to 1870.
†Allusion to Caliban's rapturous reaction to Trinculo's proffered wine in Shakespeare's
The Tempest (act 2, scene 2).

guineas, but in seating himself he had laid his broad right hand on them, and unconsciously kept it in that position, absorbed in the sensations of his palate. If he could only be kept so occupied with the lozenges as not to see the guineas before David could manage to cover them! That was David's best hope of safety; for Jacob knew his mother's guineas; it had been part of their common experience as boys to be allowed to look at these handsome coins, and rattle them in their box on high days and holidays, and among all Jacob's narrow experiences as to money, this was likely to be the most memorable.

"Here, Jacob," said David, in an insinuating tone, handing the box to him, "I'll give 'em all to you. Run!—make haste!—else somebody 'll come and take 'em."

David, not having studied the psychology of idiots, was not aware that they are not to be wrought upon by imaginative fears. Jacob took the box with his left hand, but saw no necessity for running away. Was ever a promising young man wishing to lay the foundation of his fortune by appropriating his mother's guineas obstructed by such a day-mare as this? But the moment must come when Jacob would move his right hand to draw off the lid of the tin box, and then David would sweep the guineas into the hole with the utmost address and swiftness, and immediately seat himself upon them. Ah, no! It's of no use to have foresight when you are dealing with an idiot: he is not to be calculated upon. Jacob's right hand was given to vague clutching and throwing; it suddenly clutched the guineas as if they had been so many pebbles, and was raised in an attitude which promised to scatter them like seed over a distant bramble, when, from some prompting or other—probably of an unwonted sensation—it paused, descended to Jacob's knee, and opened slowly under the inspection of Jacob's dull eyes. David began to pray again, but immediately desisted—another resource having occurred to him.

"Mother! zinnies!" exclaimed the innocent Jacob. Then, looking at David, he said, interrogatively, "Box?"

"Hush! hush!" said David, summoning all his ingenuity in this severe strait. "See, Jacob!" He took the tin box from his brother's hand, and emptied it of the lozenges, returning half of them to Jacob, but secretely keeping the rest in his own hand. Then he held out the empty box, and said, "Here's the box, Jacob! The box for the guineas!" gently sweeping them from Jacob's palm into the box.

This procedure was not objectionable to Jacob; on the contrary, the guineas clinked so pleasantly as they fell, that he wished for a repetition of the sound, and seizing the box, began to rattle it very gleefully. David, seizing the opportunity, deposited his reserve lozenges in the ground and hastily swept some earth over them. "Look, Jacob!" he said, at last. Jacob paused from his clinking, and looked into the hole, while David began to scratch away the earth, as if in doubtful expectation. When the lozenges were laid bare, he took them out one by one, and gave them to Jacob.

"Hush!" he said, in a loud whisper, "Tell nobody—all for Jacob—hush—sh—sh! Put guineas in the hole—they'll come out like this!" To make the lesson more complete, he took a guinea, and lowering it into the hole, said, "Put in so." Then, as he took the last lozenge out, he said, "Come out so," and put the lozenge into Jacob's hospitable mouth.

Jacob turned his head on one side, looked first at his brother and then at the hole, like a reflective monkey, and, finally, laid the box of guineas in the hole with much decision. David made haste to add every one of the stray coins, put on the lid, and covered it well with earth, saying in his most coaxing tone—

"Take 'm out to-morrow, Jacob; all for Jacob! Hush—sh—sh!"

Jacob, to whom this once indifferent brother had all at once become a sort of sweet-tasted fetish, stroked David's best coat with his adhesive fingers, and then hugged him with an accompaniment of that mingled chuckling and gurgling by which he was accustomed to express the milder passions. But if he had chosen to bite a small morsel out of his beneficent brother's cheek, David would have been obliged to bear it.

And here I must pause, to point out to you the short-sightedness of human contrivance. This ingenious young man, Mr. David Faux, thought he had achieved a triumph of cunning when he had associated himself in his brother's rudimentary mind with the flavor of yellow lozenges. But he had yet to learn that it is a dreadful thing to make an idiot fond of you, when you yourself are not of an affectionate disposition: especially an idiot with a pitchfork—obviously a difficult friend to shake off by rough usage.

It may seem to you rather a blundering contrivance for a clever young man to bury the guineas. But, if everything had turned out as David had calculated, you would have seen that his plan was worthy of his talents. The guineas would have lain safely in the earth while the theft was discovered, and David, with the calm of conscious innocence, would have lingered at home, reluctant to say goodbye to his dear mother while she was in grief about her guineas; till at length, on the eve of his departure, he would have disinterred them in the strictest privacy, and carried them on his own person without inconvenience. But David, you perceive, had reckoned without his host, or, to speak more precisely, without his idiot brother—an item of so uncertain and fluctuating a character, that I doubt whether he would not have puzzled the astute heroes of M. de Balzac,[3] whose foresight is so remarkably at home in the future.

It was clear to David now that he had only one alternative before him: he must either renounce the guineas, by quietly putting them back in his mother's drawer (a course not unattended with difficulty); or he must leave more than a suspicion behind him, by departing early the next morning without giving notice, and with the guineas in his pocket. For if he gave notice that he was going, his mother, he knew, would insist on fetching from her box of guineas the three she had alway promised him as his share; indeed, in his original plan, he had counted on this as a means by which the theft would be discovered under circumstances that would themselves speak for his innocence; but now, as I need hardly explain, that well-combined plan was completely frustrated. Even if David could have bribed Jacob with perpetual lozenges, an idiot's secrecy is itself betrayal. He dared not even go to tea at Mr. Lunn's, for in that case he would have lost sight of Jacob, who, in his impatience for the crop of lozenges, might scratch up the box again while he was absent, and carry it home—depriving him at once of reputation and guineas. No! he must think of nothing all the rest of this day, but of coaxing Jacob and keeping him out of mischief. It was a fatiguing and anxious evening to David; nevertheless, he dared not go to sleep without tying a piece of string to his thumb and great toe, to secure his frequent waking; for he meant to be up with the first peep of dawn, and be far out of reach before breakfast-time. His father, he thought, would certainly cut him off with a shilling; but what then? Such a striking

young man as he would be sure to be well received in the West Indies; in foreign countries there are always openings—even for cats. It
was probable that some Princess Yarico would want him to marry
her, and make him presents of very large jewels beforehand; after
which, he needn't marry her unless he liked. David had made up his
mind not to steal any more, even from people who were fond of him:
it was an unpleasant way of making your fortune in a world where
you were likely to be surprised in the act by brothers. Such alarms did
not agree with David's constitution and he had felt so much nausea
this evening that no doubt his liver was affected. Besides, he would
have been greatly hurt not to be thought well of in the world: he always meant to make a figure, and be thought worthy of the best seats
and the best morsels.

Ruminating to this effect on the brilliant future in reserve for
him, David by the help of his check-string kept himself on the alert
to seize the time of earliest dawn for his rising and departure. His
brothers, of course, were early risers, but he should anticipate them
by at least an hour and a half, and the little room which he had to
himself as only an occasional visitor, had its window over the horse-
block, so that he could slip out through the window without the least
difficulty. Jacob, the horrible Jacob, had an awkward trick of getting
up before everybody else, to stem his hunger by emptying the milk-
bowl that was "duly set" for him; but of late he had taken to sleeping in the hay-loft, and if he came into the house it would be on the
opposite side to that from which David was making his exit. There
was no need to think of Jacob; yet David was liberal enough to bestow a curse on him—it was the only thing he ever did bestow gratuitously. His small bundle of clothes was ready packed, and he was
soon treading lightly on the steps of the horse-block, soon walking
at a smart pace across the fields toward the thicket. It would take him
no more than two minutes to get out the box; he could make out the
tree it was under by the pale strip where the bark was off, although
the dawning light was rather dimmer in the thicket. But what, in the
name of—burnt pastry—was that large body with a staff planted beside it, close at the foot of the ash tree? David paused, not to make up
his mind as to the nature of the apparition—he had not the happiness of doubting for a moment that the staff was Jacob's pitchfork—
but to gather the self-command necessary for addressing his brother

with a sufficiently honeyed accent. Jacob was absorbed in scratching up the earth, and had not heard David's approach.

"I say, Jacob," said David in a loud whisper, just as the tin box was lifted out of the hole.

Jacob looked up, and discerning his sweet-flavored brother, nodded and grinned in the dim light in a way that made him seem to David like a triumphant demon. If he had been of an impetuous disposition, he would have snatched the pitchfork from the ground and impaled this fraternal demon. But David was by no means impetuous; he was a young man greatly given to calculate consequences, a habit which has been held to be the foundation of virtue.[4] But somehow it had not precisely that effect in David: he calculated whether an action would harm himself, or whether it would only harm other people. In the former case he was very timid about satisfying his immediate desires, but in the latter he would risk the result with much courage.

"Give it me, Jacob," he said, stooping down and patting his brother. "Let us see."

Jacob, finding the lid rather tight, gave the box to his brother in perfect faith. David raised the lid, and shook his head, while Jacob put his finger in and took out a guinea to taste whether the metamorphosis into lozenges was complete and satisfactory.

"No, Jacob; too soon, too soon," said David, when the guinea had been tasted. "Give it me; we'll go and bury it somewhere else; we'll put it in yonder," he added, pointing vaguely toward the distance.

David screwed on the lid, while Jacob, looking grave, rose and grasped his pitchfork. Then, seeing David's bundle, he snatched it, like a too officious Newfoundland, stuck his pitchfork into it and carried it over his shoulder in triumph as he accompanied David and the box out of the thicket.

What on earth was David to do? It would have been easy to frown at Jacob, and kick him, and order him to get away; but David dared as soon have kicked the bull. Jacob was quiet as long as he was treated indulgently; but on the slightest show of anger he became unmanageable, and was liable to fits of fury which would have made him formidable even without his pitchfork. There was no mastery to be obtained over him except by kindness or guile. David tried guile.

"Go, Jacob," he said, when they were out of the thicket—pointing toward the house as he spoke; "go and fetch me a spade—a spade. But give me the bundle," he added, trying to reach it from the fork, where it hung high above Jacob's tall shoulder.

But Jacob showed as much alacrity in obeying as a wasp shows in leaving a sugar-basin. Near David, he felt himself in the vicinity of lozenges: he chuckled and rubbed his brother's back, brandishing the bundle higher out of reach. David, with an inward groan, changed his tactics, and walked on as fast as he could. It was not safe to linger. Jacob would get tired of following him, or, at all events, could be eluded. If they could once get to the distant highroad, a coach would overtake them, David would mount it, having previously by some ingenious means secured his bundle, and then Jacob might howl and flourish his pitchfork as much as he liked. Meanwhile he was under the fatal necessity of being very kind to this ogre, and of providing a large breakfast for him when they stopped at a roadside inn. It was already three hours since they had started, and David was tired. Would no coach be coming up soon? he enquired. No coach for the next two hours. But there was a carrier's cart to come immediately, on its way to the next town. If he could slip out, even leaving his bundle behind, and get into the cart without Jacob! But there was a new obstacle. Jacob had recently discovered a remnant of sugar-candy in one of his brother's tail-pockets; and, since then, had cautiously kept his hold on that limb of the garment, perhaps with an expectation that there would be a further development of sugar-candy after a longer or shorter interval. Now every one who has worn a coat will understand the sensibilities that must keep a man from starting away in a hurry when there is a grasp on his coat-tail. David looked forward to being well received among strangers, but it might make a difference if he had only one tail to his coat.

He felt himself in a cold perspiration. He could walk no more: he must get into the cart and let Jacob get in with him. Presently a cheering idea occurred to him: after so large a breakfast, Jacob would be sure to go to sleep in the cart; you see at once that David meant to seize his bundle, jump out, and be free. His expectation was partly fulfilled: Jacob did go to sleep in the cart, but it was in a peculiar attitude—it was with his arms tightly fastened round his dear brother's body; and if ever David attempted to move, the grasp tightened with the force of an affectionate boa-constrictor.

"Th' innicent's fond on you," observed the carrier, thinking that David was probably an amiable brother, and wishing to pay him a compliment.

David groaned. The ways of thieving were not ways of pleasantness. Oh, why had he an idiot brother? Or why, in general, was the world so constituted that a man could not take his mother's guineas comfortably? David became grimly speculative.

Copious dinner at noon for Jacob; but little dinner, because little appetite, for David. Instead of eating, he plied Jacob with beer; for through this liberality he descried a hope. Jacob fell into a dead sleep, at last, without having his arms round David, who paid the reckoning, took his bundle, and walked off. In another half-hour he was on the coach on his way to Liverpool, smiling the smile of the triumphant wicked. He was rid of Jacob—he was bound for the Indies, where a gullible princess awaited him. He would never steal any more, but there would be no need; he would show himself so deserving, that people would make him presents freely. He must give up the notion of his father's legacy; but it was not likely he would ever want that trifle; and even if he did—why, it was a compensation to think that in being forever divided from his family he was divided from Jacob, more terrible than Gorgon or Demogorgon[5] to David's timid green eyes. Thank heaven, he should never see Jacob any more!

CHAPTER II

I T WAS NEARLY SIX years after the departure of Mr. David Faux for the West Indies, that the vacant shop in the market-place at Grimworth was understood to have been let to the stranger with a sallow complexion and a buff cravat, whose first appearance had caused some excitement in the bar of the Woolpack, where he had called to wait for the coach.

Grimworth, to a discerning eye, was a good place to set up shopkeeping in. There was no competition in it at present; the Church-people had their own grocer and draper; the Dissenters had theirs;[6] and the two or three butchers found a ready market for their

joints without strict reference to religious persuasion—except that
the rector's wife had given a general order for the veal sweet-breads
and the mutton kidneys, while Mr. Rodd, the Baptist minister, had re-
quested that, so far as was compatible with the fair accommodation
of other customers, the sheep's trotters might be reserved for him.
And it was likely to be a growing place, for the trustees of Mr. Zepha-
niah Crypt's Charity, under the stimulus of a late visitation by com-
missioners, were beginning to apply long-accumulating funds to the
rebuilding of the Yellow Coat School, which was henceforth to be
carried forward on a greatly-extended scale, the testator having left
no restrictions concerning the curriculum, but only concerning the
coat.

The shopkeepers at Grimworth were by no means unanimous
as to the advantages promised by this prospect of increased population and trading, being substantial men, who liked doing a quiet
business in which they were sure of their customers, and could calculate their returns to a nicety. Hitherto, it had been held a point of
honor by the families in Grimworth parish, to buy their sugar and
their flannel at the shops where their fathers and mothers had
bought before them; but, if new-comers were to bring in the system of neck-and-neck trading, and solicit feminine eyes by gown-
pieces laid in fan-like folds, and surmounted by artificial flowers,
giving them a factitious charm (for on what human figure would a
gown sit like a fan, or what female head was like a bunch of China-
asters?), or, if new grocers were to fill their windows with mountains
of currants and sugar, made seductive by contrast and tickets,—[7]
what security was there for Grimworth, that a vagrant spirit in
shopping, once introduced, would not in the end carry the most
important families to the larger market town of Cattleton, where,
business being done on a system of small profits and quick returns,
the fashions were of the freshest, and goods of all kinds might be
bought at an advantage?

With this view of the times predominant among the tradespeople at Grimworth, their uncertainty concerning the nature of
the business which the sallow-complexioned stranger was about to
set up in the vacant shop, naturally gave some additional strength
to the fears of the less sanguine. If he was going to sell drapery, it
was probable that a pale-faced fellow like that would deal in showy

and inferior articles—printed cottons and muslins which would leave their dye in the wash-tub, jobbed linen* full of knots, and flannel that would soon look like gauze. If grocery, then it was to be hoped that no mother of a family would trust the teas of an untried grocer. Such things had been known in some parishes as tradesmen going about canvassing for custom with cards in their pockets; when people came from nobody knew where, there was no knowing what they might do. It was a thousand pities that Mr. Moffat, the auctioneer and broker, had died without leaving anybody to follow him in the business, and Mrs. Cleve's trustee ought to have known better than to let a shop to a stranger. Even the discovery that ovens were being put up on the premises, and that the shop was, in fact, being fitted up for a confectioner and pastry-cook's business, hitherto unknown in Grimworth, did not quite suffice to turn the scale in the new-comer's favor, though the landlady at the Woolpack defended him warmly, said he seemed to be a very clever young man, and from what she could make out, came of a very good family; indeed, was most likely a good many people's betters.

It certainly made a blaze of light and color, almost as if a rainbow had suddenly descended into the market-place, when, one fine morning, the shutters were taken down from the new shop, and the two windows displayed their decorations. On one side there were the variegated tints of colored and marbled meats, set off by bright green leaves, the pale brown of glazed pies, the rich tones of sauces and bottled fruits enclosed in their veil of glass— altogether a sight to bring tears into the eyes of a Dutch painter;† and on the other there was a predominance of the more delicate hues of pink, and white, and yellow, and buff, in the abundant lozenges, candies, sweet biscuits and icings, which to the eyes of a bilious person might easily have been blended into a faëry landscape in Turner's‡ latest style. What a sight to dawn upon the eyes

---

*Material bought cheaply from large wholesale dealers.

†The Dutch master painters rendered the mundane details of ordinary life with realistic precision.

‡J. M. W. Turner (1775–1851), the English landscape painter whose brilliant colors and vaguely evoked images had an enormous impact on art and art criticism.

of Grimworth children! They almost forgot to go to their dinner that day, their appetites being preoccupied with imaginary sugar-plums; and I think even Punch, setting up his tabernacle in the market-place would not have succeeded in drawing them away from those shop-windows, where they stood according to grada-tions of size and strength, the biggest and strongest being nearest the window, and the little ones in the outermost rows lifting wide-open eyes and mouths towards the upper tier of jars, like small birds at meal-time.

The elder inhabitants pished and pshawed a little at the folly of the new shopkeeper in venturing on such an outlay in goods that would not keep; to be sure, Christmas was coming, but what house-wife in Grimworth would not think it a shame to furnish forth her table with articles that were not home-cooked? No, no. Mr. Edward Freely, as he called himself, was deceived, if he thought Grimworth money was to flow into his pockets on such terms.

Edward Freely was the name that shone in gilt letters on a mazarine* ground over the doorplace of the new shop—a generous-sounding name, that might have belonged to the open-hearted, im-provident hero of an old comedy, who would have delighted in raining sugared almonds, like a new manna-gift, among that small generation outside the windows. But Mr. Edward Freely was a man whose impulses were kept in due subordination: he held that the desire for sweets and pastry must only be satisfied in a direct ratio with the power for paying for them. If the smallest child in Grim-worth would go to him with a halfpenny in its tiny fist, he would, after ringing the halfpenny, deliver a just equivalent in "rock." He was not a man to cheat even the smallest child—he often said so, observing at the same time that he loved honesty, and also that he was very tender-hearted, though he didn't show his feelings as some people did.

Either in reward of such virtue, or according to some more hidden law of sequence,[8] Mr. Freely's business, in spite of preju-dice, started under favorable auspices. For Mrs. Chaloner, the rec-tor's wife, was among the earliest customers at the shop, thinking

---

*A rich, deep-blue color.

it only right to encourage a new parishioner who had made a decorous appearance at church; and she found Mr. Freely a most civil, obliging young man, and intelligent to a surprising degree for a confectioner; well-principled, too, for in giving her useful hints about choosing sugars, he had thrown much light on the dishonesty of other tradesmen. Moreover, he had been in the West Indies, and had seen the very estate which had been her poor grandfather's property; and he said the missionaries were the only cause of the negro's discontent—an observing young man, evidently. Mrs. Chaloner ordered wine-biscuits and olives, and gave Mr. Freely to understand that she should find his shop a great convenience. So did the doctor's wife, and so did Mrs. Gate, at the large carding-mill, who, having high connections frequently visiting her, might be expected to have a large consumption of ratafias* and macaroons.

The less aristocratic matrons of Grimworth seemed likely at first to justify their husbands' confidence that they would never pay a percentage of profits on drop-cakes, instead of making their own, or get up a hollow show of liberal housekeeping by purchasing slices of collared meat when a neighbor came in for supper. But it is my task to narrate the gradual corruption of Grimworth manners from their primitive simplicity—a melancholy task if it were not cheered by the prospect of the fine peripateia† or downfall by which the progress of the corruption was ultimately checked.

It was young Mrs. Steene, the veterinary surgeon's wife, who first gave way to temptation. I fear she had been rather over-educated for her station in life, for she knew by heart many passages in "Lalla Rookh," the "Corsair," and the "Siege of Corinth,"‡ which had given her a distaste for domestic occupations, and caused her a withering disappointment at the discovery that Mr. Steene since his marriage, had lost all interest in the "bulbul,"§ openly preferred discussing the

---

*Sweet cordial flavored with fruit kernels or almonds.
†A formal part of Greek tragedy, the moment when the story "reverses"—when, for example, Oedipus discovers he has killed his father and married his mother.
‡Popular oriental ballads of the early nineteenth century, by Thomas Moore and George Gordon, Lord Byron.
§A nightingale, a bird that appears often in "oriental" poems such as those transcribed in The Thousand and One Nights.

nature of spavin* with a coarse neighbor, and was angry if the
pudding turned out watery—indeed, was simply a top-booted "vet.,"
who came in hungry at dinner-time; and not in the least like a noble-
man turned Corsair out of pure scorn for his race, or like a renegade
with a turban aud crescent, unless it were in the irritability of his
temper. And scorn is such a very different thing in top-boots!

This brutal man had invited a supper-party for Christmas Eve,
when he would expect to see mince-pies on the table. Mrs. Steene
had prepared her mince-meat, and had devoted much butter, fine
flour, and labor, to the making of a batch of pies in the morning; but
they proved to be so very heavy when they came out of the oven that
she could only think with trembling of the moment when her husband should catch sight of them on the suppertable. He would storm
at her, she was certain; and before all the company; and then she
should never help crying: it was so dreadful to think she had come
to that, after the bulbul and everything! Suddenly the thought darted
through her mind that this once she might send for a dish of mince-
pies from Freely's: she knew he had some. But what was to become
of the eighteen heavy mince-pies? Oh, it was of no use thinking
about that; it was very expensive—indeed, making mince-pies at all
was a great expense, when they were not sure to turn out well: it
would be much better to buy them ready-made. You paid a little
more for them, but there was no risk of waste.

Such was the sophistry with which this misguided young
woman—enough. Mrs. Steene sent for the mince-pies, and, I am
grieved to add, garbled her household accounts in order to conceal
the fact from her husband. This was the second step in a downward
course, all owing to a young woman's being out of harmony with her
circumstances, yearning after renegades and bulbuls, and being subject to claims from a veterinary surgeon fond of mince-pies. The
third step was to harden herself by telling the fact of the bought
mince-pies to her intimate friend Mrs. Mole, who had already
guessed it, and who subsequently encouraged herself in buying a
mould of jelly, instead of exerting her own skill, by the reflection that
"other people" did the same sort of thing. The infection spread; soon

---

*A swelling on the inside of a horse's leg.

there was a party or clique in Grimworth on the side of "buying at Freely's"; and many husbands, kept for some time in the dark on this point, innocently swallowed at two mouthfuls a tart on which they were paying a profit of a hundred per cent, and as innocently encouraged a fatal disingenuousness in the partners of their bosoms by praising the pastry. Others, more keen-sighted, winked at the too frequent presentation on washing-days, and at impromptu suppers, of superior spiced-beef, which flattered their palates more than the cold remnants they had formerly been contented with. Every housewife who had once "bought at Freely's" felt a secret joy when she detected a similar perversion in her neighbor's practice and soon only two or three old-fashioned mistresses of families held out in the protest against the growing demoralization, saying to their neighbors who came to sup with them, "I can't offer you Freely's beef, or Freely's cheese-cakes; everything in our house is home-made; I'm afraid you'll hardly have any appetite for our plain pastry." The doctor, whose cook was not satisfactory, the curate, who kept no cook, and the mining agent, who was a great *bon vivant*, even began to rely on Freely for the greater part of their dinner, when they wished to give an entertainment of some brilliancy. In short, the business of manufacturing the more fanciful viands was fast passing out of the hands of maids and matrons in private families, and was becoming the work of a special commercial organ.

I am not ignorant that this sort of thing is called the inevitable course of civilization, division of labor, and so forth, and that the maids and matrons may be said to have had their hands set free from cookery to add to the wealth of society in some other way. Only it happened at Grimworth, which, to be sure, was a low place, that the maids and matrons could do nothing with their hands at all better than cooking; not even those who had always made heavy cakes and leathery pastry. And so it came to pass, that the progress of civilization at Grimworth was not otherwise apparent than in the impoverishment of men, the gossiping idleness of women, and the heightening prosperity of Mr. Edward Freely.

The Yellow Coat School was a double source of profit to the calculating confectioner; for he opened an eating-room for the superior workmen employed on the new school, and he accommodated the pupils at the old school by giving great attention to the fancy-sugar department. When I think of the sweet-tasted swans and other ingenious white shapes crunched by the small teeth of that rising generation, I am glad to remember that a certain amount of calcareous food has been held good for young creatures whose bones are not quite formed; for I have observed these delicacies to have an inorganic flavor which would have recommended them greatly to that young lady of the "Spectator's" acquaintance who habitually made her dessert on the stems of tobacco-pipes.*

As for the confectioner himself, he made his way gradually into Grimworth homes, as his commodities did, in spite of some initial repugnance. Somehow or other, his reception as a guest seemed a thing that required justifying, like the purchasing of his pastry. In the first place, he was a stranger, and therefore open to suspicion; secondly, the confectionery business was so entirely new at Grimworth, that its place in the scale of rank had not been distinctly ascertained. There was no doubt about drapers and grocers, when they came of good old Grimworth families, like Mr. Luff and Mr. Prettyman: they visited with the Palfreys, who farmed their own land, played many a game at whist with the doctor, and condescended a little toward the timber merchant, who had lately taken to the coal trade also, and had got new furniture. But whether a confectioner should be admitted to this higher level of respectability, or should be understood to find his associates among butchers and bakers, was a new question on which tradition threw no light. His being a bachelor was in his favor, and would perhaps have been enough to turn the scale, even if Mr. Edward Freely's other personal pretensions had been of an entirely insignificant caste. But so far from this, it very soon appeared that he was a remarkable young man, who had been in the West Indies, and had seen many wonders by sea and land, so that he could charm the ears of Grimworth Desdemonas† with stories of strange fishes, especially sharks, which he had stabbed in the nick of time by bravely plunging overboard just as the monster was

---

*Allusion to a essay by Richard Steele in *The Spectator*, a popular early-eighteenth-century periodical.

†Refers to Desdemona's being enthralled by Othello's tales of his travels in Shakespeare's *Othello* (act 1, scene 3).

turning on his side to devour the cook's mate; of terrible fevers which he had undergone in a land where the wind blows from all quarters at once; of rounds of toast cut straight from the bread-fruit trees; of toes bitten off by land-crabs; of large honors that had been offered to him as a man who knew what was what, and was therefore particularly needed in a tropical climate; and of a Creole heiress who had wept bitterly at his departure. Such conversational talents as these, we know, will overcome disadvantages of complexion; and young Towers, whose cheeks were of the finest pink, set off by a fringe of dark whisker, was quite eclipsed by the presence of the sallow Mr. Freely. So exceptional a confectioner elevated his business, and might well begin to make disengaged hearts flutter a little.

Fathers and mothers were naturally more slow and cautious in their recognition of the new-comer's merits.

"He's an amusing fellow," said Mr. Prettyman, the highly respectable grocer. (Mrs. Prettyman was a Miss Fothergill, and her sister had married a London mercer.) "He's an amusing fellow; and I've no objection to his making one at the Oyster Club; but he's a bit too fond of riding the high horse. He's uncommonly knowing, I'll allow; but how came he to go to the Indies? I should like that answered. It's unnatural in a confectioner. I'm not fond of people that have been beyond seas, if they can't give a good account how they happened to go. When folks go so far off, it's because they've got little credit nearer home—that's my opinion. However, he's got some good rum; but I don't want to be hand and glove with him, for all that."

It was this kind of dim suspicion which beclouded the view of Mr. Freely's qualities in the maturer minds of Grimworth through the early months of his residence there. But when the confectioner ceased to be a novelty, the suspicions also ceased to be novel, and people got tired of hinting at them, especially as they seemed to be refuted by his advancing prosperity and importance. Mr. Freely was becoming a person of influence in the parish; he was found useful as an overseer of the poor, having great firmness in enduring other people's pain, which firmness, he said, was due to his great benevolence; he always did what was good for people in the end. Mr. Chaloner had even selected him as clergyman's church warden, for he was a very handy man, and much more of Mr. Chaloner's opinion in everything about church business than the older parishioners. Mr. Freely was a very regular churchman, but at the Oyster Club he was sometimes a little free in his conversation, more than hinting at a life of Sultanic self-indulgence which he had passed in the West Indies, shaking his head now and then and smiling rather bitterly, as men are wont to do when they intimate that they have become a little too wise to be instructed about a world which has long been flat and stale to them.

For some time he was quite general in his attentions to the fair sex, combining the gallantries of a lady's man with a severity of criticism on the person and manners of absent belles, which tended rather to stimulate in the feminine breast the desire to conquer the approval of so fastidious a judge. Nothing short of the very best in the department of female charms and virtues could suffice to kindle the ardor of Mr. Edward Freely, who had become familiar with the most luxuriant and dazzling beauty in the West Indies. It may seem incredible that a confectioner should have ideas and conversation so much resembling those to be met with in a higher walk of life, but it must be remembered that he had not merely traveled, he had also bow-legs and a sallow, small-featured visage, so that nature herself had stamped him for a fastidious connoisseur of the fair sex.

At last, however, it seemed clear that Cupid had found a sharper arrow than usual, and that Mr. Freely's heart was pierced. It was the general talk among the young people at Grimworth. But was it really love? and not rather ambition? Miss Fullilove, the timber-merchant's daughter, was quite sure that if *she* were Miss Penny Palfrey, she would be cautious; it was not a good sign when men looked so much above themselves for a wife. For it was no less a person than Miss Penelope Palfrey, second daughter of the Mr. Palfrey, who farmed his own land, that had attracted Mr. Freely's peculiar regard, and conquered his fastidiousness; and no wonder; for the Ideal, as exhibited in the finest waxwork, was perhaps never so closely approached by the Real as in the person of the pretty Penelope. Her yellowish flaxen hair did not curl naturally, I admit, but its bright crisp ringlets were such smooth, perfect miniture tubes, that you would have longed to pass your little finger through them, and feel their soft elasticity. She wore them in a crop,* for in those days, when society was in a healthier state, young ladies wore crops long after they were twenty, and Penelope was not yet nineteen. Like the waxen ideal, she had round blue eyes, and round nostrils in her little nose, and teeth, such as the ideal would be seen to have, if it ever showed them. Altogether, she was a small, round thing, as neat as a pink and white double daisy, and as guileless; for I hope it does not argue guile in a pretty damsel of nineteen, to think that she should like to have a beau and be "engaged," when her elder sister had already been in that position a year and a half. To be sure, there was young Towers always coming to the house; but Penny felt convinced he only came to see her brother, for he never had anything to say to her, and never offered her his arm, and was as awkward and silent as possible.

It is not likely that Mr. Freely had early been smitten by Penny's charms, as brought under his observation at church, but he had to make his way in society a little before he could come into nearer contact with them; and even after he was well received in Grimworth families, it was a long while before he could converse with Penny otherwise than in an incidental meeting at Mr. Luff's. It was not so easy to get invited to Long Meadows, the residence of the Palfreys; for though Mr. Palfrey had been losing money of late years, not being able quite to recover his feet after the terrible murrain which forced him to borrow, his family were far from considering themselves on the same level even as the old-established tradespeople with whom they visited. The greatest people, even kings and queens, must visit with somebody, and the equals of the great are scarce. They were especially scarce at Grimworth, which, as I have before observed, was a low parish, mentioned with the most scornful brevity in gazetteers. Even the great people there were far behind those of their own standing in other parts of this realm. Mr. Palfrey's farmyard doors had the paint all worn off them, and the front garden walks had long been merged in a general weediness. Still, his father had been called Squire Palfrey, and had been respected by the last Grimworth generation as a man who could afford to drink too much in his own house.

---

*A short haircut, here alluding to a fashion of wearing the hair at about shoulder length.

Pretty Penny was not blind to the fact that Mr. Freely admired her, and she felt sure that it was he who had sent her a beautiful valentine; but her sister seemed to think so lightly of him (all young ladies think lightly of the gentlemen to whom they are not engaged), that Penny never dared mention him, and trembled and blushed whenever they met him, thinking of the valentine, which was very strong in its expressions, and which she felt guilty of knowing by heart. A man who had been to the Indies, and knew the sea so well, seemed to her a sort of public character, almost like Robinson Crusoe or Captain Cook;* and Penny had always wished her husband to be a remarkable personage, likely to be put in Mangnall's Questions, with which register of the immortals she had become acquainted during her one year at a boarding-school. Only it seemed strange that a remarkable man should be a confectioner and pastry-cook, and this anomaly quite disturbed Penny's dreams. Her brothers, she knew, laughed at men who couldn't sit on horseback well, and called them tailors; but her brothers were very rough, and were quite without that power of anecdote which made Mr. Freely such a delightful companion. He was a very good man, she thought, for she had heard him say at Mr. Luff's, one day, that he always wished to do his duty in whatever state of life he might be placed; and he knew a great deal of poetry, for one day he had repeated a verse of a song. She wondered if he had made the words of the valentine!—it ended in this way:—

> "Without thee, it is pain to live,
> But with thee, it were sweet to die."

Poor Mr. Freely! her father would very likely object—she felt sure he would, for he always called Mr. Freely "that sugar-plum of a fellow." Oh, it was very cruel, when true love was crossed in that way, and all because Mr. Freely was a confectioner: well, Penny would be true to him, for all that, and since his being a confectioner gave her an opportunity of showing her faithfulness, she was glad of it. Edward Freely was a pretty name, much better than John Towers. Young

---

*James Cook (1728–1779) explored the coasts of Canada and the Pacific Ocean.

Towers had offered her a rose out of his button-hole the other day, blushing very much; but she refused it, and thought with delight how much Mr. Freely would be comforted if he knew her firmness of mind.

Poor little Penny! the days were so very long among the daisies on a grazing farm, and thought is so active—how was it possible that the inward drama should not get the start of the outward? I have known young ladies, much better educated, and with an outward world diversified by instructive lectures, to say nothing of literature and highly-developed fancy-work, who have spun a cocoon of visionary joys and sorrows for themselves, just as Penny did. Her elder sister Letitia, who had a prouder style of beauty, and a more worldly ambition, was engaged to a wool-factor, who came all the way from Cattleton to see her; and everybody knows that a wool-factor takes a very high rank, sometimes driving a double-bodied gig. Letty's notions got higher every day, and Penny never dared to speak of her cherished griefs to her lofty sister—never dared to propose that they should call at Mr. Freely's to buy liquorice, though she had prepared for such an incident by mentioning a slight sore throat. So she had to pass the shop on the other side of the market-place, and reflect, with a suppressed sigh, that behind those pink and white jars somebody was thinking of her tenderly, unconscious of the small space that divided her from him.

And it was quite true that, when business permitted, Mr. Freely thought a great deal of Penny. He thought her prettiness comparable to the loveliest things in confectionery; he judged her to be of submissive temper—likely to wait upon him as well as if she had been a negress, and to be silently terrified when his liver made him irritable; and he considered the Palfrey family quite the best in the parish, possessing marriageable daughters. On the whole, he thought her worthy to become Mrs. Edward Freely, and all the more so, because it would probably require some ingenuity to win her. Mr. Palfrey was capable of horsewhipping a too rash pretender to his daughter's hand; and, moreover, he had three tall sons: it was clear that a suitor would be at a disadvantage with such a family, unless travel and natural acumen had given him a countervailing power of contrivance. And the first idea that occurred to him in the matter was, that Mr. Palfrey would object less if he knew that the Freelys were a much higher family than his own. It had been foolish modesty in him hitherto to conceal the fact that a branch of the Freelys held a manor in York-shire, and to shut up the portrait of his great uncle the admiral, in-stead of hanging it up where a family portrait should be hung—over the mantlepiece in the parlor. Admiral Freely, K. C. B.,* once placed in this conspicuous position, was seen to have had one arm only, and one eye,—in these points resembling the heroic Nelson,†—while a certain pallid insignificance of feature confirmed the relationship be-tween himself and his grand-nephew.

Next, Mr. Freely was seized with an irrepressible ambition to possess Mrs. Palfrey's receipt for brawn, hers being pronounced on all hands to be superior to his own—as he informed her in a very flat-tering letter carried by his errand-boy. Now Mrs. Palfrey, like other geniuses, wrought by instinct rather than by rule, and possessed no receipts,—indeed, despised all people who used them, observing that people who pickled by book, must pickle by weights and mea-sures, and such nonsense; as for herself, her weights and measures were the tip of her finger and the tip of her tongue, and if you went nearer, why, of course, for dry goods like floor and spice, you went by handfuls and pinches, and for wet, there was a middle-sized jug—quite the best thing whether for much or little, because you might know how much a teacupful was if you'd got any use of your senses, and you might be sure it would take five middle-sized jugs to make a gallon. Knowledge of this kind is like Titian's coloring,‡ difficult to communicate; and as Mrs. Palfrey, once remarkably handsome, had now become rather stout and asthmatical, and scarcely ever left home, her oral teaching could hardly be given anywhere except at Long Meadows. Even a matron is not insusceptible to flattery, and the prospect of a visitor whose great object would be to listen to her con-versation, was not without its charms to Mrs. Palfrey. Since there was

---

*K.C.B. stands for Knight Commander of the Bath, a member of the second-highest rank in a British order of knighthood; here, an indication of "Freely's" prominent descent.
†A heroic figure in English history, Horatio Nelson won over the French in the Battle of Trafalgar (1805) but died in the fighting.
‡Titian (Titiano Vecellio) was one of the most illustrious Italian painters of the sixteenth century.

no receipt to be sent in reply to Mr. Freely's humble request, she called on her more docile daughter, Penny, to write a note, telling him that her mother would be glad to see him and talk with him on brawn, any day that he could call at Long Meadows. Penny obeyed with a trembling hand, thinking how wonderfully things came about in this world.

In this way, Mr. Freely got himself introduced into the home of the Palfreys, and notwithstanding a tendency in the male part of the family to jeer at him a little as "peaky" and bow-legged, he presently established his position as an accepted and frequent guest. Young Towers looked at him with increasing disgust when they met at the house on a Sunday, and secretly longed to try his ferret upon him, as a piece of vermin which that valuable animal would be likely to tackle with unhesitating vigor. But—so blind sometimes are parents— neither Mr. nor Mrs. Palfrey suspected that Penny would have anything to say to a tradesman of questionable rank whose youthful bloom was much withered. Young Towers, they thought, had an eye to her, and that was likely enough to be a match some day; but Penny was a child at present. And all the while Penny was imagining the circumstances under which Mr. Freely would make her an offer: perhaps down by the row of damson trees, when they were in the garden before tea; perhaps by letter—in which case, how would the letter begin? "Dearest Penelope?" or "My dear Miss Penelope?" or straight off, without dear anything, as seemed the most natural when people were embarrassed? But, however he might make the offer, she would not accept it without her father's consent: she would always be true to Mr. Freely, but she would not disobey her father. For Penny was a good girl, though some of her female friends were afterward of opinion that it spoke ill for her not to have felt an instinctive re- pugnance to Mr. Freely.

But he was cautious, and wished to be quite sure of the ground he trod on. His views in marriage were not entirely sentimental, but were as duly mingled with considerations of what would be advan- tageous to a man in his position as if he had had a very large amount of money spent on his education. He was not a man to fall in love in the wrong place; and so he applied himself quite as much to con- ciliate the favor of the parents as to secure the attachment of Penny. Mrs. Palfrey had not been inaccessible to flattery, and her husband, being also of mortal mould, would not, it might be hoped, be proof against rum—that very fine Jamaica rum of which Mr. Freely expected always to have a supply sent him from Jamaica. It was not easy to get Mr. Palfrey into the parlor behind the shop, where a mild backstreet light fell on the features of the heroic admiral; but by getting hold of him rather late one evening as he was about to return home from Grimworth, the aspiring lover succeeded in persuading him to sup on some collared beef which, after Mrs. Palfrey's brawn, he would find the very best of cold eating.

From that hour Mr. Freely felt sure of success: being in privacy with an estimable man old enough to be his father, and being rather lonely in the world, it was natural he should unbosom himself a little on subjects which he could not speak of in a mixed circle—especially concerning his expectations from his uncle in Jamaica, who had no children, and loved his nephew Edward better than any one else in the world, though he had been so hurt at his leaving Jamaica that he had threatened to cut him off with a shilling. However, he had since written to state his full forgiveness; and though he was an eccentric old gentleman and could not bear to give away money during his life, Mr. Edward Freely could show Mr. Palfrey the letter which declared, plainly enough, who would be the affectionate uncle's heir. Mr. Palfrey actually saw the letter, and could not help admiring the spirit of the nephew who declared that such brilliant hopes as these made no difference to his conduct; he should work at his humble business and make his modest fortune at it all the same. If the Jamaica estate was to come to him—well and good. It was nothing very surprising for one of the Freely family to have an estate left him, considering the lands that family had possessed in times gone by—nay, still possessed in the Northumberland branch. Would not Mr. Palfrey take another glass of rum? and also look at the last year's balance of the accounts? Mr. Freely was a man who cared to possess personal virtues, and did not pique himself on his family, though some men would.

We know how easily the great Leviathan may be led, when once there is a hook in his nose or a bridle in his jaws. Mr. Palfrey was a large man, but, like Leviathan's, his bulk went against him when once he had taken a turning. He was not a mercurial man, who easily changed his point of view. Enough. Before two months were over, he had given his consent to Mr. Freely's marriage with his daughter Penny, and having hit on a formula by which he could justify it, fenced off all doubts and objections, his own included. The formula was this: "I'm not a man to put my head up an entry before I know where it leads."

Little Penny was very proud and fluttering, but hardly so happy as she expected to be in an engagement. She wondered if young Towers cared much about it, for he had not been to the house lately, and her sisters and brothers were rather inclined to sneer than to sympathize. Grimworth rang with the news. All men extolled Mr. Freely's good fortune; while the women, with the tender solicitude characteristic of the sex, wished the marriage might turn out well.

While affairs were at this triumphant juncture, Mr. Freely one morning observed that a stone-carver who had been breakfasting in the eating room had left a newspaper behind. It was the "X ——shire Gazette," and X ——shire being a county not unknown to Mr. Freely, he felt some curiosity to glance over it, and especially over the advertisements. A slight flush came over his face as he read. It was produced by the following announcement:—"If David Faux, son of Johnathan Faux, late of Gilsbrook, will apply at the office of Mr. Strutt, attorney, of Rodham, he will hear something to his advantage."

"Father's dead!" exclaimed Mr. Freely, involuntarily. "Can he have left me a legacy?"

CHAPTER III

PERHAPS IT WAS A result quite different from your expectations, that Mr. David Faux should have returned from the West Indies only a few years after his arrival there, and have set up in his old business, like any plain man who had never traveled. But these cases do occur in life. Since, as we know, men change their skies and see new constellations without changing their souls, it will follow sometimes that they don't change their business under those novel circumstances.

Certainly, this result was contrary to David's own expectations. He had looked forward, you are aware, to a brilliant career among

"the blacks"; but, either because they had already seen too many
white men, or for some other reason, they did not at once recognize
him as a superior order of human being; besides, there were no
princesses among them. Nobody in Jamaica was anxious to maintain
David for the mere pleasure of his society; and those hidden merits
of a man which are so well known to himself were as little recognized there as they notoriously are in the effete society of the Old
World. So that in the dark hints that David threw out at the Oyster
Club about that life of Sultanic self-indulgence spent by him in the
luxurious Indies, I really think he was doing himself a wrong; I believe he worked for his bread, and, in fact, took to cooking again, as,
after all, the only department in which he could offer skilled labor.
He had formed several ingenious plans by which he meant to cir-
cumvent people of large fortune and small faculty; but then he never
met with exactly the right people under exactly the right circumstances. David's devices for getting rich without work had apparently
no direct relation with the world outside him, as his confectionery
receipts had. It is possible to pass a great many bad half-pennies and
bad half-crowns, but I believe there has no instance been known of
passing a half-penny or a half-crown as a sovereign. A sharper can
drive a brisk trade in this world: it is undeniable that there may be a
fine career for him, if he will dare consequences; but David was too
timid to be a sharper, or venture in any way among the man-traps of
the law. He dared rob nobody but his mother. And so he had to fall
back on the genuine value there was in him—to be content to pass
as a good half-penny, or, to speak more accurately, as a good confectioner. For in spite of some additional reading and observation, there
was nothing else he could make so much money by; nay, he found in
himself even a capability of extending his skill in this direction, and
embracing all forms of cookery; while, in other branches of human
labor, he began to see that it was not possible for him to shine. Fate
was too strong for him; he had thought to master her inclination and
had fled over the seas to that end; but she caught him, tied an apron
round him, and snatching him from all other devices, made him devise cakes and patties in a kitchen at Kingstown. He was getting submissive to her, since she paid him with tolerable gains; but fevers and
prickly heat, and other evils incidental to cooks in ardent climates, made
him long for his native land; so he took ship once more, carrying his

six years' savings, and seeing distinctly, this time, what were Fate's intentions as to his career. If you question me closely as to whether all the money with which he set up at Grimworth consisted of pure and simple earnings, I am obliged to confess that he got a sum or two for charitably abstaining from mentioning some other people's misdemeanors. Altogether, since no prospects were attached to his family name, and since a new christening seemed a suitable commencement of a new life, Mr. David Faux thought it as well to call himself Mr. Edward Freely.

But, lo! now, in opposition to all calculable probability, some benefit appeared to be attached to the name of David Faux. Should he neglect it, as beneath the attention of a prosperous tradesman? It might bring him into contact with his family again, and he felt no yearnings in that direction: moreover, he had small belief that the "something to his advantage" could be anything considerable. On the other hand, even a small gain is pleasant, and the promise of it in this instance was so surprising, that David felt his curiosity awakened. The scale dipped at last on the side of writing to the lawyer, and, to be brief, the correspondence ended in an appointment for a meeting between David and his eldest brother at Mr. Strutt's, the vague "something" having been defined as a legacy from his father of eighty-two pounds three shillings.

David, you know, had expected to be disinherited; and so he would have been, if he had not, like some other indifferent sons, come of excellent parents, whose conscience made them scrupulous where much more highly-instructed people often feel themselves warranted in following the bent of their indignation. Good Mrs. Faux could never forget that she had brought this ill-conditioned son into the world when he was in that entirely helpless state which excluded the smallest choice on his part; and, somehow or other, she felt that his going wrong would be his father's and mother's fault, if they failed in one tittle of their parental duty. Her notion of parental duty was not of a high and subtle kind, but it included giving him his due share of the family property; for when a man had got a little honest money of his own, was he so likely to steal? To cut the delinquent son off with a shilling, was like delivering him over to his evil propensities. No; let the sum of twenty guineas which he had stolen be deducted from his share, and then let the sum of three guineas be put back from it, seeing that his mother had always considered three of the twenty guineas as his; and, though he had run away, and was, perhaps, gone across the sea, let the money be left to him all the same, and be kept in reserve for his possible return. Mr. Faux agreed to his wife's views, and made a codicil to his will accordingly, in time to die with a clear conscience. But for some time his family thought it likely that David would never reappear; and the eldest son, who had the charge of Jacob on his hands, often thought it a little hard that David might perhaps be dead, and yet, for want of certitude on that point, his legacy could not fall to his legal heir. But in this state of things the opposite certitude—namely, that David was still alive and in England—seemed to be brought by the testimony of a neighbor, who, having been on a journey to Cattelton, was pretty sure he had seen David in a gig, with a stout man driving by his side. He could "swear it was David," though he could "give no account why, for he had no marks on him; but no more had a white dog, and that didn't hinder folks from knowing a white dog." It was this incident which had led to the advertisement.

The legacy was paid, of course, after a few preliminary disclosures as to Mr. David's actual position. He begged to send his love to his mother, and to say that he hoped to pay her a dutiful visit by-and-by; but, at present, his business and near prospect of marriage made it difficult for him to leave home. His brother replied with much frankness.

"My mother may do as she likes about having you to see her, but, for my part, I don't want to catch sight of you on the premises again. When folks have taken a new name, they'd better keep to their new 'quinetance."

David pocketed the insult along with the eighty-two pounds three, and traveled home again in some triumph at the ease of a transaction which had enriched him to this extent. He had no intention of offending his brother by further claims on his fraternal recognition, and relapsed with full contentment into the character of Mr. Edward Freely, the orphan scion of a great but reduced family, with an eccentric uncle in the West Indies. (I have already hinted that he had some acquaintance with imaginative literature; and being of a practical turn, he had, you perceive, applied even this form of knowledge to practical purposes.)

It was little more than a week after the return from his fruitful journey, that the day of his marriage with Penny having been fixed, it was agreed that Mrs. Palfrey should overcome her reluctance to move from home, and that she and her husband should bring their two daughters to inspect little Penny's future abode and decide on the new arrangements to be made for the reception of the bride. Mr. Freely meant her to have a house so pretty and comfortable that she need not envy even a wool-factor's wife. Of course, the upper room over the shop was to be the best sitting-room; but also the parlor behind the shop was to be made a suitable bower for the lovely Penny, who would naturally wish to be near her husband, though Mr. Freely declared his resolution never to allow his wife to wait in the shop. The decisions about the parlor furniture were left till last, because the party was to take tea there; and about five o'clock they were all seated there with the best muffins and buttered buns before them, little Penny blushing and smiling, with her "crop" in the best order, and a blue frock showing her little white shoulders, while her opinion was being always asked and never given. She secretly wished to have a particular sort of chimney ornaments, but she could not have brought herself to mention it. Seated by the side of her yellow and rather withered lover, who, though he had not reached his thirtieth year, had already crow's-feet about his eyes, she was quite tremulous at the greatness of her lot in being married to a man who had traveled so much—and before her sister Letty! The handsome Letitia looked rather proud and contemptuous, thought her future brother-in-law an odious person, and was vexed with her father and mother for letting Penny marry him. Dear little Penny! She certainly did look like a fresh whiteheart cherry going to be bitten off the stem by that lipless mouth. Would no deliverer come to make a slip between that cherry and that mouth without a lip?

"Quite a family likeness between the admiral and you, Mr. Freely," observed Mrs. Palfrey, who was looking at the family portrait for the first time. "It's wonderful! and only a grand-uncle. Do you feature the rest of your family, as you know of?"

"I can't say," said Mr. Freely, with a sigh. "My family have mostly thought themselves too high to take any notice of me:"

At this moment an extraordinary disturbance was heard in the shop, as of a heavy animal stamping about and making angry noises, and then of a glass vessel falling in shivers, while the voice of the apprentice was heard calling "Master" in great alarm.

Mr. Freely rose in anxious astonishment, and hastened into the shop, followed by the four Palfreys, who made a group at the parlor-door, transfixed with wonder at seeing a large man in a smock-frock, with a pitchfork in his hand, rush up to Mr. Freely and hug him, crying out: "Zavy, Zavy, b'other Zavy!"

It was Jacob, and for some moments David lost all presence of mind. He felt arrested for having stolen his mother's guineas. He turned cold, and trembled in his brother's grasp.

"Why, how's this?" said Mr. Palfrey, advancing from the door. "Who is he?"

Jacob supplied the answer by saying over and over again—

"I'se Zacob, b'other Zacob. Come 'o see Zavy"—till hunger prompted him to relax his grasp, and to seize a large raised pie, which he lifted to his mouth.

By this time David's power of device had begun to return, but it was a very hard task for his prudence to master his rage and hatred toward poor Jacob.

"I don't know who he is; he must be drunk,"[9] he said, in a low tone to Mr. Palfrey. But he's dangerous with that pitchfork. He'll never let it go." Then checking himself on the point of betraying too great an intimacy with Jacob's habits, he added, "You watch him, while I run for the constable." And he hurried out of the shop.

"Why, where do you come from my man?" said Mr. Palfrey, speaking to Jacob in a conciliatory tone. Jacob was eating his pie by large mouthfuls, and looking round at the other good things in the shop, while he embraced his pitchfork with his left arm and laid his left hand on some Bath buns. He was in the rare position of a person who recovers a long-absent friend and finds him richer than ever in the characteristics that won his heart.

"I's Zacob—b'other Zacob—'t home. I love Zavy—b'other Zavy," he said, as soon as Mr. Palfrey had drawn his attention. "Zavy come back from 'z Indies—got mother's zinnies. Where's Zavy?" he added, looking round and then turning to the others with a questioning air, puzzled by David's disappearance.

"It's very odd," observed Mr. Palfrey to his wife and daughters. "He seems to say Freely's his brother come back from th' Indies."

"What a pleasant relation for us!" said Letitia, sarcastically. "I think he's a good deal like Mr. Freely. He's got just the same sort of nose, and his eyes are the same color."

Poor Penny was ready to cry.

But now Mr. Freely re-entered the shop without the constable. During his walk of a few yards he had had time and calmness enough to widen his view of consequences, and he saw that to get Jacob taken to the workhouse or to the lock-up house as an offensive stranger, might have awkward effects if his family took the trouble of inquiring after him. He must resign himself to more patient measures.

"On second thoughts," he said, beckoning to Mr. Palfrey and whispering to him while Jacob's back was turned, "he's a poor half-witted fellow. Perhaps his friends will come after him. I don't mind giving him something to eat and letting him lie down for the night. He's got it into his head that he knows me—they do get these fancies, idiots do. He'll perhaps go away again in an hour or two, and make no more ado. I'm a kind-hearted man *myself*—I shouldn't like to have the poor fellow ill-used."

"Why, he'll eat a sovereign's worth in no time," said Mr. Palfrey, thinking Mr. Freely a little too magnificent in his generosity.

"Eh, Zavy, come back!" exclaimed Jacob, giving his dear brother another hug, which crushed Mr. Freely's features inconveniently against the stale of the pitchfork.

"Ay, ay," said Mr. Freely, smiling, with every capability of murder in his mind, except the courage to commit it. He wished the Bath buns might by chance have arsenic in them.

"Mother's zinnies?" said Jacob, pointing to a glass jar of yellow lozenges that stood in the window. "Zive 'em me."

David dared not do otherwise than reach down the glass jar and give Jacob a handful. He received them in his smock-frock, which he held out for more.

"They'll keep him quiet a bit, at any rate," thought David, and emptied the jar. Jacob grinned and mowed with delight.

"You're very good to this stranger, Mr. Freely," said Letitia, and then spitefully, as David joined the party at the parlor door, "I think you could hardly treat him better if he was really your brother."

"I've always thought it a duty to be good to idiots," said Mr. Freely, striving after the most moral view of the subject. "We might have been idiots, ourselves—everybody might have been born idiots, instead of having their right senses."

"I don't know where there'd ha' been victual for us all then," observed Mrs. Palfrey, regarding the matter in a housewifely light.

"But let us sit down again and finish our tea," said Mr. Freely. "Let us leave the poor creature to himself."

They walked into the parlor again; but Jacob, not apparently appreciating the kindness of leaving him to himself, immediately followed his brother, and seated himself, pitchfork grounded, at the table.

"Well," said Miss Letitia, rising, "I don't know whether *you* mean to stay, mother; but I shall go home."

"Oh, me too," said Penny, frightened to death at Jacob, who had begun to nod and grin at her.

"Well, I think we *had* better be going, Mr. Palfrey," said the mother, rising more slowly.

Mr. Freely, whose complexion had become decidedly yellower during the last half-hour, did not resist this proposition. He hoped they should meet again, under happier circumstances."

"It's my belief the man is his brother," said Letitia, when they were all on their way home.

"Letty, it's very ill-natured of you," said Penny, beginning to cry.

"Nonsense!" said Mr. Palfrey. "Freely's got no brother—he's said so many and many a time; he's an orphan; he's got nothing but uncles—leastwise, one. What's it matter what an idiot says? What call had Freely to tell lies?"

Letitia tossed her head and was silent.

Mr. Freely, left alone with his affectionate brother Jacob, brooded over the possibility of luring him out of the town early the next morning and getting him conveyed to Gilsbrook without further betrayals. But the thing was difficult. He saw clearly that if he took Jacob away himself, his absence, conjoined with the disappearance of the stranger, would either cause the conviction that he was really a relative, or would oblige him to the dangerous course of inventing a story to account for his disappearance, and his own absence at the same time. David groaned. There come occasions when falsehood is felt to be inconvenient. It would, perhaps, have been a longer-headed devise, if he had never told any of those clever fibs about his uncles, grand and otherwise; for the Palfreys were simple people, and shared the popular prejudice against lying. Even if he could get Jacob away this time, what security was there that he would not come again, having once found the way? Oh, guineas! oh, lozenges! what enviable people those were who had never robbed their mothers, and had never told fibs! David spent a sleepless night, while Jacob was snoring close by. Was this the upshot of traveling to the Indies and acquiring experience combined with anecdote?

He rose at break of day, as he had once before done when he was in fear of Jacob, and took all gentle means to rouse this fatal brother from his deep sleep; he dared not be loud, because his apprentice was in the house, and would report everything. But Jacob was not to be roused. He fought out with his fist at the unknown cause of disturbance, turned over, and snored again. He must be left to wake as he would. David, with a cold perspiration on his brow, confessed to himself that Jacob could not be got away that day.

Mr. Palfrey came over to Grimworth before noon, with a natural curiosity to see how his future son-in-law got on with the stranger to whom he was so benevolently inclined. He found a crowd round the shop. All Grimworth by this time had heard how Freely had been fastened on by an idiot, who called him "Brother Zavy"; and the younger population seemed to find the singular stranger an unwearying source of fascination, while the house-holders dropped in one by one to inquire into the incident.

"Why don't you send him to the workhouse?" said Mr. Prettyman. "You'll have a row with him and the children presently, and he'll eat you up. The workhouse is the proper place for him; let his kin claim him, if he's got any."

"Those may be your feelings, Mr. Prettyman," said David, his mind quite enfeebled by the torture of his position.

"What! is he your brother, then?" said Mr. Prettyman, looking at his neighbor Freely rather sharply.

"All men are our brothers, and idiots particularly so," said Mr. Freely, who, like many other traveled men, was not master of the English language.

"Come, come, if he's your brother, tell the truth, man," said Mr. Prettyman, with growing suspicion. "Don't be ashamed of your own flesh and blood."

Mr. Palfrey was present, and also had his eye on Freely. It is difficult for a man to believe in the advantage of a truth which will disclose him to have been a liar. In this critical moment, David shrank
from this immediate disgrace in the eyes of his future father-in-law.

"Mr. Prettyman," he said, "I take your observations as an insult.
I've no reason to be otherwise than proud of my own flesh and
blood. If this poor man was my brother more than all men are, I
should say so."

A tall figure darkened the door, and David, lifting his eyes in that
direction, saw his eldest brother, Jonathan, on the door-sill.

"I'll stay wi' Zavy," shouted Jacob, as he, too, caught sight of his
eldest brother; and, running behind the counter, he clutched David
hard.

"What, he is here?" said Jonathan Faux, coming forward. "My
mother would have no nay, as he'd been away so long, but I must see
after him. And it struck me he was very like come after you, because
we'd been talking of you o' late, and where you lived."

David saw there was no escape; he smiled a ghastly smile.

"What! is this a relation of yours, sir?" said Mr. Palfrey to
Jonathan.

"Ay, it's my innicent of a brother, sure enough," said honest
Jonathan. "A fine trouble and cost he is to us, in th' eating and other
things, but we must bear what's laid on us."

"And your name's Freely, is it?" said Mr. Prettyman.

"Nay, nay, my name's Faux, I know nothing o' Freelys," said
Jonathan, curtly. "Come," he added, turning to David, "I must take
some news to mother about Jacob. Shall I take him with me, or will
you undertake to send him back?"

"Take him, if you can make him loose his hold of me," said
David, feebly.

"Is this gentleman here in the confectionery line your brother,
then, sir?" said Mr. Prettyman, feeling that it was an occasion on
which formal language must be used.

"I don't want to own him," said Jonathan, unable to resist a
movement of indignation that had never been allowed to satisfy itself. "He run away from home with good reasons in his pocket years
ago: he didn't want to be owned again, I reckon."

Mr. Palfrey left the shop; he felt his own pride too severely wounded by the sense that he had let himself be fooled, to feel curiosity for further details. The most pressing business was to go home and tell his daughter that Freely was a poor sneak, probably a rascal, and that her engagement was broken off.

Mr. Prettyman stayed, with some internal self-gratulation that *he* had never given in to Freely, and that Mr. Chaloner would see now what sort of fellow it was that he had put over the heads of older parishioners. He considered it due from him (Mr. Prettyman) that, for the interests of the parish, he should know all that was to be known about this "interloper." Grimworth would have people coming from Botany Bay* to settle in it, if things went on in this way.

It soon appeared that Jacob could not be made to quit his dear brother David except by force. He understood, with a clearness equal to that of the most intelligent mind, that Jonathan would take him back to skimmed milk, apple-dumpling, broad-beans, and pork. And he had found a paradise in his brother's shop. It was a difficult matter to use force with Jacob, for he wore heavy nailed boots, and if his pitchfork had been mastered, he would have resorted without hesitation to kicks. Nothing short of using guile to bind him hand and foot would have made all parties safe.

"Let him stay," said David, with desperate resignation, frightened above all things at the idea of further disturbances in his shop, which would make his exposure all the more conspicuous. "You go away again, and to-morrow I can, perhaps, get him to go to Gilsbrook with me. He'll follow me fast enough, I dare say," he added, with a half-groan.

"Very well," said Jonathan, gruffly. "I don't see why *you* shouldn't have some trouble and expense with him as well as the rest of us. But mind you bring him back safe and soon, else mother 'll never rest."

On this arrangement being concluded, Mr. Prettyman begged Mr. Johnathan Faux to go and take a snack with him, an invitation which was quite acceptable; and as honest Johnathan had nothing to be ashamed of, it is probable that he was very frank in his communications to the civil draper, who, pursuing the benefit of the parish, hastened to make all the information he could gather about Freely

---

*Convict colony the British established in New South Wales, Australia, in 1788.

common parochial property. You may imagine that the meeting of the Club at the Woolpack that evening was unusually lively. Every member was anxious to prove that he had never liked Freely, as he called himself. Faux was his name, was it? Fox would have been more suitable. The majority expressed a desire to see him hooted out of the town.

Mr. Freely did not venture over his door-sill that day, for he knew Jacob would keep at his side, and there was every probability that they would have a train of juvenile followers. He sent to engage the Woolpack gig for an early hour the next morning; but this order was not kept religiously a secret by the landlord. Mr. Freely was informed that he could not have the gig till seven; and the Grimworth people were early risers. Perhaps they were more alert than usual on this particular morning; for when Jacob, with a bag of sweets in his hand, was induced to mount the gig with his brother David, the inhabitants of the market-place were looking out of their doors and windows, and at the turning of the street there was even a muster of apprentices and schoolboys, who shouted as they passed in what Jacob took to be a very merry and friendly way, nodding and grinning in return. "Huzzay, David Faux! how's your uncle?" was their morning's greeting. Like other pointed things, it was not altogether impromptu.

Even this public derision was not so crushing to David as the horrible thought that though he might succeed now in getting Jacob home again there would never be any security against his coming back, like a wasp to the honey pot. As long as David lived at Grimworth, Jacob's return would be hanging over him. But could he go on living at Grimworth—an object of ridicule, discarded by the Palfreys, after having reveled in the consciousness that he was an envied and prosperous confectioner? David liked to be envied; he minded less about being loved.

His doubts on this point were soon settled. The mind of Grimworth became obstinately set against him and his viands, and the new school being finished, the eating-room was closed. If there had been no other reason, sympathy with the Palfreys, that respectable family who had lived in the parish time out of mind, would have determined all well-to-do people to decline Freely's goods. Besides, he had absconded with his mother's guineas; who knew what else he had done, in Jamaica or elsewhere, before he came to Grimworth, worming himself into families under false pretences? Females shuddered. Dreadful suspicions gathered round him: his green eyes, his bow-legs, had a criminal aspect. The rector disliked the sight of a man who had imposed upon him; and all boys who could not afford to purchase, hooted "David Faux" as they passed his shop. Certainly no man now would pay anything for the "goodwill" of Mr. Freely's business, and he would be obliged to quit it without a peculium* so desirable toward defraying the expense of moving.

In a few months the shop in the market-place was again to let, and Mr. David Faux, *alias* Mr. Edward Freely, had gone—nobody at Grimworth knew whither. In this way the demoralization of Grimworth women was checked. Young Mrs. Steene renewed her efforts to make light mince-pies, and having at last made a batch so excellent that Mr. Steene looked at her with complacency as he ate them, and said they were the best he had ever eaten in his life, she thought less of bulbuls and renegades ever after. The secrets of the finer cookery were revived in the breasts of matronly housewives, and daughters were again anxious to be initiated in them.

You will further, I hope, be glad to hear, that some purchases of drapery made by pretty Penny, in preparation for her marriage with Mr. Freely, came in quite as well for her wedding with young Towers as if they had been made expressly for the latter occasion. For Penny's complexion had not altered, and blue always became it best.

Here ends the story of Mr. David Faux, confectioner, and his brother Jacob. And we see in it, I think, an admirable instance of the unexpected forms in which the great Nemesis hides herself.

---

*The property that a father allowed his child, or a master allowed his slave, to hold as his own.

ENDNOTES

Silas Marner

1. (p. 3) *In the days . . . certain pallid undersized men . . . looked like the remnants of a disinherited race:* The time reference suggests the early years of the nineteenth century. The "pallid" men are displaced urban citizens, like Silas himself, who found a way to make a living in the countryside.

2. (p. 5) *in those war times:* The reference is to the Napoleonic Wars, which culminated in the Battle of Waterloo. The news of these wars barely enters the lives of the book's characters in a direct way, but the narrative frequently reminds us of them.

3. (p. 6) *to go off in a fit and not fall down:* Apparently catalepsy, Silas's disease, was not well known, although everyone was aware that people might have paralyzing strokes or fits (epilepsy). Interestingly, in a way characteristic of Eliot's use of realistic detail in this story, the people's ignorance of the possibility of cataleptic fits, which freeze the sufferer in unconscious stillness, leads them to think of these episodes as supernatural. In the story, the fits serve the function, from the viewpoint of the other characters, of a "supernatural" agent, making possible Silas's loss and redemption, while all along the reader and the narrator understand that the events are entirely natural.

4. (p. 7) *At the end of fifteen years:* The narrative begins about fifteen years after Silas's entrance into Raveloe—that is, roughly 1815. The story concludes at about the time of Eppie's sixteenth birthday, fifteen years later.

5. (p. 13) *Lethean influence of exile . . . no memories:* In Greek mythology, Lethe was the river of forgetfulness. For Eliot, the past is a condition of identity and morality. Memories anchor one's life and give it stability as they establish obligations and recall the places and people to which one's first emotions were connected.

6. (p. 16) *that habit of looking toward the money . . . brighter in the gathering gloom:* In place of the memories, and of the human connections that he had

lost after being ejected from his sect, Marner finds money. Like the community he has lost, money becomes both Marner's "purpose," and the "loam" for his "seeds of desire."

7. (p. 20) *the Christmas of that fifteenth year . . . the life of his neighbors:* Eliot is careful to locate her realistic details (and the key events of her narrative) in contexts that suggest symbolic importance. Christmas, the holiday that celebrates birth, is the season in which Marner will begin to be reborn into society and redeemed from his despair (and miserliness). The "fifteenth year," moreover, is certainly closely connected in time with the end of the Napoleonic Wars and the defeat of Napoleon.

8. (p. 21) *It was still that glorious war-time . . . anointing their wheels:* Eliot carefully suggests the impending social transition that will affect the comfortable and feudal society at Raveloe. The war and the resulting high prices were about to end.

9. (p. 26) *he would rather trust to casualties:* "Casualties" here means "chance events," the Latin root being *casus*, meaning "fall" or "chance." The theme of reliance on chance, as opposed to taking responsibility for one's actions and determining as far as possible one's own fate, is obviously a crucial one through all aspects of the book. It is likely that the name "Cass" is meant to suggest "chance," as he relies on chance to help him avoid the exposure of his marriage.

10. (p. 45) *I agree wi' Mr. Macey . . . split the difference and make themselves even:* The conversation at the Rainbow was one of the most popular parts of the novel when it was first published. It echoes some of Sir Walter Scott's treatment of traditional popular culture. The landlord, of course, is the very model of the mediator, since his interest is to make sure that all of his customers are satisfied.

11. (p. 53) *This strangely novel situation . . . preoccupation with his loss:* Marner's reception into Raveloe society marks the beginning of his redemption. The loss of the money is thus a condition of his moral salvation.

12. (p. 66) *That you must collogue with him . . . the Casses can do as they like with their land:* "Collogue" meant "collude." "Entail" is a legal arrangement that requires that at the current owner's death the property be transferred to a previously designated heir. Squire Cass is pointing out that there is no such restriction on his land so that he has absolute power in designating his heir.

13. (p. 84) *a drab joseph:* A joseph was a long coat fashionable at the time. Eliot was careful to attend to fashions, as they helped her indicate the difference between her time and the time she was recording in her narratives. Like Scott, she was attempting to evoke an earlier way of life.

14. (p. 92) *since the old king fell ill:* This alludes to the famous madness of King George III, which reached a crisis in 1811. Squire Cass's allusion suggests that the events here are taking place some time after that year.

15. (p. 102) *the demon Opium:* Opium was a popularly used drug in England in the nineteenth century; as "laudanum" it was often taken as a medication for sleeping. While Molly's addiction adds an apparently melodramatic element to the narrative, it remains well within Eliot's understanding of the culture of the early nineteenth century.

16. (p. 134) *The gods of the hearth . . . bruise its own roots:* This is one of Eliot's central themes. Here the narrator explicitly insists on the "truth of feeling" that the young Mary Anne Evans invoked to justify her return to church-going. Recognizing the irrational and indeed superstitious nature ("fetishism") of Silas's love of the home into which Eppie first crawled, Eliot insists on the importance of a reverence for the past. A coldly rational dismissal of the love for outmoded things will lead, she fears, to bruising one's own roots. Moral life depends upon remembering the past and holding it dear.

17. (p. 143) *the increasing poor-rate and the ruinous times . . . dialogue between his daughters:* In the late 1820s England was in the midst of large-scale social changes. The Napoleonic Wars were over, with a consequent economic decline; the movement from cities to developing industrial centers and the earliest development of the railways were changing the face of the country and significantly affecting farm prices as well. The traditional feudal system that was evident in the relationship of Squire Cass and his estate to the Raveloe community was collapsing. At this stage new taxes like the poor-rates were having their effect on the provincial and backward-looking way of life that the novel attempts to record.

18. (p. 149) *with her religious theory pieced together . . . elude the barriers of system:* Again, Eliot's anthropological perspective is evident. She both focuses on the universality of certain fundamental human attitudes toward life (here, the forms of religion) and emphasizes the way in which human experience and social ordering are built not out of a rational organizing of knowledge but upon the way all natural objects grow. They cannot be dealt with adequately by imposing system and reason upon them.

"The Lifted Veil"

1. (p. 174) *Give me no light, great Heaven . . . completer manhood*: Eliot composed this epigraph in 1873, but the story, originally published in 1859, was not reprinted with it until it appeared in 1878 in the "Cabinet Edition" of her collected works—the last edition she oversaw in her lifetime.

2. (p. 178) *The deficiency is there . . . laid to sleep*: Mr. Letherall is a phrenologist. Phrenology, now regarded as a pseudo-science, was in Eliot's time a credited belief system that had a powerful impact on the whole of early Victorian culture. It claimed to be able to read character by analyzing the shape of the head. Each part of the skull was thought to represent certain mental, emotional, or moral qualities.

3. (p. 192) *Lucrezia Borgia*: This painting was probably not by Giorgione; the critical thing here is the subject. Whatever the historical truth (and there is much scholarly debate), Lucrezia Borgia has long been synonymous with the most viciously deceptive of women; she is alleged to have been capable of murder and incest, among other things.

"Brother Jacob"

1. (p. 221) *"Inkle and Yarco"*: This was a tale from the Barbados, supposedly true, about an Indian princess who saves the life of a London merchant. The merchant, Inkle, in Richard Steele's version of the story in 1711, sells the princess into slavery. The story was transformed into stories, plays, and musicals, and continues to be used in different ways even today. It has often functioned as an anti-slavery story.

2. (p. 224) *Providence should be fonder of him than any of the other apprentices*: Notice the similarity of Jacob's attitude to that of Godfrey and, particularly, of

Dunstan Cass. Eliot picks up again the theme of favorable chance that is so important in *Silas Marner*. The protagonist simply assumes that since he is more important than anyone else, things will work out for him. Throughout Eliot's work, under such conditions "chance" invariably fails the egoist.

3. (p. 227) *M. de Balzac:* Honoré de Balzac, perhaps the greatest French novelist, was active in the first half of the nineteenth century, and was for the most part much admired by Eliot, although his reputation among her contemporaries was marred by the prevalent view that his works were immoral.

4. (p. 229) *David was by no means impetuous . . . the foundation of virtue:* This passage makes ironic allusion to utilitarianism, which was among the most important and influential philosophical positions of the time. (The founder of utilitarianism was Jeremy Bentham; its most famous exponents were James Mill and his son, John Stuart Mill.) Utilitarianism viewed utility—usefulness—to be the measure of morality, and argued that virtue inhered in consequences that produced the greatest good for the greatest number. While David is shown to be cognizant of "consequences," he is concerned only with himself, not with the greatest number.

5. (p. 231) *Gorgon or Demogorgon:* The Gorgons were three snake-haired sisters from Greek mythology: Stheno (the Mighty), Euryale (the Far Springer), and Medusa (the Queen); Medusa was the most famous and the only mortal among the three. The hero Perseus decapitated Medusa, and gazing upon her severed head turned beholders to stone. Demogorgon, a primeval creator god who predates the gods of Greek mythology, figures as evil in much English poetry.

6. (p. 231) *Church-people . . . Dissenters had theirs:* Eliot once again invokes the distinction made in *Silas Marner* between "Church-people" and "Dissenters." The "Church" was the Establishment, the official Church of England. Dissenters rejected the hierarchical institution and—though there were many sects—tended to agree at least that it was not the Church but the Bible and the personal experience of God that determined true religion. For the most part, the Church was predominant in wealthy areas, dissent among the working class and in the cities. Here, uncharacteristically for her, Eliot seems to be mocking the Dissenters—in the parodic name Zephania Crypt, for

example, and in naming the Yellow School. There were in fact many charitable dissenting schools named after colors.

7. (p. 232) *the system of neck-and-neck trading . . . made seductive by contrast and tickets:* Advertising and window display were rather new-fangled things, and the locals of Grimworth do not trust window arrangements and labels meant to make the merchandise attractive. David is seen as bringing in new ways (ways that in fact were to take hold historically) that cheapen and falsify commerce.

8. (p. 234) *some more hidden law of sequence:* Here is yet another subtle invocation of the theme of chance. The law of sequence was crucial to Eliot's philosophy and was central to the work of most of the philosophers with whom she had connections, most particularly Herbert Spencer, but also John Stuart Mill. In this view, every cause has its effect, every effect its cause. While "Freely" may believe in favorable chance, the passage implies that there are hidden "causes" that produce the results Freely construes as honoring his superiority.

9. (p. 252) *I don't know . . . he must be drunk:* The moment in which David disavows his brother parallels other critical moments in Eliot's longer works. Inevitably, the past returns upon those who have denied it. The most dramatic or melodramatic of these instances occurs in *Romola,* when Tito Melema (the hero-villain of the narrative) refuses publicly to recognize his father, Baldassare.

INSPIRED BY
SILAS MARNER

George Eliot liked *Silas Marner* the best of all of her works, and the admiration for this novel did not stop with its author. Also seemingly the favorite Eliot work of filmmakers, *Silas Marner* has been captured by the camera more often than any of her other books. Beginning with the eleven-minute *A Fair Exchange* (1909), directed by D. W. Griffith, one of cinema's founding fathers, the story of Raveloe's weaver has been told on film no fewer than nine times. *Silas Marner* possesses a number of notable attributes that make it a natural choice for film adaptation. Unlike the panoramic *Middlemarch*, *Silas Marner* has a manageable number of characters and plots, and it features a happy ending, which is somewhat rare in Eliot's work. As an added inducement, it portrays a host of amusing side players, the travelers at the Rainbow Inn, to lighten the solemnity of the story.

More than half of the *Silas Marner* adaptations were made in the first quarter of the twentieth century. After Griffith's work, movies with the title *Silas Marner* appeared in 1911, 1913, 1916, and 1922. In 1922 another short silent work premiered that was based on *Silas Marner*; it is known alternately as *Are Children to Blame?* and *The Little Outcast*.

After a lapse of more than sixty years, three treatments of *Silas Marner* appeared: a 1985 BBC miniseries, a major Hollywood motion picture titled *A Simple Twist of Fate* (1994), and a French television movie entitled *Les Liens de coeur* (1996). The BBC series stars venerable British performer Ben Kingsley, who earlier won the Best Actor Oscar for his work in the title role in the acclaimed *Gandhi* (1982). Kingsley is compelling as the troubled loner Silas Marner, nailing the weaver's looks and mannerisms right down to the eyes, which Eliot describes as "set like a dead man's." Writer-director Giles Foster's work was impressive enough to land him a spot directing the BBC's version of another Eliot work: *Adam Bede* (1991), which appeared six years after *Silas Marner*.

Gillies MacKinnon's *A Simple Twist of Fate* transports the story of *Silas Marner* to a small town in the modern-day Virginia countryside. Steve

267

Martin, who wrote the screenplay and stars in the film, brings his characteristic quirkiness to the role of John McCann, a cabinetmaker who serves as the updated Silas Marner. Amid pranks and moments of slapstick, Martin shows his sweet side in the excellent rapport he enjoys with the actors who play his adopted daughter, Mathilda, through the various stages of her life. Despite some comedic turns from Martin, the movie retains the novel's somber tone, ending with a custody battle between McCann and Senator John Newland for the child they both claim as their own.

Of Eliot's other works, *The Mill on the Floss* (1860) has been filmed five times, and *Adam Bede* (1859) and *Daniel Deronda* (1877) three times each. *Middlemarch* (1872) and *Romola* (1863) have been adapted in one film apiece. Still awaiting their first screen treatments are *Felix Holt* (1866) and *Scenes of Clerical Life* (1858).

COMMENTS & QUESTIONS

In this section, we aim to provide the reader with an array of perspectives on the text, as well as questions that challenge those perspectives. The commentary has been culled from sources as diverse as reviews contemporaneous with the work, letters written by the author, literary criticism of later generations, and appreciations written throughout the work's history. Following the commentary, a series of questions seeks to filter George Eliot's Silas Marner and Two Short Stories through a variety of points of view and bring about a richer understanding of this enduring work.

Comments

ENEAS SWEETLAND DALLAS

To George Eliot belongs this praise—that not only is every one of her tales a masterpiece, but also they may be opened at almost any page, and the eye is certain to light upon something worth reading—some curious dialogue or vivid description, some pregnant thought or happy phrase. *Silas Marner* is, like the rest of her fictions, full of matter and delightful manner. It is a picture of secluded village life in the midland counties in the early part of the present century, and we owe not a little gratitude to the author for the good which she has done, as well as for the amusement which she has imparted by means of such pictures. She has given dignity to the life of boors and peasants in some of our bucolic districts, and this not by any concealment of their ignorance, follies, and frailties, nor by false colouring, bombastic sentiment, and exceptional events, but by a plain statement of everyday life of the people. The charm of George Eliot's novels lies in their truthfulness. Nothing is extenuated nor aught set down in malice. We see the people amid all their grovelling cares, with all their coarseness, ignorance, and prejudice—poor, paltry, stupid, wretched, well-nigh despicable. This mean existence George Eliot raises into dignity by endowing it with conscience and with kindliness. There is nothing glittering about it. Here we have no mock heroics. There is not the slightest attempt to represent the boor as a village Hampden, not the passing pedler as a poet wanting the accomplishment of verse. The personages of the tale are common, very common people, but they are good and kind, hardworking and dutiful. It is very wonderful to see how their lives are ennobled and beautified by their sense of duty, and by their philosophy—the most consoling of creeds—that real greatness is within reach of the poorest and meanest of mankind. Wealth, glory, the pride of intellect, and the advantages of personal form—these are rare gifts, which seem to be scattered at random among the good and the bad; and in this ambitious age, when we see every one hastening to be rich and covetous of distinction, it is pleasant to be reminded that the honest man is the noblest work of God. George Eliot reminds us of it in her own genial way—transporting us into the midst of these stupid, common-place inhabitants of Raveloe—making them move before us and speak as if they lived, and making us feel a warm interest in all their petty concerns and humble endeavours. Such a novelist, while she amuses, teaches us. We open her volumes confident of most brilliant entertainment, and we close them wondering at the art of a writer who manages to reverse a time-honoured phrase and to render us, not sadder and better, but merrier and better.

—from an unsigned review in
The Times (April 29, 1861)

WESTMINSTER REVIEW

The most remarkable peculiarity and distinguishing excellence of Silas Marner, is the complete correlation between the characters and their circumstances; the actors in this story come before us like the flowers of their own fields, native to the soil and varying with each constituent of the earth from which they spring, with every difference that is implied in defective or excessive nutriment, but yet no more the creatures of blind chance, each asserting his own individuality after his kind, and none overstepping the possibilities of culture furnished by such a world-forgotten village as Raveloe. It is impossible to dissociate any of the characters from the village in which they were born and bred—they form an organic whole with Raveloe; they are not connected with it by any external, or even humorous bands, but by vital threads that will not bear disruption. The stranger Silas is at last assimilated by the little society, and only truly lives when the process has been completed. Nothing can be more profound than this picture of the manner in which all human beings are influenced by their environment, the consequence of this most wonderful fitness between the characters and the scene of their life, is that on laying down the book we do not dwell upon Silas Marner or Godfrey Cass or Dolly Winthrop, or any particular character, but are forced to embrace them all with their restricted country life; nothing short of all Raveloe satisfies the memory; there is no episode that can be detached from the story, no character that can be spared, much less conceived other than it shows itself; there is about them all a certain absoluteness like that which characterizes the works of nature.

—July 1861

HENRY JAMES

In the absence of anything new from George Eliot's hand, the two short tales included in the cheap edition of her works in course of publication by Messrs. Blackwood and now for the first time reprinted, may be accepted as a novelty. They appear at the end of the volume which contains "Silas Marner," and will doubtless procure for this volume an extended circulation. . . . George Eliot will probably always remain the greatest novelist who has written the fewest short stories. As her genius has unfolded she has departed more and more from the "short story" standard, and become, if not absolutely the longest-winded, at least what may be called the most spacious, of romancers. Of the two tales in question, "Brother Jacob," which is wholly of a humorous cast, is much the better. We say it is of a humorous cast, but it is probable that like everything of George Eliot's it may be credited with something of a philosophic import—offered as it is as an example of the many forms, in the author's own words, "in which the great Nemesis hides herself." The great Nemesis here is the idiot brother of a small criminal, who brings the latter to shame and confusion by an obstinate remembrance of the sweet things he has swallowed. The guilty brother, of whose guilt he has been an accidental witness, has bribed him to secrecy by a present of sugar-plums, and when Mr. David Faux is after the lapse of years flourishing, under an assumed name, upon the indirect fruits of his misdemeanors (a petty robbery) the too appreciative Jacob reappears clamoring for more lozenges, and throwing a fatal light upon Mr. Faux's past. The story is extremely clever, but it is a little injured, perhaps, by an air of effort, by too visible an attempt to say good things, to bestrew the reader's path with epigrams. As the incident is related wholly in the ironic, satiric manner, the temptation to be pregnantly witty was, of course, particularly strong. But the figure of the diminutively mean and sneaking young man upon whom the great Nemesis descends is a real portrait; it is an admirable picture of unromantic malfeasance. Capital, too, is the fatal Jacob, who, after the manner of idiots, leaves us with a sense of his combined vagueness and obstructiveness. The minor touches are very brilliant, and the story is, generally, excellent reading. "The Lifted Veil," which is more metaphysical, is, we think, less successful. It relates the history of a young man who, growing up in morbid physical conditions, acquires a mysterious intellectual foresight of the things that are to happen to him; together with that of a wicked lady, his wife, whose guilt is brought to light by the experiment of infusing blood into the heart of a person just dead, who revives for an instant and denounces her. The tale is woefully sombre, and there is a want of connection between the clairvoyance of the hero and the incidents we have just related. Each of these things is very wonderful, but in conjunction they are rather violent. "The Lifted Veil," however, is a fine piece of writing; and if they were interesting for nothing else, these two tales would be interesting as the *jeux d'esprit* of a mind that is not often—perhaps not often enough—found at play.

—from *The Nation* (April 25, 1878)

WILLIAM DEAN HOWELLS

The chief part of my ethical experience has been from novels. The life and character I have found portrayed there have appealed always to the consciousness of right and wrong implanted in me; and from no one has this appeal been stronger than from George Eliot. Her influence continued through many years, and I can question it now only in the undue burden she seems to throw upon the individual, and her failure to account largely enough for motive from the social environment. There her work seems to me unphilosophical.

—from *My Literary Passions:*
Criticism and Fiction (1895)

VIRGINIA WOOLF

In fiction, where so much personality is revealed, the absence of charm is a great lack; and [George Eliot's] critics, who have been, of course, mostly of the opposite sex, have resented, half consciously perhaps, her deficiency in a quality which is held to be supremely desirable in women. George Eliot was not charming; she was not strongly feminine; she had none of those eccentricities and inequalities of temper which give to so many artists the endearing simplicity of children.

—from an unsigned article in the
Times Literary Supplement (November 20, 1919)

V. S. PRITCHETT

If Miss Austen is the novelist of the ego and its platitudes, George Eliot is the novelist of the idolatries of the super-ego.

—from *The Living Novel* (1946)

Questions

1. W. B. Yeats said that George Eliot was opposed to everything that put a spring in a young man's step. Why would he have said this? What did he mean? Was Yeats right?

2. The aim of art is "the extension of our sympathies," said George Eliot. Can it be said that *Silas Marner* is a work of art in that sense? If so, for whom or what do we and Eliot extend our sympathies?

3. According to V. S. Pritchett, "If Miss Austen is the novelist of the ego and its platitudes, George Eliot is the novelist of the idolatries of the super-ego." Is Pritchett's way of looking at Eliot useful?

4. Do you see in *Silas Marner* traces of the Christian belief that was of supreme importance to Eliot when she was young but that she found untrue in adulthood? Does a kernel of the moral truth of Christianity remain in this work, even if Eliot had forsaken Christian doctrine?

FOR FURTHER READING

There is a very large body of literature on George Eliot and the three stories included in this volume. While most of the works mentioned here are books, it's necessary to include a few essays, in particular because "The Lifted Veil" and "Brother Jacob" have received relatively little attention and are often given only brief mention in books. Only over the last thirty years have the two shorter stories begun to receive serious attention. Because there is so much excellent work on Eliot, however, the list below is somewhat arbitrary and focuses either on the stories themselves or on aspects of her work and life that are directly relevant to the questions these stories raise.

Ashton, Rosemary. *George Eliot: A Life*. London and New York: Penguin, 1996. This solid biography steers clear of the tendency to idolatry that dominated earlier studies of Eliot, even after Haight's important work.

Bodenheimer, Rosemarie. *The Real Life of Mary Ann Evans: George Eliot, Her Letters and Fiction*. Ithaca, NY, and London: Cornell University Press, 1994. One of the most sensitive and intelligent studies of Eliot's life and work, this is not a full-scale biography, but it nevertheless gives a rich sense of Eliot's life and the relation between her life and her writing.

Carroll, David. "*Silas Marner*: Reversing the Oracles of Religion." *Literary Monographs* 1 (1967), pp. 167–200. An outstanding reading of *Silas Marner*, this essay is alert to the religious patterns in the book and the complications of Eliot's views of religion.

———. *George Eliot and the Conflict of Interpretations*. Cambridge and New York: Cambridge University Press, 1992. This essay deals with an important consideration of a major element of Eliot's art—its concern with the diversity of perspectives—and the moral and intellectual implications of that diversity.

Dale, Peter Alan. "George Eliot's 'Brother Jacob': Fables and the Physiology of Common Life." *Philological Quarterly* 64 (1985), pp. 17–35. Dale draws interesting connections between Eliot and Lewes's studies in science and the meaning of the story.

Gilbert, Sandra. "Life's Empty Pack: Notes Towards a Literary Daugh-teronomy." *Critical Inquiry* 3 (1985), pp. 355–384. Despite the perhaps heavy-handed cleverness of the title, this ground-breaking essay attends to the gender implications of *Silas Marner*, particularly Silas's determination to take the mother's role in nurturing and bringing up Eppie.

Gray, Beryl M. "Pseudo-Science and 'The Lifted Veil.'" *Nineteenth-Century Fiction* 36 (1982), pp. 407–423. After Knoepflmacher's chapter on the story (see below), this, along with the next item below, was the most influential essay in bringing the story back to the attention of readers and in regarding it as an exploration of materials central to Eliot's art.

———. "Afterword." In *The Lifted Veil*, by George Eliot. London: Virago, 1985.

———. "Afterword." In *Brother Jacob*, by George Eliot. London: Virago, 1989.

Haight, Gordon S. *George Eliot: A Biography*. Oxford and New York: Oxford University Press, 1968. Haight's biography was the first serious study of Eliot's life since the publication in 1884 of J. W. Cross's *George Eliot's Life*. Cross, who married Eliot in 1880, the year of her death, carefully edited and expurgated the author's letters to present her in an almost sanctified way. Haight based his biography on her letters and in a way opened the industry of Eliot biography and criticism in the last decades of the twentieth century.

Haight, Gordon S., ed. *The George Eliot Letters*. 9 vols. New Haven, CT: Yale University Press, 1954–1978. The most important work of Eliot scholarship, Haight's edition of the letters made virtually all the biographical information available.

Hardy, Barbara. *The Novels of George Eliot*. London: Athlone Press, 1959. This volume was perhaps the first study, as it certainly was the most important, to attend to the formal qualities of Eliot's art and to argue, largely through brilliant close readings, for its aesthetic richness.

Hughes, Kathryn. *George Eliot: The Last Victorian*. New York: Farrar, Straus and Giroux, 1999. This somewhat reckless but interestingly intimate biography, which is free of the kind of idolatry that had dominated since Haight's biography, focuses on Eliot's intense emotional life.

Knoepflmacher, U. C. *George Eliot's Early Novels: The Limits of Realism*. Berkeley: University of California Press, 1968. In this still-important study of the development of Eliot's fiction from *Scenes of Clerical Life* through *Silas*

Marner, Knoepflmacher reads each novel as a kind of response to the previous one.

Levine, George, ed. *The Cambridge Companion to George Eliot*. Cambridge: Cambridge University Press, 2001. This useful introduction to the full range of Eliot's life and work offers a series of essays by experts in such fields as philosophy, religion, and science.

Myers, William. *The Teaching of George Eliot*. Totowa, NJ: Barnes & Noble Books, 1984. Myers provides a finely intelligent consideration of the crucial ideas in Eliot's work.

Pinney, Thomas, ed. *Essays of George Eliot*. New York: Columbia University Press, 1963. This is the best scholarly collection of the major essays Eliot wrote before her novel-writing days.

Shuttleworth, Sally. *George Eliot and Nineteenth-Century Science: The Make-Believe of a Beginning*. Cambridge: Cambridge University Press, 1984. Shuttleworth's excellent study of the novels emphasizes their scientific implications and derivation.

Welsh, Alexander. *George Eliot and Blackmail*. Cambridge, MA: Harvard University Press, 1985. This thoroughly original study of the novels focuses on their relation to the information revolution of the nineteenth century.

Wilt, Judith. *Ghosts of the Gothic: Austen, Eliot, and Lawrence*. Princeton, NJ: Princeton University Press, 1980. In this discussion of the relation between major novelists and the Gothic tradition, Wilt spends much time on the very Gothic "The Lifted Veil."

Look for the following titles, available now and forthcoming from
BARNES & NOBLE CLASSICS.

Visit your local bookstore for these fine titles.

Adventures of Huckleberry Finn	Mark Twain	1-59308-000-X	$4.95
The Adventures of Tom Sawyer	Mark Twain	1-59308-068-9	$4.95
Aesop's Fables		1-59308-062-X	$5.95
The Age of Innocence	Edith Wharton	1-59308-143-X	$5.95
Alice's Adventures in Wonderland and Through the Looking-Glass	Lewis Carroll	1-59308-015-8	$5.95
Anna Karenina	Leo Tolstoy	1-59308-027-1	$8.95
The Art of War	Sun Tzu	1-59308-017-4	$7.95
The Awakening and Selected Short Fiction	Kate Chopin	1-59308-001-8	$4.95
The Brothers Karamazov	Fyodor Dostoevsky	1-59308-045-X	$9.95
The Call of the Wild and White Fang	Jack London	1-59308-200-2	$5.95
Candide	Voltaire	1-59308-028-X	$4.95
A Christmas Carol, The Chimes and The Cricket on the Hearth	Charles Dickens	1-59308-033-6	$5.95
The Collected Poems of Emily Dickinson		1-59308-050-6	$5.95
The Complete Sherlock Holmes, Vol. I	Sir Arthur Conan Doyle	1-59308-034-4	$7.95
The Complete Sherlock Holmes, Vol. II	Sir Arthur Conan Doyle	1-59308-040-9	$7.95
The Count of Monte Cristo	Alexandre Dumas	1-59308-151-0	$7.95
Cyrano de Bergerac	Edmond Rostand	1-59308-075-1	$3.95
Daisy Miller and Washington Square	Henry James	1-59308-105-7	$4.95
Daniel Deronda	George Eliot	1-59308-290-8	$8.95
David Copperfield	Charles Dickens	1-59308-063-8	$7.95
The Death of Ivan Ilych and Other Stories	Leo Tolstoy	1-59308-069-7	$7.95
Don Quixote	Miguel de Cervantes	1-59308-046-8	$9.95
Dracula	Bram Stoker	1-59308-114-6	$6.95
Emma	Jane Austen	1-59308-089-1	$4.95
Essays and Poems by Ralph Waldo Emerson		1-59308-076-X	$6.95
The Essential Tales and Poems of Edgar Allan Poe		1-59308-064-6	$7.95
Ethan Frome and Selected Stories	Edith Wharton	1-59308-090-5	$5.95
Frankenstein	Mary Shelley	1-59308-115-4	$4.95
Great American Short Stories: from Hawthorne to Hemingway		1-59308-086-7	$7.95
Great Expectations	Charles Dickens	1-59308-006-9	$4.95
Grimm's Fairy Tales	Jacob and Wilhelm Grimm	1-59308-056-5	$7.95
Gulliver's Travels	Jonathan Swift	1-59308-132-4	$5.95
Hard Times	Charles Dickens	1-59308-156-1	$5.95
Heart of Darkness and Selected Short Fiction	Joseph Conrad	1-59308-021-2	$4.95
The Histories	Herodotus	1-59308-102-2	$6.95
The House of Mirth	Edith Wharton	1-59308-153-7	$6.95

(continued)

(continued)

The Prince and the Pauper	Mark Twain	1-59308-218-5	$4.95
Pygmalion and Three Other Plays	George Bernard Shaw	1-59308-078-6	$7.95
The Red Badge of Courage and Selected Short Fiction	Stephen Crane	1-59308-119-7	$4.95
Republic	Plato	1-59308-097-2	$6.95
Robinson Crusoe	Daniel Defoe	1-59308-360-2	$5.95
The Scarlet Letter	Nathaniel Hawthorne	1-59308-207-X	$4.95
Selected Stories of O. Henry		1-59308-042-5	$5.95
Sense and Sensibility	Jane Austen	1-59308-125-1	$5.95
Six Plays by Henrik Ibsen		1-59308-061-1	$8.95
Sons and Lovers	D. H. Lawrence	1-59308-013-1	$7.95
The Souls of Black Folk	W. E. B. Du Bois	1-59308-014-X	$5.95
The Strange Case of Dr. Jekyll and Mr. Hyde and Other Stories	Robert Louis Stevenson	1-59308-131-6	$4.95
A Tale of Two Cities	Charles Dickens	1-59308-138-3	$5.95
Tao Te Ching	Lao Tzu	1-59308-256-8	$5.95
The Three Musketeers	Alexandre Dumas	1-59308-148-0	$8.95
The Time Machine and The Invisible Man	H. G. Wells	1-59308-032-8	$4.95
Tom Jones	Henry Fielding	1-59308-070-0	$8.95
Treasure Island	Robert Louis Stevenson	1-59308-247-9	$4.95
The Turn of the Screw, The Aspern Papers and Two Stories	Henry James	1-59308-043-3	$5.95
Twenty Thousand Leagues Under the Sea	Jules Verne	1-59308-302-5	$5.95
Uncle Tom's Cabin	Harriet Beecher Stowe	1-59308-121-9	$7.95
Vanity Fair	William Makepeace Thackeray	1-59308-071-9	$7.95
The Varieties of Religious Experience	William James	1-59308-072-7	$7.95
Villette	Charlotte Brontë	1-59308-316-5	$7.95
The Voyage Out	Virginia Woolf	1-59308-229-0	$6.95
Walden and Civil Disobedience	Henry David Thoreau	1-59308-208-8	$5.95
The War of the Worlds	H. G. Wells	1-59308-085-9	$3.95
Ward No. 6 and Other Stories	Anton Chekhov	1-59308-003-4	$7.95
The Waste Land and Other Poems	T. S. Eliot	1-59308-279-7	$4.95
The Wings of the Dove	Henry James	1-59308-296-7	$7.95
Wives and Daughters	Elizabeth Gaskell	1-59308-257-6	$7.95
Wuthering Heights	Emily Brontë	1-59308-044-1	$4.95

BARNES & NOBLE CLASSICS

If you are an educator and would like to receive an
Examination or Desk Copy of a Barnes & Noble Classic edition,
please refer to Academic Resources on our website at
WWW.BN.COM/CLASSICS
or contact us at
B&NCLASSICS@BN.COM.

All prices are subject to change.